DOLPHIN DRONE

A MILITARY THRILLER

JAMES OTTAR GRUNDVIG

Skyhorse Publishing

Skyhorse Publishing books may be purchased in bulk at special discounts for sales promotion, corporate gifts, fund-raising, or educational purposes. Special editions can also be created to specifications. For details, contact the Special Sales Department, Skyhorse Publishing, 307 West 36th Street, 11th Floor, New York, NY 10018 or info@skyhorsepublishing.com.

Skyhorse® and Skyhorse Publishing® are registered trademarks of Skyhorse Publishing, Inc.®, a Delaware corporation.

Visit our website at www.skyhorsepublishing.com.

10 9 8 7 6 5 4 3 2 1

Library of Congress Cataloging-in-Publication Data is available on file.

Cover design by Laura Klynstra
Cover image: Shutterstock

Print ISBN: 978-1-5107-0931-7
Ebook ISBN: 978-1-5107-0932-4

Printed in the United States of America

Dedicated to:

my father
Ottar Grundvig
(1913—2009)

my sister
Anne Renette Markham
(1948—2009)

Remembering their deep affinity for the oceans.

Author Acknowledgments

I WANT TO express thanks and deep gratitude to Skyhorse Publishing's founder and President, Tony Lyons, the preeminent risk-taker in the hyper-competitive book market of New York City; to my editor Alexandra "Alex" Hess and her latent passion for the military thriller genre and her "humanizing" the story even more; to the book's copy editor Mark Amundsen for asking the right questions; and to Louis Conte, a consultant to Skyhorse Publishing, for making the introduction to the publisher on a different book.

I also want to thank my literary agent, Greg Aunapu of Salkind Literary Agency, for his insights as freelance journalist and agent of the publishing industry and his knowledge of the US Navy Marine Mammal Program (NMMP) and its trained dolphins, which is quite impressive for anyone inside or outside the publishing world.

I would also like to thank the US Navy Marine Mammal Program, former NMMP spokesman Tom LaPuzza, one of the 1961 program's founders Dr. Sam Ridgway, and since 2007 is the president of the board and paid director of MMSC, Robert C. Schoelkoph for their help and guidance on the training, feeding, and health care monitoring of the navy dolphins.

Finally, for writers who take up this "lonely profession"—from which the author is rarely ever alone—and who follow those who lit the beacons through the darkness to the dawn of a completed work, I am eternally grateful to the late literary agent Jack Scovil; the late writer, novelist and professor Richard Elman at Bennington Writers Workshop, who told me to "write with force"; and to my lifelong writing pal and creative "sounding board," Reverend Sherry Blackman.

Chapter One

A CHILL BIT Merk Toten's neck and shot down his left arm under the wet suit sleeve. It tingled, igniting a swarm of tremors in his wrist. He snapped his hand to shake it off, but couldn't. The shaking arose at the worst possible time; and his timing, he knew from the past, was piss-poor.

He wondered, why the weakness had appeared then? At that exact moment? Why at dusk? Why on a mission, kneeling in a two-man rubber boat in the Strait of Hormuz with no arms, exit strategy, or backup plan? Three CIA drones had been retasked to Yemen, while the SEALs deployed two Mark V assault boats in a defensive posture several klicks back outside the ports of Oman. That bothered him.

Irritated, Merk stilled his hand strumming his fingers on the gunwale. The RHIB—rigid-hulled inflatable boat—painted black like the accessories on board, sat camouflaged in the charcoal waters. What light remained came from the laptop. He peered out into the darkness, adjusting his eyes.

Farther up the strait, Merk saw a seam where the black water fused with the darker sky. He fixed his eyes on that seam and waited, thinking about the underwater survey he had planned for months: A pair of elite navy dolphins that he had trained for a year, dove down in the strait mapping Iran's new subsea pipeline. When built, the oil conduit would stretch across the thirty-five-mile-wide strait to Khasab Port in Oman.

What concerned him was being exposed in the dark sea. Any glint of light would become a liability for the US Navy "dolphin whisperer." So Merk closed the laptop. In doing so, he broke off his ability to communicate with the dolphins roaming the seafloor. Sure, he could recall them by dipping a sonar-whistle in the water to summon them by their birth names—whistles given to a calf rising to the surface to breathe its first breath—but that wasn't the same as having an open two-way channel to com with them.

Just as quickly as the tremors weakened his wrist, his senses flooded with dread: the chugging of a motor alerted him to the presence of another vessel—garrulous and throaty at first, then growing louder . . . until a green and white fishing trawler breached the black veil of night. The bow lurched forward, slicing the sea open like a zipper. The sight of the vessel punched Merk in the gut. He wondered why a trawler cruised through the strait at that late hour. He glanced at his teammate, Morgan Azar, an African American Special Forces biologist and veterinarian. Azar mouthed, *What's that doing here?* Merk shrugged. Lt. Azar swiped through intel reports on a tablet, trying to figure out how the trawler managed to evade the Office of Naval Intelligence's surveillance net. "Nothing comes up," he whispered.

"Must be Iranian. It's the same green and white as their flag," Merk said.

Azar read an ONI note: "Satellites tracked two fleets of fishing boats leaving port at 1400 and 1600 zulu. The last fleet passed through more than three hours ago."

"At sea?" Merk looked down the strait, scratching the greasepaint on his cheek. Miffed, he turned to the trawler, trying to figure out how it became a straggler. Was it delayed because of a crew issue? Did it have engine trouble? Whatever the reason, Merk and Azar crouched behind the gunwale, holding fast as the ship's waves rolled toward them, watching the fishermen start to unfold piles of nets across the deck.

Merk dialed into a mental checklist, ticking off items he had prepared for the mission. He had painted or taped all of the accessories in the RHIB black. Or did he? He ran through the list: plastic-clad laptop, beacons, flashlights, scuba gear, flare gun, and first aid kit. Check. He had smeared his face with black greasepaint. Check. He wiggled his digits in the fingerless gloves and pressed them against the inflated bow. In darkness, he and Azar should be invisible.

The first wave surged the rubber boat. The second wave bobbed it up and down. A third swell rocked the RHIB sideways. Merk eyed Azar, who pointed with his eyes back to the trawler. Merk looked over. The fishing ship slowed down hard, plowing bow waves as it lurched into a drift. Did the crew spot them? Did they sense something?

"Why are they slowing down right over my fins?" Merk clenched his hands into fists.

"Did they pick up a stray acoustical signal?" Morgan Azar asked.

"How could they? The laptop is closed." He tapped the device.

"What about a fishfinder?" Azar queried, watching the trawler.

"Something's not right." Merk flashed two and then five fingers, signaling Lt. Azar that the Pacific bottlenose dolphins would stay underwater longer without coming up for air. The hand-sign meant another five to seven minutes, or twice the normal dive time for the sea mammals to surface and breathe.

Eyeing the trawler, Merk recalled that kind of long, tense wait from before—exposed in enemy territory with no exit. Only the last time, it was off the coast of China a decade ago. That neuro-association prickled his fingertips; he felt his heartbeat pulse in his wet suit.

* * *

SCANNING THE BOTTOM of the seafloor a half-klick south, the navy dolphins swam down to a depth of thirty meters. They were contouring the layout of the gas pipeline that would one day deliver crude oil from Iran's South Pars Phase-12 offshore platform to Oman's refineries.

* * *

AS THE TRAWLER drifted away, Merk opened the laptop and swiped the glidepad. The laptop cam biometrically scanned the whites of his eyes to access the software. He looked up at the ship, drifting, slowing; his fingers hovered above the color-coded keyboard. The yellow key sent a signal packet in the cetaceans' language up to a military satellite that beamed the data back down to a DPod—a dolphin communication pod—bobbing on the surface.

The black, hockey puck–shaped DPod converted the data stream into digital whistles. Radio waves don't travel well in saltwater. Like a submarine that deploys an antenna or buoy on the surface to enhance communication, Merk deployed the DPod to better stream video captured underwater by the dolphins' dorsalcams.

Merk watched the screen and hit a second blue key, commanding the dolphins to conduct a swim-by of the trawler, and to breathe.

Lt. Azar zoomed night-vision binoculars on the trawler's waterline and saw it was fully laden. He signaled to Merk that the fishermen weren't heading to the Gulf of Oman to fish—not loaded with cargo, not at one knot. Something was up in the vessel, he agreed. But what? Another sign that the ship wasn't bound for the fishing shoals could be seen by the naked eye: a pair of telescopic boom cranes—"rabbit ears," Azar called them—were folded upright with not a single net attached to either hook.

The signal mast swayed back and forth. The low rumble of the engine ground to a halt. The ship drifted into position ready to perform its task.

"Let's cut and run," Azar said.

"Negative."

"Merk, let's abort. Play it safe."

Merk refused, shaking his head. "We have to see what they're up to."

"We came here to collect data. You got it. Let's bolt. The fins are at risk as much as we are," Azar said, stabbing a finger in Merk's chest.

Merk stared at him.

"You wanted this mission with no guns, no weapons. You got it. But not in a trade-off for the lives of the dolphins."

Chapter Two

WITH DOUBT RUNNING through his mind, de-encrypted pictures began to stream from the dolphins' underwater survey. Merk opened a dozen photos on a split screen. Infrared images showed not a pipeline, but its layout across the seabed. Concrete anchors with glow-sticks marked the trail. He turned the laptop around and showed the digital images to Morgan Azar.

"Shit hot. You got what we came for," Azar said, tapping the laptop.

"Negative. We need to find out what that ship is up to."

"Toten, pull out, goddamn it. Abort. You sound like you're still a SEAL. You left spec warfare for a saner job in the Navy Marine Mammal Program. Remember?"

"The survey has changed," he said, pointing to the colored keys. He raised a finger over the red abort key, and looked him dead in the eye: "Remember the chlorine gas. First Syria, now ISIS is using it against the Kurds."

"You and I are like the dolphins you've trained. We follow orders. Fall in line. Keep the chain of command intact. There's nothing for us here to improvise."

Merk ignored Azar, focusing a pair of night-vision binoculars, panning across the sea to recon the vessel. He zoomed in on the cargo buried beneath the nets, but couldn't identify what the fishermen were hiding. Fed up with arguing, Lt. Azar counted the number of men on board—eleven, about double the crew for a trawler that size, with another three to five, he figured, in the cabin.

The high-tech binoculars allowed both men to capture digital images of what they saw and relay them in real-time to SEAL Team Three command at the Joint Special Operations Task Force-Gulf Coordinating Council in Qatar; to CENTCOM in Tampa, Florida; and to a team of CIA analysts in Langley, Virginia.

"You and I know the CIA doesn't have a single asset in Iran to ID the cargo," Merk said.

Lt. Azar lowered the binoculars, and said, "That's not our mission. You know we're naked out here." He sat by the outboard motor, waiting for the signal to start the engine. Merk dipped a sonar-whistle in the water; it pinged the dolphins' name-whistles, calling them.

A few minutes later, one bottlenose dolphin surfaced, clearing its blowhole in a jet of spray and pinched a breath of air. Merk saw a shark bite on the dorsal fin and knew he was looking at Tasi, the female dolphin in the pod. Inapo, the other Hawaiian bottlenose dolphin, a 550-pound male, breached the surface alongside Tasi.

Merk waved them over. He checked the micro dorsalcams on both biologic systems and then inspected the GPS tags clipped to the base of their dorsal fins. He double-checked the tags to see if a mobile app worked on the tablet. The mobile device showed a split screen of the dolphins with their geocoords; the infrared shots of the dorsalcams captured a part of Merk's face—or what he called a "hot selfie" for the thermal heat it picked up of his jaw and cheeks.

Merk fitted a sensor with a float tied to a short cord over Tasi's rostrum. He flashed a hand-sign; the dolphin dipped below the surface flowing over to the trawler.

Inapo rose and pecked Merk on the lips. He petted the mammal and mounted a sensor device over the rostrum. With a slashing sign, the dolphin darted away to sweep under the vessel and tag the hull with a GPS tracker. Both the CIA and navy brass in the Pentagon would be privy to know where the fishing ship was heading—out to sea or back to port.

Merk waited another minute for the dolphins to get in position. He glanced back at Azar, gave a "now" look. The lieutenant started the motor, turned the throttle, and glided out to close on the slow-moving ship. As Azar steered the craft off the starboard flank of the trawler, Merk swiped the tablet awake. He tracked the dolphins' movements onscreen: virtual blinking fins moved in real time, their positions triangulating every few seconds by a trio of military satellites.

Merk opened Dolphin Code, the intra-species software he invented with DARPA scientists and engineers. In communicating with the dolphins digitally, the software collected the data and stored it in the navy's "Blue Cloud." The color-coded program allowed Merk to press a single key or a series of keys to give the mammals up to 100 different goals, tasks, or commands to carry out in their vocalizations of trills and whistles.

With a swipe of a finger, Merk uploaded the radar tracker on the fishing trawler and superimposed it over the geospatial map of the Strait of Hormuz. That allowed him to monitor the dolphins' progress in shadowing the vessel. He lifted the binoculars and zoomed on the lights of the trawler that dimmed near blackout . . . a couple of fishermen slid open the stern gate . . . other men pulled the nets off the hidden cargo, revealing iron spheres with contact spikes. Merk signaled to Azar that the fishermen were going to drop sea-mines into the strait. And yet, the articulating arms of the cranes never swiveled into position to perform the task; the mines were being deployed by another on-deck method.

The fishermen walked the lead anchors with a mooring cable off the back of the ship. Once the anchor slid out the gate, it pulled the mine into the water in a splash, and the mine disappeared in a carpet of foam. The operation told Merk that the Iranians were using a rail system mounted on the deck to slide the mines, an offloading method quicker than using the cranes.

Another quarter klick south, the fishermen planted the next two mines, one after the other sinking below the surface. The fishermen pulled the nets off the last piles, revealing four more sea-mines. The ship slowed in a drift, giving the crew time to set the mines in a cluster. When the next pair of mines dropped into the strait, Merk saw the ship's waterline rise above the surface.

Lt. Azar cut the engine and let the RHIB glide. He paddled the craft by oar close enough to observe, far enough away to remain out of sight.

Merk pressed a Dolphin Code key, ordering Tasi to plant the float on a mine, and said to Azar, "Tasi is going to tag a mine for the admirals. The Pentagon needs this intel."

Trailing in the wake of the fishing ship, Tasi received the signal via a transponder chip embedded behind her melon. The dolphin pinched a breath of air and dove under.

On the laptop, Merk watched Tasi plunge below . . . diving down . . .

He tracked her descent by watching the depth meter rollover as she made her way to the sea-mines. Merk knew the depth of the strait near the tip of Oman was twenty-five meters—about the draft of a fully laden supertanker. Alongside seven islands that Iran controlled in the strait, with an eighth belonging to Oman, the mines were being placed in thirty to fifty meters of water, right in the heart of the shipping lanes. The location of the seamines presented clear evidence of Iran's intent to combat the United States at every turn and opportunity.

"It's the 'Tanker War' all over again," Merk said, referring to the 1980s ship war in the Persian Gulf. Morgan Azar refused to discuss the geopolitics of the past, even though nothing had changed in nearly half a century.

* * *

TASI DOVE TO the bottom . . . echolocating to get a fix on the depth of the seafloor.

The last mine's anchor landed nearby in a muted thud.

The sound told her she was close to the mines . . .

In the darkness, Tasi swam past the cluster, pulsing the mooring cables attached to the buoyant mines, while steering clear of touching the contact spikes.

Chapter Three

O N THE FISHING vessel, an armed guard paced around the deck. Off the starboard, he glimpsed the dolphin Inapo surfacing alongside the ship, taking a breath, spying on the guards.

A glint on the dorsalcam lit up when the guard shined a flashlight. Another guard swung an AK-47 assault rifle, training it on the creature. He opened fire. The shots ripped the surface of the water just as Inapo dove under. The gunfire stirred other guards to spread around the vessel and search the water off the trawler for the navy dolphin.

One guard scouted the darkness beyond the stern. He saw the silhouette of the rubber boat. He pointed into the night, trying to get a fix on the target, panning the water with a flashlight. Several guards moved to the stern and took aim with rifles.

At the bow, a guard pounded on the cabin, alerting the captain about the intruder.

From the RHIB, Merk and Azar watched the commotion of the Iranian Revolutionary Guards on the ship. A trio pulled a canvas off an inflatable boat with an outboard motor, dragged the craft to the gate, and pushed it into the sea.

"They marked us," Merk said, as Azar cranked on the engine. Merk looked at the open water behind them and knew that if they fled toward Oman the Iranian pursuit boat would catch them. He opened a box and handed a flare gun to Azar, and then took over the outboard motor and gunned it. Merk steered the RHIB not away, but toward the trawler. Azar didn't like the risky move. The

RHIB boomed across the sea at a speed that earned the SEAL nickname "boghammer."

The Iranian pursuit boat sped toward them. One guard opened fire; another unloaded a staccato burst.

Azar ducked, while Merk stayed low with bullets zipping overhead. Azar released the safety latch on the flare gun, aimed with the RHIB zeroing in . . . Merk swept the boat in a wide arc . . . swerved out in an S-curve . . . and then cut back hard to intercept the path of the pursuit boat. He gunned the engine. Azar fired the flare—

The hot green pellet shot in a comet trail and burst when it struck the gunwale, tumbling in a flash across the pursuit boat, ricocheting off the motorman into the sea. Blinded by the flare, the Iranians couldn't relocate the RHIB . . . Merk bore down on them . . . and rammed the bow of the pursuit boat at an angle. The impact tossed a guard about as he fired wildly. A bullet struck Morgan Azar above the chest, knocking him off balance. He lurched to the side, tipping over . . .

The collision dumped two Iranian guards into the sea. Clipped, the pursuit boat twisted, rising out of the water. Airborne, it careened, landing on top of the third guard, blasting him under the surface. The collision knocked the RHIB nose-up, lifting it on the side. With the hull rising, Merk gripped the outboard motor; Azar fell into the sea. The RHIB slammed the surface, bounding before correcting itself with Merk tilting the motor out of the water to slow down.

He cut the engine and looked on board for the laptop, but couldn't find it. *It must have tumbled into the sea*, Merk thought. He scanned the area where the laptop fell overboard, but didn't see anything, then looked back at the wounded Azar, floating on the surface. Azar managed to turn on a rescue beacon on his vest and waved Merk to search for the dolphins.

The trawler turned around and headed toward the RHIB. Without the laptop, Merk had no way to com with Tasi or Inapo. Seeing the trawler bear down on him, he started the motor, fishtailed the RHIB around, and raced away.

* * *

UNDERWATER, TASI SWAM below a sea-mine and grazed it without touching a protruding contact spike, releasing it from the anchor. The metal sphere rose like an overinflated balloon to the surface. The dolphin darted off, whistling for Inapo to clear the space.

* * *

ON THE SURFACE, the trawler opened up speed. Guards fired into the darkness in the area where Merk was fleeing after ramming the pursuit boat. As the captain pushed the engine, knowing the trawler's heavy cargo had been offloaded, he gazed down at the fish-finder screen and saw a blurred image of a mine rise to the surface, right in front of the bow.

The fishfinder flashed the ascending object at five meters . . . four meters . . . rising . . .

About to hit the mine, the captain slammed the engine off. The trawler lunged in a jolt. The ship rocked hard, bouncing up and down. Holding on, the captain and first pilot peered out the cabin window trying to locate the mine—when it struck the bow and exploded.

The blast blew apart the ship, tearing open the engine room and fuel tanks in an arcing fireball that toppled the boom cranes into the water. Secondary explosions hurled the guards over-board in jets of fire, their bodies flailing as they splashed into the sea.

In the RHIB, Merk looked back with despair at the fiery wreck of the trawler. Having raced past Azar, he searched the sea, but couldn't locate his wounded teammate's green beacon. Merk turned the boat around and felt for the night-vision goggles or flare gun, but couldn't find either device. So he took a chemlight from his vest, twisted it on, and tossed it into the sea.

He guided the RHIB toward the chemlight, calling out Azar's name. "Morgan . . . Morgan . . . Hey, Azar . . . Come back." No response. A long moment passed.

And then: Merk spotted Morgan Azar floating facedown in the water. He zoomed over to him, cut the engine, and hauled his teammate on board, flipping him over. Azar wasn't breathing or coughing, not a wisp of life.

Merk stretched out Azar's limbs, unzipped his wetsuit and, with two hands, pushed down on the chest, compressing it, rapidly pumping thirty times. He then tilted the veterinarian's head back, opened his mouth, stuck a finger inside to clear the air passage, and breathed two hard breaths into his lungs. Pump and blow. He resumed pumping Azar's chest again and again, thirty times. Still nothing. So Merk pressed his lips to Azar's mouth and blew two more deep shots of air into his lungs. A trace of air leaked out of the mouth, along with a faint echo of a heartbeat. Merk cocked his arm and punched Azar in the sternum. The jolt shocked the motionless body into a spasm, but then it stopped. He listened for a heartbeat, but the faint echo was gone.

Merk searched the rubber boat, but didn't find the first-aid kit where the shots of adrenaline were stored. Like the laptop and flare gun, the first aid kit must have fallen over. "Jesus, Azar, don't die on me," Merk said, surveying the burning debris field. He searched for signs of the dolphins. "Fuck . . . " he said, panning the surface. No sign of them.

The sea was empty except for the wreckage, except for a few floating corpses, except for the smoldering debris. Now Azar was dead, lifeless, like everyone around Merk. He knew it was his fault that the veterinarian died, his fault for pushing the core mission of the dolphins from surveying an underwater pipeline to spying on the Iranians laying sea-mines in the strait. Now Merk had the problem of the two missing biologic systems. Did they escape the blast radius of the mine? Were Tasi and Inapo knocked out? Were they alive, injured, drowning, or dead?

He started the motor and rode toward the trawler engulfed in flames with the remains of the hull listing, sinking, smoke spewing from the hot water. Merk called out, "Tasi . . . Inapo . . . Tasi . . . Inapo . . . " guiding the rubber boat back and forth like a farmer plowing a field.

Merk drove over the body of a dead guard; he steered around the next smoky corpse, when Tasi breached off the port side, screeching a victory squeal. She leapt onto the gunwale, startling Merk. He embraced the dolphin and strapped her on the side of the boat.

Inapo leapt onto the port gunwale. He, too, squealed a victory whistle. But all was not well.

Chapter Four

A<small>T ZERO-DARK-HUNDRED</small>, A Navy SEAL climbed on a boulder alongside a deserted road on the outskirts of Jaar, Yemen. From the perch, the SEAL dialed a pair of night-vision binoculars and panned it over low-slung houses across the city. He swept the infra-red lens from west to north until his eyes fixed on a laser-painted marker on the upper wall of a low-rise building.

Confirming another SEAL had painted the target, he took out a laser-gun, sighted the target, and fired a laser on the terrorist head-quarters, painting the wall above the first laser mark. He turned on a Satcom and pressed an encrypted code, waiting a few seconds to signal again. . . .

* * *

U<small>P</small> M<small>ARKET</small> S<small>QUARE</small> from the target building, CIA clandestine operator Alan Cuthbert strode in the middle of the dusty street toward a closed teashop. He felt his Satcom vibrate two times under the dark blue Bedouin *tob*, and knew the target had been painted. That was the first check of three he needed before ordering the drone strike, the last steps in the kill chain.

Cuthbert picked at grains of sand in his brown bushy beard. He tapped his knuckle on the shop door, scanning the street behind him in a city that had been fought over by three factions: the Shiite Houthi fighters, who ousted the former Yemeni president in January 2015; al Qaeda on the Arabian Peninsula; and Saudi-sponsored military guard. In an air of paranoia, Cuthbert watched a young boy head down the silent street away from him, toward the target house.

He thought about intervening to save the boy from harm, then erased the idea. Anxious to meet the recruited CIA asset named Bahdoon for the first time, Cuthbert knew better than to tap the door again. He waited, eyeing the street, when he heard a creak of the floorboard inside, followed by footsteps approaching. The door opened. A diminutive Yemeni man, clean-shaven, dressed in an Italian designer suit and tie, startled the CIA operator, who stepped inside. Bahdoon's appearance belied the troubles his nation suffered in yet another civil war.

Wearing wire-rimmed glasses, Bahdoon offered Alan Cuthbert a seat at a wood table. The Oxford style, short-cropped hair caught the agent off guard, too; so did the lack of facial hair. On the table sat a tin teapot. What threw Cuthbert off even more—there were no bodyguards in the shop. Stranger still, Bahdoon didn't pat him for weapons. They sat down. On the chance of the tea being spiked, the agent waited for the host to sip first, before he poured a cup.

"Yemen tea is good for your endurance," Bahdoon said, sipping.

Cuthbert took a sip and watched the top-secret asset's eyes, then said in code: "The stars are aligned," referring to the terrorist safehouse being laser-painted. "But we still can't drink tea on the moon." Again that was code, asking Bahdoon to give the second of three confirmations before Cuthbert ordered the drone strike and then exited Yemen by boat later that night.

"Hmmm, you are strapping," Bahdoon said, sipping. "You know what they say."

"About what? Size? Strength?"

". . . Drones."

Cuthbert shrugged. Bahdoon sipped the tea and placed the teacup on the side beside the saucer. He flipped the saucer over, removed a note taped to the bottom, and handed it to the agent. Cuthbert unfolded the paper, read three numbers of mobile phone SIM cards with RFID identifiers. He took out a smartphone and scanned the numbers with a secure mobile app. He uploaded the image, swiped it to an encrypted cloud, and pressed "send," forwarding it to CIA analysts back in Langley's Drone Counterterrorism Unit, tasked with operating the military drones in countries, such as Yemen, where no US troops are based.

"Are drone strikes your life's work?" Bahdoon asked, pouring more tea.

"Nah, bagging terrorists is my sweet spot," Cuthbert said.

"What about the ones you have killed? Their spirit lives on." Bahdoon took a sip.

"Huh? Who are you referring to?"

"Abu Musab al-Zarqawi and Anwar al-Awlaki," he said. "Zarqawi was the builder of training camps. A brute. He was the founder of ISIS when he sprang from a Jordanian jail in 1999. Awlaki, the graceful American preacher, has been more alluring dead since the 2011 drone attack. It helped launch ISIS's radical jihad. Awlaki's impassioned speeches live on YouTube and on the dark web. They are some of the most persuasive recruiting tools for jihadists. The one on the *Afterlife* spoke to Muslims the world over on how to prepare for death."

Alan Cuthbert held up the piece of paper, saying, "Yeah, I read the transcript. He used the analogy of two planes striking each other over India. Death came fast to those passengers."

"Instantaneous, like a drone hit," Bahdoon said, lowering his voice. "I heard Houthi rebels are in Zinjibar scouting the port for mercenaries. Be vigilant."

Cuthbert nodded, tapped his smartphone, noting, "Even if you shut this off, there's a second battery in the internal clock that's still ticking."

"The men sleep with their mobile phones shut off at night. But they have scouts and runners, children looking out for their safety," Bahdoon said. "There, you must be careful. When you leave, move swiftly. Follow no one in uniform. Those men are AQAP."

When the Satcom vibrated against his waist, Cuthbert knew the CIA and NSA had confirmed the RFID numbers belonged to the terrorists sleeping down the street in the laser-painted building. With SIGINT confirmed, he stood up and nodded to Bahdoon, placed an envelope packed with euros on the table, and nodded again. Bahdoon spread the money out and lifted a note in the stack. He opened it and read a list of weapons. "First weapons to be delivered in three days," Cuthbert whispered. He shunted out the door, thinking, *This is our first drone strike in Yemen since the civil war erupted.* The war forced the CIA to pull its assets out of the country.

Outside, Cuthbert gazed down the street to the building at the end of the square. He saw no one and headed the other way. Lurking behind a food cart, the young boy flicked a laser-pointer on the agent's back, marking him. Cuthbert pressed a hot button through the Bedouin *tob.* It signaled the CIA reachback operator, the expert at the joystick of the Predator C drone at the drone base in Djibouti, who, in concert with a CIA analyst, would fix the target. That gave Cuthbert half an hour to drive out of Jaar to Zinjibar and escape by boat in the port city.

As Alan Cuthbert ambled around the bend of the street, flanked by a mix of clay bricks and modern glass and steel buildings, he heard a blade scrape against a stucco wall. Without looking back, his heart raced, his blood pressure elevated, goading him to take longer strides. His eyes scanned the arid street in front of him. His steps hurried. The blade sound scraped louder, then vanished, replaced by the patter of footsteps approaching from behind.

A man's voice called out, "Sir . . . wait. Wait, sir . . . Sir?"

Cuthbert wheeled around, sizing up a gangly man with an unkempt beard. He gazed over the man's shoulder down the street to a second, larger uniformed man approaching. "Sure," the agent groused, and removed the *aba* from his head. He flipped the silk bolts aside, whipped out a knife from the mantle; the blade flashed as he rammed it through the left hand of the man, who lunged at him. He shrieked in pain. Cuthbert stepped on the man's foot and drove an elbow into his throat, chopping him to the ground; he writhed as blood ran out of the impaled hand.

Cuthbert ran when the uniformed man charged, lumbering in pursuit. The agent disrobed, turned on his smartphone, and pressed a coded text alerting the two laser-paint SEALs that he was on the run heading toward them.

Down the street, the agent saw a pair of armed soldiers scamper toward him. He glanced at the smartphone and, with a digital map of Jaar, slowed down to swipe it larger. Seeing an escape route, he dashed down a side street. More shots were fired, but missed him. He glanced back to one soldier stooping down to take aim and shoot a series of volleys; the other soldier, joined by the uniformed man, pulled out a pistol and fired several rounds.

As more shots strafed the ground near him, Cuthbert ran along the walls of the buildings, making a clean shot at his large frame difficult. Shells tore up the stucco wall, sandblasting his face and forehead with chunks and debris, with grains hitting him, his left eye in a spat of dust. He covered the eye, took a step, and a foot stuck out tripped him. The agent stumbled to the ground, scraping his face. Cuthbert rolled over and looked up with one eye at a US SEAL, who pointed him to stay down. The SEAL whipped around a long-barrel MK-17 SCAR assault rifle and fired a two-shot burst at the charging soldier, knocking him to the ground. He swerved the barrel around and squeezed a muzzle flash of three shots that tore into the large uniformed man, dropping him to the street.

Cuthbert looked to the end of the street and saw a third soldier run away.

"The tango has gone for help. Let's go. Move it," the SEAL said, pulling the CIA agent off the ground as he wiped dust out of his eyes.

They scurried down an alley, zigzagged up another street, and ran into an abandoned building. In the alcove, they saw a drug-addled squatter quivering in the fetal position. Covering his mouth from the stench, the SEAL pulled a tarp off a motorcycle, handed Cuthbert the assault rifle, and started the engine. The CIA agent climbed on and off they sped out of the building and out the center of Jaar, heading to the border, to the surveillance nest where the other SEAL had painted the target on the terrorist building. Cuthbert clicked the Satcom three times.

* * *

INSIDE THE SIXTH floor of CIA headquarters in Langley, Virginia, Red Cell CIA analysts watched the plasma screen. The infrared night view of Jaar, where few lights glowed, showed silhouettes of green and black buildings, rows of them, passing under the drone as it flew overhead until it spotted and locked onto the laser-painted wall of the building. One analyst pointed at the screen, while another located the target on a laptop and confirmed the GPS coordinates of the target against the laser markings, saying, "Target all green. Light 'em up."

* * *

INSIDE A BUNKER at the Djibouti drone base, the reachback operator fired the drone's first of two Hellfire missiles from more than 500 klicks away. The comet trail shot off in front of the drone, arcing down toward the target. The analyst saw virtual crosshairs streak to the laser-paint, when the Hellfire missile locked on the building. Just before it struck, the reachback operator fired the second Hellfire in a double tap strike, Navy SEAL style.

The first Hellfire missile burrowed into the concrete wall of the old building and erupted into a fireball. A huge ascending explosion collapsed the walls and rooftop, crashing them on top of the floors below.

The second Hellfire missile's heat-sync zeroed in on the explosion and slammed into the teetering building. The next blast broke the structure apart, pancaking the floor slabs to the ground in a cloudburst of flames and debris.

"We got 'em," the CIA analyst said, tapping the reachback operator in a fist-bump. "The tangos are dead."

"Roger that. They are," the reachback operator said, watching the ensuing inferno on an infrared live-feed.

Chapter Five

"**G**ODDAMN IT, TOTEN, you don't know your ass from your elbow. What were you thinking taking on the Iranian Guard Corps?" Captain Davis Whittal shouted, circling Merk like a trapped prey.

Merk sat in the middle of the captain's conference room at the Jebel Ali US Naval Base in the United Arab Emirates. He stared at the fit young captain's waist, then watched the veins in his neck throb with each biting word.

"Merk, you were unarmed, unfocused, and had no goddamn backup. Lt. Azar is dead. Dead . . . so rein yourself in, sailor. . . ." The captain paced back and forth. "I don't care what black program you work for. You're still in the United States Navy. We don't lose good men on a hunch, or gut instinct. What were you going to do when they spotted you? Huh?" He nudged Merk's shoulder.

Numb, Merk sighed, reflecting on the loss and stared aimlessly at the floor. Captain Whittal walked away, then turned 180 and stepped back, hovering over Merk, who began to pluck hairs from his eyebrow, one by one, in an unconscious self-mutilating trance.

"The cause of death is being determined as I rip your ass apart." Captain Whittal leaned in Merk's face and, dropping his voice a few decibels, said, "And yet you somehow got valuable intel last night out in the strait. Shit, what am I to do with you?"

Looking up at Whittal, Merk had nothing to say; the death of Azar cast an immense shadow over him and his reputation like an ice overhang.

"Toten, why didn't you abort when you spotted the Iranians? Why did you ignore Morgan Azar's pleas to pull out and bolt? ONI investigators are going to need to know the whys. And they will find out when they grill you. . . . Tehran is foaming at the mouth to attack us in retaliation," the captain said.

"Retaliation? For what? The puke Quds Force didn't know we were there?"

"You're not listening. Read my lips and let my words sink in. . . . You're no longer a SEAL, lieutenant. You haven't been for a while. You left that branch of the navy a decade ago. You had one objective last night," Captain Whittal railed, kicking a chair across the room with such force that it crashed into a wall. "Beyond getting your teammate killed, you broadcasted to the Ayatollah that US Navy dolphins are spying on them in their water."

Whittal kept chiding Merk, tapping his shoulder, bumping him, getting in his glum face, shouting: "You could've lost the Dolphin Code to the enemy, instead of the sea."

"But I didn't, did I? Next time, I'll tether the laptop to my leg," Merk said, pissed off.

"Shit, Toten, you're conflicted."

"Conflicted?"

"Affirmative. Like I said, 'your ass from your elbow,'" the captain shrieked. "What were you doing last night? Were you in Six mode? . . . Do you miss being a trained assassin?" He stepped away and paced in front of the dolphin whisperer. "I'm asking, because when my SEALs conducted inventory of the boghammer, they didn't find anything. Just a spent flare gun shell."

"Hell, I wish you could ask Lieutenant Azar about the flare. He fired it."

"I'm wondering if you've permanently morphed into a no gun, pussy pacifist, or . . . are you just a puke lifer, like your navy mustang father?"

"Leave my old man out of this. He's dead."

"So is Azar. You could've had the systems killed, too."

Merk shook his head, since he knew both Tasi and Inapo were very much alive. Two navy dolphins that should receive Medals of

Honor for bravery under fire and carrying out tasks, not to mention their ability to improvise, got what? Some R&R downtime in a pool, a checkup, their teeth brushed, fed fish for their reward. That, Merk knew, was a bad deal.

Merk unzipped the top of his wet suit and pulled his arms out of the rubbery sleeves. He stripped down to his waist, revealing to Captain Whittal the faded Navy SEAL Trident tattoo on his right bicep and an orange-and-silver *parang* tattoo—"broken daggers"— on his right breast. But it was the left side that caught the captain's eye. Like an aged map of the Louisiana Purchase, a burn scar covered the left flank of Merk's back, wrapping around his side and arm and across his ribs up to his left breast. The sight of raw fused skin, tight as a snare drum, coarse like gravel, stopped the captain cold from pressing on with his verbal barrage.

Merk stood up, exhaled a calm breath, finding his center again, and asked, "Captain, when will the fins be released to my supervision?"

"Toten, we're not talking about the systems right now. You have to give a deposition on the circumstances relating to Lt. Azar's death. NMMP Director Hogue will do the grilling from San Diego. She will then see if the fact-finding discussion will require a JAG probe."

"Look, I don't want to feed Tasi and Inapo or even check their vitals. They need to be examined in water, in their environment, for post-traumatic stress. No different than soldiers coming back from the field of battle."

"You and the biologic systems will be flown to the Naval Special Warfare Unit Three at the Asu Bahrain Navy Base at 1500 hours. You can examine them there," Whittal said. Realizing he was no longer penetrating Merk, that his words were being ignored, that the dolphin whisper's focus was elsewhere, that Merk had shut out the pain, compartmentalized it, pushed Azar's death to the back of his mind, the captain said, "Toten, your request to use the French naval base here is denied. You'll be stationed in Asu until your next mission, which should be soon."

Merk grabbed a towel and headed to the captain's quarters to shower and get changed.

After he got dressed, Merk returned to the conference room. On a live feed, he spent an hour answering questions from Naval Marine Mammal Program Director Susan Hogue and five ONI officers and investigators stationed on both US coasts and one at an undisclosed forward operating base in the Mid East. Merk filled the reports, one after the other, flipping through tablet screens, providing digital testimony on the events that transpired in the Strait of Hormuz, from Iran's mine-laying operation and his decision not to abort, to ramming the Iranian pursuit boat that led to Morgan Azar being shot, his drowning, and death.

* * *

HOURS LATER, MERK finished the paperwork and headed outside. He stepped into the intense wall of heat, but it was the industrial odor of the oil refineries and natural gas processing plants across the port that magnified the loss of Morgan Azar. He worried about the health of his dolphins, not enough to be distracting him from thinking about his girlfriend though. There in the mechanized port of oil and gas and steel, he recalled her fine scent, the touch of her hair flowing through his fingers, and the warmth of her flesh pressed against his body.

He remembered her and then looked down the terminal to the fenced-in officer's recreation building. It housed an outdoor swimming pool, shielded from the sun under tent-like canopies.

He wondered how Tasi and Inapo were doing, how they were holding up in the pool of water, as he headed to the medical examiner's office to read Morgan Azar's autopsy report and see his body, his face, one last time.

Chapter Six

SMOKE POURED OUT of the collapsed roof. The bombed stone building, which centered the market square in Jaar, smoldered in hot rubble. Citizens' faces wrought with despair and belligerence, looked on, their eyes red and inflamed like embers in a fire. Mob rage flared with more and more onlookers pouring into Market Square.

The surgically accurate CIA drone strike caved in the slab roof, collapsing stone walls on two sides. Rescue workers, villagers, and policemen pulled the bloodied, lifeless bodies of children out of the wreckage. They picked their way around the broken beams and piles of debris to a row of waiting ambulances turned into makeshift hearses.

How could the US blow up an elementary school? It was tragic to blow up the *Médecins Sans Frontières*—Doctors Without Borders—at the Kunduz hospital in 2015, but quite another thing to raze a school full of children when Navy SEALs were on the ground to laser-paint the target and signal intelligence, confirmed in order to avoid a repeated mistake. Perhaps worse, the American court system threw out a civil suit against the US president, congress, and the CIA for hunting down and killing Anwar al-Awlaki, a US-born militant cleric who had joined AQAP, in a drone strike in Yemen 2011. The attack also killed al-Awlaki's teenage son.

How would justice be served with militants and civilians being killed by drone strikes across a country shattered by civil war? And now children were dead. Yemeni soldiers joined the swelling throng that screamed, pumped fists, and waved knives, chanting "Death to America."

The devastation of the drone strike tore open a school and not a terrorist safe house, as intelligence analysts had guaranteed with "ninety-eight percent accuracy." It wasn't the first time the controversial CIA drone program took innocent lives, or that children were victims of a remote, distant crime by the US's autonomous, unmanned air vehicles.

Behind a news team filming the destroyed school, Bahdoon, the Yemeni-born, French-educated psychiatrist, videotaped the rescue operation. He captured the visceral anger of the people in the street with his smartphone. He adjusted his wire-frame glasses, filming as he looked for other dramatic pictures to shoot. A pair of tall, armed Somali warriors, dressed in rags, wearing light blue headscarves—*hijabs*—hovered in Bahdoon's shadow. He stopped recording, removed his glasses, and wiped the dust out of his eyes. Bahdoon rubbed the lenses clean on his shirt and put the glasses back on. He saw a Yemeni soldier carry a woman's arm out of the ruins and started filming again, capturing the grisly scene, tracking the soldier as he strode to a police vehicle and put the arm in the cooler, as if putting fish on ice.

The mob reacted to the dismembered arm. They screamed, shouting louder, cursing with bloodthirsty revenge. Some yelled for death. But the satellite that identified the CIA target hung in low earth orbit, while the CIA team that fired the drone's Hellfire missiles sat in a climate-controlled mobile trailer in one of the secret drone bases in the United Arab Emirates, Afghanistan, or Djibouti, Africa. Each base was located more than five hundred miles away, making it hard to haul those responsible for the attack into the square to be stoned or beheaded.

Bahdoon was aware of that reality, just as he was cued into the power of social media. The videos he captured that day were already going viral around the world, not just on al Qaeda or ISIS websites, but across American and European channels, hitting news airwaves, Twitter feeds, YouTube, Facebook pages, and a myriad of social, mobile chat, and video platforms. Bahdoon the propagandist was keen on exploiting the social sentiment of the people against the West, who, he knew, would recoil in horror at the attack. Children blown to pieces, an elementary school destroyed. The school bombing put the US military machine on notice for days, if not weeks. And it might be the tipping point to force the CIA to scale back its drone operations in Yemen.

Bahdoon knew how to pull the psychological levers. He was educated in France and the United States. In less than a day the bombing would turn into a damning indictment against the US drone program with the UN, countries around the world, and Western journalists coming to report on the horror. So Bahdoon ordered the locals to line up the grieving, distraught parents. Their images would raise global awareness with their fury directed at the United States, the "Great Satan," who destroyed the school in the drone strike.

After filming an elderly husband and wife embracing in pain over the loss of their child, Bahdoon turned off the videocam. He stepped to the Somali guards and said in their native tongue, "Call the scout at the dock and ask him how many Coast Guard ships are in port."

One Somali guard took out a mobile phone and called a scout at the seaside pier in Zinjibar. During the war on terror, both Jaar and Zinjibar had been fought over, captured, taken back, recaptured, and lost again to AQAP fighters—a.k.a., Ansar al-Shari'a—in their ongoing battle with CIA-sponsored Yemeni government forces, which ultimately lost to the Iranian-backed Houthi rebels. The Somali guard listened and nodded again and again. He flicked two fingers, letting Bahdoon know there were two Coast Guard cutters in port.

Bahdoon stepped behind the Somali guards to make a call to the highlands north of Jaar in *Rub' al Khali*—the Empty Quarter—one of the largest sand deserts in the world, stretching from Yemen and south Saudi Arabia, east across Oman into the UAE.

Speaking Arabic, Bahdoon said, "Imran, take the camels to the well." He ended the call without receiving confirmation on the other side; he grinned at the Somali guards and wiped dust off his brow. Bahdoon had something far more powerful than a civil lawsuit in a US court on his smartphone. He had the raw images of a CIA drone strike on the "innocent lambs of Yemen."

He tweeted the photos dripping with blood on jihadi and Twitter accounts he hacked.

Chapter Seven

A N A-FRAME TENT sat at the base of a sand dune. Camels slurped water in a trough, watched by a few tribesmen. The animals were showpieces for US military satellites and spy drones, in case a UAV was retasked to watch the tent from above.

Inside the tent, Qas, a twenty-five-year-old hacker from the Syrian Electronic Army, scraped dust off his scarred face as he watched Imran listen to Bahdoon's coded message. He kept his hands by the laptop keyboard, wary that the NSA or the US National Reconnaissance Office could hack his keystrokes. Imran, a beefy, mustachioed Syrian army sergeant, turned off the satellite phone, and repeated the coded message in Arabic to Qas: "Take the camels to the well."

The shorthand meant cyber-hijacking a tanker in the Gulf of Aden.

But Qas froze. So Imran slapped him in the face. He grabbed the boy by the nape of his neck and shoved a pistol in his eye, growling, "You no longer work for Assad's army, you work for me. You don't obey me, I'll cut open your scar and bleed you."

The engineer nodded, carefully lifting his fingers over the keyboard, waiting for Imran to withdraw the firearm from his face. Qas was a tall, wiry-frame geek with a crooked nose, broken several times; a pair of scars from the civil war in Syria hardened his resolve. The wounds dated back to the start of the "Water War" in 2011, when Syrian farmers protested the politically driven water policies that crushed agriculture during a drought.

When Imran withdrew the pistol, Qas swiped the laptop awake. He clicked open a link to a slew of Trojan horses, malware that had been installed in the supertanker's navigation system a month before with a flash-drive. It was an inside job. More viruses were installed remotely when the captain's first mate opened a spear-phished email. With the viruses activated from their dormant state, Qas had monitored the ship for a week and now uploaded a super-imposed map of the Gulf of Aden. He showed Sergeant Imran the oil tanker's course running through the northern waypoints of the gulf, and asked, "How many degrees north do you want to pull the ship off course?"

"Degrees? Six," Imran answered confidently, watching the ship's blinking image move at sixteen knots. "Will they know?"

"How far they drift north? No. The hijacked Automatic Identification Systems transponders is double blind," Qas explained. "We change the ship's course. The pilot changes it back to what he thinks is right. But the new course sends the ship to where we want it to go."

"Praise Allah. The tanker will be in range of the Somali team in thirty minutes," Imran said, glancing at his watch.

"How much longer do we need to stay here? This tent's hot as an oven," Qas said.

"After the operation is carried out. We move tonight across the cooling sand," Imran said.

Nodding, Qas said, "When the tanker comes in contact, I will disable the water cannons and other pirate defenses."

Chapter Eight

THE ORANGE LEVIATHAN plowed through the Gulf of Aden laden with two million barrels of crude oil, heading west toward the Red Sea.

Low, slow, the three-football-fields-long supertanker followed the anti-pirate shipping lane waypoints off the coast of Yemen. This alternate course was made in an attempt to steer clear of the Somali pirates, who, after a steep decline in raids, hostage captures, and ransoms, began to crank up scouting activities again around the Horn of Africa, casing the ships that sailed into the waters every day, but not attacking them.

Of the 20,000 vessels that pass through the gulf each year, transiting to and from the Suez Canal through the Red Sea, Somali pirates used to attack one in 600 ships. Since 2011, that ratio had plummeted. The decline in the rate of attacks was due to the NATO-led counter-piracy program. That included erecting regional piracy call centers and the deployment of the Vessels Protection Detachments (VPD)—the hiring of armed guards placed on board the ships by the shipping companies. Two years after that strategy was implemented, it shifted piracy away from Somalia to West Africa, off the coast of Mali and Nigeria. Confident that the pirate attacks had waned in the gulf, frugal shipowners reduced the VPD crews to pairs and even a lone trained sniper. Such was the case for the Norwegian-owned, Singapore-flagged supertanker *Blå Himmel*—*Blue Heaven*.

On the bridge, Peder Olsen, a machined ex-counterterrorism sniper, stood by the ship's Danish captain, as well as the pilot and first mate—both Filipinos. While they chatted in accent-rich

English, Peder, from Norway, scouted the blue sea to identify potential threats. Hot, dehydrated, he had enough being in the sun, patrolling decks and catwalks. The broad-shoulder mercenary with cropped blond hair had a bad case of sunburn. It made his neck and scalp tender with pain.

Peder knew the scouting of the pirate boats was a passive activity. So he focused his attention on the ships and tankers that might smuggle Iranian oil and weapons through the gulf. He chugged a bottle of water, took off his sweaty tee shirt, wiped a damp towel across his strapping chest and arms, and pulled a clean tee shirt over his head. As he pushed his arms through the sleeves, he turned his focus to the sea when the pilot pointed to a pair of wooden dhows off the port side.

That spring day, Peder kept an eye on the ship's blindspot, as the black hulled fishing boat angled toward the supertanker's starboard aft just outside the wake.

The Somali fishermen had been tracking the vessel for a day, passing intel through a broken chain of fishing boats. The Somalis trolled for information from a network of local Yemeni fishermen with satellite communication equipment, some stolen, some salvaged from previous raids, others bought from the spoils of the shipping companies' ransoms from past hijackings. But it was the remote work of Qas, the Syrian Electronic Army engineer in the Empty Quarter, who took command of the ship's navigation system without the captain knowing.

In NATO's quest to collect data for the big picture on the growing piracy threat, they required commercial ships to radio their charts. The broadcasts of ships' flag, ports of loading, course, and destination compounded the folly, since the network of soft protection openly shared radio transmissions with pirates and fishermen who eavesdropped from near and far.

In 2002, the AIS ship-tracking software system was implemented worldwide, continually transmitting critical shipping data between seafaring vessels—again handing over the specifics of route, course, speed at sea level, and position to the scouts and hackers every ten seconds. Qas hacking the ship relayed that information back to the pirates.

The captain and Peder, a sniper from Norway's *Forsvarets Spesialkommando* (FSK)—"Special Forces"—monitored neither the weather nor the AIS tracker of an American-flag container ship heading toward them thirty nautical miles west. Instead, like the pilot, their attention shifted to the third boat on the radar cruising in their shadow of the starboard flank.

Peder spoke in Norwegian, which is similar to Danish, saying: "Captain, we must keep an eye on that craft. It looks suspicious." He picked up binoculars, dialing the zoom. He tracked the forty-foot dhow as it raced across the sea. His trained eye identified the craft as a pirate mothership—a floating platform from which pirates launch skiff attacks to ensnare targeted vessels. That's what he deduced from eyeing a large canvas sprawled over a hidden object. Did the canvas cover hauls of fish or bundled nets? Or did skiffs lie in wait underneath?

The captain, a dignified, gray-haired Dane, put his hand on the first mate's shoulder, and ordered, "Take the crew down to the engine room and lock them in."

"*Ja, ja*, run. Hurry," Peder urged the Filipino, giving the pilot a first aid kit as he headed out the door. The pilot took the ship's manifest and exited the bridge.

The captain hit the button to start the water cannons, but nothing happened. He hit the button again—no response.

Chapter Nine

PEDER PULLED A barrel-bag from under a cabinet and placed it on a seat. He aimed binoculars at a distant point beyond the bow and watched the dhow cut in front of the tanker. Seconds later, it launched a pair of skiffs with what looked like a mix of Yemeni and Somali pirates. The speedboats tore across the sea, moving ahead of the supertanker. But then, like in an eerie dream, the skiffs swept in a mirror figure eight and gunned it back toward the tanker.

"What the hell?" Peder observed, confused by the tactic.

"Are you sure that's a pirate ship?" the Danish captain asked, zooming his binoculars.

"*Ja*. The skiffs are hauling," Peder said. He eyed the coast of Yemen through the heat haze. "Captain, are we on the right course?" The captain checked the navigation, the GPS coordinates, and the electronic compass. Peder looked at him as if he were a bookish professor, then took out a compass. He swiveled it around in his palm until the needle aligned with the north cardinal point.

"Here, look—" Peder said, holding the compass over the ship's electronic compass that showed the ship's instrumentation was off by several degrees. "Something's wrong, captain. Have you been hacked?"

"Hacked?"

"*Ja*, cyberterrorists," Peder said, growing incensed at the captain's lack of situational awareness. "Maybe it's why you can't turn on the water cannons."

The mothership left the skiff and headed west toward the unseen American container ship, relatively close in nautical miles, but still out of sight in the haze.

Peder put down the binoculars. He watched the skiffs back into the shadow of the supertanker. With the mothership racing ahead, the other twin fishing dhows—well behind the vessel—released a trio of skiffs into the water. One by one, the boats, powered by twin-engine outboard motors, began to crisscross in the tankers' wake to surround the vessel.

"Jesus Christ, they're going to attack," the captain said, alarmed.

"Jesus isn't here." Peder unzipped the barrel-bag. He assembled a folding-stock assault rifle with grenade-launcher. He zipped a bag filled with ammo, slung it over his shoulder, and said, "If I can't turn away the skiffs, we're fucked."

The captain pressed a distress beacon, signaling a SOS to NATO and an international defense force stationed on the Yemen-owned island of Socotra off the Horn of Africa. But the base, equipped with rescue and attack helicopters, naval littoral ships, and Navy SEALs and Special Forces battalions, was located hundreds of miles east in the Indian Ocean from their present position. Knowing that, the captain picked up the radio and contacted the American vessel ahead. He warned the American captain about the pirate mother-ship moving toward his vessel's direction in a coded message. Then he called mayday, spewing: "This is *Blå Himmel, Blå Himmel.* Mayday, mayday. We are under pirate attack."

A staccato burst of gunfire punctuated his words. Bullets ripped across the steel deck below. Screams of panic followed the next exchange of gunfire. Pounding footsteps vibrated the metal stairs and across the decks and catwalks, as crewmen fled or hid to take cover.

An errant rocket-propelled grenade arced over the bridge, scorching the air in a hot vapor trail. The RPG projectile missed with a boom, exploding over the sea.

Peder opened a side portal. He placed the barrel-bag outside, turned to the shaking captain, and warned, "Be careful."

A burst of shots pelted the metal deck and bridge; the captain ducked. When the shooting stopped, he opened the starboard door, slid outside onto the landing, and listened to the throttle of the skiff engines. He gazed over the rail: the three skiffs from the dhows trimmed alongside and tied on to the supertanker. Skinny, dark-skinned Somali pirates, many of them teenagers, climbed up grapnels and rope ladders, like invasive lizards scurrying up a tree.

The pirate boarding party wore dark blue tee shirts and shorts, forgoing the white tees and tan shorts worn on previous raids, giving the tiny specks out in the gulf a hue harder to detect against the deep blue.

The captain peered down the stairs and saw one Filipino crewman lying in a pool of blood. A tall, sinewy pirate, gripping an AK-47 assault rifle, stepped over the body and raced up the steps. The captain retreated back into the bridge. He picked up the radio to call the distress signal again, when the door flung open with a hostile pirate aiming a rifle in the captain's face.

In a deep, heated voice with a thick Somali accent, Samatar said, "Cup, no rad." He swatted the radio out of the captain's hand, pushing him away from the controls. A second pirate slipped behind Samatar and took over the ship, slowing it down to ten knots . . . then eight . . . then held her steady at six knots. "Cup, take me to da box."

Samatar stared at the captain's twitching lips and inspected his hollow gaze. The pirate slapped him across the face, pressed the gun's hot barrel against his cheek, grinding it into the bone, singeing the Dane's fair skin, barking, "Box, man. Show me the box now." Samatar grabbed the captain and shoved him out the door into a captured Malay crewman, held under gunpoint by a trio of teenage pirates.

"Again. The box? Show me," Samatar demanded, cocking the pistol to fire.

The captain shrugged. Samatar shot the Malay crewman in the face—a jet of blood shot out. The victim's legs gave way; the pirates caught the lifeless body; the head slung to the side. Samatar dug his fingernails into the captain's neck and pressed the smoking hot barrel against the Dane's cheekbone, saying, "Money. Take me to da box."

The Danish captain flinched when Samatar clucked a trigger sound with his tongue, pulling the gun away. The captain pressed his burned flesh, asking, "Box? You mean the safe?"

"Yeow, Cup." Samatar slapped the captain across the back of the head, shoving him down the stairs toward the captain's quarters.

Shocked, prodded, and goaded, the trembling captain gripped the handrail and stumbled down the metal steps. He gazed ahead to a couple of pirates chasing a squat Vietnamese sailor—the only other non-Filipino in the crew—across the main deck, where all the crude oil was stored underneath in massive vats. The quarry scurried toward the bow. A moment later another team of pirates climbed on board from the mothership skiffs, cutting off the sailor's path of escape. Trapped, the sailor threw his hands in the air and surrendered. One pirate searched his pockets; the other pirate knocked him down with the butt of the rifle.

As the captain relived the Malay crewman being shot in the face at point-blank range, he knew that in the first minutes of boarding the escalation of violence had peaked. Why the shock of violence? Why the cold-blooded killing of a crewman? A dead hostage is not a bargaining chip.

In his quarters, the captain followed the advice of Peder to "submit." He opened the safe without any tricks or resistance. He stepped back as Samatar stuffed stacks of US dollars, Swiss francs, euros, British pounds, and Norwegian kroner into a backpack. The haul netted more than sixty thousand dollars total from Åsgard Lines A/S.

Samatar zipped the backpack shut, slung it over his shoulder, and dragged the captain outside.

Chapter Ten

O UT IN THE glare of the sun, the captain shielded his eyes. Samatar, donning mirrored sunglasses, dragged the captain past the housings covering the giant oil tanks that sprouted up from the double-hulled vessel.

Amidships, Samatar pushed the captain across the entire length of the tanker toward the bow, where pirates stood around a pair of captured sailors, who kneeled over the body of the Vietnamese deck mate.

At the bow, Samatar threw the captain on top of the felled sailor. He clicked a radio and spoke in rapid-fire Somali tongue, barking orders to one of his men: "No. Follow the plan. You see an American eagle watching . . . a boat off the tail . . . NATO ships . . . dump the black gold in the sea. Don't let your father down." Samatar listened for a moment. After a pause, a reply shot back: "Okay, Sama."

Seven stories beneath the bridge, below the fuel tank that fed the ship power to travel across oceans, through the pump room at the base of the hull that separated the reservoir of oil tanks from the stern, sat the engine room. Tucked inside, the first mate and half the crew had barricaded themselves in with the three engines of the U-shaped stern. With the ducted propellers facing inward, the U, as opposed to the V-shaped design, made the screws churn the sea into a single vortex of power to propel the tanker to sail faster. The noise of the engines drowned out the shouts of the pirates banging on the walls and doors to breach the engine room.

Trapped, hiding in the rear of the room, where the shafts of the screws stuck out from the engines through the stern hull, the first mate and crew listened to the muted sounds of banging and braced for the worse. They couldn't hear all the words of the pirates, but they did hear the broken English that cursed them, that spat out threats, that demanded they open the door or die.

As the escalating Darwinian battle between predator and prey of the pirate attacks ramped up, month-by-month, year after year, the Somalis had come newly prepared for the crewmen hiding behind barred steel doors. The young teen with two front teeth missing took out a wad of Slovakian plastic explosive—Semtex-H—and stuffed a blasting cap in the clay brick, formed the putty over the door handle, then ran a wire around a column. With a signal to other pirates, the teen set off the shaped charge connecting the wire to a mobile phone. He tapped a picture.

The door exploded open, shredding the steel.

The pirates charged in through the smoke, firing into the ceiling to avoid damaging the engines. Shrapnel from the blast ricocheted, wounding a couple of cowering crewmen. The first mate trembled, holding his ears in deafening pain. Behind him, other crewmen quivered with their chests on their knees, their hands raised in surrender.

The Somali teen with the missing teeth slapped the first mate hard. He pushed him into the arms of henchmen, who whisked him out of the engine room. The pirate took out a radio and called topside, telling Samatar that the engine room was secure and the remaining crew were now hostages.

Chapter Eleven

A<small>T THE BOW</small>, Samatar received the radio message that the supertanker was under his control. He lifted the captain off the deck, turned to take him to a metal ladder to stuff him in one of the skiffs, when a gunshot cracked the heat haze.

A bullet ripped through the backpack and clipped Samatar's shoulder. The shrapnel from the exploding shell blew open the backpack, scattering money, like leaves blown off a tree. With strength fading, Samatar spun around to see where the shot came from. In the pivot, he grabbed hold of the captain's arm and pulled him into the line of fire. Before he could shield his body with the Dane, the next shot struck Samatar, blowing a hole in his stomach.

Samatar let go of the captain, twisted and hit the deck. The captain fell by his side. The Dane looked at the shock in Samatar's eyes, then rolled away as the other pirates returned fire. Samatar held his entrails against his body to keep them from spilling out and gazed vacantly at the deck.

The pirates unloaded a volley of gunfire at the bridge.

On the roof of the bridge, bullets whizzed over Peder's head. He flattened his body and fired one last shot that killed Samatar a quarter mile away. He knew it would be seconds before the pirates pinpointed the sniper nest. So he looked around, surveying the chimney stack rising above the bridge and figured that it was too big and bulky to climb down safely to the stern to abandon ship. Instead, he grabbed the rifle, rolled over, sprang up, and dashed across the roof toward the port stern.

A burst of shots whizzed by him—so close that he felt air molecules slice apart.

At the edge, Peder threw himself down and lowered his body onto the steel beam of an outrigger. He ambled across it, keeping his balance with outstretched arms. As Peder neared the end of the outrigger, extending over the sea, he tossed the rifle into the water and leapt off the superstructure. A swell broke fifty feet below . . . He fell in a controlled jump toward the wave, scissor-kicking the air, until his feet came together and plunged into the sea, like a fence post.

Underwater, the tanker's massive wake plowed over him; the rumble of the triple screws forcing him down, churning, pushing him away. Counterintuitively he flapped his arms upward to sink deeper. When the pressure built up in his ears, he knew what to do from his days as an underwater welder: he pinched his nose, gently breathed out, popping the pressure in his ears. With his descent arrested, he looked up at the ship's wake streaming overhead and fought the urge to surface and the need to breathe.

Peder floated upward, kicking, until he breached the surface like a cork, breathing hard and heavy, spitting salt water out of his mouth, choking, coughing over and over again.

Peder opened a Velcro flap and pressed a radio beacon, signaling to the NATO pirate response team for search and rescue.

Chapter Twelve

THE SUN BEAT down on a pair of lorries carrying white-hulled speedboats through the dusty roads of Bosaso, in the Bari province of northern Somalia. The vehicles rocked and bobbed down street after street, turning in front of stores, squeezed by a fish-processing plant, snaked past mud-caked Land Rovers parked in a narrow alley, and bounded and jostled toward the coast with a couple of passersby giving the delivery truck a second look.

In the pirate capital of Puntland, it was an open secret that the crafts were being delivered not to fishermen, but to the local group of pirates run by Samatar's brother, the Puntland warlord Korfa, who took over the pirate tribes of Somaliland to the northwest when NATO forces cracked down on piracy in the Indian Ocean and Gulf of Aden around the Horn of Africa. This effectively put their trade of hijackings and hostages-for-ransom out of business.

The port city of Bosaso housed 500,000 people. Swaths of sun-bleached, low-rise, clay and brick buildings cut views of the horizon, except when one looked out to sea, where a mosque dome topped nearly every block. Bosaso was the gem of Somalia, rising above the war and poverty. The poor man's Morocco, with a skyline absent of construction cranes, was sandwiched in a bowl of mountains to the south. Situated on the Gulf of Aden, Bosaso became the hub that received the UN food relief program deliveries; brought in caches of Chinese, Russian, Iranian, Pakistani, and North Korean weapons; smuggled desperate Somalia emigrants across the gulf to Yemen; and once hauled in a third of the annual take of pirate hostages during its peak.

It wasn't only Mogadishu that had been scarred and held without the leadership of a true government for a generation. Somaliland, which fell under the swift and brutal control of Islamic law, fought several bloody clashes with the Somalis of Puntland beginning in 2003. Brothers Korfa and Samatar played both sides of the war, fueling skirmishes, and ending them in violence.

On the outskirts of the city, a Yemeni boy dismounted a donkey by a watering hole. He left the animal with local farmers, ran through a flock of sheep, and cut across the road in front of the tandem lorries carrying the skiffs. Over an arid hill, a seaside villa came into view. The boy raced the vehicles to the house, where a family of poor Somalis waited outside, their expressions browbeaten, their bodies slack.

At the door, an armed pirate stuck a rifle in the boy's chest; the boy flashed a hand-sign.

Inside the cool stone and clay house, another pair of guards aimed AK-47 assault rifles at the boy. A third guard, standing in front of a Chinese dragon curtain, waved the child to enter the living room. The Yemeni boy took a seat on a straw mat and waited. He listened to the strange dialect of an African mother, her wide hips wrapped in a dark blue tunic, cradling her baby a few feet from a sinewy black man. He wore a sleeveless shirt that revealed the slight bulge of an oddly shaped hump on his left shoulder blade. Was the mass a fatty deposit? A birth defect? A cancerous growth? Or was it a battle-wound that didn't heal properly?

With an angular face and leopard-like eyes, the man lounged in a wicker chair. He heard the mother's pleas, the trembling of her voice as a pet snake slithered up his arm and across the buffalo hump to his good shoulder. He kept an eye on an HD TV on the wall with the screen showing nothing but static. The link to a satellite feed was broken. He pressed a remote, shutting off the TV.

Korfa, the warlord of the Dharoor Valley Clan, was pirate number one in Puntland. He was the micro-loan officer to the poor, the sheriff, the enforcer, the buyer of foreign spies and government officials. To the locals of Bosaso he was known as the "Ferryman" for transporting hundreds of Somali refugees across the gulf to Yemen year after year. And when the civil war broke out in Yemen, he ferried some Houthi tribesmen and Yemeni terrorists and their families back to Puntland.

"How am I going to take care of my baby here in Somalia?" the mother asked, while her baby clawed at her breast to feed on milk. Korfa nodded at the mother, staring at her plump, milk-swollen breasts. She pulled open the tunic, revealing a sand-dollar-size nipple the baby clutched and suckled. As the baby fed, the warlord felt the warm surge of blood fill his groin, fattening his cock against his thigh on its way to a hard erection, when hushed Arabic words were exchanged at the door.

A bodyguard stepped to Korfa telling him in Puntland code that the Sheikh's men had arrived from Somaliland. Korfa signaled the visitors to wait. He took out a pair of mirrored sunglasses, stared at the mother, saying in Somali tongue: "You will be safe with my son and my sister. Remember they are refugees from the valley, like you. When the UN or Red Cross ask you about my boy and sister, what will you tell them?"

The mother held her baby tight, replying, "They are refugees of war and famine."

"Say that and nothing more, and your voyage will be smooth." Korfa stood up, handed her pictures of his son and sister. He motioned a guard, who picked up a backpack of food and handed it to the mother, then escorted her outside.

Korfa looked over at the Yemeni boy. He saw a tear stream down his face. The warlord put the snake on the floor. The boy jumped backed and hid behind a guard, who bent over and picked up the snake. Scared of the viper, the boy stepped back and bumped into a pair of AQAP recruits, who had entered the villa casing the rooms for cameras and weapons. Once the room was cleared, Yemeni General Mustafa walked inside. He was second in charge of Somaliland.

General "Muse," as insiders knew him, reigned over the clerics, who preached Islamic Sharia Law, and managed his AQAP soldiers, who enforced its moral codes and gender limits.

Korfa gave General Mustafa a hard look, signaling with his eyes that he would need a moment with the boy. He eyed the child, asking in Arabic, "Why the long face?"

The Yemeni boy, now shaking, intimidated by the presence of the general and his AQAP henchmen, gulped, "We captured the whale . . . "

"Good. Then the tanker is heading to port. . . . Why the long face?"

"When Samatar took the captain to the skiffs, a sniper shot him."

"Dead? Sama dead?" Korfa erupted and grabbed the boy by his skinny shoulders. "You say my brother Samatar is dead? My own flesh and blood?" Korfa bellowed in rising anger. He belted out a catcall to the ceiling, as if he could see God's angry face from the unseen the sky. "Did Sama's men stand like statues and watch him die? Did they catch the assassin?"

The boy froze unable to answer.

"Good God, what the fuck?" Korfa snatched a Kalashnikov from his bodyguard, swung it around and smashed a vase and glass bookcase with its butt. He ripped the shelf frame off the wall, smashing pots and pictures, stepped on the glass with his bare feet and whipped the assault rifle into the TV, shattering the flat screen in a crack of smoke. Shocked, bristling at the news, Korfa turned around, the veins in his temples throbbed with a rapid beating heart. Out of the corner of his eye, he saw AQAP soldiers chatting like birds in small talk.

General Mustafa, a man of mixed Egyptian and Yemeni blood, giving him bronze skin with Egyptian features, frowned at the boy, and then looked at Korfa: "Where are the Syrian satellite phones I gave you?"

The general was oblivious of his soldiers' disrespect behind him.

"Gave me? I bought them from you, like I did the skiffs outside on the lorries," Korfa replied, anger strained his face. He pointed at the boy—"This Yemeni is my runner. As for the Satcoms, they're up in the mountains. If spies or Americans try to triangulate where I stand, all they'll find are goats and a booby trap. Boom!" He bellowed, spreading his arms in a blast arc. Korfa stepped around the boy and drilled a cold stare at the soldiers. "What are you hyenas chatting about? My brother, Sama, is dead."

The soldier shrugged, staring not in Korfa's eyes, but at his shoulder hump. Korfa saw that as a second slight from an AQAP field grunt. Korfa drilled another stare into the soldier, who averted his eyes. Korfa put his arm around the boy, and said, "Call the mothership and tell the crew to bring the captain to port." The Yemeni boy nodded and dashed out of the villa. Korfa turned to General Mustafa: "What would you do if you lost your right arm to a sniper?"

General Mustafa wondered where the question was leading. "I'd hunt the beast down and behead him, filming his death live on a jihadi website." The general took out a smartphone and showed Korfa the video of dead children being carried out of the ruins of a school in Yemen.

"Who has seen this?" Korfa asked, pointing at the video in the general's palm.

"The world. It's on Twitter, YouTube, everywhere . . ."

"Who is the man? Who is the genius behind luring America to attack a school?"

"A propaganda doctor, named Bahdoon," the general said.

"Send him to Somaliland to meet the hostages," Korfa said, turning his attention back to the soldier. He stepped past the general and eyed the soldier, saying, "The sniper who killed my brother . . . I will hunt him down, his friends, his family, his children, pets, cousins, professors, and kill them all. If the bastard is still alive, I'll smoke him out of a tree stump like termites."

With that, Korfa shoved the AQAP soldier outside. In the shock of daylight the field grunt turned around and became confused by Korfa's rage. He gripped a pistol. But Korfa grabbed his hand, and clamped onto the firearm, removing it from his grip. Korfa tossed the pistol to one of his Somali guards, who now numbered a dozen. "Who do you work for? Somali government? . . . Kenya?"

"No, no. I work for General Adad in Syria. . . . Let go of my hand," he said, as a stack of pamphlets slipped out of his tunic onto the ground. Korfa kicked the pamphlets aside and saw the dead, bearded, Jordanian terrorist leader Abu Musab Zarqawi holding an assault rifle.

"You're lying. You're not al Qaeda, you're the Caliphate ISIS. You're here to recruit my people to Islamic jihad?" the warlord groused. General Mustafa and Korfa's bodyguards formed a circle around the pirate chief and the ISIS spy as they faced off. "Muse, why didn't you vet this scorpion? He will kill my people, plant his black Islamic flag in my land, then kill you," Korfa said. He pulled out a pistol, snatched the soldier's hand and, with eyes burning in hot embers, he clucked his tongue mimicking the sound of a gunshot. The spy flinched. Korfa pushed him to the ground, tearing open his tunic that revealed his bare chest. The spy wasn't wearing a wire, but he did have a concealed dagger inside the waistband and a tattoo on his biceps of a "Z" made of rifles.

Korfa turned to the general, saying, "Vermin like him are not welcome in Somalia." Then he shot the spy in the chest and listened to the air wheeze out of the man's lungs. His last breath for life filled the air.

The pirate warlord stepped on the pamphlets of Zarqawi, grinding them in the dirt.

Chapter Thirteen

FROM THE HELICOPTER flight deck of the USS *New York LPD-21*—a San Antonio-class amphibious assault ship built with twenty-four tons of recycled steel from the wreckage of the World Trade Center towers that fell on 9/11—SEAL Commanding Officer Nick "Nico" Gregorius, a stocky Greek-American with thick black hair, checked equipment, weapons, supplies, diving gear, trimix gas tanks, rebreathers, and ammunition prior to loading on board the UH-60 Black Hawk.

The boatswain's mate master-of-arms stood over the weapons cache confirming the inventory with a handheld scanner. He directed the crew to load the supplies into the cargo bay.

A landing signal officer, holding a pair of glowing batons in one hand, lifted the visor shield of his helmet and approached CO Gregorius. He showed him an instant message and pointed to the stairwell door behind him that went down into the ship's storage area. The CO nodded and headed into the ship—that was the leading edge of the US Navy's Assault Ready Group for mobile and rapid deployment missions in the littoral space.

The USS *New York* carried a crew of 365 sailors and 700 battle-ready marines from the Marine Expeditionary Unit. The ship was more than ready to combat pirates in a clash. Called to duty from the Persian Gulf after the *Blå Himmel* was seized, the USS *New York* picked up two SEAL platoons stationed at Point Alpha Base and cruised into the Gulf of Aden.

It launched one of two Predator drones to track, monitor, and survey the American-flag vessel *Shining Sea.*

The captain's executive officer, or XO, greeted Nico Gregorius in the below deck hangar. He informed him that he was being led to sickbay. They meandered down a flight of stairs, through the mess hall, to the amidships medical office. The XO flashed his ID badge and took the SEAL inside the room that held the sunburned, fatigued sniper Peder Olsen.

CO Gregorius checked the snoring Norwegian's med charts and EKG monitor. He turned to the XO. "What do you want me to do?"

"The order came from the top, commander," said the XO, reading an IM on a tablet. "It states you're to awaken the patient with whatever means necessary to learn what he saw."

The CO gave the XO an *are-you-fucking-kidding-me* look, as he pried open one of Peder's swollen eyelids. Under the puffy slit, he saw the pupil was dilated. "I need the coldest water you have on board this vessel. Cold, but not too clean."

"We got some house gray water below deck," the XO said and ordered it over the radio: "Send a mechanic to the desal filter room and bring up a cold, cold bucket to sickbay."

"Gray water, clean enough for laundry, I like it," the CO noted, checking Peder's pulse.

Five minutes later, the construction mechanic arrived in navy blue coveralls carrying the bucket of water. Gregorius examined Peder's sun-blistered face. He unhooked a monitor, raised the arm with the IV drip, and then tapped the mechanic's elbow, prodding him to dump the water on the sniper. Cold water splashed all over Peder's head and chest, pouring onto the bed, soaking the sheets and mattress, running and dripping onto the floor.

Jolted awake, Peder sprang up shaking his head. He came to, brushing the water off his lap. CO Gregorius put his hand on Peder's soaked head, saying, "Norseman, you are on board the USS *New York*. You jumped off the *Blue Heaven*. Do you hear me, you blond puke?"

Peder managed to squint one eye open. He spat, pursed his lips, and mouthed, *"Jaaa."*

The SEAL CO worked Peder on a line of questioning that established where he was when the pirates seized the supertanker; how they hijacked it trailing in the blind spot; how the AIS navigation system had been hacked; and how he suspected the pirates used the mothership as a decoy. Peder then admitted that he shot the lead pirate before jumping ship.

Chapter Fourteen

IN THE COCOON of silence beneath the surface of a large holding pen, Merk Toten curled his body into a ball, resting his knees on his chest. He felt his kneecaps touch his skin.

Expelling breaths through a snorkel, Merk feathered the water with the swim fins to keep neutral buoyancy. He watched the chalk-blue haze in front of him, sensing a dolphin spying on him. The unseen biologic system pulsed him with its sonar clicks. In a blink of an eye, the dolphin defined Merk's shape, his heart rate, the density of his sinews and bones, the health of his organs, and the remaining air in his lungs. Unsure from which point the dolphin would attack, Merk panned the blue bowl—when the snout of the dolphin soared overhead.

The moment he tracked Tasi, the torpedo-shape of Inapo sliced behind him, grazing Merk with his pectoral fin. The gentle bump at high speed spun Merk into a barrel roll. Tumbling backward like a top, he let go of his knees, stretched out his legs, and unfolded his body to arrest the spinning motion. But in doing so, he was vulnerable to being hit by Tasi.

Merk turned around, crossed his arms, and blocked a heavy blow with her snout. The force of Tasi spearing him, the combat diver, jarred the snorkel out of his mouth. With the dive mask knocked cockeyed, salt water flooded his eyes, temporarily blinding him. Inapo swung over, butted Merk back down, snatched the dislodged snorkel, and swam it to the surface, separating the breathing apparatus from the diver.

Above, the muted sound of footsteps strode across the floating metal dock.

Tasi, the navy dolphin with a shark bite scar on the back blade of her dorsal fin, breached the surface, tossing the snorkel onto the dock. The snorkel spat out a rill of water as it landed at the feet of a naval attaché in white uniform, wetting his patent leather shoes. Behind him stood CIA agent Alan Cuthbert, dressed in camouflage army fatigues.

Merk took an elevator ride up to the surface with Inapo. Cupping his hand on the dolphin's beak, he let go as they soared out of the cove. Merk twisted his body a quarter turn, landing his butt on the dock. He rolled backward and sprang to his feet, dripping wet in front of the naval attaché.

Out of uniform, Merk wasn't obligated to salute the higher-ranking officer. Instead, he extended his wet hand and shook the attaché in a firm grip. Alan Cuthbert looked on in disbelief, eyeing the water running down the ridges and striations of the burn scar that covered the left side of Merk's body. "Am I fired, heading back to San Diego?"

"Negative, Lt. Toten. You're hired, going to Somalia," said the naval attaché, looking over at Tasi and Inapo spying on their conversation.

"Really, sir?" Merk said, shocked to hear it after failing to save the life of Lt. Morgan Azar in the Strait of Hormuz. "Excuse me, sir." Merk turned to Tasi and Inapo, who floated—waiting for the next command. He signaled his fingers in pinchers to go "eat."

The dolphins swam across the cove, hidden behind a tall sand-colored blind that kept the marine mammal holding pens away from prying eyes in the Persian Gulf. Tasi and Inapo fluked to a female animal handler. She dangled fish in a bucket. The dolphins breached and struck their bodies in a loud midair slap. They bounced apart and splashed into the cove. Tasi and Inapo resurfaced in front of the handler, clearing their blowholes in jets of mist.

"Finesse and force," Merk said, pointing to the dolphins. "Tasi the female is all brains, very cunning. The male, Inapo, is loaded with testosterone like a bull."

"I can see that. Tasi and Inapo . . . they are the Guam-bred systems, aren't they?" The naval attaché took a towel from an animal handler and gave it to Merk to wipe off. "Toten, Special Ops Command has a new assignment for the MMS. It's Black Lit."

Merk understood the code words for "blacks ops in the littoral environment"—"Black Lit"—as more than classified. The mission would be clandestine in nature as opposed to covert action. That meant the op would conceal the sponsor, in that case the US Navy, instead of merely concealing the mission. In the former, the president would have zero knowledge that it existed, since it was off the books in the black budget. In the latter, the profile of a covert mission was grounded in an intel briefing with the executive-in-chief, often with Congressional oversight. Merk became curious as to why he was called to participate in a Black Lit operation.

"Where can we talk?" Alan Cuthbert asked.

The naval attaché looked around, not sure where to talk to in utmost secrecy. Merk pointed to a naval salvage ship on the other side of the blind, and said, "I was told the ship has a dive chamber on board. It seats eight. The stainless steel doors and walls dampen all outside noise. Close to soundproof."

"Pure oxygen, I'll take it," the attaché said, leading Merk to the chamber.

Stationed in an annex of the US Navy Base in Asu Bahrain, northwest of the Qatar peninsula, the Navy Marine Mammal Program's half-dozen dolphins were on loan to train and guard naval ships stationed in the Persian Gulf.

Merk toweled off and slipped on a "Go Navy" tee shirt. He led the naval attaché and Alan Cuthbert into the high-pressured hyperbaric diver chambers, or HBOTs. Sent overseas from one of six Norfolk, Virginia, rapid dive units, the HBOT was the ideal place to talk in private.

Once inside the cramped quarters, which had chairs, a wood table, and a bench, the chamber operator with a saturation technician closed the steel door and locked it shut. Merk hadn't seen Alan Cuthbert since they worked together in ferreting out an al Qaeda infiltrator in Hawaii a few years back.

The naval attaché picked up on the familiarity between the men, and asked, "Merk, how did you guys know each other?"

"It was a discussion about methods."

Cuthbert looked at Merk and then at the attaché, but said nothing.

"Methods? On what? Interrogation? Tracking terrorists?"

"Interspecies communication," Merk said. "We compared notes on dolphin spy-hopping versus man-made CIA Predator drones. Drones that one day be made for the sea to replace Tasi."

The attaché nodded, pretending he understood, and showed images on a laptop. A grainy infrared video showed a SEAL team boarding the US-flag container ship at 2217 hours. He said: "Toten, the *Shining Sea* was one of two vessels hijacked yesterday. When the SEALs boarded the ship, they didn't find any sailors. The bridge, main deck, engine room, and panic room were empty. No crew. Not even the body that spilled the blood during the pirate attack."

"I read the briefs. Like the captains being off-loaded into the pirate mothership. Does the evidence suggest the pirates transferred the American crew to the *Blå Himmel?*" Merk asked. "The oil cargo must be richer than the goods stored in those containers, no?"

The naval attaché showed footage from a Predator drone trailing the tanker heading to Somaliland. He explained that they never found the pirate mothership, and went on in detail about the lone escapee, Peder Olsen, the former Norwegian Special Forces sniper turned mercenary. He played a video on his mobile phone of Peder, sunburned, doused with a bucket of water, barely audible, confirming a kill before abandoning ship.

"The spec warrior wasn't the captain, but a hired gun. He must have killed a big lion and knew it," Merk said. "Why else abandon the hostages? He lived to fight another day."

"You read his actions like you know him," Cuthbert said, tapping the table.

"Gut, SEAL gut." Merk looked at the naval attaché, asking, "The pirate killed by Peder, who was he?" The attaché shrugged. So Merk turned to Cuthbert: "What list does the CIA and FBI share on the most wanted pirates in Somalia?"

"We have a dossier of three dozen inner-circle pirates from the Horn of Africa," he replied, "with ten of them operating in the north provinces along the Gulf of Aden."

"Anyone you know on that list?"

"A pirate named Samatar. His name translates to 'Doer of Good,'" Cuthbert said.

"Who's his warlord?"

"No one. Co-warlords. He shared power with his brother, Korfa, in Puntland."

Merk sat back with a quizzical look, then turned to the attaché: "Has anyone contacted Peder's family in Norway?"

"Sure. The Norwegian shipowner must have done that," the attaché sort of answered.

"You might want to inform his family about the pirate he took out. They're going to need twenty-four hour protection. Then I'd be concerned about why the supertanker is heading to Somaliland closer to the Red Sea instead of Korfa's home state of Puntland," Merk said.

"Anything else?" the naval attaché asked.

"What groups are bargaining for ransom demands?"

"Demands? It should be one demand, right?"

"Maybe three ransoms," Cuthbert interjected, holding up as many fingers.

"Why abandon the American ship? Hostage logistics? Something didn't go as planned, like Peder killing Samatar?" Merk wondered. "Alan, what's your story? Why are you here?"

"If you haven't heard, I got set up in Yemen."

"By whom?"

"We thought he was a good CIA asset. We vetted his background, his education in the West, his family tree, his business associates. For a Yemen businessman he was clean. Clean, legitimate business. No ties to AQAP or the Islamic State," he said. "The other night, one of our drones took out a building he told us was a terrorist safe house. But it ended up being a school. Children's bodies were pulled from the rubble, all videotaped for the world to see."

"You're kidding? No terrorist affiliation, but the asset sets you up to fail," Merk said.

"It happened on the same night you were on the Strait of Hormuz with Lt. Azar," the naval attaché pointed out, adding, "Really sorry about what happened to Morgan."

Merk half nodded, his eyes retreated in a pensive stare. "Same night? The night Iranians planted sea-mines. The drones were retasked to Yemen that night, Azar and I knew that. And the CIA doesn't have any assets in Iran either, do you?"

"Merk, the FBI hostage rescue team is being flown from Cairo to a town in Sudan, across the Somaliland border," the naval attaché said. "The White House summoned a private contractor to make contact with the pirates and the shipowners in Virginia and Norway."

Cuthbert elbowed Merk, saying, "Your former SEAL CO Dawson in Coronado and his partner, retired Delta Force commando Christian Fuller, are the private negotiators."

"Dante Dawson? The last I heard he retired."

"Affirmative. From the navy, not from action," the attaché said. "His new co is called Azure Shell."

Alan Cuthbert nodded in deep thought. He ran his finger round and round the table surface, eyeing the grain of the wood, looked up and said, "Is there a link? . . . A link between what you stumbled on in the strait and my asset setting me up in Yemen?"

Merk nodded: "There has to be."

Chapter Fifteen

WHEN THE CH-53E Super Stallion helicopter landed late that afternoon on the stern deck of the USS *New York*, the XO greeted Merk and escorted him to the Combat Direction Center, or CDC.

Merk refused to go. He wanted to stay behind to watch the NMMP veterinary team unload Tasi and Inapo, take them down on the elevator, and transfer them from the stretchers into inflatable holding pens in three-foot-deep salt water draped by tall safety nets.

Merk trusted few Navy personnel and fewer subcontractors with the care of his dolphins; he was especially protective of the Pacific bottlenose dolphins from Guam. Prior to a mission, he wanted their stress levels reduced. That included indoor air quality being particulate free; that loud noises wouldn't disturb, startle, or harm them; and that they wouldn't be exposed to passive pressure from nosy, camera-clicking ensigns or become amusement for small crowds.

What concerned Merk about new naval vessels? They tend to carry heavy metals in the air in the form of dust and filings on the floors, walls, ceilings, and vents, if the rooms, corridors, and stairwells weren't fine-cleaned before launch. He followed Tasi and Inapo down into the dank industrial storage hangar of the ship. As soon as the hardboxes rolled off the lift, the odor of hydraulic fluid permeated the air. The hairs on the back of Merk's neck stood up and his skin grafts started to itch, reminding him of the sense of danger he felt the night an oil-slick fire burned in the harbor off mainland China in the Taiwan Strait.

Merk surveyed the below deck chamber. To the rear, he saw the source of the acrid smell. In the backlit hangar, the silhouette of the ship's other Sea Stallion sat idle with a battery of mechanics working on the main rotor. He strode toward the helicopter and noticed hydraulic fluid dripping in a puddle next to an open gangbox. Parts, tools, and hoses were strewn across a plastic sheet on the floor. Covers and couplings from the rotor were piled on carts, as engineers inspected the rotor blades. Merk knew it would be hours before they finished the repair and reassembled the helicopter to fly. He figured the floor would be washed down with ammonia cleaner—an abrasive odor that he didn't want the dolphins exposed to. And with the mission details still undefined, Tasi and Inapo could be holed up in the bowel of the ship for days, depending if and when the Black Lit op would be launched or the order to abort was called.

Not willing to wait on a request going through the chain of command, from the cargo deck up to the USS *New York*'s commander, to move the dolphins to a new temporary location, Merk sought out the cargo master, who was busy scanning barcodes with a handheld device. The young officer took inventory of the NMMP supplies before they were moved by forklift to a storage bay. The cargo master, a lanky marine with a Southern drawl, gave Merk a once-over look and continued to scan the boxes and coolers of fresh fish, as if Merk weren't there.

"How long is the chopper repair going to take?" Merk asked.

"Well, fuck me, bud, looks like you got one helluva request," the cargo master said with a shitless smirk. "Let me see if the mechanics can't speed things up. You know, salt air triples maintenance time on helos and such."

Merk began to speak when a mechanic dropped a lug wrench in a loud clang, startling Tasi to thrash about. The sight of the stressed dolphin rippled through Merk. He clenched his fists, cleared his throat, and growled, "You wouldn't let your mates sleep down here with the hydraulic piss leaking on the floor, would you?"

The cargo master scanned the last box, waved the forklift operator to store the supplies, then locked Merk in a stare. "You, your flippers are on board my ship. We have one bird down and I'm running a tight schedule with the combat cargo master. He's not navy blue like you and me. He's an ornery leatherneck planning to send the Marine Expeditionary Unit into Somalia . . ."

Merk folded his arms and listened. He recalled tolerant thoughts of how he held it all in when his alcoholic navy father used to erupt like a volcano in a drunken rage. He thought about the autistic teenager who helped map out the sounds of dolphins with music and math. And he thought about holding his girlfriend's hand as he looked in her black pearl eyes.

". . . That means I have to coordinate supplies, food, weapons, and ammo with the CCM and his assistant for hundreds of action-starved marines. You land here out of the blue, waste no time demanding the red carpet for your diva dolphins," he said, jabbing a finger in Merk's chest.

Merk snatched the cargo master's hand, twisted it over, and pulled him in close, saying in measured anger, "I've had a bad fucking week. My friend died. My dolphins came out of combat. I lost my laptop in the drink. Now, where are you going to store my fins?"

Grimacing in pain, the cargo master yelped, "Ouch. Shit . . . okay, okay. Back up to the flight deck they go."

"Roger that?" Merk squeezed harder, applying more pressure.

"Oh, yow, yes . . . roger that."

Chapter Sixteen

T HE PETTY OFFICER guided Merk through half of the 684-foot-
long USS *New York* toward the CDC, the communications nerve
center located under the antenna tower of the ship, where he would
join a meeting in progress. Merk pulled the petty officer aside to call
the XO to get permission to visit the Norwegian sniper Peder Olsen
in sickbay before entering the CDC.

With permission granted, a nurse led Merk into the room.

Peder Olsen was deep in slumber; there were gauze bandages
wrapped around second-degree burns, with cortisone cream covering blisters on his face, forehead, and neck. Merk recognized the
lowest level of a burn ward and remembered his days aboard a ship
recovering from one skin graft procedure after another. Olsen had
an IV drip with heart and brain monitoring wires strung across his
torso and head like computer cables that seemed to be more for
show than anything else for the strapping mercenary.

Merk stepped around the other side of the bed and examined
Peder's right hand. It was swollen and burnt red by the sun. The
ring finger on the same hand, where Norwegians wear their wedding bands, showed a redder sunburned ring around the finger
where the band had sat wedged for years. Merk suspected Peder had
removed his wedding band prior to boarding the *Blå Himmel* for the
high-risk assignment of being the ship's hired gun. What he didn't
know was whether the Norwegian was a mercenary, or something
more, such as an informant or an embedded asset gathering intel
for NATO or Norway's Special Forces.

"When was he awake last?" Merk asked the nurse.

"Nine hours ago," she said, reading the patient's chart on a tablet. "When he's up, inform the XO. I need to speak to him." Merk exited the room.

* * *

IN THE CDC, Merk stood to the rear alongside a technician and surveyed those seated around a conference table: Naval engineers, a weapons officer, an ONI officer, a communications officer, the commander, the XO, and a tired SEAL CO Nico Gregorius, who reclined in a seat with a knee resting on the edge of the table. Nico scratched his day-old stubble.

On the wall, banks of flat- and curved-screen monitors and computer terminals kept the ship's twenty-eight officer crew up to date on shipping activity in the gulf, live shots from Predator drones, and the latest news on the pirates, Somalia, and the owners of the hijacked ships. A wall screen replayed the night-vision video the SEALs captured of the passing vessels. Seeing that Merk was in the CDC, a technician played the clip of the SEALs and a platoon of marines boarding the US container ghost ship, *Shining Sea.*

The infrared video revealed little about the pirates or the missing crew. Other than a pool of blood from one of the wounded or slain crewmen, there was little to go on. The pirates either aborted the hijacking of the ship or followed through to abandon the vessel in the first place.

Merk wondered: *Was it a logistical mistake that caused the pirates to leave the* Shining Sea *early? Or did they do it as part of a master plan?*

What was unique about the double hijackings: The pirates successfully seized two ships on the same day in the same shipping lane. They escalated violence at the start of boarding both vessels. Perhaps more under the radar, the Somali pirates returned to the heavily internationally patrolled Gulf of Aden to target the ships, after expanding their territory into the Persian Gulf and Indian Ocean off the coast of Kenya. But did they have help?

The high-echelon targets were always oil and gas and its wealthy owners, from Arab nations and royal families, to the Western oil conglomerates that serviced them. *Why did the pirates hijack the container ship?* Merk wondered. The commander motioned him to speak.

"What do you have on scope and timing with the MMS pod?" Merk asked.

"You'll be airborne with your marine mammal systems at 2100 hours zulu. We use the cover of night to drop you inside the twelve mile international line off the coast of Somalia, with geocoords that are equidistant between the provinces of Somaliland and Puntland," the commander said. "Nico will ride with you, conducting his own inland recon. He'll provide cover for you and the MM systems."

Merk checked the red-eyed SEAL CO, saying, "Nico, you got the stamina for this?"

"No worries. I sleep one hemisphere of the brain at a time, like your fins."

The navy personnel erupted with laughter.

Grinning, Merk nodded in approval, liking the CO's knowledge of dolphin neurobiology.

"You've come a long way, Toten, from your hellish survey last week. The scope of the clandestine op is in here," the commander said, sliding a black folder stamped "Top Secret" across the table. "After you commit the details to memory, the XO will relieve you of the brief. This op doesn't exist. Not when you get captured. Not when you return. It has no code name."

"Fine. I'm a phantom," Merk said, glancing around the room. "Why the Somali pirates? Why now? Why are we getting involved in an FBI procedure?"

"We got word. Somali pirates had help," the commander began to explain. "AQAP and the Syrian Electronic Army, maybe others. We wonder if the attacks on the two ships were ordered by the Revolutionary Guard Corps in Tehran or by the Houthi rebels they sponsor in Yemen. The mullahs might seek revenge for your mission that blew up their mine-laying operation in the Strait of Hormuz."

"Revenge is not my cup of tea," Merk said. "Iran has all the motivation it needs to undermine the US. Like them, we're all birds in a cage, following orders, honoring hierarchy."

Chapter Seventeen

I N A GROUND floor conference room at CIA Headquarters, the CIA director, a graying, athletic man with a politician's suave looks, nodded while handing over a blue border folder meant for the State Department, marked "Top Secret." "The Azure Shell team will be a day late to negotiate with the pirates," the CIA director told the deputy DO. "Does the FBI know that?"

"You're supposed to be at the White House PDB in an hour," the deputy DO said.

"I canceled that BS fest. I've been called back here on a couple of fronts," the CIA director said. "Let's go to the Seventh Floor."

* * *

ON THE SEVENTH Floor of Langley, down the hall from his corner office and private kitchen, the CIA director broke off a videoconference with the head of MI6, Britain's foreign counterterrorism division. A disagreement erupted over what was happening in tracking the movement of tribesmen and the Syrian Electronic Army personnel in the Empty Quarter Desert, the growing unrest in Jaar, and other onetime al Qaeda stronghold cities in southern Yemen.

The poor arid country, led by a fragile government and an even weaker economy—oil exports account for ninety percent of Yemen's GDP—had to defend hundreds of miles of oil pipelines against saboteurs. Two main pipelines ran from the southwest corner of the Empty Quarter in the Massila oilfield to ports along the

Gulf of Aden, with a third pipeline running west to the Ras Isa oil terminal on the Red Sea.

The argument with the intelligence ally was enough to send the CIA director bolting out of the conference room and head down to the Sixth Floor Ops Center. There he huddled with his deputies, including the head of the CIA's ultra-secret Special Activities Division, SAD, an ex-navy SEAL from SEAL Team Six, and senior analysts from the CIA's Information Operations Center Analysis Group— IOC/AG. Surrounded by wall screens, a pair of desktops, tablets, a plasma TV, fed with an array of real-time surveillance devices pulled from a global network of military, spies, informants, and high-tech eavesdropping devices, the director let his eyes absorb intel on the two red-hot fronts: the reigniting ISIS-inflamed civil war in Syria, Iraq, and pan North Africa, and the resurgence of AQAP in Yemen.

On one wall screen, a microcam, snaked inside a pole of a tent in the Syrian desert near the Iraqi border, captured a female North Korean missile engineer, Kim Dong-Sun, seated with four Syrian Army generals and a fellow North Korean scientist. They discussed the blueprint design of a missile launch site through an interpreter. The talks were going down live.

The CIA director shook his head. With mounting angst he badgered the analysts: "How long have they been breaking bread?"

"Thirty . . . maybe thirty-six hours," one Red Cell analyst replied.

"Jesus." He looked over at the SAD director, and ordered, "Mobilize whatever forces you have on the ground and kidnap that bitch before she leaves. You know what she's doing? Well, I don't need Clandestine Services to tell me. . . . She's finishing plans to erect a long-range missile site aimed at Europe. Congress wants to handcuff our ability to interrogate key assets? Bloody idiots."

"You're serious about snatching the engineer?" the director of operations spoke up.

"Why not? The glare of the media might just shock them into action. Don't forget they mocked our agents in the War on Terror with the AG's show trial," the CIA director said. "Every time I went to visit the president, his cabinet, and congressmen—who had lost faith in the war, who had lost their spine to back this agency, who had lost their way in Yemen, who had pulled out of that conflict prematurely without finishing the job—I got the sense that they didn't fully appreciate what the stakes were. They didn't get it. But now, now when the dust settles on this Syria-ISIS-Kurdish-Libya-Iranian shitstorm, they'll wish they were no longer in office, that they were retired, spreading their gospel bile on the lecture circuit. Instead, they pushed their naïve bullshit agenda of peace on the world, underfunded and undermanned the war, and blocked the army's surge required to defeat the Islamic militants—and defeat them by air. They never handed the baton to NATO or asked us to take charge and kill the enemy."

One satellite image appeared to show a guard standing on the roof of the school/terrorist safe house in the Jaar square. That caught the CIA director's eye. He ordered analysts to look at past pictures of the roof at night for comparison, and then asked, "What's an armed guard doing on the roof protecting an empty school building at night? Is he a villager or an AQAP tango?"

The deputy DO wondered, too. Then the CIA director stepped over to a plasma screen showing dorsalcam images of a navy dolphin conducting swim-bys of the subsea, trans-strait oil pipeline, and then Iran's laying of the sea-mines. He looked around the room, and challenged his staff: "Hey, Red Cell Team, tell me one of those dolphins triggered the release of the mine?"

A female analyst spoke up: "Director, that's affirmative. All spy satellites confirm the hit on an Iranian fishing cover ship. I spoke to Susan Hogue last night. She's the head of the navy's Marine Mammal Program in San Diego. Hogue confirmed the direct action. One of the navy's dolphin team members made it out alive; the other one was shot and drowned during the escape. He was a former Special Forces operator turned veterinarian. His name was Lt. Morgan Azar."

The CIA director shook his head to his deputies. Annoyed, he said, "Did you hear that? Tehran almost got us good with a fishing trip. Well, now we know what to look for when we retask our spy satellites. Is Red Cell operative Alan Cuthbert in position?"

"Yes, director. He landed at Fort 24 two hours ago," the analyst said.

Chapter Eighteen

THE THUDDING ROTORS vibrated Merk's chest. They purred in his wrist as he absorbed the droning white noise, which made him drowsy until he nodded off. Soon REM sleep twitched his eyelids as the Black Hawk helicopter was en route to drop him and Navy SEAL Commanding Office Nico Gregorius, along with the dolphins, inside Somalian territorial waters.

The transport helicopter crossed the Gulf of Aden flying above the surface of the sea under radar. The operation used the veil of night to penetrate Somali airspace, when few fishermen or pirates were out at sea, especially after the double hijackings.

Backed by a lethal gunship in an Apache Longbow helicopter trailing a half klick behind, they were escorted deep into Somalia coastal waters. The Longbow was armed with eight "fire and forget" air-to-surface, RF-Hellfire missiles with advanced precision-kill weapon-system rockets, a platform designed for the littoral battlespace with the Longbow Fire Control Radar. Tasked with intercepting a pirate skiff—if for some reason the Somalis still lingered offshore—the pilot and copilot-gunner were ordered to track and follow, but not engage the target, since the aim was to gather intelligence on the location of the mothership, which still had not been located.

In the Black Hawk, the napping Merk sat on the floor of the cargo bay. He had made it a point not to hang with the dolphins. Close ties with the advance biologic systems, as the Navy Marine Mammal Program referred to its dolphins, was frowned upon. No excessive bonding or close relationships with the sea mammals.

Merk understood the game and heard it all before. He held his back to the dolphins.

Tasi and Inapo were lying in slings suspended in hardboxes with gurney-casters, the brakes in locked position. Thin poly sheets draped the dolphins' bodies, with slits cut for the dorsal fins, blowholes, and eyes. Articulating branches of micro-sprinklers sprayed their epidermis, keeping the sea mammals' skin moist during air transport, which dried them out, stressed them by bumping their core-body temperature up toward feverish levels. That was another health problem Merk wanted to avoid at the start of a mission.

A replacement Army Special Forces marine biologist—it would have been Lt. Azar had he not died in the Strait of Hormuz—monitored the mammals' vital signs, recording medical data on a tablet. After she finished the spot check, she prepared liquid vitamins mixed with minced kelp, kale, and Norwegian fish oil, and loaded the concoction into a handful of oversized syringes. She opened a cooler and inspected the fresh herring and mackerel the Pacific bottlenose dolphins consumed as reward during training exercises that consisted of locating mines or unexploded torpedoes.

Feeling a burr in his behind, Merk awakened. He opened his eyes. Disoriented for a second, he refocused his whereabouts and then reminded himself that the new op was not an undergoing training exercise. The mission was real. It was the second live littoral operation within a week for Tasi and Inapo inside enemy water. He wondered how they would perform, how they would fare under stress, how they would still remain an asset in the age of drones, robots, mobile apps, digital intel, cloud computing, big data, and the Internet of Things. The navy dolphins were moving sensors; and it was his job to collect the data.

Over the next twenty-four hours Merk would learn just how well his year of training Tasi and Inapo at a secret base in Guam had paid off. The NMMP brass would be evaluating him. "Conflicted" or not, as Captain Davis Whittal labeled him in the debriefing on what happened in the strait, Merk had to look beyond weapons and passivity and balance following orders that put the dolphins in harm's way versus his desire to one day set them free in the wild.

On a tablet, Merk watched the drone video of the missile strike on the school in Yemen. He looked at the time of the attack and realized it took place within forty minutes of the Iranians dropping mines in the strait. He didn't believe in such "rainbow" coincidences; there had to be a connection. But what?

SEAL mode came creeping back into Merk's mind.

Chapter Nineteen

O N THE WAY to Somali, Tasi and Inapo appeared calm on the surface; their vitals and core body temperature were normal. Stress didn't show up in their behavior, not during dry transport, not when he trained them in Guam and then later for NMMP and DARPA brass under a top-secret cover on a remote Hawaiian island. How would they react to a second mission in a week?

Merk didn't know the answer. But the data he collected on their behavior, sleep, and eating patterns might point to a sudden outburst or breakdown in discipline. Still, he was going into uncharted territory with them, and any other pod of navy dolphins he had worked with in the past for that matter.

When the Black Hawk reached the insertion point a few miles off the coast of Somalia, it hovered off the coast, halfway between Bosaso and Maydh, an ancient holy Arabian city in the Sanaag region that centered Somalia's north coast. The Black Hawk's cargo door opened; a pair of SEAL divers jumped backward into the sea.

The helicopter's cargo bay opened. In patchy water, the cargo master lowered a Zodiac inflatable boat to the divers. In succession, the cargo master made the delivery of arms, ammo, food, supplies, and equipment down to the divers. Tasi and then Inapo were lowered in their hardboxes to the sea. When the lamb's wool–lined stretchers sank below the surface, the dolphins wiggled out of the slings and swam around the drop zone, inspecting the perimeter to guard the divers.

After the hardboxes were hoisted back up to the cargo bay, a winch lowered Merk and Nico into the Zodiac. The divers handed supplies to them and were lifted up to the helicopter.

Merk flashed a hand-sign to the dolphins, signaling them to leap onto the rubber boat. Tasi landed on board a liner draped over the starboard gunwale in a spit of spray. Merk strapped her down and rubbed the shark-bite dorsal fin for good luck. Then Inapo dove under the hull of the Zodiac, corkscrewed up, and slithered onto the opposite gunwale. Merk held Inapo in place, pulled the strap over the mammal's missile-shaped body, tying him down.

Nico turned south to the empty sea, flipped down night-vision goggles, and scanned the silhouette of the rocky horizon in the distance. The Longbow pulled alongside, hovering fifty feet above the waves, its four main rotor blades whooshing in the air, rippling creases in the sea. Its reverse-tricycle landing gear deployed as if it were going to set down on the water. The pilot and copilot-gunner, who used FLIR and the Longbow radar mast that can see through fog, searched ahead to make sure the sea space was clear. With a flash of a laser pointer from the cockpit, Nico signaled they were heading to shore. He turned on the engine and rode the craft; Merk stretched out between the dolphins, keeping them calm on the bumpy ride to shore.

Behind the CO, Merk watched the helicopters bank away. First, the transport and then the Longbow swept back toward the USS *New York*. He gazed in Tasi's eye to check her mood. She appeared calm. Inapo gave off a different, moody vibe.

Nico gunned the inflatable boat. The stiff wind rippled Merk's face, which was blackened with grease paint like an ex-Navy SEAL. To calm the dolphins down, Merk drummed his fingers on the rubber tube. Even with the muted droning noise of the outboard motor and the vibrations from the bumpy ride, the dolphins listened to Merk's fingers through their jawbones resting on the gunwales. Having been raised by his navy father, Bill Toten, hopping from base to base, the one constant was his old man teaching Merk the dots and dashes of Morse code since he was a child. In turn, Merk passed that communication of sound on to the dolphins he trained. He tapped his fingers in dots and long dashes, signaling the dolphins to rest, to shut down one hemisphere of the brain and slumber in a state of half awake, half asleep. The last series of dashes—taps—relaxed Inapo enough to halt the mammal's dead-eyed look and squeak at Merk.

The dolphins would ride on the rubber boat close to shore, before being released. Had the mission been set in the hostile arena of the Persian Gulf, off the coast of Iran, or near the delta of the Tigris and Euphrates Rivers in Iraq, where the Islamic State, the Kurds, and Iraqi forces were fighting over the Kuwaiti oil fields, Merk would have found a way to deep-six their mission.

For Nico the ride in to Somalia was different. The admirals and analysts at Special Operations Command (SOCOM) had originally identified the barren island of Jasiira Maydh, eight miles north of Maydh, for Merk and Nico to set up a staging nest. On further analysis of the mile-long rocky island with football-stadium-high bluffs, no vegetation or fresh water, and a lunar, fissure-torn, guano-covered surface, the island gave the CO and brass at SOCOM pause. It would have put Merk and Nico offshore, out in the open with little relief from the sun, while being stuck on a rock with no escape route. So the gambit to operate onshore in a CIA safe house was estimated by some analyst to be less risky.

Less than a mile offshore, in front of a one-story box sticking up on the toe of a hill, Merk zoomed on an object floating on the sea a couple hundred yards ahead. He held up a fist for Nico to shut off the engine. The inflatable boat slowed to a glide, then to a drift rocking in the waves. The CO trained night-vision binoculars on the dark object. Initially, he thought it was a bough of driftwood or a dhow. In the choppy sea, the object bobbed, making positive ID harder.

After a long moment, a pair of silhouettes, human figures, could be seen kneeling in the object that grew into the outline of a fishing skiff. Merk listened over the whistle of the wind until he heard the faint throttle of an outboard motor. He looked back at Nico and flashed two fingers for two fishermen. The CO unzipped a shoulder bag and took out a folding-stock rifle with a night-vision scope. He opened the stock and aimed the rifle at the fishermen; Merk reached over and lowered the barrel, shaking his head. Nico gave a hard look; Merk took out an audio-telescope, turned it on, and aimed the acoustical nozzle in the direction of the skiff. He slipped on earpods, and listened to the engine drown out sound in the distance.

Merk played with the squelch fader on the transceiver until he filtered out the static noise of the fisherman's putting engine, while tuning up the sound of their voices. As he zeroed on the idle, but insect-like chatter of their foreign tongue, he realized they weren't pirates or terrorists. He could sense that by the tone of small talk. Still, they had eyes, ears, and tongues that could spread the word to the pirates if they spotted the small US cell inside Somalia waters.

Knowing secrecy was paramount, Merk unclipped the straps on the dolphins. With his twin hand-signs, the dolphins leapt off the rubber boat and sliced under the waves. They raced toward the fishing skiff, fluking across the surface. When they came within a short distance of the craft, they dove under, mirroring one another's moves, silently communicating.

Merk motioned Nico to watch at the skiff closing on their position, when one dolphin leapt over the boat, grazing a fisherman.

Startled, the man ducked; his mate shut off the motor. They turned on flashlights and panned the sea searching for the wraith that unnerved them. The man stood up to shine the light at a steeper angle below the surface, looking here and there—when the other dolphin shot up, rammed the boat from behind, jolting it hard. The fisherman stumbled and dropped the flashlight into the sea. Spooked, his mate motioned him to sit down as he started the engine, and sped off into the night, racing away from the area.

Merk and Nico shared a laugh and then picked up paddles to row ashore.

Chapter Twenty

T HE BOX ON the dark horizon, when up close, became a white seaside house on a mound with a dock jutting into a lagoon. Merk glanced at Nico, signaling that the house was their destination. When they drew within a hundred meters of shore, the outline of a person pacing in front of the seaside villa stood out as the new concern.

"Who's that? Anyone expecting us?" Merk whispered, knowing the hijacked ships were far west in the next state of Somaliland. He dialed the binoculars, zooming to see if the guard was armed. Although he didn't see a rifle in the hands or slung over the shoulder, it didn't mean the guard was unarmed. Merk motioned Nico to proceed with caution. Again, the "all clear" intel on land from the Office of Naval Intelligence, Navy SEALs, and CIA was off—by a mile. The safe house wasn't empty. Nico had some explaining to do, but it wasn't going to happen then.

Merk took out a high-pitched whistle and blew it. The call, silent to human ears, summoned Tasi and Inapo to swim back to the rubber boat and ride them to shore. There, Merk would observe whether the safe house was indeed *safe*, or was an advanced CIA hideout that had its cover blown. He aimed the audioscope and listened to the guard's flip-flop sandals crunch on the granular surface. The footsteps paced back and forth, stopped, pivoted 180 degrees, then strode back. Without another guard to chat with, the sounds detected were of little use. He faded out the footsteps and eavesdropped on other sounds in the background. Beyond the wind chafing the eaves of the Spanish tile roof there was nothing audible to note.

Unable to wait for Nico to announce a Plan B—if there was one—Merk needed to take a closer look of the guard to see whether he was armed. With a nod that he was going in, Merk slipped on dive goggles, snapped his feet into swim fins, and rolled over the gunwale.

The water was balmy with a strong leeward current.

Tasi glided over and offered her dorsal fin; Merk grabbed hold and hitchhiked a ride to shore. He stayed low as Tasi rode him in, plowing through the waves that rose in the surf. The black crests rolled, breaking in streams of heavy white foam. Feeling a wave lift him, Merk released his grip and bodysurfed to shore. He kept his head up, hands out in front to block against any rocks striking his face, and glided in on the breaking swell.

The surf washed Merk up a stony beach. As it ebbed with another wave about to break on top of him, he heard footsteps crunch toward him and then stop. He saw sandals with black feet and polished toenails, which froze him. He was staring at a woman's feet. But the sound of a handgun cocking stilled him. Merk felt another wave break over his legs as he pulled the dive goggles off and looked up at a tall, built African woman with long braided hair that slipped down the back of her shirt, aiming a handgun at his forehead.

Merk raised his hands; being caught spiked his blood pressure. Then out of the corner of his eye, he glimpsed one of the dolphins skimming the shallows, sliding sideways. And with a burst, the dolphin tail-whipped a column of water over the guard. Drenched and startled, the woman slipped and fell. Merk grabbed her ankles, pulled her toward him. He pinned her face to the ground with his forearm, and wrested the handgun from her grip.

"Who are you?" she spat out in English with a Kenyan accent.

Merk held her down, removing the magazine from the pistol and emptied the bullet from the chamber, wondering the same question about her.

It was the first time he held a gun in decade. And it was cold.

Chapter Twenty-One

I N THE SAFE house by the sea, Nico introduced Merk to the Kenyan secret police officer, a CIA asset code-named Nairobi. For the past five years, she had infiltrated the pirates' hostage-for-ransom supply chain in southern Somalia, working with US military and intelligence advisors. The CIA moved Nairobi north to the breakaway region of Somaliland and, within a year, she had infiltrated the outer circle of enforcers, negotiators, arms runners, skiff captains, fishermen, gunners, and boarding crews that reported to the pirate brothers Korfa and Samatar.

"I'm a deal away from being inside the last ring of nine mothership captains," Nairobi said, not amused by being caught off guard by the dolphin splash attack.

"Nine, hmmm?" Merk mouthed, glancing at Nico with a look of doubt.

"No wonder AQAP has moved in to partner with the radical Islamists of al-Shabaab," Nico said, playing along Merk as he watched Nairobi's facial expressions.

"And the pirates," Merk added.

The Kenyan army had trained agent Nairobi to be a money broker with the shipowners and insurance side of the hostage-for-ransom business. On the surface, she worked to release scores of hostages, while infiltrating deeper into the pirate underworld to identify the names, contacts, and key leaders who populated the complex web of Somalia warlords; Islamic assassins, both local and Yemeni-based terrorists; and the pirates in the trade of hijacking ships. Then there was the brutally effective ISIS war fueled by a winning propaganda machine, drawing thousands of Western believers, wannabes, converts, and disillusioned and disconnected citizens. Radical Islam offered them hope. An out. A job. A goal. Free society offered them nothing, failing the youth by offering a wage-suppressed, debt-ridden, slavery subsistence.

"What's your story?" Merk asked,

Nairobi ignored him. She didn't input any *KorSam*—Korfa and Samatar—piracy network information on a computer, but rather on a piece of paper she folded and stored out in the open, wedged in the pages of a children's book about Noah's Ark in a bookcase, which she showed Nico. Other times, she went on to explain to him, she posed as a UN humanitarian coordinator negotiating terms with the warlords to deliver food and aid to the poorest villages. Still other times she acted as a double agent, spying on and planting true and false intelligence with the pirates about the Islamic militants and their common enemy, the United States. All of those activities in aggregate allowed her to move freely within the pirate towns and among the local fishermen without raising an eyebrow of suspicion. But as a woman, she had limited access in the Somalia cities and regions controlled by the misogynist, male-dominated world of Islamic extremism.

Nairobi worked around that handicap by using her body for sex-as-trade bait when she needed to barter with the money-as-religion warlords, pirate leaders, planners, and negotiators. Few could resist the five-foot-ten, walnut-brown skinned woman with a dimple on her right cheek, a vivacious smile framed with long hair braided into a tail now resting on her broad shoulders like a snake. Nairobi had an athlete's muscular, powerful build. As a foreigner living in Somalia for five years, she used the cover story of being a fugitive from Kenya, forced to flee her country after killing a politician in a sex-triangle scandal.

The CIA planted that story in Kenyan newspapers and Somali media outlets to give the story heft and authenticity, she told Nico, insisting that the "rumors grew into legend." Her favorite: she had cut off the balls of the politician, slit his throat, and bled him to death face down in a hammock, while barbequing antelope with his political enemy. She neither confirmed nor denied the story, since Islamic radicals despised the leaders of Kenya, calling them infidels and the next target of Al-Shabaab extremists.

After listening to her exploits, Merk refused to be swept in by her ardent speech on US—Kenyan relations, or be taken by her sultry, thoroughbred good looks. He kept a distance and remained skeptical about Nairobi until the day she proved her loyalty in action, not words. Nico noticed the cold shoulder and nudged Merk with a knee and gave him a look to be social.

"What's your real story? Beyond war?" Merk asked, taking out a new Dolphin Code laptop from a waterproof bag.

"What do you mean?"

"Any children? Any desires or wants in life?"

"Yes, I have two children. A boy and a girl. Eight and three," she said.

"Do they have cool names like my dolphins?"

"What are their names?" she asked, showing Nico and Merk where she hid a machete behind the bookcase.

"Tasi and Inapo. Female and male. Both I trained for a year in Guam and then Hawaii."

"It must be beautiful in the Pacific. I've never been, just online."

"And the names of your children? True African names?"

"Akello, the boy. His name means 'Born After Twins.' His father was a twin," she said. "My daughter is named Fathiya. It means 'Triumph' in Swahili."

"What do they like to do?" Merk asked, sat down and swiped on the laptop. Using an eyeball-vein scan he accessed the secure hard drive.

"Akello likes to carve wood. Makes alligator heads from logs, eagles from a large branch, and tribal masks from bark," Nairobi explained with mist in her eyes; she clearly missed them.

He uploaded satellite images, photographs, topographical maps, and sea-lane charts, then opened a pane of a live shot of the drone patrolling the Somalia coast, hunting for the missing vessels and pirate mothership. By integrating an array of live feeds, maps, and digital pictures, he identified the lagoons, coves, estuaries, valleys, ridges, and mountain landmarks by image, name, land contours, and GPS coordinates. The Dolphin Code program streamed a live split-screen of the micro-dorsalcams worn by both Tasi and Inapo, from their point of view, swimming in tandem along the shallows of the Somali coast.

"And Fathiya? Her name sounds so close to the English word 'faith,'" Merk noted.

"Fathiya likes to play the piano and sing."

Merk verified that the dorsalcams were acoustically sensitive to whenever a dolphin echolocated the space ahead, transmitting the biosonar feedback to the laptop, where it transcribed the frequency into an acoustic signal. With another software program developed by a military vendor in San Diego, the wavelengths were translated into a shadowy image, like that captured by ground-penetrating radar. Image quality was not high-definition or detailed, but it gave Merk insight on whether the dolphin was targeting a small fish or a something larger like a tuna, shark, boat hull, or sea-mine.

Merk ran a program that extracted the images the drone captured at night with a high-res infrared camera. It catalogued each subject, while displaying the geocoords with time rolling over in seconds and minutes in the lower right corner. Using the GPS data, Merk directed the systems to head to a specific location to conduct a sea level swim-by for a closer look. The first target was a cluster of ten skiffs scattered on shore. Some were flipped over; others pulled halfway on land; still others were dumped with bows stacked in all directions. It seemed as if the skiffs had been abandoned overnight. With the cluster sitting two-dozen klicks west of the safe house, it would take the dolphins a few hours to reach. Yet, the littoral environment was as a good place to start the search and surveillance mission.

After hiding the outboard motor in a toolshed, and deflating the rubber boat and stowing it in a shallow cave along with food rations, water, and SEAL body armor, Nico opened the rifle case and pulled out a quad of American, Israeli, German, and Russian assault rifles. He handed them to Nairobi, along with boxes of ammunition. She opened a false door behind a wine cabinet and stored the weapons inside, except the AK-47. Nico opened the next barrel-bag and dumped a pile of euros and dollars across the table. Merk took notice; the piles of cash made him uneasy. Merk stared at Nico, but the CO averted his gaze. The SEAL handed over hundreds of thousands of euros and dollars to Nairobi. To be used. To be spent. To buy off the pirates. And to bribe warlords and officials. None of the freewheeling purchases sat well with Merk, since it exposed the CIA to a blind spot to buy intel in a land of spies, thieves, and double agents.

Nico ignored Merk. He used his Greek charm and flair, and engaged Nairobi in jovial talk. He feigned interest when the CIA asset ran through options on the places to hide inland if the pirates or Islamic militants closed on the safe house. She told him where to hide, who to watch for, and which way to escape. The well-rehearsed list made Merk suspicious. He wondered when was the last time a CIA agent sat down with Nairobi, vetted her, and debriefed her face-to-face, despite him connecting with her children stories; they were real, he knew. Taking the cue from Merk's mood, Nico stepped outside to scope the layout of the safe house for webcams, listening devices, and signs of watchers outside.

While Nico searched the safe house for bugs and spycams, Merk typed a code directing the dolphins to follow the coast west and report back on any hot items along the way. He locked the GPS coordinates of the skiffs and uploaded them into the program, so that when the dolphins came within a klick a signal on the laptop would alert him they were about to arrive.

Nairobi stripped out of her wet clothes. Underneath, she wore a tee shirt with no bra and *Body Glove* swim shorts, revealing her curvy glutes and long, sinewy thighs. The Kenyan agent changed tack and was all business when she stuffed the euro packs into money belts, stowed a couple of stacks of dollars next to the weapons behind the wine cabinet, taped another stack under the dining room table, and put the rest in a backpack. She stepped behind a blind, stripped out of her wet underclothes, got dressed. She stepped out from behind the blind and slipped into tattered navy blue coveralls, clothing likely taken from a mechanic of a hijacked ship, buttoned it to her breasts, revealing cleavage, and slung the backpack over her shoulder.

Dangling car keys, Nairobi picked up a cooler and headed to the front door, announcing, "I will go to the fishing village west, some forty miles. I can buy intel on the hostages there."

Nico handed her a Chinese military Satcom; showed her how to use it, saying, "Nai, if you call, keep your observations brief and general. Don't use names on the open channel."

"Sure, no names?"

"Good. When you're done, trade the Satcom to the pirates, so we can triangulate a GPS vector on Korfa's whereabouts."

She nodded, stuffed the Satcom in the backpack, picked up a clothes bag, and headed out the door.

Chapter Twenty-Two

"SHOULD WE TRUST her?" Nico asked, listening to Nairobi drive away.

"You know her history?" Merk asked. "Her kids were real enough. That wasn't rehearsed . . . Triumph, what a great name is Fathiya for a girl."

"Yeah, Merk. What you asked and what the CIA spooks told me."

"Let's look for a means to shadow her. Then move out."

"I can tell you a dozen reasons why we should stay here tonight."

"Nico, you answered your question. We don't know her, despite her children. If she's a double or is being spied on, the safe house will be visited tonight. My dolphins are at sea. I can't be separated from them. Not for a day."

"C'mon, Toten, we just got here."

"I'm not staying. Don't trust this house." Merk opened drawers, sifting through clothes, then rifled through a closet, pulling out scarves and towels to protect against the sun. "We go stealth, blend in. No body armor, no ammo, no guns."

"Now you've gone off the deep end. I'm not moving around the pirate mecca of the world, stripped of firearms. Not going to happen," he said, picking up the AK-47 assault rifle.

"You know how Nairobi has more muscles than we do. Bet more endurance, too."

"Toten, is that anyway to talk about our host?"

"Go out and check the perimeter," Merk said. "Look for trip wires, cams, hidden mics. See if the locals are watching us."

Nico grimaced, hit the lights, and bolted out the door. Merk glanced at the laptop and held a penlight in his mouth. He examined the ceiling fan and lighting fixtures for snooping devices. He didn't see any on first pass, then swept wall to wall, checking under lampshades, behind furniture, artwork, and around a bulky TV set. After scouring the kitchen for bugs, Merk noticed Nairobi didn't own a landline phone. Without a secure line, he wondered how she communicated with her CIA handler, if she did at all. Maybe she hadn't done that in years. There was one way to confirm Nairobi's CIA sponsorship, and that was the same with Merk's on-again, off-again girlfriend, who worked at the CIA's Clandestine Services unit. But by infiltrating Somalia, there was no way he could risk trying to contact his lover while operating in a dark country, radio dead. And who knew whether she was working in some black operation herself at the time. All he could do was recall running his hands through her long hair the last time, taking a whiff of her scent, and being aroused—thoroughly aroused.

After a sweep of the grounds outside, scouting the mountain range to the south with night-vision binoculars, Nico returned, informing Merk that Nairobi drove west along the coast, and that there were no signs of spies, surveillance nests, or audiovisual devices. He told him that he set up motion sensors to guard the house on the landside, while hanging the audioscope and a webcam under the eaves of the roof. After setting up the squawk box, which would alert them of an intruder by sight or sound, Merk showed Nico a pencil-rod webcam set behind a painting, whispering, "Let's get out of here. Don't have a good vibe on a safe house that isn't safe."

"Got a second car outside," Nico said, searching the drawers for the keys.

"Let's tail her. I can work remotely with the fins." Merk double-checked the images downloaded from the drone. Using the Dolphin Code software to com with the drone, he followed the stream of live shots with a coded timer in the lower right corner of the screen. It showed there was six hours of drone flying time before the USS *New York* would call it back.

Merk closed the laptop and stuffed it and the tech accessories into a backpack. Outside, Nico hopped into the driver's seat of Nairobi's second car, a Chinese SUV. Merk kicked the rear fender to feel the metal density in the body of the vehicle. The soft resonance told him the car was made of scrap metal; it would rust shortly after a crash.

Merk sighed and climbed into the vehicle. He folded a red-and-white checkered square Bedouin scarf, called the *kufeya*, into a triangle and placed it on his head. He fitted an *igal* of camel wool over his skull, securing the scarf in place. The *igal* was decorated with fine metallic beads and threads.

The CO glanced over and chuckled at Merk's headgear: "You're so busted."

"Yeah, well, Nico. Think tribal."

As Nico drove off, Merk opened the laptop and watched the dolphins near the cove of the first target area he tasked them to sweep. Tasi surfaced and glided toward shore. The dorsalcam picked up the first cluster of skiffs pulled halfway out of the water. Inapo swam ahead, circled back, and surveyed the cove from the other side—as he was trained to do.

In unison, they worked the key points of the cove with each system taking turns leaping on the edge of shore. That allowed them to digitally capture shots they couldn't get in the surf. It also enabled them to place their jaws on the beach to feel for vibrations through their jawbones, tuning in on any vehicle passing by on the coast road.

"You miss her?" Nico asked.

"Who?"

"Your girlfriend. The one you see twice a year."

"I don't know why I agreed to this. To come into enemy territory. Am I mad? This is crazy to go this deep again?"

"Yeah. She's military right? Banging some marine?"

Merk shook his head, and replied, "No, Nico. She's smarter than you. She's CIA intel. You know, an analyst."

"Why would a geek be interested in a puke SEAL retread like you?"

"Who knows? Maybe she has a thing for dolphins and I'm her bridge to a free swim with the fins."

As Nico needled him, Merk began to phase out his words and think of her, as he swiped different panes of the quad split screen in and out of zoom to see the progress of the dolphin's surveillance along the coast. Nothing special came out of the images Tasi and Inapo captured. A pile of used fishing nets told Merk the skiffs belonged to fishermen, not pirates.

With neither Tasi nor Inapo picking up vibrations of intruders or vehicles, they swam to the next target a few kilometers west—one of two marinas that a year before were not visible from any spy plane or satellite, but were captured earlier that night for the first time by the drone.

Merk knew drones were useful and effective beyond blowing up terrorist targets, hospitals, or schools. But unlike navy dolphins, they had to return to base to recharge, refuel, or rearm.

Merk gazed out of the window to the dark sky over the dark sea, thought of his girlfriend, her dark eyes with a spark of life in them, and then remembered grabbing hold of Nairobi's calves as he pulled her down when he climbed on shore in Somalia. He knew the next few days would be different, hectic, dangerous, with little time to think about any women.

Chapter Twenty-Three

DEEP INTO THE morning, Merk deployed the dolphins farther west in a search for the Somali pirates, when a series of high-pitched whistles came back, not from Tasi or Inapo, but from the drone. Within the software, embedded between the trills, flashed a message that the Dolphin Code software began to decipher and translate the sounds into a broken string of words.

Merk read the message, recognizing that it didn't originate from the USS *New York* or the NATO pirate task force, but from CIA headquarters in Langley. Should he trust its content? Was it a coded message meant for Nairobi? Or did he receive something else?

In the chain of words he felt a wave of anticipation that it might be his girlfriend trying to contact him. But then within the words was a latent message, a code within a code. Bracing himself, he read every word with dread: "Hot . . . Load . . . Gone . . . Missing . . . in Syria."

Anticipation gave way to disbelief. Merk knew what those words meant—a dirty bomb or some sort of hot material, chemical, chlorine, radioactive, or biological, was on the move in war-torn Syria. There were few assets on the ground to stop it.

What the hell? Did the CIA confirm this? he wondered, keeping the news from Nico. Merk recalled Iran's attempt to plant sea-mines in the Strait of Hormuz and then the images of the CIA strike on the terrorist safe house in Jaar, Yemen, on the same night, within the same hour. Something wasn't right and he finally made the connection. Whoever gave the false intel to CIA Agent Alan Cuthbert was also sponsored by Iran. It was the diversion of luring three CIA drones away from the Persian Gulf that night to fly over Yemen airspace that told Merk that the propaganda tsunami of striking a school and the mining of the Strait of Hormuz were coordinated at least a month in advance.

But who was the mastermind behind those dual, seemingly unrelated events?

Chapter Twenty-Four

ALONG THE IRAQ border, north of the Syrian town of Abu Kamal on the Euphrates River, stretched a chain of burnt-out forts and outposts that lay in ruins from the ISIS offensive in the spring of 2014. With the help of Iranian air power and battalions, by agreement with the Syrian government, a 100-mile stretch of desert had been carved out, driving the ISIS forces farther north into Syria and across Iraq, then down along the reinforced border with Saudi Arabia.

Strengthened with US military backing and Russian sorties, the Kurdish army with thousands of Iraqis cleared out a similar terrorist haven of ISIS fighters on their side of the border. That left a joint venture between US Special Forces advisors and the Iraqi police task force to monitor the refugees and insurgents flowing over the broken border crossings.

During the day, Iranian gunships, drones, and spy planes watched from the sky, while ground patrols branched out, scouting along the border and following the corridor for ISIS warriors, suppliers, smugglers of cigarettes and kerosene, exiled Baath Party commanders once loyal to Saddam Hussein, deserted Syrian soldiers, Syrian rebel factions, and al Qaeda groups and offshoots that wanted to attack the West and the United States.

The US countered that activity at night with high-tech hardware, from infrared cameras able to detect the heat signatures of rodents on the ground, to Long-Range Acquisition System (LRAS) night-vision scopes capable of picking up humans several klicks away on dark moonless nights. Beyond degrading the Islamic State, Iraq deployed more of their policemen and army guards at Fort 24 than at any other border crossing along Syria. It was an attempt to stop the influx of suicide bombers, al Qaeda bomb-makers, ISIS fighters, and former Hussein loyalists from destabilizing the fractured government in Iraq any further, whether north fighting ISIS over Mosul, or in the villages on the outskirts of Baghdad.

Across the border from Fort 24 in Syria's northeast desert, a flat, arid plateau with a ridge of berms rising low to the east along Iraq, a group of Syrian Army generals met with a pair of North Korean engineers and a middle-aged Iranian nuclear scientist named Ferdows.

Among the leaders in the group stood Syrian four-star General Adad, a rotund, bombastic man with graying hair and sun-leather face. Adad ran through a list of items on a marked-up blueprint. Loving to hear himself talk, the general surveyed a swale to the south and pointed to planned locations for a missile launch, a supply house, a couple of false buildings, and a control center. He pointed to a road in the distance, fingering where a connector road would be constructed that ran across the sand in a figure eight driveway, as shown on the plan, that would encompass the site. With the wave of his hand, he boasted about how the site layout was his idea, even though the plan was cloned from an existing base in North Korea, first, then Iran.

As Adad spoke, flanked by a trio of Syrian guards armed with Kalashnikov assault rifles, a translator listened to and verbalized his words into Korean so the visitors would understand the general's remarks. Since Ferdows was fluent in English, French, his native Persian of *Farsi*, and Arabic, Syria's official language, no translation was needed for the Iranian scientist.

The balding, bespectacled Ferdows listened intently, taking in elements of the design piece by piece, jotting them down in a tablet design app. He removed his wire-rimmed glasses and squinted southwest, where he visualized Israel standing on the other side of Jordan. The idea to build a North Korean long-range missile launcher in eastern Syria, like similar facilities erected in Iran, armed with Iranian nuclear-tipped rockets, brought a grin of satisfaction to his face. Syria couldn't let the rebels or ISIS insurgents overthrow the general's government. They had to be kept out of the eastern desert border. To ensure that level of containment, General Adad blew up a dam, destroyed access roads and infrastructure to water, in effect cutting off supplies to the Caliph and his army of the Islamic State of Iraq and al-Sham (ISIS), a.k.a. the Islamic State of Iraq in the Levant (ISIL). ISIS's primary goal was to liquidate Shia Muslims in Iraq and Syria, the Putin-backed Syrian regime, the Kurds to the north, and Iran emboldened by the US nuclear treaty. That threat was still real and not going away. General Adad understood that better than most; he also knew cutting off fuel and water were key to keeping the Islamic State's power contained in the north, along the border with Turkey.

The North Koreans listened to the general. The old Korean man was a frail ballistics engineer, while his female colleague, Kim Dong-Sun, was a missile specialist. The Korean pair checked the contours of the land and the locations where each component would support and supply the missile battery.

Dong-Sun was a petite colonel devoid of emotion. She wrapped her long hair in a bun and tucked it under a cap, which accentuated her angular, stone face, plain without makeup, and that afternoon coated with sand dust. Her narrow, Siamese cat-like eyes, black, shifting, took in the desolate landscape. Whenever she glanced at the fat, portly body of General Adad, which was alien to her countrymen's smallish, thinner figures, she cringed.

Dong-Sun looked over the shoulder of General Adad, seeing the plans with hand-written notes in Sanskrit for the first time since they were emailed to the Syrian military from North Korea's Physics Department of Kanggye Defense College a month ago. The Syrian engineers had done a decent job of plotting what she designed. The only item she saw missing were the Chinese solar panels she engineered that would provide backup power in case the underground cables, which ran from the mountain valleys of the west at the earthen Tabqa hydroelectric dam to the nearby border with Iraq, were severed by the civil conflict or damaged by sabotage.

Dong-Sun was about to broach the subject when out of the corner of her eye she spotted apparitions drifting in the heat haze along the

Syrian side of the berms by the Iraqi border. She had been silent for the better part of the hour-long briefing. She knew her place in the misogynist Syrian world was to stand resolutely still, hover in the background, be silent, be gracious, stay out of sight, speak when spoken to—she was used to the same boorish treatment back home in the male-dominated Asian societies of China and the Korean peninsula.

The engineer watched the visitors float across the melting sand. Silently, steadily they strode over the watery mirage. For a moment she was transfixed by the optical illusion, by the way their legs wriggled in the heat waves, by the way their lower bodies melted in the undulating mirror of sand. With a tap on the wrist, she interrupted the translator, pointing to the visitors. Redirected by the unwelcome party, he stopped translating.

General Adad didn't hear the chatter of the translator. So he glanced at him and followed his sightline over to the intruders. As the Syrians turned east, adjusting their eyes to the heat rising from the desert, the foursome came into view: Armed Syrian soldiers escorted a white male and female couple, in their twenties, dressed in khakis and tee shirts, looking American.

Dressed in an olive green North Korean officer's uniform, pants, and a tunic with blue liner, big buttons, and starch-stiff lapels, Dong-Sun opened a flap on her utility belt, pulled out a pair of binoculars, and zoomed in on the couple. The man was sturdy with a robust frame, had curly brown hair and a beard. The woman was tall and thin, her straight blonde hair tied in a ponytail. Both were covered in dust. The armed guards carried many cameras slung over their shoulders.

"Western maggots. They smell like American journalists," Dong-Sun said in Korean. The translator stared at her. She shot a stare back, prodding him to translate her observation. He did so reluctantly. She looked at the tablet that Ferdows stowed under his jacket.

The guards stepped in front of General Adad in a defensive posture that both bewildered and amazed her. They spread their legs apart, stiffened their wide frames in an open stance, and lifted the AK-47s chest-high without lowering their heads to eye the rifles' scopes. Taken back by their unorthodox stance, by the fat targets they made of their bodies, Dong-Sun handed the binoculars to her colleague and moved Ferdows aside. She studied the poor aim and terrible posture the Syrian marksmen made in taking a stance against the threat.

The engineer shook her head, took out a lemon from the utility belt and, with a paring knife, cut the fruit in half. With a swipe she peeled the rind back and cut the halves into quarters. She bit into the lemon, sucking on the sour juices, watching the guards' tense shoulders, at their once-relaxed demeanor stiffened into frowns. Dong-Sun spat out a seed and the chewed quarter before spitting out the rind, then inserted the next lemon slice into her mouth.

In watching her drain the juices out of the lemon, Ferdows made a sour face. He and his countrymen recoiled at the uncouth Korean.

"Look at them. They are backpack reporters," she said in Korean. "American debt is so big, TV news can't pay production crew wages." She noticed their hawklike stares, spat out the next lemon quarter and, using her hands to hold an imaginary firehose between her legs, she shouted at the Syrian guards in Korean: "You stand like fat elephants, holding your guns like trunks. Are you fat and slow like elephants?"

Not understanding a single word she said, the guards glanced over to the fiery Korean colonel, while trying to keep an eye on the captives. Kim directed the translator to translate what she said. He winced and shook his head pleading not to. "Translate," she shrieked. He started to translate her words and the generals looked back at her in shock as she crudely dressed down Adad's guards.

Fed up with all the masculine eyes glaring at her, as if she were the one who held the Kalashnikovs like a limp garden hose, Dong-Sun motioned General Adad that she would demonstrate for his guards how they should stand and aim the rifles. Curious to see what she would do next, Adad motioned the nearest guard. The soldier looked at the general in dismay.

Kim Dong-Sun stepped over, tapped the guard's elbow, lifted the rifle to his shoulder, sat it on his meaty upper arm, and tilted his head down. She tried to angle his big frame sideways, but he refused to budge. So she stepped behind him, looked at his large butt, and remarked, "Do all Syrian cows have fat tails?"

The translator was appalled. But Dong-Sun didn't wait for him to speak. She kicked the guard in the back of his leg, forcing him down on one knee. She pulled his shoulder back and yanked his torso sideways. His stance and aim were still poor, out of line. So she snatched the rifle from the other guard, shouting, "Watch. Learn."

With deliberate, robotic movements, Dong-Sun stood sideways, sucked in her gut as if she had the fat man's belly, saying, "Make your body thin, like blade of grass." She dropped to one knee, put the rifle on her shoulder, pressed the stock snug to her cheekbone, eyed the sight at the tip of the rifle, aimed it at an imaginary target in front of the captives, and then fired a shot that blew a spray of sand at the boots of the captive bearded man.

He flinched, wiping grains of sand dust off his beard and out of his eyes. The woman stopped to help him, but the border guard yanked her away, goading her on without her colleague. The other border guard swore in Arabic, wondering what the errant shot was all about.

General Adad, together with his generals, waved their hands, shouting that it was okay, that the crazy Korean engineer was a woman learning how to shoot.

Without knowing what he said, Dong-Sun stood up, ignored the bellowing men, handed the rifle back to the other guard, and then circled around the kneeling one, squeezed his shoulder, and straightened his aim. "Go, now. Fire," she yelled. But he didn't shoot. "Fire. All clear," she repeated. Still, he hesitated. So she tapped his elbow; he recoiled a shot over the heads of the captives, who ducked alongside the now-angry border guards.

The kneeling guard threw the assault rifle on the ground in frustration. She picked it up, stood sideways, reed-thin, and walked the guard through the steps from holding her form to steadying the rifle, and aimed the sight beyond the target.

The brooding General Adad watched the engineer with dark amusement.

* * *

THE SWIRL OF speculation blew up like desert sand in the tense Sixth Floor Ops Center. The CIA director and his team viewed the covert meeting between Syrian and North Korean scientists. The satellite image showed the minutest of details, from the time on General Adad's black Movado watch to the chevron stripes on Colonel Kim Dong-Sun's army uniform.

"There they are—" the CIA director shouted, unable to contain his anxiousness over the operation going south. He pointed to the border guards goading the CIA agents, dressed as journalists, to the Syrian generals. "Looks like world heritage day, minus the UN blue helmets and ISIS desert fighters," he remarked. He took a breath, adding, "We have Koreans, Syrians, Americans . . . Hell, we probably have an Iranian nuke engineer planted somewhere in there."

At 0400 zulu, the thumb-tapping CIA director stood with his team of intel specialists and directors. His fatigued, bleary-eyed minions had worked overtime late into the next day, driven by fear that the hot Syrian dirty material would find a way to be shipped out of the war-ravaged country, despite the CIA and Pentagon retasking more than a dozen drones to scour the Syrian borders and battlefields to pick up the infrared trail of plutonium, uranium, or some type of gas agent.

The team had been driven into the ground, analyzing the swatches of electronic NSA-eavesdropped files, and CIA back channel HUMINT with file after file on suspected militants and Islamic State terrorists devouring the bulk of their time and resources. The Syria-Iran-Yemen AQAP connections dominated the new Red Cell analysis. But the CIA director had a sinking feeling that the hot load was headed to or had already made it across the border. If that were the case, then there would be little hope to intercept it until it reached its target destination.

"What's she doing?" the deputy director of operations asked.

Dong-Sun took the rifle from the guard, demonstrated how to control breathing to calm the body, release tension, and relax the brain's alpha waves, while focusing her mind on the singular task at hand. In a standing position, she aimed the rifle and fired a volley that clipped one of the cameras dangling by the Syrian border guard's side. With a burst of the lens, the agents hit the ground covering their heads; the guard jumped back shaking.

"Jesus Christ, that was close. Is she training Adad's men how to shoot?" the CIA director yelled, the artery in his neck rippling. Mad as hell, he turned to Red Cell analysts: "Did one of you damn ants find anything on Ms. North Korea being an expert marksman?" The analysts froze. They didn't utter a word; another pair stared down at the table. "Hell, Ms. North Korea is a rifle specialist first, and a missile engineer second, and we don't know this? That's nuts."

As the SAD director flipped through the pages of Dong-Sun's dossier, the director of clandestine services stepped over to the CIA director and whispered in his ear. With his index finger, the CIA director motioned to contact the Signal Command at Fort Meade to arm the Hellfire missile on the drone hovering over the Syrian desert. All hell was about to break loose.

Chapter Twenty-Five

Furious by the brazen shot, General Adad leaned into Dong-Sun's face swearing in Arabic. She handed the AK-47 back to the guard and covered her mouth and nose from the odor of the general's bad breath. He could have used her lemon to cleanse his palette. He blinked more rapidly as his voice and blood pressure rose. Wary that his temper was about to erupt, she eyed the border guards pulling the Americans to their feet and pushing them onward.

Ferdows took the blueprints from General Adad's hand, as the border guard with the confiscated cameras signaled the Americans to stay put. He strode quickly, glancing back at the hostages. Dong-Sun watched the bearded American pull a small object, like a pen, out of his shirtsleeve. Sensing danger, she stepped behind Ferdows and General Adad to use them as human shields. She didn't want to die in war-torn Syria.

With a click of the pen a starburst grenade, hidden inside a camera, exploded in a percussion blast, instantly killing the Syrian soldier. The shock wave radiated out, knocking over the generals, Adad and Ferdows, back on top of diminutive Dong-Sun. The generals, closest to the border guard's motionless body, writhed in pain, covering their ears as blood seeped out.

The CIA agents yanked the other border guard to the ground, wresting the AK-47 and pistol from him. The female agent turned around and fired the pistol, shooting General Adad's bodyguards. The bearded agent stabbed the border guard in the ribs, driving the blade into his ribs until his eyes flared open in shock, while his will to fight slackened.

Taking a page out of Osama bin Laden's al Qaeda playbook—when he dispatched a pair of assassins dressed as journalists to blow up the Afghan Northern Alliance leader Ahmad Shah Massoud two days before the 9/11 attacks—Alan Cuthbert and his fellow CIA operator moved in to secure the site.

A jeep rumbled up the road in a cloud of dust, cut across the flats toward them where the connector road had been designed. The female agent picked up the plans, while Agent Cuthbert pulled a quivering Ferdows off of Dong-Sun. With the cap blown off her head and her long hair disheveled, draping her stunned face, Cuthbert lifted the engineer to her feet as the jeep skidded to a halt. Waiting to see who was in the vehicle, the female agent frisked Dong-Sun's backside. The agent felt the outline of a pistol tucked down the belt of her narrow waist, and pulled out a Browning automatic.

She clicked the safety off, gripped the pistol behind the swaying Dong-Sun, ready to fire. The engineer stood still, raising her hands. She looked back at Ferdows rolling over on his side feeling his clothes for the tablet. He found it under his shirt.

A burly Baathist colonel stepped out of the jeep in a Syrian army uniform. He bore a thick mustache and scanned the stunned and wounded in a dark gaze. He reached inside the cab and pulled out a shotgun, leaned his elbows on the hood, aiming the barrel at the agents. Alan Cuthbert glanced over to his colleague. Coming to an accord with just a look, he thrust his hands above his head as he approached the jeep. He and the colonel exchanged a few words in Arabic, when the agent stopped. The Baathist colonel lifted the rifle off the hood and aimed at Cuthbert's chest. The colonel checked a birthmark on the agent's left forearm, saying, "Cuthbert, yes. Confirmed," and waved the female agent to bring Dong-Sun over.

With the wounded generals sprawled on the ground, writhing, moaning, immobilized, the colonel pushed the female agent aside, lifted the chin of Dong-Sun, and stared at her blank gaze.

He twisted her around, as Alan Cuthbert bound her wrists behind her back with snap-ties. The female CIA agent pulled the North Korean engineer around the other side of the jeep, and dumped her in the backseat.

Chapter Twenty-Six

A T THE BORDER, the CIA agents abandoned the jeep, stuck in a berm.

They whisked Kim Dong-Sun with the ex-Saddam loyalist over the border. The Baathist colonel, a mole buried deep in Syria's civil war, was the reason why the CIA was able to pull off the brazen daylight kidnapping. A battery of Iraqi Army soldiers and policemen applauded the capture. Behind the cordon, a quad of American military officials waited to bring the North Korean engineer inside for low-intensity interrogation.

Dong-Sun scanned the dark-skinned faces of the Iraqis, then saw the pale American officers pulling back, opening a side door of Fort 24, a tan brick and bitumen building perched on an arid hill. An array of radio antennas pointed to the sky. Fort 24 had survived the Syrian civil war and the area of what ISIS once claimed in erasing the border between Iraq and Syria.

Inside a small room with no mirrors or windows, the CIA agents dumped the North Korean in a chair, cut the plastic ties off her wrists, and pushed her seat up to a wood table with a glass of water on top. Dong-Sun finger-combed her hair out of her dusty face, took a sip of water, and studied the faces of Alan Cuthbert, the blonde female agent, then eyed a scruffy US Marine sergeant sitting between them. A fourth person entered the room. He was a short nerd dressed in civvis. He, she knew, was an interpreter on the surface, a CIA agent under the guise of a contractor specialist.

Kim Dong-Sun shook her head. She reached across the table and took a pen and pad from the female agent, then began to scrawl in English a request and then drew a man with a beard.

The note read: *Let me speak to the man alone. Turn off the cameras to the room.*

Dong-Sun slid the note across the table to Alan Cuthbert, who read it. He smirked and slid the note over to the female agent, who motioned everyone to step outside.

Cuthbert closed the door behind her, signaled to the camera in the corner of the ceiling to shut off, then sat down with the laptop and his smartphone, making sure they were recording their conversation. He then rolled out the blueprint of the missile launch site and stared at Dong-Sun, as if the engineer, based on a hard look, would divulge state secrets and plans in a second.

"Kimchi, you don't need an interpreter to talk to me. So tell me what these plans mean," he said, flicking grains of sand out of his beard. "You're a pretty good marksman for a woman."

Dong-Sun picked up on the racial slur and gender slight and frowned at the burly CIA agent. Sitting still like Buddha, Dong-Sun stared at Cuthbert, who lasered a death stare back.

"What the hell? Why won't you talk?"

"Are we live with your bosses?" she said in a thick Korean accent, tapping the laptop.

Alan Cuthbert nodded, saying, "Sure. We have an open live feed to CIA's Sixth Floor Operations Center, with the CIA director and his team. They watched the kidnapping unfold live." He then spoke to the laptop, announcing, "Director, this is Baghdad station chief at Fort 24 border crossing. We're in possession of North Korean ballistic missile engineer, Kim Dong-Sun." He wouldn't state his real or any other name in front of her.

Dong-Sun managed a razor-thin grin. She took a sip of water, and—slammed the glass down on Cuthbert's fingers. He yelled, grabbing his hand in pain. She lunged across the table, chopped the off-balance agent across the forehead and pushed him to the floor, rolled over the table and locked the steel door, putting a chair against the doorknob. She smashed the glass, took a jagged shard and hovered it over Cuthbert, motioning him to stay on the floor. The engineer then spun the laptop toward her as guards banged on the door, trying to break into the room.

She showed her face and spoke into the laptop mic in American English: "This is CIA Agent Jenny Myung King of SOG Clandestine Services. Hi, Director, I can see you . . . " Jenny King eyed the shocked and speechless Alan Cuthbert still on the floor. She repeated her name, her senior CIA officer rank and pay level of GS-15, and then revealed the top-secret code name of the missile site Special Ops mission she was involved in: "Operation Sandblast Scree."

She ripped off her North Korean army tunic, tossed it on the floor, shouting, "Your field morons have blown my cover." She banged her fist on the door, yelling, "Wait. Stop the noise. Wait a minute." As Cuthbert climbed off the ground, signaling to the camera that he was "okay," Jenny spoke to the laptop: "They have ruined nine months of deep surveillance. They have blown my clandestine op. They have wasted thousands of man-hours and hundreds of thousands of dollars paying off local assets. Now let me bring the Langley ass-clowns of Red Cell up to speed . . . I already kidnapped the real Dong-Sun thirty-six hours ago. The person you need to interrogate is Syrian General Adad and the Iranian nuclear scientist Ferdows. But your pack mules left them in the desert. Isn't that right, Alan Cuthbert?"

Agent Jenny King turned away and sat on the edge of the table, burying her face in her hands to absorb her frustration. She looked up at the ceiling, shouting, "God, you guys suck."

Feeling sick to his stomach, Cuthbert kicked the chair away from the door and opened it, eying the woman he thought—no, he believed—was the real North Korean engineer, "Sorry, Agent King."

"Worse than kidnapping me was leaving Ferdows's tablet behind," Jenny said.

"What's on his tablet?" Cuthbert asked, rubbing his forehead.

"Tehran's plans of moving hot material across the Syrian deserts to Homs . . . from there to the West and maybe the US to detonate," she said. "This is the closest we have ever gotten."

Mouthing he was sorry again, Cuthbert sat down and said, "We can make this right."

"No, you can't," she said, as the real CIA station chief stood at the threshold of the door.

"Yes, King, I can," he said, then swung the laptop around to face him, as he explained his on-the-fly plan for Agent King with the CIA executives. "We send the North Korean King back to Iran to make the CIA's gross mistake of kidnapping her go away."

"Alan, that might work," she admitted. "They don't know I'm a CIA agent."

"No one does in here. Except a few of us," he said.

The station chief stepped inside the room and shut the door, motioning Cuthbert to hold it a minute while he stood on a chair and pulled the cable out of the camera.

"Go on, Alan, tell me how you will make it work," she said, dropping the glass shard on the table.

"Tehran has screwed us ever since the 2015 nuclear treaty. They set me, the agency, and the US up to fail in Yemen with the planted bad intel on the drone strike."

"You mean the terrorist headquarters that was actually be an elementary school, where body parts of children were pulled from the rubble?" she said.

"Yes, that one. Funny thing, we accidentally got back at them the same night when a US Navy dolphin op uncovered a Quds fishing trawler mining the Strait of Hormuz."

"Was that survey run by Merk Toten?" she asked.

He nodded yes.

"Did Merk make it out alive?" she asked, concerned about the health and well-being of her boyfriend.

"You can say that. I sat down with him for his next mission. He's now deep in a Black Lit op in Somalia. Like you, it doesn't exist."

Chapter Twenty-Seven

*P*irate ship, mothership, citizenship.
     Those were the words that flickered through Merk's mind as he observed the destitute poverty—the hovels, the lean-tos, the shantytowns—that dotted the broken coast of rocky coves and sea cliffs amid stretches of pristine sandy beaches, one with the rusting hull of a hijacked ship run aground.

Inland, he glimpsed garbage strewn near the poor dwellings; worn clothes dried on the same lines as fishing nets; elderly men drinking spirits in the shade with armed Somali militants looming in the background, smoking rolled cigarettes.

On the leeside, the turquoise blue sea boasted the ocean's wealth. Sitting there day after day, cooked by the copper-hot Somali sun, lured their eyes to gaze out at the sea and dream about the riches of the world passing by in the shipping lanes every day. The Gulf of Aden seemed to be their only hope in a destitute land, to seek and steal a fortune. Whether it was trawling the shoals for fish, depleted after years of overfishing by foreign ships, or extracting money in the hostage-for-ransom trade that, after rising from the shadow of obscurity in 2008, had been successful for the "Pirates of Puntland," who became a scourge for international shipping and a model for Nigerian pirates to copy the same business model.

Of the thousands of ships and vessels, box carriers and oil tankers that passed the coast of Somalia each year, why wouldn't a warlord dispatch packs of youths on skiffs to steal from the rich? It was only money. Just numbers. Money for lives and cargo. They usually received the money; the hostages often got released unharmed. Yet it grew into an arms race.

Pondering the limitations they were about to face in the search for the pirates, an alert flashed on screen: "Receiving Com."

Chapter Twenty-Eight

MERK LOWERED HIS sunglasses and eyed a pane open on the laptop. An aerial shot of a new drone flying over the coast near Somalia's western port city of Berbera came into view.

At an altitude of two miles, the drone's high-resolution eye captured the long strand of beaches that marked Berbera, once a tourist hot spot for European divers. Now it was all but deserted. Beyond a couple of beached fishing boats, with nets draped over them, or a few youths sauntering barefoot on the sandy hook peninsula of the natural harbor, there was a row of unused fishing boats strung together at a single anchor, a wrecked dhow tilting on a sandbar.

A quarter mile west of the port by the fuel storage tanks, the immense black-orange hull of the *Blå Himmel* rose out of the shallow water, listing starboard. Its watermark visible, exposing the lower hull to splotches of barnacles, the bow of the supertanker had run aground half a football field from shore.

Waves passed on both sides of the ship, as if the hull acted like a man-made jetty to buffer beach erosion. But as Merk enlarged the shot full-screen, he saw no one lingering by the vessel in the surf, on its decks, in the bridge, or anywhere else onboard. Even the on-land fuel depot was deserted. He didn't see an oil slick, which meant the double-hulled *Blå Himmel* sat on a soft bed of sand. That told him the pirates knew where they would strand the ship, on the sandbars of Berbera, daring international forces to come inside Somalia's territorial waters to retrieve it.

Was it a trap? He wondered.

The drone's camera, controlled remotely by UAV operators out of Chabelley Airfield at Djibouti base, zoomed on the fore starboard deck to a dried puddle of what appeared to be blood. The more Merk studied the red swatch, running it across an imaginary sight line of a sniper back to the top of the bridge at the stern of the ship, some 750 feet away, the more he was convinced the blood belonged not to the captain or crew, but to the slain pirate leader, Samatar. He wouldn't need blood type or forensic analysis. What the Norwegian mercenary, Peder Olsen, whispered to him was enough for Merk to know that the pool of blood belonged to the dead pirate leader.

Off the bow several rows of footprints dotted the beach to and from the sea. Some prints were defined step for step; others were rubbed out, as hostages must have been dragged against their will through the sand. Merk was certain the pirates had a greeting committee when they arrived late that night. But what he didn't see, such as wheel ruts from vehicles hauling cargoes or hostages away, puzzled him.

Before Merk informed Nico on what he observed, the gap to gather intel just grew larger. Directed to swim to the next bight in the coast populated with fishing huts but with no slips or docks, a dozen klicks outside of Berbera, the dolphins wouldn't arrive to the site for a few hours. He would then decide whether to move to the stranded supertanker when they arrived.

From the GPS chip in the Chinese cell phone, which kept a tab on Nairobi, Nico said she had driven past the fifty klicks she mentioned. She took a fork in the road, deviating from the coast at Berbera, driving inland south through a pass in the Sheikh Mountains. With Nairobi continuing on that road, Merk knew there would be several more hours of intel blackout—at least on his side—of what was taking place near or away from the tanker. That spelled trouble since the first seventy-two hours after a hijacking is the most critical time to locate hostages and learn their fate.

Another alert flashed on the laptop. The webcams Nico and Merk had installed in Nairobi's house chimed in a live feed. Merk blew up the cams into a multi-view screen, showing: outside the front of the house, inside the kitchen, and in the living room. He tapped

Nico's arm, nudging him to look at the laptop. Nico scanned the road ahead, checked the rearview mirror—they were alone—and pulled over. They looked at a pair of intruders peeking in the windows, checking the property on both sides of the house, and then picked the lock and entered the front door.

Inside, the intruders moved from room to room, opening closet doors, inspecting the dishes in the sink, reading the labels on bottles in the wine cabinet, unaware there was a hidden closet behind the fine wines. They rifled through the mail Nairobi deliberately left on the table. Merk wondered if they would look under the table and find the stack of euros she had taped to the underside. After a few minutes in the kitchen, the intruders fanned out to different rooms. Any thought about Nico and Merk returning to the safe house vanished. As a result, their exit strategy out of Somalia would have to be rerouted. They could no longer go back the way they came to Puntland. There was no going back to the safe house at all.

And that bothered Merk.

"I'm going to drop you off at the beach so I can shadow Nairobi," Nico said.

"That should work." Merk gazed out to the slivers of the blue sea blinking between the breaks of the bluffs and rock outcroppings as Nico drove along the coast.

Chapter Twenty-Nine

THE ARMED GUARDS wore blue jeans and white tee shirts. Khmer Rouge–like scarves draped their heads, shading their scalps from the intense spring sun.

Their scowls grew sharper; the worry lines cut furrows in their foreheads. They stepped forward to block the entrance to the compound, flanked by crags halfway up the Sheikh Mountain Pass. With a glance, the guards raised AK-47s, aiming them at the windshield of the approaching car. The vehicle skidded to a stop.

Powering down the window, Nairobi stuck out her hand and shook the silver bangles on her wrist, alerting the guard who was behind the wheel. One guard strolled over to the door, his swarthy face crinkled in the arid heat, his eyes bloodshot. He stole a glance at Nairobi's cleavage, asking whom she wanted to visit. But when she answered, it wasn't his boss Korfa she asked for, but the hostages of the *Blå Himmel* and the *Shining Sea.*

The guard made a face, mulling her unusual request, in light of the slaying of Korfa's brother Samatar. He looked back at the other guard. After a pause, he nodded at her. As the guard opened the fortified gate, the first guard banged his fist on the car door, asking her in the animal trader dialect of Somaliland's modern city of Hargeisa, "Did you bring the cloth?"

She lifted up a folded purple cloth with blurred bands of white and violet around the border. Then she held up an old edition of the Qur'an, showing the book's frayed spine, the pages yellowed with age.

The guard waved Nairobi through. She drove into the compound. Inside the gate, half a dozen teenage pirates carrying Uzis and AK-47s guided her to park under a dead tree, offering no shade from the heat. When Nairobi stepped out, an elder fisherman frisked her. He ran his hands over her thighs, swept them under her crotch, and squeezed her firm butt. She stood still, containing her disgust at being groped. She watched the leering eyes of the boys without complaint as the elder patted her blouse, grazed her ribs, pinched the wires under the bra. The elder removed her sunglasses and checked her eyes. The brightness dilated her pupils; she squinted.

She covered her eyes, scanning a pair of new Audi sports cars parked under a camouflage canopy. They were stored in shade. Caught in the disequilibrium of the light and the news that she had arrived at the funeral of Samatar, Nairobi followed the elder into the dwelling fortified out of a natural cave. The pirate hideout, covered with *wadis*—sandy rivers—pouring down from the Sheikh Mountains into one of many springs and underground wells in and around the pass, was an ideal place that provided sanctuary to stay out of the prying eyes of US drones, satellites, and spy planes. Because it was located inland, away from the coast, away from any major city, the CIA rarely looked at the greenery and the mountains of western Somaliland. And until a week ago, Nairobi didn't know of the compound's existence.

Nairobi had visited Samatar and Korfa plenty of times the past few years, at their home in Puntland, negotiating on a fishing skiff at sea, bartering a deal with the Somalia Coast Guard, making intel drops outside a mosque to win their trust, in another compound, or in a string of huts and safe houses closer to where she lived on the coast.

So the new secret location of Korfa's hideout gave her pause. It demonstrated how fast the pirates had moved under the twins. They consolidated power, wiped out rivals in the north, and ramped up and executed plans. She also knew how Korfa and Samatar resisted overtures from Yemeni tribesmen, AQAP, and other militant Islamic groups to join and build up radical Islam in their homeland. But their form of Muslim worship was far more nuanced than the male-only, austere practice of the Taliban or the Saudi Arabian-sponsored Sunni Islam Wahhabis schools.

Korfa's clan mixed religion with African mysticism; trusted their women to carry out segregated but important religious rites, functions, and doctrines. He didn't like Somali women being covered up, not head to toe. With their burgeoning trade of money-for-hostages and double brass balls, the twin brothers branched out, expanding both their territorial empire and network of foreign sponsors and trade partners. Some even migrated to Nigeria to help ramp up the pirate attacks of Western Africa or support Boko Haram attacks in the north.

Like Alexander the Great, their father's domain wasn't big enough to contain their ambition. Now they saw moving beyond Somalia's borders as the next step in their rise to power. That was the threat that scared the US intelligence agencies the most about Somali and why the Pentagon sent Nico, Merk, and the navy dolphins on the Black Lit to gather intel.

In the main entranceway of the cave, boxes of supplies were stacked to the ceiling. They contained items from dry goods and vacuum-packed food to arms and ammunition. Nairobi sensed Korfa's men were preparing for something big, that they planned on being holed up for some time—all the supplies told her that. The pirates were ready to go underground, to live in the network of caves in the Sheikh Mountains for months or longer.

Sensing the chess move, Nairobi had mentally prepared for that day to discuss the hostages and how she could become the liaison in the negotiations with the foreign shipowners and insurance companies. But all that changed with the death of Samatar. Korfa was going to honor his brother before any business was going to be conducted, before he launched any plans seeking revenge. The more she thought, the more she realized the hostages were being held at some other location outside the compound in the mountain pass.

The elder led Nairobi into an alcove. It was dimly lit with oil lanterns. As her eyes adjusted to the light, she saw Korfa's women—a curvy mistress, his graying aunt, and a couple of young female cousins—standing in a burial pit the guards had dug out by hand. The women draped light green cloth on the pit's walls, chanting prayers in preparing the hole to receive the body.

Nairobi nodded politely, handed the purple cloth to the aunt, and stepped around the pit. At the back of the alcove, she saw Korfa cleaning the body of Samatar. She noticed the gunshot wound had been sewn up and Korfa had worked on preparing the body like a tree, rinsing the flesh of the trunk with holy water, moving down the boughs of the legs, wiping away the blood from the fatal wound, and wiping off Samatar's arms.

The pirate warlord stared at Nairobi as he dipped the washcloth, wringed it damp, and dabbed it on the stiff muscular biceps and forearms of the corpse Samatar. She saw for the first time vulnerability in Korfa's hardened eyes. When he pointed to the Qur'an, she no longer saw a warrior, a pirate, or a warlord, but a believer in both his faith and lifting his oppressed people out of the thrall of poverty. That made it difficult for her to spy on the charismatic, warlike man.

Samatar's eldest of three sons, a fourteen-year-old boy, limped over to his uncle Korfa and handed the robe and tunic his father had worn on his march to Mecca a decade earlier. Knowing the religious significance of Samatar's clothes, Nairobi opened the Qur'an, looked at Korfa, and waited for his guidance on which chapter and verse to read.

Without looking back at her, Korfa said, "An Nur. Medinan Twenty-Four. Forty-Six."

She flipped through the Qur'an until she came to the Chapter *An Nur* ("The Light"), and read from verse 46: *"We have indeed sent down Signs that make things manifest: and Allah guides whom He wills to a way that is straight. (47): They say 'We believe in Allah and in the Apostle and we obey': but even after that some of them turn away: they are not Believers."*

Samatar's eldest son began to recite a prayer next. Korfa grabbed Nairobi's wrist, squeezing the bangles, and whispered, "Nai, I want the name and country of the sniper."

Chapter Thirty

E AST OF BERBERA, Nico drove up and down the coast, reconning the seascape to make sure that the location where he dropped Merk off was isolated so the dolphin whisperer could remotely com with the dolphins without being spotted. They settled on a strand five klicks outside the harbor, where the beach came to an end, transitioning from flat sand to terraces of stone slabs. Around a point, a broken cove formed a shelter with boulders backed by rocky mounds.

Merk stripped off the Bedouin headdress, grabbed his gear, and told Nico that he had forty-eight hours to gather intel on the pirates before they exited out of Somalia somewhere west.

The SEAL CO nodded, watched Merk pick his way over the boulders and disappear down in the cove. He turned the vehicle around and drove to Berbera. From the GPS vector of the Chinese military Satcom he gave Nairobi, her vehicle sat halfway up the Sheikh Mountains Pass.

For the next hour, Merk dug in, setting up a surveillance nest within the confines of the cove. He stored MREs, canteens of water, and other foodstuffs in different nooks and crevices, wary that the items needed to be safe from high tide that could flood the cove, turning it into a tidal pool. He changed out of his clothes into a wetsuit, took a pair of digital binoculars, and scouted the horizon on the gulf. He panned the sea searching for skiffs, the large dhows like the mothership, and larger vessels like freighters and tankers. The sea was mysteriously empty, still. With the hijacked Norwegian tanker found in Berbera, he expected to see navy ships. But there were none. The absence of a decisive naval response made the view all the more strange and disconcerting, yet at the same time it whetted his curiosity.

Merk settled down in the shade of the mounds, monitoring the progress of Tasi and Inapo. He was replaying a clip of the dolphins trailing an armed Somali Coast Guard boat heading out to sea, as opposed to moving west along the littoral to the stranded oil tanker near Berbera harbor. That told Merk either the Somali government was on the take with the pirates or they had intel that an ambush would await them at the port city. He copied and pasted the geocoords of *Blå Himmel* into the Dolphin Code and transmitted it along with the location of the cove so that the systems would swim to him first. He needed to inspect their condition before directing them to head on to scout the harbor and keep watch over the tanker for the next twenty-four hours. The dolphins would be tasked to monitor all activity surrounding it.

For a while, the dolphins tracked the Somali Coast Guard out to sea. With a click of the Dolphin Code colored keys, Merk directed Inapo to swim under the hull of the motorboat, fluke sideways as he had been trained to do, plant the dorsalcam on the fiberglass bottom, and roll away. The dorsalcam had an adhesive strip that when pressed would seal it to the surface and break from the dorsal fin when the mammal pulled away. Hidden inside the pencil-rod cam sat a GPS tab with a motion sensor, which recorded the speed of a body in water. Although minus one dorsalcam until he fitted Inapo with another, Merk could track the movements of the Somali Coast Guard boat, relay that information to the US Navy, which in turn could watch it with a drone, spy plane, or military satellite to see if they rendezvoused with any of the pirates.

After tagging the boat and confirming it via Tasi's dorsalcam, the Coast Guard boat headed out to the gulf.

Merk called the dolphins back to shore.

Chapter Thirty-One

NICO DROVE UP the foothills into the high mountain elevations of the Sheikh Pass. The GPS indicated that Nairobi had parked her vehicle inside the compound that he had passed on the right as he drove up a steep incline. He rose back and forth on a switchback mount, rolling out onto a plateau. He pulled off the road behind a guardrail and hid the car out of sight of passing vehicles. He took out a folding stock sniper rifle, communication gear, a backpack with food and water, and hiked a good way from the vehicle.

The CO set up a surveillance nest on a bluff. The ledge held a commanding view of the valley below, with mountain streams cutting across and running under the Sheikh Pass. In the background, he noted the road snaked down the foothills and curved toward Berbera in the heat haze sea far away.

With the high-powered telescope, Nico spotted the camouflage canopies housing a slew of luxury cars. Then he saw Nairobi's vehicle parked under the dead tree. He zoomed on four guards roaming the premises inside the compound.

Chewing on an energy bar, the CO reminded himself he had to wait and be patient for Nairobi to emerge out of the underground complex.

Chapter Thirty-Two

A s THE SUN arched across the midday sky, the dolphins made their way toward the cove. Merk monitored all the channels he had at his disposal, but was disappointed by the inactivity of the US military. The drone had neither returned nor been replaced.

Both the sky above and the gulf in front of him were empty, at least from his viewpoint, while the dorsalcam attached to the hull of the Somali boat showed images every now and then of the Coast Guard pulling over fishing skiffs for inspections and to conduct interviews as the few remaining resources of the Somali government tried to string together bits of intel and feed them to the offshore naval forces. Perhaps NATO and the international navies were busy tracking down the other hijacked ship, the *Shining Sea*.

Merk opened a backpack. He took out a scuba mask, a pair of swim fins, mini trimix tank with a regulator, and a backup dorsalcam. As he checked the equipment, children's voices broke the silence. Like wind chimes, they were soft and airy at first, but then became more pronounced. He glanced around the cove, closed the laptop, and shoved it in the backpack, stowing it sideways in between boulders. He left the scuba gear on a stone shelf and stepped out of the cove to see the young visitors.

He made sure he didn't step on a seashell or stone that would announce his arrival. Merk stretched his arms and gripped a boulder like a globe, craning his head around it to spy on the kids. Rising slowly, he peered over the rocky surface until he spotted the first boy, a young Somali about six years old. Behind him his pal with a bushy afro waded into the surf. They idly skipped stones across the water, uttering a few words in their native tongue. Although Merk didn't understand the language, from their light tone, he felt the children were doing what kids have done for millennia: play, explore, socialize, and interact with nature.

While Merk stayed out of sight, a third voice of another boy shouted directly above him. Startled, he looked up at an older boy, with coffee-brown skin and a fixed smile, pointing out to sea. Then the other two boys called out pointing at Merk as they waded deeper in the surf. The older boy looked down at Merk, who stepped away from the boulder raising his hands to show he was unarmed.

The older boy's grin froze, his lips started to tremble. Nervous, he asked in broken English with a Somali accent, "Who are you?"

Realizing that the other boys had turned their attention to the sea, Merk gazed beyond them and saw Tasi and Inapo gliding to shore. Taking advantage of the timing, Merk answered, "I am fisherman."

"You, fish?" the older boy asked nervously. "With what?"

"Dolphins," Merk said, pointing to the dolphins moseying over to the boys in the water, each species checking the other out. Merk stepped into the sea. Not wanting to show too much or reveal what he was up to in their country, he flicked his wrist with an open-fingers sign to the dolphins. Tasi and Inapo rose out of the water sculling backward on their tails. They twisted around, dove into a wave in a splash, swimming out to sea.

"Wow," the youngest boy said in amazement. "He fishes with dolphins." His American English was better than his pals, which Merk figured out he likely picked up watching American TV on the Internet or a mobile phone.

"Why you here?" the older boy asked, climbing down from the boulder. "No tourists in our land. Tourists flew away like birds."

Merk looked at him, and said coyly, "To learn why they flew away."

"I know why," the boy with the afro said, sticking his chest out with pride.

"You do? Why did they leave?" Merk asked.

The boy showed his right arm and back of his hand. His skin was pocked with scabs of dried blisters, clusters of strawberry pimples, and fresh wounds, as if burnt from inside out of his flesh. Merk took the boy's hand and examined the breakout lesions more closely. Not wanting to speculate on what caused the scarring, he looked in the child's sheepish eyes, which withdrew with eye contact, and asked, "What caused this?" Without waiting for the boy to come around to answer, Merk pulled up the left wetsuit sleeve and showed his own burn scar, saying, "Fire ate my skin. What harmed yours?"

"Water," the older boy said, pointing out to sea.

"Water?" Merk followed his finger out to the horizon, and asked, "What kind of water?"

"Poison water."

Chapter Thirty-Three

AFTER LISTENING TO Agent Jenny King's reasoning to save her blown cover as the North Korean missile specialist Kim Dong-Sun, the CIA director told his deputies to leave his seventh floor office. He sat forward and scanned his desktop, picked up a pencil, and snapped it between his fingers. After a pause, he called in a favor, striking a key on a laptop that connected him to the one army general he trusted in the Joint Chiefs of Staff at the Pentagon.

As soon as the executive assistant patched the call in to the general, the CIA director dumped any pretense of word or tone. He left no doubt how Operation Sandblast Scree was in a tight spot, how it might be linked to the stolen hot load on the move across Syria, and how the CIA needed help to move back into Syria "tonight" to retrieve the real North Korean engineer. The only problem he saw for the US Special Forces would be taking the hostage and hauling her across a border that was now crawling with Syrian forces, Iranian Quds Force, and ISIS spies and scouts in the wake of kidnapping CIA Operator King as the North Korean engineer.

"General, all I want to do is bring the real missile engineer back to the Iraqi station for interrogation," he said.

The general listened. He ran through a few "logistical challenges," did some calculations in his head, and then said from a black ops vista it was not only "do-able," but could be done that night. Still the old friend, feeling the director's stress, rationalized with him not to think about international laws they might end up breaking, since the new operation would be blanketed under the auspices of national security if word ever leaked out about the operation.

Moreover, he told him that as for the "hermit kingdom," the late Kim Jong-il deserved some cold retribution for torpedoing a South Korean submarine in spring 2010, as did his son Kim Jong-un, who enflamed the border relations by shutting down a joint-venture factory between the two Koreas, firing missiles, and threatening to attack America at the slightest provocation.

From that moment on, the army general formulated a clandestine operation, the existence of which neither the president nor his cabinet would know anything. To ensure the safety of embedding CIA operative Jenny King as the North Korean engineer into Iran, a senator on the Defense Intelligence Committee would be told the following day about the black op, with its details to emerge as the operation got under way. Another precaution the CIA director and army general took was to ensure the cover story about Agent Jenny King was between them, and that the marine helicopter pilot and crew who flew her across Iraq to the Iranian border would be told that they were transporting the real Kim Dong-Sun.

Speed, stealth, and secrecy were the elements needed for the success of the new operation.

It took little under an hour of poring over the pesky details and logistics Agent King had given to her superiors at the CIA, for Joint Special Operations Command (JSOC) to task the 1st Special Forces Operational Detachment-Delta—a.k.a. Delta Force—for the mission.

The JSOC general called the director and informed him that he had a Delta Force—DF—detachment in Baghdad ready for interdiction. In a video briefing, he said the DF cell would be airborne by nightfall, then slip across the border near Fort 24 to "re-acquire" the North Korean officer from the underground catch basin Agent King had temporarily stuffed her in until the agent's mission in the Syrian desert was supposed to be over, forty-eight hours later. But that plan was fouled up when the CIA agents, dressed as journalists, kidnapped one of their agents, who was in deeper cover as part of SOG's Clandestine Ops.

The JSOC commanders at Centcom, along with the CIA director, all knew how risky the operation would be, especially with the CIA attack on the Syrian missile launch site in the desert earlier that day. Those who knew General Adad understood the warhorse would use every resource to scour the desert searching for and finding links and evidence to nail the CIA to the cross for its role in the attack on his army, while derailing Syria's plans to build a long-range missile site. The launch area and border would be teeming with soldiers in full-lockdown mode, itching for a firefight.

An hour later, the Delta Force cell was scrambled and flown to an undisclosed entry point near the border, north of Fort 24. The CIA analysts selected that location after reviewing satellite images captured on a sliver of land with the least foot and patrol traffic. It would be easy for the commandos to slip across the border.

Since Syria believed the CIA had already kidnapped the real North Korean engineer right out of General Adad's summit in the desert, how much more flak could the US intelligence agency be hit with in taking the risk to go back over the border to retrieve the real engineer?

That's how Jenny saw it; the CIA director agreed. But they couldn't wait to see if Delta Force would succeed in the mission.

Chapter Thirty-Four

AGENT JENNY KING dressed up again as North Korean engineer Kim Dong-Sun. The platoon of Marines whisked her out of Fort 24 to a waiting helicopter. The Black Hawk flew across the desert spaces of ISIS-controlled Iraq to its northeast mountain border along Kurdistan, Iran.

As the first phase of the new Operation Fire Sanctuary unfolded, the CIA director phoned his counterpart in Tehran's secret police, explained the mistake his agents made in crossing the border into Syria, and that he wanted to make the mistake go away by handing the North Korean engineer over to Iran in less than twenty-four hours of her capture, so Tehran could return her to her native country. The director also explained that, because of the ongoing civil war in Syria, the ISIS skirmishes in southern Iraq, where no victim was too small or young, and the numerous mass graves recently discovered, the US in no way was going to appease Syria by paying it tribute. With that, the director emphasized that it was in the best interest of both nations, regardless of what caused the sinking of an Iran fishing trawler laying sea-mines in the Strait of Hormuz, to move on and contend with the crisis of Sunni extremist flare-ups.

No word would leak to the press about the missile launch site, nor would Israel be notified of Syria's plans to defend itself if Iraq fell completely into the lap of the enemy.

After a conference call with Tehran clerics, including the Iranian prime minister, Iran agreed to meet the US Marines ferrying the North Korean engineer at the Diyala province's lone road border, controlled by the Kurds. Money from Washington would motivate

Kurdish leaders to allow the crossing at its border. The CIA director called it an "expensive bridge toll."

In the past, Kurdish demonstrators had blocked the main road in protest when Iran cut off the water supply from the al-Wind River, one of the five main tributaries that feed the Tigris River. But with the water flowing again into the fertile plains of Diyala, the main road was open—yet heavily guarded by Iranian soldiers, with the Ayatollah's Revolutionary Guard en route to transport Dong-Sun. Without a Korean translator on the Iranian side at the crossing, the US figured the handing over of Kim Dong-Sun would run smoothly. What they didn't have a handle on was where the Islamic Revolutionary Guards Corps was going to take her once inside Iran. That became the CIA director's chief concern.

Would they take King back to Tehran? To a military base? Or to a nuclear weapons site?

If the transfer went down without a hitch, both sides agreed to keep the real events that led to the shootout and kidnapping at the Syrian missile site under wraps. The CIA didn't need any more negative press. The international media was still bashing the agency on the drone strike of the school in Jaar, Yemen, even after the agency put out evidence to the contrary that the structure wasn't a school, but a terrorist safe house after all. The bodies of the children killed, the CIA suspected, were flown in from Syria and used as props. The press was investigating that new claim; the UN was looking into it as well.

The FBI's request to take DNA samples was denied. Where did the bodies of the children disappear to in Jaar? Then a new problem arose. No one could find the corpses after they were supposedly driven to a hospital between Jaar and the coastal town of Zinjibar.

No matter what the CIA or UN would discover about those claims, the damage had already been done. The hatred toward the "Great Satan" United States had kicked into overdrive. The images of the bloodied bodies of children, along with the woman's amputated arm—a teacher?—weren't going away from the world's collective memory or the social media channels anytime soon. The damage was fixed and indelible.

On the other hand, Syria didn't need to be linked to a long-range missile program with North Korea while the country was being torn apart by civil war, threatened by the Islamic State, and propped up by Russia, while several in the US intelligence community were skeptical that all of the Syrian regime's chemical weapons—toxins, biologic chemicals, and lethal agents—had been destroyed aboard the Danish ship.

For the delivery of Kim Dong-Sun, the US Marines were given strict orders to make the flight to the border crossing comfortable for her. Getting the message, four young jarheads threw a blanket on a wooden crate in the rear of the cargo bay, plopped the North Korean engineer down, and gave her a canteen of water and an energy bar. Due to the logistics of ongoing ISIS strikes and bombings, the flight required a refueling at an air base outside of Kurdish-controlled Kirkuk. The northern city of Mosul had fallen to ISIS and became its stronghold.

For Jenny to convincingly play her role as the North Korean engineer, she slept on the first leg of the trip, feeling each burr of the rotor vibrate through the metal deck, up the slats of the crate, and drum into her thighs, buttocks, and spine.

The longest day she could remember just got longer.

When the helicopter landed to refuel, a marine sergeant and a Delta Force colonel climbed on board and checked the engineer's condition. She opened one eye, saw the officers standing in front of her, and opened the other eye, then cursed at them in Korean. They stepped back, motioning the engineer to calm down. They showed her a map of where they were taking her, and then gave her a backpack and a cooler stuffed with fruit, yogurt, vegetables, and cereal.

Dong-Sun grabbed a lemon. She began peeling the rind, split it open, and squirted lemon juice in the face of the buzz-cut Marine sergeant. He squinted, his eyes watered as he wiped his face with the back of his hand, and then glared at her with wet red eyes.

On orders from JSOC, the Delta Force colonel handed Kim Dong-Sun two backpacks with woman's clothes, size 0, that would fit her lithe frame, toiletries, and two envelopes of cash in the amount of twenty thousand dollars in denominations of twenties, fifties, and hundreds. She made a grouchy face and bit into the lemon, sucking on its sour juices to refresh her dried-out palette. Eating a lemon raw repulsed the marine sergeant—which was her point, to revolt him enough to make him deboard the helicopter when the refueling finished. He waved good-bye; she kissed him off and followed that with a staccato burst of Korean swear words that turned into an endless stream of profanity. Although he didn't understand the meaning, he got the message loud and clear.

The sergeant stepped out of the helicopter, yelling, "Get the bitch out of Iraq ASAP."

The CIA and Joint Chiefs of Staff knew when they handed Kim Dong-Sun over to the Iranians they would search the backpacks of clothes and cooler of food in their search for any device that might be hidden. They would review her papers and North Korean passport, which Jenny took from the real engineer. And with a half year immersed in deep training of the real Kim Dong-Sun, from Jenny King modulating the engineer's speech and stiff mannerisms, combined with slight modifications to her looks, she felt she could pull off the ruse—until she got to Tehran. There it would be anyone's guess as to what would happen next, whom she would meet in person or by videoconference from North Korean military. So the risk of being caught as a double agent still lay ahead and increased the deeper she moved into enemy territory.

Knowing that gamble, the CIA station chief removed a brass button from her grey North Korean military uniform sleeve, opened it up, hollowed out the shell, inserted a micro GPS chip, sealed the button, and had it sewn back onto the sleeve. Once the marines handed her over to the Revolutionary Guards Corps, Langley could track her movements through Iran, as long as she wore the uniform and didn't go deep underground into one of Iran's hardened nuclear facilities.

After refueling, the Black Hawk lifted off for the second leg of the flight.

Chapter Thirty-Five

A T THE COVE, the boy with the toxin-blemished skin picked up a rock, stooped over a sandstone slab, and scratched three letters: "I-U-U."

Merk read the shorthand and recognized what it meant: "Illegal, Unreported, Unregulated."

The ex-navy SEAL was taken aback by the teenager knowing the acronym about illegal ocean dumping. Merk figured he must have heard it used by fishermen or his parents or among some local villagers, like the Somalis who complained every day about the plight and hardship of their country being a dumping ground for the world. Merk had heard the rumors, he had seen some of the photographic evidence, now he heard the words direct from victims who lived there.

The boy nodded, tapped his foot on "IUU," and then pointed out to the gulf.

"You have toxic dumping in the Gulf of Aden?" Merk said in disbelief. Shielding his eyes, he peered out to the sun-bright sea.

"Long ago," the boy said.

"Got it. The collapse of your government in 1992," Merk said, panning the horizon. "How far out?"

"Not too far. A kilometer or two," he said.

"Bastards." Merk ran his fingers over the boy's toxic burn scars. He opened the laptop, uploaded the Dolphin Code program, telling Tasi and Inapo to swim to shore. "We'll make a deal. I send my dolphins to search for the poison water, and you don't tell anyone that I came here. If you do, I go to jail, and the dolphins will be in trouble."

"Yeow," said the eldest child, patting his friends on their shoulders.

The scarred boy nodded, rubbing his scars on Merk's burn-scar left arm, as if he were making a blood oath of secrecy, a pact to keep their silence.

As the navy dolphins swam to shore, the boys got excited. They saw the glint of the micro, pencil-thin dorsalcams and metal tags— GPS tracking—mounted at the base of the dorsal fins. High-tech dolphins. They had never seen anything like those creatures in their lives.

Merk took out a four-inch probe with an elastic strap and waded into the water. He flashed a hand-sign to Inapo to lift his pectoral fin so Merk could mount the probe. He flicked on a switch, ran the probe like a wand through the air, and saw a tiny blue light flicker rapidly. Knowing the probe was working, Merk floated in between the dolphins, introducing them to the children. "This is Tasi. In Guam, her name means 'Ocean.'"

"Tasi? Ocean? Cool," the youngest child repeated.

"Tasi was bitten by a shark on the fin right here—" he showed the shark-bite scar on the dorsal fin. The boys sighed, feeling for the dolphin; the child with the toxic skin rubbed his wound, petting the dolphin in solidarity. "This is Inapo. In Guam his name means 'Wave.'"

"Wave and Ocean, great," the eldest child said.

Merk tapped the dolphins behind the melon. In a flash, Tasi and Inapo somersaulted, brushed Merk's legs, swerved underwater, and darted out to sea.

"Where's Guam?" the eldest boy asked.

Merk waded out of the shallows, shook the water off of his legs and arms, squeezing excess water out of his hair, and said, "It's on the other side of the world. Close to Japan."

"Wow," the boy said.

"Go. Don't say a word. I will help you," the dolphin whisperer said, then took a picture of the kids with a tablet, and learned where they lived, in two houses on the same street.

Merk waded back into the water. He knew he had to keep what the dolphins discovered a secret until he left Somalia.

Chapter Thirty-Six

THE DOLPHINS SWAM a few miles offshore, towing a DPod with them for enhanced subsurface communication. They dove beneath the waves . . . diving down, down, down . . . following the undersea shelf. They split apart along opposite sides of a wall, descending beneath the surface.

Tasi glided down to a plateau at a depth of 500 feet.

* * *

ON SHORE, MERK sat out of sight in the shade of the cove. He tracked the dolphins' deep dive on a 3-D undersea map of the gulf, knowing that its deepest floor was near Yemen, more than a mile deep. At 2,000 feet he would recall the dolphins if they didn't find anything. That would allow them time to swim up to the surface to breathe before he would decide what to do next: dive or abandon the search. Even dolphins can be exposed at extreme depths.

* * *

DEEP UNDERWATER, TRAINED to explore subsea landmarks, Tasi spotted a ledge and, farther below, a slope that flattened out between broken ridges. She fluked down, inspecting the brown coral seabed, and began echolocating the marine life.

The dolphin glided up and over a series of swales, before spotting a seamount ahead. As she closed on the mound, man-made debris came into view. First, a couple of pieces of steel she pinged with biosonar, then the rusted lid of a drum, and then on the other side of the mount three long boiler-sized containers, the near one half-buried in sand.

The middle boiler leaked a trail of air bubbles rising out of a tiny hole like an eelworm.

* * *

ON SEEING THE boilers through Tasi's infrared dorsalcam, Merk typed code to the DPod directing Inapo to swim over to Tasi to inspect the discovery with the special probe.

Minutes passed. Merk watched the blinking GPS lights of the dolphins converge on screen. He opened a split-screen, watching the POV of the dorsalcams as Inapo joined Tasi in examining the boilers. Inapo swam around the backside and hovered over the farthest of the three boilers, lowering the pectoral fin with the probe inches from the rusted steel wall; a reading pinged. The probe caused a sine wave spike that jolted the needle on a digital meter. Realizing what Inapo found, Merk ordered the systems to swim to the surface out of harm's way and return to shore.

When he heard a squeal sound chiming over the laptop, Merk stood up. He imagined himself in the Somali boys' shoes, watching the wealth of the world cruise by the beaches day after day, bypassing the broken land. The footage captured would remain a guarded secret, even from the navy, until Merk had a chance to review the findings. For the moment, he was happy to get Tasi and Inapo out of there. But the discovery gave him pause. Were the pirates just out for ransom money? Or was revenge of being poisoned fueling their anger toward the West?

If it were the latter, then maybe the Somali pirates would join terrorist affiliates planning to attack the United States. That would fundamentally change how Washington and the CIA had understood and analyzed piracy in the Horn of Africa. It would profoundly change how the West would have to deal with the new threat vector. But who were their sponsors?

Chapter Thirty-Seven

THE CROSSING OF the broken Syrian border in the south was going to be a major undertaking for Delta Force with a lot at stake. The exposure of time, doing it under the cover of night, combined with the space—a six-mile jaunt across open desert to where the real North Korean engineer had been stowed by CIA agent Jenny King—put the commandos in the line of fire.

In order to clear a path and stay out of sight of ISIS scout teams, roving Syrian rebels, and patrols of the Syrian Army, Delta Force team needed to create a diversion.

At 2120 hours a klick south of Fort 24, a tanker truck blew apart in an ascending fireball. The explosion could be seen and felt for miles. The blast wave rocked the CIA station and shook several Syrian soldiers in the area on the other side of the border. They raced to the border, took cover, and trained assault rifles on the burning wreck.

North of Fort 24, the Delta Force cell of eight commandos led by a seasoned CO crossed the border on foot. They stayed north of a river, followed its winding path miles into Syrian territory. They used night-vision goggles and a pair of audioscopes to sweep the terrain, making sure the path was free and clear as they moved a quarter klick at a time.

The Delta Force CO checked the geocoords at the six-mile mark. He scanned the dark horizon north and spotted a row of palm trees planted alongside a new highway—a *road to nowhere*, since the Islamic State and local tribesmen cut it off from the oil-rich towns.

Amid the chaos of the Syrian civil war, Damascus claimed to the UN that the new road was a "feeder" highway for farmers. But US intelligence knew better. The Syrian military had built the road with the plan to transport arms and supplies to the missile launch site that was under construction, while it built up an array of camps to launch an offensive against ISIS when the time was right to drive the terrorists from the eastern border region.

The Delta Force CO split his team in two. He sent one cell along the east side of the road, while leading the other cell down the west side, with both cells to converge in the middle of the road, until they located the catch basin that held the real Kim Dong-Sun.

By the time they reached the two-lane highway, with gutters and culverts yet to be completed, a pair of headlights, like beady snake eyes, slinked down the road from the west.

The DF CO hid his cell behind crates of materials and precast concrete pipe. The other Delta Force cell, unable to find similar cover, hit the ground and rolled into a swale, lying flat on top of their weapons so that the metal wouldn't catch or reflect light as the vehicle drove by.

For a long, tense moment they kept still, feeling their hearts race, listening to the vehicle approach, the tires whining louder and louder across the concrete pavement, the light beams expanding wider, until the vehicle passed by as if riding directly over them. It would be another minute before the vehicle drove far enough down the road to where the commandos felt secure to climb to their feet and move on to search for the catch basin.

Delta Force knew that the highway ended a mile or so from where they stood. If those in the vehicle conducted a patrol from inside the cab, they would return by the route they came in short order. By the time Delta Force reached the manhole cover on the side of the road, they saw the vehicle headlights begin turning around in the distance to head back.

A pair of commandos pried opened the manhole cover. The DF CO stuck a snub-nose flashlight down into the catch basin, made sure there were no booby-traps and that the hostage was alone. The flashlight lit up the gritty concrete box. In the corner sat a bound and gagged Kim Dong-Sun, her pants caked with mud from washout sediment that gathered on the concrete floor.

The tired, frail North Korean engineer shielded her eyes from the bright light.

One by one, Delta Force commandos lowered into the catch basin. They understood if Syrians in the vehicle spotted them slipping into the hole or stopped to inspect the catch basin, the operation would be blown and they would likely die in a firefight, trapped below ground in a concrete coffin with the North Korean scientist the CIA had kidnapped.

Delta Force CO pulled the manhole cover back in place as the headlights straightened down the road and beamed on the catch basin. He stepped down, shut off his flashlight, and waited. The commandos hunkered down, aiming their assault rifles at the manhole cover, saying not a word. Shafts of light flickered through the finger holes in the manhole cover. The vehicle passed by without stopping.

Another minute ticked away before the DF CO signaled the field medic to check on the condition of the hostage engineer. The medic, with the help of another Delta member, gave Kim Dong-Sun water, setup an IV drip in her arm—she was dehydrated and shivering. After five minutes, the medic gave her a sedative to put her out for a few hours. He let the IV run its course for another few minutes—making sure she would be alive when they crossed back over the border—before he removed the needle, swabbed the puncture, pressed a Band-Aid, and then put her 105-pound body in a sling.

Commandos lifted her up to the manhole, as the others raised her out of the catch basin.

With an all-clear signal, Delta Force hauled the North Korean engineer from the area. Four men carried the sling for a klick, and then the other four Delta Force warriors carried the load for the next klick. Each cell took turns carrying Kim Dong-Sun the six miles back to the border crossing and into Iraq, where they rendezvoused with a Humvee.

CIA operator Alan Cuthbert ended up driving the North Korean engineer to a waiting helicopter that would fly them to a secret CIA drone base in Saudi Arabia. Upon arrival at the base in the Saudi mountains, CIA agents prepared to interrogate the real Kim Dong-Sun for days.

Chapter Thirty-Eight

NIGHT. FOUR HOURS after the Black Hawk landed at the main road border crossing in Diyala, Iraq, a squad of Iranian Revolutionary Guards Corps piled out of two army trucks.

A cordon of US marines backed by a Kurdish battalion escorted Kim Dong-Sun—a.k.a. CIA agent Jenny King—to a Kurdish leader named Behar. In the dim light, Jenny noticed that Behar's face was scarred. She wondered what caused it, pointing to the wounds. Behar looked at her, and after a pause, said, "Chlorine gas. Barrel bombs dropped from Russian helicopters."

Behar walked Kim Dung-Sun over the border and handed her North Korean passport and papers to the lead revolutionary guard, a tall, bearded man with sun-creased face. He reviewed the papers, handing it back to his assistant. She gulped, waiting for the papers to be confirmed. The assistant whispered in the unkempt lead guard's ear; he nodded once and waved the North Korean engineer to follow him to the trucks.

Agent Jenny King walked now into enemy territory, about to be driven deep into Iran.

Keeping her undercover act in line, Jenny knew better than to look back at Behar or the US marines who ferried her to the Iranian border. Such a glance would raise a flag with the revolutionary guards, and maybe plant a seed of suspicion about her true identity.

Waving a flashlight, the lead guard put the North Korean engineer in the back of the truck with a squad of bearded soldiers. The truck turned around with the second army truck and drove Agent

King on her way deep into Iran, heading up the mountain pass in darkness.

CIA Agent Jenny King wouldn't know her destination until she arrived. She estimated that it would be sometime the following day, if she was lucky.

Chapter Thirty-Nine

N IGHT FELL ON the Sheikh Pass in Somaliland.

Nico had spent most of the day in the surveillance nest passing time, waiting for something to happen. *Hurry up and wait* was the SEAL motto he recalled on surveillance ops. Like most of the dreary assignments, he knew not much happened over long stretches of time. He setup a mini tripod with a webcam that digitally captured activity inside the compound gate of anyone entering or exiting the mountain hideaway.

After Nairobi had arrived, Nico saw little activity at the entrance, other than a changing of guards. Only later did one other vehicle show up, around dusk. Nico replayed the video, watching it on a smartphone. It showed a slight man with Arab features wearing glasses step out of a jeep. The SEAL CO found that odd, since almost everyone in the compound was of African origin. And here arrived a Middle Eastern businessman, well dressed in a gray tunic and wearing glasses.

The sight of Bahdoon arriving at Korfa's compound threw Nico off. The CO replayed the video, trying to see if he captured a clean shot of Bahdoon's face for a screen grab, so he could run the image through the DIA, Office of Naval Intelligence, the CIA, and FBI terrorist databases to see if there was a match, and with it a name and background.

Nico knew whatever was taking place inside the compound had to be important. What he couldn't figure out: What side was Nairobi on? Did she serve two masters? The CIA *and* the Somali pirates? He didn't know, but he recalled Merk's caution.

Then a tall man dressed in fatigues and wearing red-and-white *kufeya* scarf led Nairobi outside. He whispered in her ear as a phalanx of armed guards escorted them to three waiting Range Rovers—all ransom money vehicles in Nico's eyes.

Bahdoon weaved through the wall of guards and stepped inside the second Range Rover with the Tall One and Nairobi.

Is the Tall One the "Ferryman?" Nico asked himself.

Nairobi and the Tall One sat in the backseat of the second Range Rover; Bahdoon rode shotgun in the front passenger seat. That meant she was leaving her vehicle behind, along with the tracking device that Merk planted on the car.

"Damn it. How the hell am I going to follow her now?" Nico said aloud.

The CO wanted to track Nairobi and the pirates, but couldn't. At least not right away. He saw trailing the convoy close behind as a fool's errand, since night would reveal the headlights of his vehicle. Nico would have to wait for them to drive a good distance before he shadowed them. Waiting to see which way the convoy turned when it left the compound, he wondered if the pirates would make a right up the hill toward him and drive on to the small shantytown of Burco, a haven for smugglers, pirates, and recruits. Or left, down the Sheikh Pass to Berbera by the sea, where there was a prison and oil installation near the harbor pier.

When the compound gate opened, the first Range Rover turned left, followed by the second vehicle, and then the third. They were all heading down to the harbor, where the hijacked tanker ran aground in shallow water. Nico not only had to wait for all three vehicles to clear the dark road below, but he had to wait for a pair of guards to finish smoking cigarettes. They flicked the butts on the ground and stepped back inside the compound, closing the gate.

With a single guard on sentry duty inside the compound, Nico climbed in the Chinese vehicle and started the engine. He kept the lights off as he turned around, and steered the SUV downhill, keeping his foot off the gas until he coasted by the compound. And then he floored it.

Nico switched on the headlights and headed toward Berbera, in what he suspected would be the start of a long night.

Chapter Forty

B EING A FORMER Navy SEAL, Merk knew he couldn't stay in the cove that night. His cover was compromised, no matter how cautious and quiet the children might be. He figured one of them would say something, a word, a passing remark of a dolphin, a visit by an American. Nor could he travel along the coastal road, as he was unsure whether Somalia had put checkpoints in place or had enacted a curfew. And traveling down the beach was not an option, since he felt at some point he would be spotted out in the open.

He directed the dolphins to swim ahead west and locate a small boat, while he followed them down the beach on foot. Merk kept his head on a swivel, glancing behind to make sure the strand was deserted, listening for voices of people and the sounds of passing vehicles. He panned the sea for activity, surveying the beach ahead. It appeared empty. The eerie stillness along the beach was punctuated by gentle waves whispering every now and then, as they ebbed and flowed.

A klick or two down the beach, a ping chimed from the laptop. Merk stopped, pulled the laptop out of the backpack, opened it, and saw a small craft with an outboard motor through Tasi's dorsalcam. He took out a pair of night-vision binoculars to see if he could spot the boat and dolphins down shore. Panning the silhouettes along the bight coastline, he spotted a few houses, a pile of nets with a couple of boats pulled on shore, then further ahead off a point the dolphins swimming around the moored craft just offshore. Merk hit a key on the laptop instructing Tasi and Inapo to stay put until he got there.

Merk slid the laptop in the backpack, slung it over his shoulder, jogged down the beach.

When he arrived, he eyed a small run-down house with its lights out. The shades were drawn; a truck parked out front. But it was a couple of dilapidated wooden chairs by the back door that hinted to Merk there were people sleeping inside. He waded into the water up to his waist, quietly slipped the backpack in the boat, and then untied the line of the Boston whaler at the mooring buoy. Unable to untie the last knot, Merk took out a serrated knife and frayed the rope one strand at a time, cutting the line to give it the effect that it had frayed apart.

He rolled on board and signaled Tasi to push the craft away from shore. He then tied a loop on one end of the rope, slipped it over Inapo's snout, and signaled the dolphin tow the boat out to sea. But Inapo gave Merk a quizzical look. Merk waved the dolphin over, looked him in the eye, and said, "Don't go soft on me now. We can't make noise until we are out there," he pointed. Inapo squeaked a high-pitched whistle, and towed the boat out to sea.

A half klick offshore, Merk pulled the ripcord several times until the engine turned over. With a deep throttle, he revved the power and pushed the prop into the water, taking off. Tasi and Inapo broke away from the boat and swam ahead toward the piers of Berbera, where Merk could faintly make out the silhouette of a small cargo ship listing in the harbor. Based on the size, he knew that the abandoned, rusting ship was neither the hijacked supertanker *Blå Himmel* nor the American-flagged container ship *Shining Sea*.

Merk cut the engine and, for the next few hours, let the boat drift as he monitored the dolphins searching the piers and inner harbor of Berbera. At daybreak, the dolphins would survey the supertanker. The dolphins' underwater reconnaissance netted Merk zilch on the activities of the pirates. The piers weren't patrolled; only a couple of jeeps were spotted on the beach by the tanker, as the pirates surely kept an eye on their prized catch. He wondered what Nico was up to in shadowing Nairobi in her quest to break into the pirate's inner circle.

Under a starlit night, Merk lay down to get some shut-eye. He used a backpack for a pillow, felt the sensation of floating. At dawn, they would resume the search.

Chapter Forty-One

NICO DROVE AROUND the seaport of Berbera. After midnight the town became a virtual ghost town. Other than a few thugs and teenage gangbangers loitering on the streets, there was little activity. The prison lights were banked dark, except for the perimeter fence with a couple of downspout lights flooding the grounds under the watchtowers.

Across a field, a pair of guards patrolled the giant fenced-in oil depot. But like the other buildings in Berbera, many of them were older structures designed in Ottoman architecture. He didn't dare drive around the storage tanks to the beach where the jeeps had been spotted earlier watching the supertanker grounded by the steel pier that jutted from the onshore fuel depot.

Nico drove down a deserted street and parked the vehicle under a tree. When he climbed out, he checked the front and back seats to make sure he didn't leave anything behind with the US military brand.

On foot, Nico strolled down one deserted street after another, looking in the driveways, spying on the parking lots behind office buildings, gas stations, and 500-year-old mosques, while staying out of lines of sight from a man milling about a street corner. Nothing turned up in the way of sighting any of the Range Rovers or Nairobi. Did they drive on to Hargeisa, the capital of Somaliland? And was it to another warlord or a rendezvous at the airport?

Nico eyed the buildings for a high vantage point that he could climb, stay out of sight in daylight, as he searched the coastal city for a clue to the whereabouts of the convoy.

On first glance, he noted too many of the Berbera buildings were low-rise, one and two stories high. His eyes fell on the giant oil storage tanks that covered several acres by the water. The depot would be the best place to setup a surveillance nest. But the oil storage tanks had drawbacks. For one, he would have to slip by the guards unnoticed; who knew what the sentry detail would be the next day or whether the pirates would be offloading crude oil from the hijacked ship.

Second, he confirmed the pirates were stationed on the backside of the depot in the jeeps.

Third, once the sun came up the next morning, hiding on top of the storage tank would grow hot in a hurry even with the white albedo paint reflecting the rays of the sun out to space.

But what concerned him was that if they offloaded the tanker the next day, Nico would have workers crawling over the storage facility. Still, that location put him in the center of town, with an eye on all four main roads leading out from the port city—the Sheikh Pass where he came from, the other inland road to Hargeisa to the southwest, and the coastal roads that stretched east and west. Nico opted to find a way atop one of the tanks, slipping past the guards unnoticed.

Nico cut through a few yards, pulled a worn canvas off a boat, rolled it on the ground, and threw the roll over his neck and shoulders like an oxen yoke.

He moved like a wraith across the street, hiding behind a car outside the oil depot fence. He saw that the perimeter chain-link fence wasn't crowned by razor-wire, and found only one security camera—aimed at the front gate. He figured he could get into the depot without much trouble. Seeing that the storage tanks ran a dozen deep back to the sea, he decided to follow the road to a deserted office building, staying out of sight of the guards.

Behind the main facility, he spotted three giant storage tanks inside another fenced-in compound guarded by a single security guard with no camera. The guard hung out by the gate, tugging on the fence fabric, idle and bored. The guard picked up stones and tossed them, just passing the hours until he would be relieved. At no time did he lift his head to check on the fuel tanks that towered over him. Nico looked back at the main depot. He waited for the patrolling guard to make his loop around the facility, and then followed the fence perimeter toward the sea of the smaller depot. On the backside by the beach, Nico picked the rear corner to climb the fence. He put on a pair of cut-proof gloves.

He stabbed his fingers in the chain-link mesh and scaled the corner of the twelve-foot high fence. When he reached the top, he pulled the sharp forks down, wired it to the post, then swung his body up and over the top, with a prong grabbing onto his pants, tearing into his thigh. He pulled at the snag, freeing his leg, and slid down the fence to the ground. Knowing he had his tetanus shot four years ago, the SEAL CO ignored the metal cut to his thigh. Nico checked the jeeps. No movement. He didn't see the guard, so he selected the rear storage tank, the one closest to the pier where fuel supplies were offloaded into gas mains, and climbed the steps.

Up a flight of stairs that circled halfway around the tank, Nico scaled a ladder and reached the roof of the oil tank. Once on top, he stayed low, checking the surroundings. The only vantage point taller than the storage tanks was the supertanker bridge run aground. The listing vessel appeared abandoned, not an ideal location for pirates to take position—not when NATO commandos might swoop in at any moment.

But if a pirate or Somali official took a tour of the ship the next day, they might spot Nico hiding on the roof. So he unrolled the canvas with the plan to crawl under it just before dawn broke to hide in plain sight.

For the next hour, Nico panned the quiet port city and streets with night-vision goggles. He searched for a sign on the whereabouts of Nairobi or the Range Rovers. But after a long hour, he knew he had lost them. Nairobi and Korfa must have driven off in some other direction out of town. But where? Back east toward Nairobi's house? Or west to Djibouti border at the mouth of the Red Sea?

Across the border in Djibouti, the US built up the naval expeditionary base, Camp Lemonnier, to patrol the Somali pirates around the Horn of Africa, support the Arab Spring uprising since 2011 that spread across northern Africa into the Middle East, and train and sponsor rebels in Yemen to suppress AQAP and Houthi militia.

Today, "Camp Lemonade," as Nico referred to it, fed the Syrian rebels arms and weapons in the CIA's quest to overthrow President Bashar al-Assad's regime, while operating at the newest drone base. Camp Lemonnier provided critical infrastructure support for NATO's anti-piracy campaigns launched, in concert with the Japanese military, on patrols that covered the Gulf of Aden from the Red Sea to the Horn of Africa since 2010.

That was the year when the unified naval command was able to turn the tide against the outbreak of Somali pirates, but only to see such attacks bloom off the West Coast of Africa.

Nico realized he couldn't wait until dawn. He had to notify the command on board the USS *New York* to be on the lookout for the convoy of Range Rovers, with Nairobi, that was either in and around Berbera, or heading in one of two—no, three—directions; the third being the capital Hargeisa of Somaliland. If they drove to the capital, Nico figured it would be for a meeting at an office building or at the airport.

The CO broke radio silence and sent an encrypted text to the USS *New York*, requesting a drone to fly over the roads heading out of Berbera. He then laid his tired body down to grab some shut-eye.

Chapter Forty-Two

D AWN AROUSED THE shimmering blue gulf.

Adrift in the boat, Merk stretched his limbs, rising from a power nap, feeling the rays of the sun warm his body. He rolled over on his stomach and opened the laptop, accessed the Dolphin Code software, and then heard the winding of a motorboat engine. The sound grew louder. The boat approached rapidly, its motor revving high and higher with anger. Merk slipped the scarf over his head, wrapped it around his face to hide his American features and sat up.

The motorboat closed on the craft Merk stole the night before. Two Somalis crouched in their boat: a motorman and a point man, who aimed an AK-47 assault rifle right at Merk. The point man wore the red-and-white Bedouin scarf; he motioned the motorman to cut the engine. Before Merk put his hands in the air, he pressed a yellow color-coded key—a distress signal for the dolphins to come to his aid. He listened to the point man shout obscenities, peppering him in a language he didn't understand.

Irritated by Merk's silence, the point man cocked the gun as the motorboat hit the stolen craft. Merk tapped his ears, acting as if he were deaf. The Somali didn't buy it and fired a warning shot over Merk's head. He berated him. The gunman stepped on the gunwale to board. Trapped, Merk kicked the side hard, rocking the point man to fall into his boat. As he stumbled forward, Merk kicked the assault rifle out of the pirate's hands and into the sea. The point man landed hard on his ribs. He rolled over holding his side, then whipped out a broad-blade dagger and lunged it in a backswing.

Merk deflected the dagger, as the blade sliced through the wet suit sleeve, drawing blood. He grabbed the Somali's biceps, pulled him in close, headbutted him, and then kneed him in the chest. The blast stunned the point man, knocking the wind out of him.

When he fell back, Merk hooked the point man's leg and rolled him overboard.

The motorman stood up yelling, waving a pistol. Flush with anger, he stepped toward the bow when, virtually out of nowhere, Inapo soared out of the water, drilling the motorman in the back, disorienting him as he plunged into the sea.

From behind, the point man reached up and grabbed Merk's scarf and pulled it over his neck, twisting the cloth hard, strangling him. Choking, Merk lost his breath . . . his face turned beet-red . . . his nostrils flared as he snorted through his nose for air, spitting last gasps with his legs kicking and squirming.

As he was about to pass out, Tasi breached behind the point man and swatted him with a hard tail whip, blasting the assailant under the surface. Merk felt the pirate's limp hand slip off his neck, the scarf running through the man's fingers. Merk opened his mouth in a silent scream for air, his mouth stretching wider and wider, gasping for air to breathe, to fill his lungs. Merk's chest heaved and heaved until his throat finally pumped oxygen down into his lungs . . . *er-huh* . . . *er-huh* . . . *er-huh* . . . hyperventilating, a state of delirium. He saw the expanding blue sky above amid bursts of stars, sunspots that flashed before and dazzled his eyes.

Tasi finished off the point man, nosing the lifeless body under the surface.

Sucking air, Merk rolled over, coughing, twitching, spitting . . . out of breath, his lungs burned and bellowed until he grabbed his throat clutching the scarf. As he regained normal breathing, he looked around dazed, scanned the gulf . . . then turned over and panned the coast. He watched Inapo pull the motorman underwater, out of sight. Exhausted, Merk rolled over and rested his chest on his hands, looking at the reflection of his weary face in the bright water.

Tasi fluked over and rubbed her beak against Merk's face to comfort him. She squealed a sorrowful cry. "Tasi, think those kids are going to tell we're here?"

Tasi trilled in agreement, splashing water in his face.

Chapter Forty-Three

N ICO CRAWLED OUT from under the canvas on the storage
tank roof. He slithered to the edge and peeked over the wall.
Below, he saw vehicles pull up to the oil depot office building. He
looked at officials down by the beach examining the supertanker
and saw the jeeps had driven away. It appeared the pirates weren't
going to offload any crude oil that morning, since other officials
dressed in army fatigues inspected the offloading pier adjacent to
the supertanker.

What he couldn't figure out was what were the pirates going to
do with the supertanker. It made no sense, unless they were going to
use the two million barrels of oil on board as collateral to go along
with the ransom for the hostages.

Nico stooped down on the platform that ringed the roof of the
tank, hiding behind the knee wall and railing on top of it. He took
out binoculars and scanned the supply dock where Berbera workers
offloaded a small cargo ship, as if the hijacked supertanker listing
across port didn't exist. He panned farther out to sea, tracking a trio
of fishing boats, dhows with no mothership, a sailboat, and then farther out still a motorboat with a lone man riding it in a loop around
the outskirts of the harbor in line with the supertanker, and then
abruptly cut the engine. Nico could make out the red-and-white
checkered scarf, but not the man. He zoomed out of long focus
and panned the bridge and decks of the supertanker, but didn't see
anyone on board.

The hostages had been offloaded and taken to an inland storage
facility, that much he knew. The CO was about to stand up when he

heard the gate to the fuel depot open below. Nico ducked and listened to the voices of three or four men enter the fenced-in area. He crawled behind the knee wall toward the ladder, and then peeked down the steps to see three military men and a manager of the oil depot. The manager pointed to the supertanker and then over to the three giant storage tanks inside the compound, implying they could offload the oil from the ship.

* * *

OUT BEYOND THE port, Merk adjusted the *kufeya* scarf on his head, typed commands on the laptop ordering the dolphins to split up and check both piers—the big supply dock that ran parallel to shore and a warehouse, and the long road that shot straight out from the oil depot to the fuel depot pier.

At the supply dock, Inapo swam underwater, gliding around the barnacle-coated pilings, and surfaced under the concrete deck. From the view on the dorsalcam, it didn't appear to be much out of the norm. So Merk switched to a full-screen view of Tasi swimming under the fuel depot pier. She panned the fuel lines suspended over the edge, unconnected to the ship.

Tasi swam a figure eight under the pier, weaving in and out of the pilings toward shore and then glided back; then the dolphin dove under, swimming alongside the giant hull that listed out of the water. Beyond the keel being grounded, the rest of the ship appeared normal. Tasi's probe didn't detect leaking oil or a fuel spill.

The dolphin doubled back to the stern, then circled around the giant props. Trained to take a furtive breach and spy approach, Tasi rose behind the props, using the steel blades as cover. She pinched a breath with the blowhole and dove under again.

On the starboard side of the hull, which tilted several degrees, Tasi slowed her fluking. She coasted, inspecting the steel above and then below the surface. Amidships, she stopped when she found an odd box attached to the side of the hull in a depth of five feet.

Merk zoomed in and out with the dorsalcam, looking at what appeared to be a bomb.

How could that be? He wondered. It wasn't there the day before when the SEAL team visited the ghost tanker after the hijacking. To what purpose would blowing a gaping hole in the vessel stuck in port do for the pirates, unless it was booby-trapped for another reason? Pirates hijack ships and take hostages for ransom, not mayhem. Or did Korfa change the formula?

Merk signaled Tasi to swim on, checking for another box. At the bow, on the same listing side, the dolphin found a second device. Now Merk had to break radio silence, just as Nico did, and send the digital images to the USS *New York* to be distributed and analyzed.

Time was now the crucial factor.

* * *

ON THE ROOF of the storage tank, Nico heard the officials climb the stairs. He crawled backward, peeked over the knee wall, and saw it was too high to jump. He looked at the rumpled canvas and ruled that out to hide under. So he crawled around the platform, moving away from the ladder opening. When the first man stepped onto the roof of the storage tank, he stopped and lay flat, hiding in the footwell between the tank's raised roof and the knee wall.

Nico slid out a pistol, placing it on his chest. He waited to see if they would walk over and spot him. He breathed a shallow breath, looked up to the spacious blue sky and listened. . . . The men chatted in Somali tongue, probably something about offloading the oil, storing it in the depot, confirming the capacity of the storage tanks. Perhaps they saw the canvas and wondered who left it behind. Perhaps they plotted what they would do if NATO or American forces stormed the bay to reclaim the vessel.

The men turned around and climbed down the storage tank. They left without discovering the SEAL hiding on top. Nico exhaled, holstering the pistol.

Chapter Forty-Four

INSIDE A GIANT empty hanger used to address thousands of Marines stationed at or about to be deployed from Camp Lemonnier, the US forward operating base located in Somaliland's niche neighbor of Djibouti, a couple of CIA case officers sat at a round table with the micro security firm Azure Shell.

Dressed in blue jeans with a Somali flag tee shirt, ex-navy SEAL Team Six CO Dante Dawson drank iced herbal tea. An African American with a V-shaped body, thick mustache, and bulging biceps, Dante wanted more details than the CIA officers were willing to share with him and his partner, Christian Fuller, a former FBI counterterrorism sniper.

Fuller, a lanky Caucasian raised on a farm in Nebraska, didn't trust CIA intermediaries; never did. Maybe it was the Beltway's Bureau-versus-Agency rivalry, the penchant to blame one another. September 11 was the fault of the FBI for failing to track the terrorists learning how to fly at the US flying schools; while the CIA owned both the failure to kill Osama bin Laden prior to the World Trade Center and Pentagon attacks, and the Benghazi raid on the September 11, 2012, when terrorists killed two navy SEALs and the CIA station chief to the region—a.k.a. the ambassador—at a CIA safe house. Either excuse rubbed the bearded Fuller the wrong way.

"You're going to have to do better than the goatshit you're passing off as intel," Dante said, a bit pissed, feeling jetlagged. "We have ransom money to deliver. Money for lives. So what else can you agency pukes tell us about the second hijacked ship? The container vessel—"

"*Shining Sea*," injected the CIA case officer.

"Affirmative. Where's she now?"

"Offshore in Zeila, the ancient city across the border in Somaliland," the case officer said. "Not far from here."

"Good. And the supertanker sits idle in Berbera, affirmative?" Dante pressed.

"Yes," said the other CIA agent, who was an Asian American with a boyish face.

"We're not delivering ransom money for the ships," Fuller said, unhappy with the dentist approach of pulling teeth to extract answers from their agency counterparties.

"The warlord Korfa, where's he? Have you set up an open line to com with him for ongoing talks?" Dante asked.

"Uh, we don't know," said the case officer with a shrug.

"Great. What else are you holding back? It's what we need to know before we cross the border into pirate country," Dante griped, standing up. He flexed the pecs on his barrel chest. At first, they didn't answer. "Fuller, give me the Satcom." Fuller handed the Satcom to Dante. He keyed in a password, entered a code, and connected direct to Centcom headquarters in Tampa, Florida. "This is former SEAL Team Six Dante Dawson of Azure Shell calling the DCI rep of the 1st Special Forces Op Detachment Delta."

"Okay, okay." The Asian American agent waved his hands to end the call. "Do not call Delta Force."

"Sure. You were saying?"

"We don't know where Korfa is. But we do know his brother was shot dead on board the tanker, with his body brought to a compound along the Sheikh Pass. A SEAL tailed Korfa into Berbera, but he lost him in the port city."

"Keep going."

"We got word from the SEAL that our asset, codenamed Nairobi, disappeared with the Ferryman," he explained.

"And . . . ?" Fuller patted the kid agent on the shoulder.

"There's a plane from Syria en route today to Hargeisa Airport. We believe there's a connection between the Somali hijackings and the regime in Syria," he explained.

"Roger that. It's called blood money," Fuller said, dripping with sarcasm.

"Two for two. What other details could we use to save our lives and the butts of the hostages?" Dante asked, staring hard at the Asian American agent.

"There's one more," the case officer said. "US navy dolphins just recorded what looks like bombs attached to the hull of the tanker run aground in Berbera."

"Jesus, man, my old pupil . . . Merk Toten on the scene?" Dante said with a broad grin. "Damn. Has the CIA or navy intel confirmed whether the objects are bombs?"

"Not yet. The DIA is working on it with a squad of SEAL EOD divers in Coronado."

"Explosive ordnance divers," Dante said, nodding to Fuller. He turned to the case officer, asking, "What's our best entry point into Somaliland? Zeila, Berbera . . . or the airport?"

After a long silence, the Asian American agent replied, "The airport in Somaliland. It's inland, but that's probably where the hostages were taken. We are retasking the one drone we have for Zeila to get first reports on the hijacked container ship."

"The State Department will put a call into the government in Hargeisa, requesting to open a line of talks between you and the pirates," the case officer said.

"Got it. You better not be missing any more details," Dante said, pointing a finger at the agent. "What we learn, we'll com through Langley, not you."

Chapter Forty-Five

THE BLACK HAWK helicopter lifted off from Camp Lemonnier. It banked north out over the Bab-al-Mandab Strait, the "Gate of Grief," so named for the dangers it posed to sailors, captains, and cargo ships alike on navigating the narrows.

The Azure Shell hostage negotiators, Dante Dawson and Chris Fuller, peered out the cockpit window. The southwestern corner of Yemen sat across the waters, on the other side the mouth of the Red Sea, with rugged mountains rising above a barren strip of desert.

Ignoring the CIA's guidance to fly directly to Hargeisa Airport, Dante called his "sea daddy," four-star admiral Quail Sumner, at the Pentagon to receive clearance to fly over Zeila and inspect the hijacked container ship, *Shining Star*, from the air. He then clicked open a photo gallery on a tablet and swiped pictures taken of the Kenyan CIA asset Nairobi exiting the compound with Korfa; aerial drone photos of the listing tanker *Blå Himmel*; and underwater dorsalcam shots of the two planted devices on the ship's starboard hull. The bombs looked real enough. He passed the tablet to Fuller to get his take as an ex-FBI counterterrorism specialist.

The copilot glanced back at the Azure Shell team, asking, "Hey, Dawson, how many hostage negotiations have you guys pulled off?"

"Six," Dante replied.

"Make that eight," Fuller said.

"How many together?" the copilot asked.

"Did he say successful? . . . Uh, three," Fuller said.

"We handled a few million. But who's counting when you're talking about lives saved," the former CO said. "We did lose two hostages when a teen pirate fired due to frayed nerves. The kid was a rookie. But hell, the gunfire did change the tempo of the negotiations after that."

"Did it make you nervous?" the pilot asked.

"When you're unarmed, middle of an empty desert with a drone, maybe, hovering in the sky covering your hind flank, sure, we perspired a bit," Dante said.

Fuller pulled up video clip interviews with the *Blå Himmel* mercenary, Peder Olsen, who had been transferred from the USS *New York* to the US forward base on Socotra Island, off the Horn of Africa, where the US military had been building up forces on that island and Masriah Island, off the coast of Oman, to counter the Somali piracy and prepare for a clash with Iran.

The massive buildup began in early 2012. It was born out of Iran's nuclear program and military threats to close the Persian Gulf, including the ISIS invasion of Iraq two years later. What Fuller found odd was that the USS *New York* flew Olsen to the US military base on Socotra and not the NATO counter-piracy base. Also left out of the ongoing negotiations with Somali pirates for the release of the two ships' crews was United Kingdom's Piracy Ransom Task Force, which didn't exactly bother Dante Dawson or Fuller—their absence would make the duo richer. But it did make him wonder, why deliver Olsen there instead to the anti-pirate fusion center, which was established for NATO's Gulf of Aden Operation Ocean Shield—OOS—initiative?

Curious, Fuller accessed the OOS Somali dhow database through the global NATO Shipping Center, NSC. He opened both the Reuters AIS ship tracking system and the NSC weekly pirate report. But he didn't find much, other than the dates and names of the hijacked ships. The dhow database wasn't much help either. So he went back to the CIA Somali pirate database and accessed drone photos of the Norwegian supertanker, a schematic showing where Peder Olsen was—on the stern roof of the bridge—when he shot and killed the pirate leader Samatar 300 meters across the tanker at the bow of the ship. As an FBI and SWAT team sniper, Fuller wondered why Olsen decided to take that shot. Was that the only target he fired on the bow?

Fuller pulled up drone photos that showed a pool of blood where the pirate fell on the bow deck. He zoomed in and maneuvered the picture around 360 degrees, looking past the blood for tiny bullet holes in the steel or gunwale. But he didn't find any. If there were other pirates with Samatar, why wouldn't Olsen take them down, too? Fuller showed Dante the aerial photo.

Dante studied them and examined the area around the blood, looking for stray bullet holes in the deck. "Maybe Samatar's body-guards fired back," Dante suggested, handing the tablet back to Fuller as he gazed out the window to the other hijacked ship, which was moored in the bay of Zeila. With binoculars, he surveyed the container boxes stacked on the deck of the *Shining Sea*. He panned the bridge and derricks, but didn't see a single person on board. Unlike the supertanker, the container ship appeared upright, in deep water, sitting unscathed.

"Pull out—" the copilot said to the pilot, pointing to an ancient stone tower.

Dante and Fuller looked down across the beach to the tower, where they spotted a couple of pirates aiming RPG-7 grenade launchers at the helicopter. The pair stood in the threshold of the broken door, pointing up at the invading Black Hawk, while another pirate, armed with AKM assault rifle, kneeled on the crumbled turret on top of the tower.

The pilot banked the Black Hawk out over the gulf, climbing away. A few stray shots were fired; a RPG grenade scorched the air, rising . . . soaring . . . The pilot corkscrewed the Black Hawk down toward the sea, spinning, as the grenade ripped by the tail, barely missing the rear rotor. He swung the helicopter out of the drive and raced over the sea, with Dante and Fuller holding on, laughing at the close call.

"We lost hostages, not our lives," Dante said to the pilot, clutching his chest. "Damn."

The pilot flew over the arid land and there, across the vast desert expanse in the heat haze of the horizon, stood Hargeisa, the heart of the runaway region of Somaliland.

Chapter Forty-Six

A DOZEN MILES off the coast of Berbera, Merk rode the stolen skiff out to sea with the navy dolphins swimming alongside, fluking, darting, diving, leaping, hopping over the waves. They raced out in front, crisscrossing the bow.

Merk sent an encrypted message to the USS *New York* to be extracted by the Black Hawk that had carried him, Nico, and the dolphins to the drop zone off the coast of Somalia days before. He cut the engine and waited in open sea. He scanned 360 degrees to see if any ships, dhows, or skiffs were heading his way. For the next hour things remained calm.

Breaking the stillness of the blue sky was the blurred image of a Black Hawk flying in from the northeast. As it flew closer, Merk took out a chemlight, twisted it with an infrared beacon, and held it so the pilots could identify him as the US navy dolphin trainer.

When the Black Hawk cruised within a half klick of the stolen skiff, it flickered a pulsing blue light under its cargo bay, signaling Merk they spotted him as friendly.

Merk pulled off the Bedouin scarf, stuffed it in the backpack, powered down the laptop, and slid it into a waterproof bag. He pulled off the robe, handed the backpack to Tasi, and she nosed the floating pack to the extraction point. Navy divers jumped out of the hovering helicopter into the sea. The cargo bay opened and lowered a lambskin-lined basket down to the water.

The divers lifted Tasi and the backpack up to the cargo bay. The basket returned, and they loaded Inapo and hoisted the marine mammal back up to the Black Hawk. Merk swam to the divers, who hauled him into the basket and lifted him up. One diver swam over to the skiff and planted a shaped charge on the hull below the waterline. He inserted a remote trigger, then swam over to the basket, where he was the last to be lifted into the Black Hawk.

* * *

IN LESS THAN three minutes, two dolphins and three men were hoisted on board the helicopter with the basket pulled inside the cargo bay and the payload doors closed.

As the Black Hawk hovered in reverse, backing off the skiff, the diver pressed a code into a Satcom and detonated the shaped-charge, which blew a hole in the fiberglass hull. In a spat of smoke the craft took on water and began to list, dipping below the surface as the sea poured in.

As the skiff sank, Merk said, "That's it. That's where the pirate mothership disappeared. The Somalis sank it." He relayed his insight to the navigator, who texted it to the USS *New York*. Within a minute, the gulf swallowed the boat, leaving no trace of Merk or the navy dolphins ever having been in Somali waters. They were now being flown to Camp Lemmonier, their new forward operating base.

* * *

FOR NICO GREGORIUS, hiding on the roof of the oil storage tank all day, stuck in the port of Berbera, was a waste of time. He knew he would have to wait several more hours for nightfall before he could move out and go track down Nairobi.

By late afternoon, he received a coded message. He deciphered a text informing him that hostage negotiators were en route to Hargeisa Airport to meet with the Somali warlord Korfa and his pirate lieutenants. While Nico lay in wait listening to the occasional voices and sentry footsteps below to break up the boredom, he ran several options through his head: find a way to exit Somalia or migrate inland to the capital to provide intel or, at a bare minimum, backup for the US hostage negotiating team being flown to Hargeisa.

From past negotiations, Nico understood that dealing with Somali pirates took weeks, even months to conclude. Something unusual was up; he couldn't put his finger on it.

Chapter Forty-Seven

IN THE WAR-TORN ghetto of Hargeisa, a food and goods market thrived between rows of shanty structures and abandoned rusty lean-tos. Halfway down the bazaar market of Hargeisa, pitted between food stands, sat a fish-processing warehouse, its wood door painted olive green.

To the rear of the processing space stood a concealed door, which led to an empty storage room. Inside, Korfa sat at a table drinking tea. He stared at Nairobi; her face was battered and her left eye was swollen shut. A pair of bodyguards hovered over her and lifted Nairobi's limp body to sit upright in the chair. In the dim light, stitches crossed a bloodied eyelid, as tears streamed from her good eye. She fidgeted as if trying to pick up a cigarette that wasn't on the table.

"Nairobi, want some tea?" Korfa asked in a calm voice.

Trembling, she nodded.

He poured tea, pressed the cup to her lips, allowing her to sip. "My men found this in your safe house," Korfa said, plopping down stacks of euros and dollars on the table. "This wasn't there last week when I searched your home. Who are you helping? The CIA?"

She shook her head. "Somali army?" She shook her head once more, and flinched to block another blow to her head, but all Korfa did was pick up the cup and offer her another sip. "Okay. Who?"

"US navy," she said in a raspy whisper.

"SEALs?"

She nodded.

"How many?"

She raised two fingers.

"Two? That's it? Not a full SEAL platoon? I find that hard to believe," he said, coming unglued. He didn't want to be assassinated like his brother. He stood up, circled behind her.

Terrified, she glanced behind, bracing to be struck again. He put his hand on her shoulder and pressed gently instead, reassuring her that no more harm would come to her as long as she worked for him. She nodded, and broke down sobbing.

"Nai, we are meeting a US negotiating team in a few hours—after dark. You're going to help me close the deal. Hostages for money, simple, right?" Korfa said, motioning the guards to take her away until she would be needed.

Out of the shadows, Bahdoon stepped to Korfa, and said, "General Adad has landed."

Korfa nodded. The pirate warlord flashed one finger for the number of men who would join him to meet Syrian General Adad at the airport, and tapped Bahdoon on the shoulder.

Korfa and Bahdoon followed a dozen armed pirates out the back door of the warehouse into an abandoned building across a vacant alley. A tall pirate put down a RPG grenade launcher, opened double padlocks, and stepped inside a filthy cement floor room where the *Blue Heaven* crewmen were being held hostage. A dozen sat on the floor with their arms tied behind their backs, duct-tape slapped over their mouths.

Sporting a bloodied head bandaged and missing a tooth, the ship's Filipino first mate watched over the crew. Had Korfa found the hostages set free by the first mate, he would've castrated him under Somaliland law.

After a swift, brutal beating, Bahdoon sat down with the broken first mate and got inside his head. Within half an hour Bahdoon had flipped the captor, persuading him to work for him, and not the ship's crew.

Bahdoon stepped out from behind the armed pirates and handed two canteens of water to the first mate to give to his crewmen one at a time. The first mate started with the captain, in the far corner of the room. He ripped the duct tape off the captain's mouth and pressed the canteen to his parched lips. Water ran down the captain's face as he gulped like a thirsty dog.

The tall pirate clicked digital photos and shot a video of the hostages being given water by the first mate.

The crew was alive, beaten, but faring well under such foul conditions, with their mental health deteriorating each passing day; their images would be sent out in two batches. First, to the shipowners and NATO anti-piracy command on Socotra Island, and then on the World Wide Web and social media sites for all to see.

Korfa planned to light a firestorm of international fear by bringing the world audience to the plight of his people in Somalia; of the US and European forces invading the lands of Islam; of the toxic waste dumped off the shores of Somalia, poisoning a generation of Somali children; of foreign countries stealing their fish; of Somali people starving, malnourished, dying in a civil war that the CIA sponsored with the former puppet leader Barre in the 1980s. Korfa no longer relished being just a warlord. He wanted a ton of flesh, not a pound, for all the injustices put on him and his people. Spurred on by the death of his brother Samatar, he would kill to get it.

Bahdoon uploaded the digital files to an al Qaeda cloud portal with the cryptic note:

Beheadings will start at dawn, one every six hours, unless our demands are met. Failure to deliver, attached images will be shared with the world. Somalia's Heart Bleeds

—Pratique Occulte

Chapter Forty-Eight

A LANDING SIGNAL worker emerged from the white control tower, hopped in a cart, and was driven out to a waiting plane with Arabic lettering painted on the tail along with a diplomatic emblem. The dark-skin Somali wore a grimy baseball hat and yellow safety vest, and held a pair of yellow paddles in his hand.

They rode across one runway to the distant tarmac at the far perimeter fence of the airport. Just inside the chain-link fence, crowned with coils of concertina wire, sat the plane with its airstairs folded open by the cabin door.

An armed Syrian soldier stood at the bottom of the airstairs, waving the cart to ride over. The driver crossed the runway and parked, turning off the engine. The soldier approached the driver as the signal worker took off the safety vest and handed it and the paddles to the driver. He pulled off the hat and tossed it in the cart. Korfa showed his face and studied the soldier, saying in Arabic, "General Adad is waiting for me. I am Korfa, brother of the slain warlord Samatar," he said to the soldier, who clicked a radio mic twice.

An assistant to General Adad peered out the cabin door, spotted Korfa, and motioned the soldier to let the Somali warlord board the plane. Korfa climbed the airstairs. Bodyguards greeted the warlord at the cabin door and patted him down as a precaution. Korfa pulled up his shirt showing his bare chest and abdomen scarred from knife fights and bullet wounds. Confirming the Somali warlord wasn't wearing a wire or carrying weapons, the Syrians escorted Korfa into the jet and closed the door behind him.

A young female Syrian officer, assistant to General Adad, offered Korfa a drink of scotch, whisky, or gin. The Somali warlord wagged his finger *no* and reached for a bottle of mineral water. After a few minutes, General Adad emerged from a back office, sitting his weary frame in a leather chair across from Korfa. They shook hands. The general offered the warlord a Cuban cigar, but he declined that, too—Korfa neither drank nor smoked.

"How is the project coming along?" Korfa asked in Arabic.

"We were on track . . . we were ahead of schedule until being attacked at the missile site," the general said, reaching for a glass of twenty-one-year-old single-malt scotch, on the rocks with a twist, from his assistant. "It was the CIA, dressed as journalists. An al Qaeda deception. Reporters, we thought, snooping around the Iraqi border," he said, taking a well-deserved swig.

"I have the same problem here in Somalia. Too many spies."

"You have a problem? I have ISIS to the north and al Qaeda to the south in Yemen."

"A couple of American SEALs landed yesterday," Korfa said. "They are hunting for me while a US plane will be dropping off the hostage negotiating team across the runway."

"When are you supposed to meet them?" the general asked, chewing ice.

"In twenty minutes," he said without looking at his watch.

"I see. Don't you have to go then?"

Korfa shook his head, and replied, "My double will be there. Right after we make the trade of the tanker hostages for money, we will release the images of the hostages being fed water. But General Adad, we keep the Danish captain."

"Why, Korfa? Why risk that?

"Betrayal."

"Revenge? Don't Americans want to confirm the captain is alive?"

"Of course. We tell, no, we then show the negotiators that he escaped. Street photos on our social media sites will prove the Danish rat runs through the ghetto of Hargeisa and is alive." Korfa drank the sparkling water. "Until we shoot him for escaping."

A Syrian army copilot emerged from the cockpit, announcing, "General, the US bird has landed. Across the tarmac on the other end of the airport."

General Adad signaled his assistant to bank the lights in the jet. He led Korfa to the port windows, where they peered into the darkness. Down the far end of the runway, they saw the flashing lights with rotor blades whirring in the dark air. A silhouette of a quartet of armed navy SEALs led hostage negotiators Dante Dawson and Chris Fuller out of the Black Hawk to a waiting jeep.

"How did you arrange the Americans to show up so fast? It usually takes weeks," General Adad asked with a wave of his hand.

"We sent a message to Washington through our hot channel," Korfa said. "What are you going to do with the missile site now?"

"Build it," he said, adding, "But with a new site in Yemen. We need to unleash the holy hell of my Syrian Electronic Army." He banged his fist.

Korfa turned away from the window and looked the general in the eye.

"Why wait, Ferryman?" asked the general. "Cut me in on half of the ransom money and I will bomb the US base when the second batch of hostages land in Djibouti. My Syrian e-Army is already inside the base's firewall."

Korfa unzipped his pants, unhooked a money-belt, and handed it to the general.

General Adad opened the Velcro pockets, seeing they were stuffed with cash from Nairobi's safe house. The general grinned as he watched the jeep, carrying the ransom negotiators, drive out the gate.

Chapter Forty-Nine

THE JEEP'S WORN shock absorbers jostled Dante and Fuller about in the backseat. They felt every bump, pothole, and turn as the Somali pirate drove them from the airport through the good part of Hargeisa, and then plunged into the poor section of the capital of Somaliland. In numbing detail, past eye-flinching poverty, abandoned properties, scarred slums, with the poor moping about, drained of life. Dante had seen it all before, but that night it felt different.

The blunt images flickered with each swerve of the jeep. The mercenaries saw a dirty mother sitting on the curb barefoot, breast-feeding her baby in rags; trash piles strewn here and there with rats crawling over the refuse; the one-arm drunk twitching and stagger-ing, sucking on a bottle of whiskey. Life was hard for most people in the world—Dante understood that. Broken, hungry, filthy condi-tions amid the squalor that most people of the world endured daily reminded him of growing up in the South Side of Chicago. Dante knew how far he had come from the violent streets, up through the navy SEALs ranks and into semi-retirement. Forming a hostage secu-rity company in Azure Shell kept his skills, spirit, and mind from going dull.

As the Jeep turned down another narrow alley, they caught a glimpse of a woman lifting her dress, bent down at the knees, urinat-ing in the middle of the street. The driver honked the horn, hit the high beams, finally chasing her off. The alley was located behind the market street, where the acrid stench of urine and rotting fish heads overwhelmed their senses. Fuller's eyes watered; Dante covered his nose.

Ahead in the shaky headlights, pirates escorted a line of hostages across the alley from the green building into the fish warehouse— when two men made a break. They dashed away from the jeep's headlights.

On the curb, the tall pirate waved the hostages to hurry into the warehouse when out of the corner of his eye he saw the Danish captain and the Filipino pilot knock over a guard and sprint down the alley, their once-bound arms cut free. One pirate aimed a RPG launcher, ready to fire, when the tall pirate lifted the weapon in the air and drew a pistol. He squeezed one round and shot the pilot in the thigh, dropping him to ground. He yelped, squirming in pain, holding his wounded leg. The Danish captain glanced back at the fallen pilot, and then to the tall pirate, who aimed the pistol skyward and fired the next round in the air.

The gunfire signaled two pirates to chase after the captain. The pirate with the rocket launcher wheeled around, kneeled, scoping the RPG at the jeep as it pulled up and shut off its headlights. The tall pirate sent more guards to grab the wounded pilot and drag him into the warehouse. Then the ragged Filipino first mate ambled out of the green building unescorted. The sight was strange, but for Dante it was the first mate's catatonic stare that unnerved him.

The tall pirate, backed by armed guards, strode over to the jeep and pounded on the hood. The driver stepped out of the jeep, sweating, nervous, batting his eyes about. Finally, he looked at the tall pirate and opened the back door, waving the negotiators to come out. Dante and Fuller stepped out, each carrying a black laptop case slung over their shoulders.

They were led into the fish-processing warehouse. Once inside, the smell grew harsher, the lighting dimmer. The odor of the fish lingered, far more acute than outside in the alley.

The hostages were moved into a false-wall room, where Korfa's double sat at the end of the wood table, donning shades and a *kufeya* scarf, with a laptop facing him. He motioned the Americans to wait as the bodyguards frisked and patted the hostage negotiators one more time.

"Can't be too careful," Korfa Double said in a British accent. "You shot my bro, Sama."

"We didn't shoot anybody," Dante said calmly, not wanting to escalate a delicate first meeting into something intense or unwieldy. Hostage negotiations were always unpredictable, rarely by the book, and could turn upside down in a flash.

Dante stared Korfa Double in the eye. With the hostages stowed in an adjacent room, Korfa's double was in charge. He wore an earsleeve, allowing the real Korfa to watch and coach the negotiations from the Syrian jet at the airport. With a webcam hidden in the ceiling streaming a live feed to Korfa, the double swung the laptop around showing Dante where the hostages were being kept—next door.

Guards waved the hostages out of a freezer. They were shivering, trying to warm up inside the humid plant, before they would be herded back into the freezer for another icing. "Twenty minutes in the freezer, ten minutes out," the double said. "The longer our talks go, the worse shape they will be in. Maybe one or two will freeze to death if you talk too much."

"Who ran away outside?" Fuller asked.

"The captain," the tall pirate said, standing behind him. "There are no heroes."

"Know—" the double said, opening meta images of street people of Hargeisa taking pictures and video of the Danish captain running for his life through the market and streets of the Hargeisa ghetto. "He won't run far. Not with his white skin. How much ransom did you bring?"

"Right now? . . . A cool million," Fuller said.

"That's short by three," the double replied. He waved Dante and Fuller to sit down and swung the laptop back to face him. They sat down and put their laptop bags on the table.

"Yeah, we know that. It's by design. We're dealing with two different shipowners in two different countries," Fuller said.

"We will give another million dollars for the release of the *Blå Himmel* supertanker in Berbera and the release of the *Shining Sea* container ship we flew over in Zeila," Dante said. "For the last million, we need her crew set free."

"Ummm, maybe," the double said.

"We give you this money for the hostages next door and the captain," Dante said.

"Go out and catch him yourself," the double said, shaking his head with laughter, his voice deep and calm like the real Korfa.

*　*　*

INSIDE THE SYRIAN jet, Qas, the young Syrian Electronic Army hacker, emerged from the back office. He sat down at a desk with multiple computer screens, and then set up the real Korfa to talk into a mic, coaching his double in the warehouse, as he watched the negotiations live.

". . . Shipowners and insurance companies have another problem," Dante said, remotely.

The real Korfa spoke into the mic, saying, "Don't say a word. Let him speak."

"Look, we know there are two bombs planted under the tanker in Berbera," Dante pointed out. "They're on the starboard hull."

"To hell with the owner," the double said. "Why look at me? The port guards did it to stop Americans from stealing the hijacked ship back at night."

Korfa spoke into the mic: "Remember, we don't trust you. We are trading ransom money for lives. The ship will come later, since you came short of cash."

The double held up his finger, repeating word for word the first two lines. Fuller gave Dante a look, but kept silent.

General Adad sat down next to Korfa, watching the double repeat the words to the negotiators online. "Your double is good," the general observed.

"He should be. He went to acting school in London," Korfa said.

* * *

IN THE ROOM, the Korfa's double repeated the claim, "You dare come here short of cash?"

"Best we can do on short notice," Fuller interjected, pounding the table.

The Korfa double gave the former FBI special agent a hard look, then glared at Dante, saying, "Hand over the money, walk out with those next door. When we catch the captain, we will bring him to Zeila in exchange for half a million dollars."

Dante looked at Fuller and communicated with his eyes, blinking Morse code for doing the deal. Fuller nodded as he contemplated the revised offer. He tapped his index finger on the table, and then opened his laptop bag, showing stacks of one hundred dollar bills. Dante proceeded to do the same, swung his laptop case around, pulling out stacks of euros.

"Let's do this," Dante said. He stood up and extended his hand to shake with Korfa Double to seal the deal. But the double removed his sunglasses and stared coldly at the ex-SEAL. "Okay, we will see you next in Zeila with the other hostages," Dante said.

"You won't see me there. You will see the ghost of my brother Samatar," the double said cryptically, not once raising his hand to shake.

Dante and Fuller stepped away from the table. The tall pirate escorted the Americans out the door into the vacant alley. They would wait for the hostages to be turned over to them by the jeep. The big transport truck waited by the end of the alley.

Ten minutes later, the hostages were taken out of the freezer one last time and herded outside. They were shaking, quivering, flashlights blinding their eyes, disorienting them further. At the rear of the line, psychiatrist Bahdoon walked alongside the turned first mate, chatting with him, and handed the Filipino an amulet of a Somali two-faced animal deity: one face of a bull, the other of a cow.

The amulet had roots in pre-Islamic Somali myth. Bahdoon said of the figure: "This is your protector, the god Waaq. The universe is

balanced on the bull's horn. You belong to Pratique Occulte now."
The doctor touched the single horn on the amulet.

* * *

IN THE SYRIAN jet, Korfa and General Adad watched the hostages
being led out of the fishing warehouse. He pointed at Bahdoon talking with the first mate, and boasted, "My doctor flipped that man in
less than two days. He's now a follower of the Occulte."

"Korfa, you know why we met tonight," the general said, sipping
scotch. "The whole world has turned against ISIS, against the old
regime. The West keeps arming the rebel army, along with Qatar.
They accuse the old guard Syria of using chemical weapons."

"Yeow. We Somalis are labeled dogs and pirates. We are beneath
the Western standard of living, education, skin color, religion,"
Korfa complained about the overt racism.

"Osama bin Laden taught us something. He taught Islamic people after the fallout of the Arab Spring that we need to act loose,
decentralized, yet come together against the force of the Great
Satan and hit the devil from all sides," General Adad said. "In the
world's eye, Syria is scarred. That's what's shown on the news. But we
are fighting with our brothers Hezbollah, AQAP, and Iran, with Iraq
erupting with sectarian violence against ISIS, ignited by the Syrian
civil war, with recruits from Assad's old regime."

"In America, Pratique Occulte has cells, but not with my dark
skin," the warlord said.

Qas looked out the window to a second Black Hawk landing at
the far end of the runway.

"Good, they are going to fly the hostages out of the country,"
Adad said to Qas, and then looked at Korfa, "Do you have what you
need?"

"Yeow. Ready to go. Pick a city, choose one, choose a day, choose
a time. Bahdoon and I will act against the target."

"In three days I will choose. Inside the borders of my Syria is not
where we will fight the enemy," he said, pointing to Qas, "Meet the
captain of the two stolen ships." General Adad stood up, stepped

over to the window, and saw the gate open. Outside, the jeep drove onto the tarmac and then the truck followed with the hostages. As General Adad watched the unloading of the hostages into the helicopters, he aimed his finger like a gun and pulled an imaginary trigger at the helicopters, saying, "'Black Hawk Down'. . . again."

Chapter Fifty

AT CAMP LEMONNIER, the Black Hawk helicopter refueled and a new crew of pilots, on standby, climbed into the cockpit to fly Merk and the dolphins to the next mission.

Marines stored supplies of MREs and thirty gallons of water on board, alongside dolphin first-aid kits, sheepskin-lined tarps, coolers of fresh fish, extra laptop batteries, Satcoms, ammo, flares, Kevlar vests, helmets, and night-vision goggles.

In the mess hall, Merk wolfed down three turkey burgers, sans the bread. Then he ate a bowl of fruit salad, seaweed salad, kelp, spinach, and carrots, and chased it all down with fresh cranberry juice and a quart of milk.

Merk took a shower. He checked his body for cuts, sores, and boils. He applied a cloth to the cut on his forearm and lifted his chin to inspect his neck where the pirate strangled him. He didn't see any deep marks or bruises. He snapped an aloe stalk, dripped the aloe juice on the burn scar of his left forearm, and kneaded it into the damaged skin. Looking in the mirror, he had a flashback of clutching the dolphin that saved his life. In doing so, the dolphin's body spared half of his torso from being burned, while the creature succumbed to the sea of flames.

The navy dolphin, which ended up dying in his arms minutes after he caught fire, dove him underwater to extinguish the flames. That dolphin was the only biologic system in the US Navy Marine Mammal Program to die in combat. It was a distinction Merk never wanted to own.

After putting on shorts and a SEAL Team Six tee shirt, Merk joined the CIA agents, who had grilled Dante Dawson and Chris Fuller earlier, in the joint agency intel fusion center. There they briefed him, SEAL Lt. Commander Kell Johnston, and a SEAL sniper on the next mission—the dorsalcam reconnaissance of the US container ship *Shining Sea* above and below the surface.

Merk was fine with taking the meeting. He wanted to clear the air on a few items. He didn't have to wait. The CIA case officer dropped drone photographs of small craft and navy dolphins searching the sea. Merk slid the photos, one after the other, to Kell Johnston, who studied them carefully.

"You know who they are?" The agent pointed at the soldiers in the boats.

"Sure. Iranian motorboats and . . . former Soviet-trained navy dolphins," Merk said, nailing the answer. "Strait of Hormuz is where they're searching, correct?"

"Affirmative," the agent said. "What could they be looking for, lieutenant?"

"Well, either there was a leak on our top secret mission," Merk began to explain, ". . . or one of the revolutionary fishermen survived our collision."

"I choose the latter," the case officer said.

"Can you confirm that?" Kell Johnston asked.

"You're both on a need-to-know basis," the Asian American agent interjected.

"Of course. The CIA toils only in the shadows," Merk said. Unimpressed with the CIA, he handed the photographs back to the case officer. "Your search is fruitless. It's like pissing in the wind. You won't find anything."

"How do you know that?" the steamed case officer asked, pulling up the operation's inventory list on a tablet. "I see you lost a—"

"Laptop. It was ruined by the salt water when it sank ninety feet to the bottom. And the DPod, I sank that remotely when I returned to base," Merk replied. "And I lost Lt. Morgan Azar to a selfish, stupid move on my part. I got the intel at the expense of my friend's life. Nothing sucks more than that. It's been like a bone spur embedded in my heart. The feeling won't go away. How about you? What part of your humanity have you sacrificed on a mission?"

"Lt. Toten? Really?" the Asian American agent said.

"If I were you, I'd focus on the dolphins in the photos, not the Iranian guards."

Frustrated with the answers, the case officer turned on a digital wall map showing two large islands off the coast of Zeila. Sacadadiin Island was the larger of the two islands, about half the distance closer to shore of the bombed ancient city. Dense vegetation and thick mangroves covered most of the terrain, partially inhabited, visited daily by fishermen, tour boats, and others.

A few miles into the gulf stretched a sandbar-like spit of an island called Ceebaad. That forlorn land was sparsely covered with a quilt work of scrub pine, low green bushes, and wind-swept sedge grass. Barren and sandy in some spots, a rubble coast surrounded the elongated triangle-shaped island.

The case officer said, "There's no fresh water on Ceebaad, little on Sacadadiin Island."

"We'll setup a camouflage blind to provide cover for Toten and the dolphins to operate," Kell Johnston said.

The agents showed the SEALs the locations of where they should position perimeter cameras to watch for boat traffic around the island. The Asian American agent gave Merk a flash drive with a one-page document that identified several targets for the dolphins to carry out surveillance activities.

The case officer took a remote and clicked on a split-screen showing Korfa and the Korfa Double. "You need to study this," he told Merk.

"Why? I'm a marine mammal recon guy, not a cold warrior SEAL," Merk said.

"Hey, Toten, you're the one who asked to conduct an exit interview of the Norwegian sniper before we send him back to Norway," the case officer said, getting annoyed.

"Run that by me again."

"Lt. Toten, on the right is the real pirate warlord Korfa. We are one 100 percent sure with our facial-recognition software from photos taken by one of our assets—"

"Nairobi?"

"Yes. Based on her work for the past five years." The agent took a laser pointer and ran the red dot on the 81 percent match of the facial features in the double's face. His cheeks were millimeters too high; the nose five degrees more crooked; the lips thinner and mouth one size smaller, among other features from the hairline, including distance between eyebrows across the bridge of the nose. "It was a close match. It fooled the hostage negotiators. But they secretly filmed Korfa's double. Sunglasses in a dark room became a dead giveaway."

"What are you going to do with Nairobi?" Merk asked.

"Break off contact until we need her again," the case officer said.

"If her cover is blown, are you going to let her be raped and tortured?" Merk asked. "She has children. Young beautiful kids."

"Like the navy, we follow orders. Not from sunny San Diego, but from the analysts and directorates in Langley," the case officer countered.

Merk looked at the lieutenant commander, saying, "Kell, maybe you want to get word out to CO Gregorius. Nico is still in Berbera. Have you heard from him?"

"Toten, stay the fuck out of this. You're not a SEAL anymore," the case officer snapped.

Frustrated by the careless disregard for the professionals who put their lives on the line, Merk pounded the table and stormed out of the meeting, saying, "You better pray I drown."

* * *

AT ZERO DARK hundred, Merk and the dolphins were loaded on board the Black Hawk; a cell of four navy SEALs and Lt. Commander Kell Johnston joined the flight. The helicopter swooped over the Mandab Strait heading toward a rendezvous with the *Shining Sea*.

Chapter Fifty-One

WITHIN HALF AN hour the helicopter reached the insertion point in the gulf, crossing some invisible border between Djibouti and Somaliland that stretched across the dark water to Yemen.

The cargo bay opened. A basket lowered a pair of SEAL divers into the bay north of Ceebaad Island, some eight miles offshore. They checked the surroundings, saw a laser-signal from the cargo master, and the basket lowered the SEAL sniper with Lt. Commander Kell Johnston into the water.

The divers escorted them on shore, pulling a floatation box of guns and ammo, and dragged it onto the rock-strewn beach. As Kell took out infrared binoculars and panned the northern half of the island to make sure they were alone, the divers swam back to the drop zone. Once clear, they signaled the cargo master to lower the dolphins, one at a time, followed by Merk, with the biosystems' supplies stowed in an inflatable rubber boat with an outboard motor.

Using night-vision goggles, the SEALs cleared the island one area at a time.

Above, the Black Hawk pilots deployed the FLIR system, scanning the distance of the long island, which narrowed to a point in the south. The infrared didn't pick up any heat signature of man or animal. Merk and the SEALs backup team stood alone on Ceebaad, at least until the next morning. Lt. Commander Johnston and the SEAL sniper dragged the boat and supplies on shore. They dug three pits in the patches of sand, placed the supplies in the holes, and covered the objects with camouflage cargo nets.

Once set, the Black Hawk hoisted the divers on board and banked away in stealth mode, flying back to the forward naval expeditionary base in Djibouti.

While Lt. Commander Kell Johnston discussed the night sentry duty with the sniper, from mealtime to sleep time, how and when to search the barren island with no fresh drinking water, Merk waded into the sea. He splashed the water with his hand and, within a minute, Tasi and Inapo emerged from slumbering in the black water.

Merk waded deeper to check the dorsalcams. He tested them on a smartphone screen to make sure they worked. Next, he examined the GPS tracking tags at the base of the dorsal fins and pinged them like a dating app on a satellite map of Ceebaad Island. Once confirmed the geocoords were accurate, Merk flashed a hand-sign to Tasi and Inapo. The dolphins squealed and fluked off, swimming around the north side of the island, heading toward the silhouette of the low hills and mounts of Sacadadiin Island in the near distance.

Merk waded back onshore. He sat down with the laptop and used a biometric scan of his eyes' veins to grant access to the laptop hard drive, in-memory chip, as well as the navy's Blue Cloud. Within seconds, he tracked the navy dolphins heading to the moored hijack ship on the other side of Sacadadiin Island off the Zeila coast. They cruised at a leisurely pace of six to seven knots, or about a third of their top swimming speed.

As he waited for the dolphins to reach the container ship, Merk took a short break. He stretched his limbs and peered up to the heavenly bodies that dotted the black dome sky. He remembered when he was a boy, he used to search the heavens for answers to his broken bond with his father, the loss of the mother he never knew. For the first time, he made the connection that he had fallen into the flypaper of another broken relationship with his love for Jenny King. It would be that way, if it lasted, until either they retired or took new jobs. For Merk, his bond with the dolphins was the glue in a relationship he coveted the most.

Merk made out the silhouette of the SEALs patrolling the middle of the island and heading toward the southern tip. He rolled on one knee and checked the progress of the dolphins. To his surprise they were swimming slower than before, at three knots an hour. Why?

He opened blowhole charts, heartbeat rates, lab results on blood samples—negative. He scanned the veterinarian's meticulous notes for any obscure comment or observation about the physical health and well-being of either dolphin. Merk read through the food charts—mackerel, squid, herring, worm eel—and then the list on amino acids, glutathione, and nutrients with heavy doses of vitamins. Nothing leapt off the page. Were the dolphins tired? Was it something in the water? He closed out the medical fitreps and sent a Dolphin Code message directing Tasi and Inapo to split apart and swim faster to the container ship.

For the next several minutes Merk monitored the blinking GPS dots as they moved across a digital map toward the known satellite location of the box carrier *Shining Star*. It didn't take long for Merk to deduce that Inapo, who swam ahead tripling his slow speed, appeared fine, and yet something was wrong with Tasi. Knowing daylight would arrive in three hours, Merk had to intervene—Tasi would never make it to the target and back to Ceebaad Island before daybreak.

He closed the laptop, stuffed it in a waterproof backpack, and sprinted to the rubber boat. Merk pushed the craft into the sea, lowered the outboard motor, and started it.

Merk guided the boat down the coast, opening the throttle, ramping up speed.

He saw Lt. Commander Kell Johnston and the SEAL sniper sprint across the island, waving him to stop, calling his name.

Merk slowed the craft and flashed a chemlight sign to Kell that one of the dolphins was down and that he would return soon. The second chemlight sign told Kell to have the SEAL extraction team at Camp Lemonnier on emergency standby.

Chapter Fifty-Two

W HEN NIGHT FELL on Berbera, Nico Gregorius climbed down from the roof of the oil storage tank. He trailed close behind the guard and, when the armed man turned the corner walking around another tank, Nico snipped a hole in the fence and slithered out.

Like a cat, he moved across the seaside city, staying low, ducking behind trees and bushes and parked vehicles when people strolled on the street or when cars drove by. In the neighborhood across from the oil facility, the CO moved through yards and houses, up one dirty street, and down a junk-strewn alley. He checked the cars—most were locked—*of course,* he thought. Very few people in northern Somali trusted the pirate scourge.

Then down a side street his luck changed. He found a beat up Russian-made car with the door open and the keys under the seat. He turned on the engine and drove off, noting that half a tank of gas would be enough to get him to Hargeisa. As he turned the corner onto the main road, he flipped on the headlights. Within minutes, Nico followed road signs that led to the Hargeisa-Berbera Highway, an arid stretch of roadway that would take him inland.

After traveling an hour, Nico reached the outskirts of the capital city, where he saw a haze of lights floating over Hargeisa like a halo. He pulled over and turned on his smartphone, to ensure the CIA and ONI could track his movements. He needed to see if there were any updates to the intel he sent earlier in the day. Nico clicked on a video file in the mission cloud, showing Dante Dawson meeting with Korfa.

Notes from the cash-for-hostages ransom negotiation included the geocoords of the fish processing plant in the street market, in the run-down shanty part of the city. The Danish captain had escaped, but was re-apprehended. And that Nairobi hadn't been seen. The update was a couple of hours old. Nico drove on to the slums.

He entered the deserted alley that ran parallel with the street market, slid out, and walked on foot to the green building, where the hostages had been kept, across the alley from the fish plant. Nico took out an audioscope, unfolded the stock, inserted an earpod in his ear, and aimed the scope at the plant door. Adjusting a knob, he faded down the low alpha wave hum of the freezers and refrigerators and heard male voices speaking the local Somaliland dialect.

Nico eavesdropped not on the contents of the conversation—the CIA would decipher the recording of what they discussed—but to figure out the number of men in the room. What was he up against? Five men? Eight? A dozen? Who else was inside the plant?

He listened and noted four different male voices; perhaps one of them was Korfa. He couldn't tell. He figured there had to be another pair of guards in or near the room, maybe more if the warlord was inside. The SEAL CO folded the stock, dismantled the audioscope, and slid it in the pack. Nico took out two pistols, holstered them, and then armed an Uzi machine gun and removed the safety latch. He stuffed an extra ammo clip inside his belt.

Nico played with the door handle and found it unlocked. That meant the pirates would use the door for an exit in case Korfa's facility was raided. He slipped inside and saw, to his surprise, no guard stationed by the door or around the corner in the dimly lit hall. Nico followed the voices to a hidden room. A tall bookcase had been pushed aside on rails. A sliver of light fanned out from the cracks around the wood door and jamb. He put an eye to the crack by the hinge and peeked inside, moving his eyeball around until he saw the tall pirate standing by the wood table, speaking to whom he thought was Korfa.

Nico took a flash grenade from his vest, turned the doorknob ever so gently, and pulled the door back an inch. When he heard a slight creak in the doorjamb, he yanked the door open and tossed the grenade inside the room, turning his back to the door, looking away from the blinding light.

In a star-bright burst, the grenade stunned those inside, temporarily blinding the pirates.

Nico lunged into the room and ducked. Holding his eyes with one hand, the tall pirate sprayed the door with a staccato burst of gunfire with the other. Nico fired the Uzi, clipping the tall pirate in the knees and thighs, dropping him to the floor where he shrieked in pain.

Another guard at the door, who didn't appear to be blinded by the flash, chopped the Uzi out of Nico's hands . . . the guard grabbed him by the vest and whipped out a dagger . . . Nico pulled out a pistol and fired three shots into Korfa's chest, blowing him out of the seat . . . just as the guard plunged the blade in Nico's other arm.

Hearing footsteps of another pirate behind him, Nico spun the guard around, who took the blow of a cleaver to his neck and shoulder. Pulling the hacked guard down with him to the floor, Nico fired several rounds into the cleaver-wielding pirate. He and the squirming guard hit the floor hard. Nico pushed the corpse off, rolled away, got up on one knee and, through the haze of hot smoke, saw Nairobi sitting on the floor on the other side of the room. As he scrambled toward her, two simultaneous shots burst. One bullet struck Nico in the back above his kidney, dropping him to the floor. The second shot, fired by the injured Nairobi, hit the guard who entered the room behind Nico. That shot pierced the guard's heart, killing him instantly.

Nico slumped to the floor. Dazed, he tried to gather his senses, bracing against the knifing pain, feeling strength drain from his chest and limbs. He shook his head, pulled out the Satcom, and sent a text message that Korfa was dead and that the CO was going to die with Nairobi. Hearing footsteps thumping down the hall, Nico pressed an emergency code on the Satcom, erasing its disk and wiping data clean off the in-memory chip.

As his focus became blurred, the dying SEAL CO saw the dead Korfa lying across the floor, clutching a pair of sunglasses. To Nico's surprise, the real warlord Korfa burst into the room, aimed an AK-47 at Nairobi, and shot her dead before she could fire the next volley. Her death broke the bond with her children, who would never get to see her again, or hear her voice, or share her joy and laughter. Akello and Fathiya were motherless and didn't know it yet.

Korfa kicked the bottom of Nico's foot. The SEAL CO rolled over, blood streaming from his wound, his eyes rolling back in his forehead—whites. Unable to see the warlord standing over him, he could only listen.

"You shot the wrong Korfa," the warlord said, picking up the Satcom as Nico died.

Bahdoon entered the room unarmed. He surveyed the firefight. The dead: double agent Nairobi, Korfa Double, and the US SEAL CO, among a half dozen pirates. He asked, "Korfa, what are you going to do with the American body?"

"Ransom, of course. Money, money, money. Bahdoon, you handle psy warfare. I will demand twice the ransom for the treachery the Americans committed in trying to assassinate me," Korfa said, bristling in anger.

The guards lifted Nico's lifeless body and slumped it in a chair. Korfa put his arm around the dead SEAL and posed for a digital picture, which Bahdoon captured on a smartphone and would then upload on a social media platform to go viral.

"This reminds me of the TV crews last week in Jaar. The show I put on with the dead children on TV was fantastic," Bahdoon said with dark glee. "We'll blame ISIS. The US lost the propaganda war with the drone strike. Now they'll lose the psy war before the attack."

"Bahdoon, remember I'm the Ferryman, not a butcher. So how are you leaving Somalia?"

"My Indian passport is waiting for me in Paris, along with an airline ticket," he said.

"I'm heading out through Nigeria and from there as an oil trader," Korfa said.

Chapter Fifty-Three

MERK SPED THE rubber boat tight to the dark mangrove-clad coast of Sacadadiin Island. He eyed the digital map on the laptop screen showing Inapo closing on the hijacked ship, while Tasi had just cleared the southwestern point of the island.

Swimming at fifteen knots, Inapo breached the black water, the dorsalcam capturing the broad stern of the vessel. As the dolphin approached the *Shining Star*, the starboard side came into view, the multicolored container boxes stacked skyward like child's blocks. At that point, Merk made the decision to go with only one MM system conducting reconnaissance that night. What he needed to do beside fish Tasi out of the gulf was figure out why she became belabored while swimming to the target.

When the rubber boat approached within one hundred meters of Tasi, the dolphin splashed furiously. The dorsalcam view bounced around—choppy shots of the sea, the island edge, a rotating night sky. Merk cut the engine and glided over. Her dorsal fin sank below.

In full view of the *Shining Star*, forming a towering silhouette against the low lying horizon of Zeila bay, Merk took the chance of being spotted. He grabbed a flashlight and circled the beam around the water, looking for any sign of Tasi—foam on the surface where she thrashed about, a disturbance of air bubbles ejected from her blowhole. Some clue, but found nothing.

"Jesus Christ. C'mon, c'mon, Tasi . . . Where are you? . . . ?" he muttered, frantic.

Merk moved the flashlight back and forth across the surface, and then reached for the sonar-whistle. He grasped it and, about to lower it in the water, felt a thump under the rubber boat. He looked around, and Tasi floated upside-down out from under the bow. Merk tethered a rescue line to his ankle and dove in the water. He swam to Tasi, rolled the stunned dolphin over, and began to pound her side hard, stunning her to wake up. He blew a powerful breath into her blowhole, causing her to eject water and then pinch several breaths. The dolphin came to, opening an eye, glancing around, yet she was dazed and weak.

"Tasi, I'm going to lift you up. But you need to help by jumping in the boat." With that Merk pulled the rubber boat over, pulled the slack out of the line, holding the now short cord in his mouth, and hoisted the mammal up. Tasi fluked hard, rising up where Merk pushed her into the rubber boat. Exhausted, he hung on to the side. When his strength returned, he pulled himself into the rubber boat, sprawled flat on his back next to Tasi. He wiped water out of his face and howled like a wolf with victory.

Merk rolled the tarp over her, sliced a hole for the dorsal fin to stick through, and then headed back to Ceebaad Island, letting Inapo conduct the survey of the ship's hull alone.

* * *

AT THE STERN of the Shining Star, Inapo broke the surface, cleared his blowhole, and dove underwater. The navy dolphin swam to inspect the vessel's props. The massive propellers were intact, but with a lone haunting scar. A crewman from the hijacked ship had been tied to a massive blade. His hands floated gently in the current; his hair flowing upward like strands of sea-grass; his face and body bloated. A corpse to serve as a warning sign for the US Navy.

Inapo shot a burst of sonar clicks from his melon into the chest of the victim to confirm the heart was not beating. The dolphin detected no pulse, no sign of life. Inapo swam around the starboard side, panning the long hull. He found a metallic object floating beneath the surface.

Swimming by the object, the dolphin dove to the seafloor and came up under the sphere with a hard metal shell of a sea-mine.

Inapo clicked the object, as the dorsalcam captured the contact spikes. The sonar feedback told the dolphin that the mine was armed. Relaying the intel back to Merk via the Dolphin Code, Inapo swam around the ship to locate more mines.

* * *

THE LOW-SCRABBLED TOPOGRAPHY of Ceebaad Island came into view. Merk opened the throttle racing the rubber boat with Tasi to the far side of the island. As the boat turned the corner, Kell Johnston and the SEAL sniper flagged Merk over. He swerved the craft around the north end of the island, shut off the engine, and glided to shore. Merk lifted the tarp and noticed Tasi was low on energy. He rolled the heavy creature over the side into the water.

Tasi drifted away. She peeked her head above the surface waiting for Merk to give instructions. He flashed the sign to stay at rest. Merk told the SEAL sniper to bring the cooler over so he could feed the dolphin, while he and Kell tracked the progress of Inapo surveying the *Shining Sea*. Unsure how to feed the mammal, the sniper held up a mackerel and looked at Merk for guidance.

"You know how to aim a firearm and squeeze the trigger, don't you?" Merk said.

"Sure I do," the SEAL sniper said, gingerly lowering the fish to Tasi's mouth. The dolphin reached up and snatched the mackerel out of the sniper's hand, grazing his fingers with her conical shaped teeth. Startled, the sniper stumbled backward and fell in the water.

"Toten, what's wrong with your animal?" Kell asked.

"Don't know. But I can't have a liability out there with daybreak coming," Merk said, carrying the laptop over to a storage area and placing it on another cooler of food. He typed in commands on the color-coded keyboard, opening a split-screen that showed a live shot of the dorsalcam with Inapo looping under and around a third sea-mine. The other half of the screen showed images the system had caught earlier. Merk opened the clip of the dead crewman bound to the propeller; the first sea-mine off the starboard side; and a second mine near the bow.

"We have a murder," Kell said, pointing at Inapo poking the corpse's head.

"The pirates wouldn't mine the harbor if they wanted to keep the cargo," Merk said, carrying the laptop to the stone beach. He placed it on a rock, turned up the volume so he could hear an alert ping in case Inapo tried to contact him. He waded into the shallows and dove underwater, swimming out to Tasi.

For the next ten minutes, Merk and Tasi gently swam together, mirroring one another. They played, splashed, and frolicked; all the while he examined her from beak to tail. He felt for wounds, scrapes, gashes and sores under the belly, the most sensitive part of a dolphin's skin, but found nothing. He ran his palms down her sides, but again didn't find any wounds, scars, cuts, scrapes, or bruises. He eyed the dolphin; she stared back at him.

Merk wasn't any closer to figuring out what was wrong with the MM system. Did she suffer from a virus or illness? Did the back-to-back-to-back missions exhaust her? He sloshed out of the water with Kell asking, "You find anything?"

"No. She appears clean," he said, puzzled. "Maybe a virus."

"Well, that's life. Wait till you take her back to the bioteam at Camp Lemonnier."

"'Life'?" Merk repeated, looking at Kell, then asked, "Do you have an audioscope?" Merk waved the sniper to join them. He led the SEALs into the water, pushed the rubber boat out, handed the tarp to Kell and the sniper to unfold, and then tapped Morse code on the hull.

Tasi surfaced. She moseyed over and, with help from the SEALs, slid inside the craft. Merk and the sniper rolled Tasi on her side. He motioned Kell to aim the audioscope on the belly of the dolphin, moving the nozzle from her chest, then along the digestive tract to the tail. Merk waded around, pulled the receiver out of Kell's ear, motioning him to aim the audioscope.

He heard Tasi's heartbeat, and then over her belly the echo of a second, rapid heartbeat. The heartbeats were as clear as a SEAL double tap. "Tasi is pregnant," Merk rejoiced.

Chapter Fifty-Four

THE CONVOY OF military trucks drove through, over, and around the mountains of northwest Iran on the way to the ancient holy city of Qom, south of Teheran. The slow, bumpy two-day grind wore on Agent Jenny King, who was disguised as the North Korean missile engineer Kim Dong-Sun.

Iran's Revolutionary Guards Corps kept her company for the ride. They hinted to King they were driving her to Fordow, one of seventeen known nuclear weapons sites in Iran. The secret site, in which UN inspectors only learned about in 2009, was built as a nuclear fuel enrichment plant at an old Revolutionary Guards Corps' base. But Fordow wasn't a missile site facility. So why were they taking Kim Dong-Sun there?

The truck drove up a long, steep road. It followed the rough incline into the narrow gap of a mountaintop, crossed over the summit, and on the downward slope the hidden base of Fordow came into view in a dusty, rugged bowl of rock.

A borrow pit sat next to the entrance with excavated earth, rubble, spoils, and a contaminated water aeration pond holding bluish-silver flowback water in a geotextile-lined pool. That reminded Jenny of chemical-laden hot fracking pools back in the states. Dusty gray roads swept this way and that around the base, with one road slanting down to the gate of an underground tunnel. The lone freestanding three-story building stretched as long as an aircraft carrier to the base of a mountain. The cover structure hid an ongoing dig of the underground facility to expand, Agent King figured, the 3,000 centrifuges that were already humming to enrich uranium from the eyes in the sky of satellites, spy planes, and stray drones.

The truck drove down the road to the tunnel, rumbling, bouncing, jostling about, kicking plumes of dust in its wake before stopping at a gate. The driver handed papers to armed guards wearing masks. They checked the vehicle and then asked Dong-Sun for her passport and papers.

Jenny King handed the North Korean engineer's stolen passport with her photo replacing the real Dung-Sun's photo. She explained to the guards that the Americans took her papers when she was kidnapped and hauled across the border into Iraq. With the papers missing, the guard made a radio call, eyeing with suspicion, and waited.

A few minutes later, the Iranian nuclear engineer Ferdows, with whom she worked with at the missile site in the Syrian desert, emerged. The old scientist looked into the rear of the truck and saw the North Korean missile engineer sitting in her dirty uniform. He made eye contact with her; she nodded with a stone face. Ferdows put his hand on the guard's shoulder, and whispered. The guard waved her to step out of the vehicle. He led her and Ferdows down into a side door of the underground facility. A pair of Revolutionary Guards trailed the engineers, entering a tunnel by way of an elevator shaft that traveled far down into the earth.

If she wasn't so tired or disoriented from the long ride—Ferdows had flown back to Iran from Syria, he told her—she might have counted whether the elevator rode down six stories or seven.

The metal door lifted open. Ferdows led Dong-Sun down a passage, through a corridor, and into a heavily guarded weapons room. She figured that the hall of German-made centrifuges had to be nearby, behind one of the three walls in the large rectangular room, populated with scientists and Iranian army and naval officers, checking out the latest Iranian drone—great for photography, poor for taking out either soft or hard targets. Another table had disassembled parts of a torpedo and oddly, beside it, framed photographs of navy dolphins with Iranian divers.

Jenny wondered if the dolphins were left over from the Soviet era. A decade ago, Russia had given Iran ten-to-twelve trained navy dolphins for Iranian waterparks. But did Putin's Russia give Iran more dolphins? And what if the mammals never made it to the waterparks? Jenny knew from her own analysis that Russia had trained 500 dolphins in its marine mammal program, while the US NMMP at its peak in 1987 had 120 dolphins in the program, with 100 today.

Did the Tehran government also take a dozen or so trained biosystems for military use? If so, it was the first she heard of it. And having dated Merk Toten on and off the past couple of years, he mentioned the first half of the story—Russian dolphins sent to Iran for waterpark entertainment—but not the other half for military purposes, which now began to sink in with her and make sense with all that was going on in the Persian Gulf, Yemen, Syria, and Somalia.

Why wait for a missile site to be built in the Syrian desert when Iran was ramping up a plan to attack the West with an armed torpedo or a kamikaze dolphin? Both were low tech, both were disposable, both were low risk, high reward endeavors. The tactics made it easy to deny or to blame on someone else. *So why not use both?* she wondered. Why not attack the West with a torpedo or two and several navy dolphins? The possibility of a dolphin drone fascinated her. The thoughts about timing and logistics perked up her tired bones. She was awakened, riveted.

With a notion of what Iran was capable of, the fatigue that permeated every pore and bone in her body vanished. She was alert again, thinking, contemplating, figuring out what the global plans were for the Iranian-Syrian-North Korean alliance, with a sprinkling of an al Qaeda offshoot. The possibilities blew her mind. Now King had to survive her deep foray into Iran's nuclear weapons program and get word back to Langley that something nasty was going to be launched in the coming weeks. The mother of all terrorist attacks, out-dueling the Paris attacks.

Ferdows stopped at the table. He met with a general and introduced the North Korean engineer he worked with in Syria, saying in Farsi, "This is the comrade who was kidnapped by the CIA. All forty-five kilos of her." Laughter erupted. "Before she was taken, she taught Adad's soldiers how to shoot straight. You should have seen the look on their faces."

The men rippled with laughter; a scientist banged the table joining the hilarity.

"What a puny woman," a revolutionary guard said with more bursts of laughter.

"Don't forget," the scientist chimed in, "you only need a small amount of yellowcake to set off a big chain reaction."

The laughter spread, with Jenny finally joining in, even though she didn't understand a single word. Even hardened Revolutionary Guard Corps could laugh. Who knew? When the joke had run its course and the laughter died down, Jenny scanned the weapons room and didn't spot any other Asians in the space. She was grateful she wasn't put on the spot to answer to a North Korean military officer, who might know the real Kim Dong-Sun.

The scientists and engineers stepped back as Ferdows pulled Jenny toward the table. He swept his arm over the torpedo elements, guidance system, and unassembled parts. She looked at the pieces, but took a closer look of the trained dolphins in the photographs, seeing they were wearing devices on the pectoral fins and harnesses with spikes over their mouths.

Ferdows asked: "Can we insert a load into the torpedo and still use the guidance system?"

"Who designed this?" she asked, knowing the best defense to a technical question she knew little about was to ask more questions—since her training was on missiles, not torpedoes.

Another bearded engineer unrolled the blueprints of the torpedo, which had American naval design logo and a DARPA stamp on each drawing.

"Ah, American," she observed in broken English. "Do you trust design?"

"Of course," Ferdows said with confidence. "General Adad's Syrian Electronic Army hacked these plans last year from a naval contractor in San Diego."

"And the guidance system? Who designed it?" she asked, examining the parts.

"Another American company in the Pentagon's Iron Triangle," Ferdows answered.

"How much space will it lose from the new payload?" Dong-Sun asked.

"Half a hand wide," he replied, using his old wrinkled hand as a reference.

"What are those animals? How will they be used?" Agent King asked, pointing to the pictures of the Russian navy dolphins.

"Six of them will go. They are escorts, some carrying a decoy payload, others the real device," Ferdows said, adding, "We learned to trust technology over time."

"I trust humans less," Agent King said. "Where are the dolphins now?"

"En route from Canada," he replied.

Jenny now knew that America was the target for the attack in the West. In less than half an hour inside the Fordow nuclear enrichment facility, she learned how the dirty bombs were going to be delivered—by water—coming into some port city in the United States. She didn't push her luck in asking which city, as she was sure the real answer, if it were already selected, wouldn't be shared with the engineers and scientists. She turned to Ferdows, announcing, "I need to eat, wash up, sleep on the torpedo design. I need to discuss this with my design team back in Pyongyang. Then I can have answer for you in the morning."

"Make sure it's by sunrise," Ferdows said. "The general wants to fly you out to the new missile site in the Kurdish mountains tomorrow morning. The recipient will choose a target in the next few days. Torpedoes need to be ready for shipment."

"So soon," Dong-Sun nodded. She took out an old North Korean–made digital camera, and captured pictures of the torpedo and its guidance system. She overheard the engineers speak in Farsi, but zeroed in on two French words their talk included: *Pratique Occulte.*

Why those strange words? she wondered.

Chapter Fifty-Five

———————

A T DAWN, AMID orange sunlight shafting through clouds over
the Gulf of Aden, a pair of Longbow attack helicopters shadowed the Black Hawk that picked up Merk, the dolphins, and the
SEALs along with the supplies. The camouflage nets and foxholes
were abandoned for the pirates or fishermen to figure out how they
ended up on Ceebaad Island.

Merk said not a word to a female biologist about Tasi being pregnant. Both dolphins were cleared for the mission, so Merk would
let the NMMP bio-staff run tests and conduct exit checkups on Tasi
and Inapo to see what they might find, if anything, about Tasi's
pregnancy.

If the second group of hostages were going to be traded and
released for ransom money, then Merk was sure that he and the navy
dolphins' tour of duty of Somalia were over, and they would either
be sent back to Qatar or across the ocean to NMMP in San Diego.
They had exceeded their duty, serving the navy, the Pentagon, and
the intelligence community.

* * *

BACK AT CAMP Lemonnier, the mobile NMMP team separated the
dolphins to run full medical examinations. The CIA agents, with
Dante Dawson in tow, took Merk to the brigadier general's private
dining facility to eat breakfast and do a deep dive on the intel he
gathered.

Merk gave his order to the waiter for cranberry juice, sashimi, seaweed salad, and bowls of blueberries and steamed vegetables. He gazed around reading the somber looks on the agents' faces, then nudged Dante under the table. The ex-navy SEAL CO gave Merk an *oh-shit* stare, and said, "CO Nico Gregorius tried to rescue Nairobi last night . . ." His voice trailed off.

"He did what?" Merk said with a look of surprise.

"Nico shot the Korfa double that Fuller and I met. In a firefight in trying to rescue Nairobi, the warlord and his henchmen killed Nico," Dante said, looking long and hard at Merk.

"CIA asset Nairobi is presumed dead," the CIA case officer added.

"Jesus. Nairobi? Her daughter Fathiya, Triumph, what happens to her?" Merk mouthed in disbelief. It was just the other day that he grabbed her by the leg and pulled her down as he came ashore on Somalia the first time. For Nico he was less surprised. Merk understood the danger of the assignment for himself, the dolphins, and in particular for the SEAL CO, as they had been there numerous times before. But for Nairobi it was somehow quite a shock. Perhaps it was related to his feelings he had about Tasi being pregnant in some subconscious way. At that table seated with those men, Merk Toten felt more conflicted about his hardened SEAL past and what to do with the navy dolphins than ever before: release them to the wild or defend the United States, bound to come under attack.

Whatever his decision, Merk couldn't let Tasi birth a calf in the confines of the Navy Marine Mammal Program. He would have to break protocol, something that had been drilled into him by his Navy mustang father since he was a child.

"Nicholas was able to film and record parts of the firefight. When he was bleeding on the floor, his last act of bravery was to wipe the Satcom clean," the Asian American agent said. "Sorry, man, my condolences." He patted Merk on his shoulder.

Merk downed a glass of water. "When's the Norwegian mercenary going to arrive?"

"He's here. Landed an hour before you arrived," the case officer said.

"Dawson, you and I need to chat with him after breakfast."

"I can't, Toten. Tight window. Better eat fast. I'm outta here at 1100 hours. Will be driving to the Somaliland border to make the next trade of money for hostages."

"Dante, don't you question that? The release of the hostages is happening way too fast. My fin found a dead sailor tied to the propeller of the *Shining Star*. That's a warning General Custer would have heeded entering Indian country."

Chapter Fifty-Six

A T NOON, THE Marine-led convoy drove the Azure Shell hostage negotiating team to the coastal border between Djibouti and Somaliland.

At the request of the Pentagon, the Djibouti Coast Guard followed the meet off coast to ensure that no pirates were going to do an end around at the point of exchange. The arid strip of land—near Zeila—was located a couple of miles inland from the sea where eighteen Oromo immigrants from Ethiopia had died of thirst and starvation some years back. Dante shared that piece of history with Christian Fuller, who rolled his eyes, and said, "Is that our omen or the dead man tied to the prop? Great, let's trade money for the living on the grave of the dead."

A half-mile back a pair of Black Hawk helicopters supported the six-vehicle convoy on the Djibouti side of the border. But it was the CIA drone that flew high across the border that added another layer of security, filming the ruins of Zeila, the mine-clustered *Shining Sea* in the bay, and the fifty-mile wasteland desert that stretched inland to Hargeisa.

What the CIA didn't notice at first, or anyone else at Camp Lemonnier, was that when General Adad landed at Hargeisa Airport, he did more than deliver Qas and another Syrian Electronic Army hacker to Korfa. Adad also dropped off an Iranian-made *Hemaseh*—"Epic"—drone, which Qas and an engineer had assembled in the hangar after the first group of hostages was flown out of Somalia. Way up in the blue over the Somaliland border, the Epic Drone flew a mile higher than the American UAV. With camera and infrared equipment stolen by Chinese hackers from the US military and a defense contractor, the Iranian drone began to track the movements of the UAV, while capturing the border meeting high up in the sky.

Bahdoon, the Yemeni psychiatrist, drove a jeep to the border. He parked the vehicle and pulled a gas mask over his head and face. He adjusted the straps, made sure the filter cartridge canister was set. He opened the door and stepped out unarmed. He walked by himself toward the border, to where Dante and Fuller stood waiting with steel cases of cash in hand for the trade. A cordon of armed marines backed the Azure Shell negotiators, along with the Coast Guard at sea, Black Hawks a klick behind, and the US drone at five thousand feet.

"Look at this scorpion," Dante said to Fuller, a bit miffed by the gas mask.

"I see it, stinger and all."

"Hey, Somali, take the mask off. The air is fine out here to breathe," Dante shouted.

"Christ, what happened to wearing al Qaeda black pajamas?" Fuller said, eyeing the buttoned-down, khakis-wearing doctor.

Bahdoon waved Dante to cross the border to confer on behalf of the hostages' release. Using a mobile phone app as a voicebox, he asked, "Do you have all the money this time?"

"Yes. For the dead American SEAL, the Danish captain, and hostages from the *Shining Sea*," Dante said, pointing to the suitcases. "The money is all here, two million large."

"No, no, no. What about the ships?"

"You're emptying oil as we speak in Berbera. You mined the container ship off Zeila. You killed a sailor and tied him to the propeller. Now you want more money for bad behavior? It's not going to fucking happen," Dante said, standing his ground.

Bahdoon didn't argue the points. He stood where Korfa didn't dare to stand, near the border, in fear of being shot like his brother or assassinated like his body double. The warlord wasn't about to take any chances. Bahdoon nodded and ambled back to the jeep. He pressed a number on a mobile phone, summoning a bus to drive the hostages to the border.

Both sides waited for the olive-green bus to arrive. Dante and Chris Fuller waited and watched, when finally the bus pulled around the dusty bend and arrived at the gate.

As the hostages climbed out of the bus, shielding their eyes from the bright sun, which they hadn't seen in days, one Marine began filming the release. In good faith, Dante stepped over the border and dropped off one case of money. Until he saw the Danish captain and CO Nico Gregorius in a body bag, he wasn't going to release the other case of money.

A young pirate handler picked up the suitcase and carried it on board the bus, to see if all of the money was there. Five minutes went by when the bus flashed its headlights, signaling that the trade had been accepted. It took another few minutes with no sign of activity in the bus that gave Dante pause. He started to wonder if the final trade would go down at all. Just when he was about to tell Fuller to enact Plan B, a Land Rover drove up behind Bahdoon at the border. For a long, tense moment the Land Rover, too, sat idling.

"Full, what's going down?" Dante whispered. "Why the gas mask?"

"Psycho warfare? . . . Or he's hiding his identity," Fuller observed.

Dante turned around and stared at Bahdoon, studying his posture, watching his hand motions and gait, his height—five-foot-six at most—weighing around 140 pounds. "Mm-hmm," Dante agreed with Fuller's assessment. "Film his ass so we can find out who he is." The former FBI special agent nodded, and subtly clicked a button on his Satcom signaling the marine to zero in and film the pirates.

Before the marine could target Bahdoon, the man climbed into the jeep and backed away. But Dante was able to film the gas mask pirate doing just that with his smartphone. A pair of Somali pirates stepped out of the Land Rover—they too were wearing gas masks. One led the harried Danish captain at gunpoint toward Dante at the border. The other pirate dragged a body bag out of the vehicle and dumped it on the ground—a clear sign of disrespect. Dante's neck veins bulged. He was livid. He clenched his fists and bit his lower lip, gnashing his teeth.

A couple of marines took aim at the Somali pirate escorting the captain to the border crossing. Dante held up a fist for the Marines to lower their weapons. The pirate, breathing hard through the gas mask filter, stopped the captain in front of Dante, pointing at the other suitcase of money, the firearm now pressed to the back of the captain's head.

Fuller took a couple of marines over the border with him to check on the contents of the body bag. A marine unzipped the bag; Fuller stooped over and matched the dead SEAL CO Nico Gregorius with photos of him. He pulled the CO's dental records, and checked it against the teeth in the corpse's mouth. They matched. He then scanned Nico's finger- and palm-prints.

Fuller looked back at Dante and nodded, then wiped a tear leaking from his eye. He and the marines carried the dead CO back across the border. Another marine carried the second suitcase across the border and placed it in front of the jeep. When the contents of the suitcase were inspected inside the Land Rover, the vehicle flashed its headlights, signaling the pirate to release the Danish captain.

With the beat-up captain weak in the legs, Dante put his arm around the Dane and escorted him across the border, handing him off to a couple of marines, who took the *Blue Heaven* captain into medical care.

Dante snapped a photo of the pirate heading back to the Land Rover, then turned around and crossed the border back to Djibouti.

All that remained of the attacks were the hijacked ships. There, NATO and Centcom would call the shots on how to proceed to defeat or contain the pirate cells in Somaliland. But if it were up to Dante, he would have the CIA drone hovering above bomb the Land Rover right that minute and forget bargaining for the ships or the cargos.

Chapter Fifty-Seven

THE CIA AGENTS blocked Merk from talking to Dante about grilling the Norwegian sniper Peder Olsen, since Dante was no longer in the military. They insisted that the former SEAL CO could only be used as an intermediary in hostage negotiations. For Merk, they went further and put a call to their FBI counterparts in Washington to keep Merk away from Olsen altogether.

The CIA shafted Merk. He felt the knife stab in his back. He knew something deeper was going on than the typical agency turf war. So he went to the intel fusion center to conduct the interview himself. He called on a favor from an E-9 Marine sergeant major, who led the Norwegian sniper into the dining hall. When Merk arrived, Peder sat on a chair backward, his meaty forearms folded on the backrest. The sniper stared at Merk with a cocky smirk. Noting his sunburn was on the mend, Merk motioned a young, green ONI officer to leave the building. The young naval intel officer said nothing as he exited the door. Merk double bolted the door and strode back to Peder.

"So you are the dolphin trainer I heard about," Peder said in a testosterone-fueled tone.

Merk stood in front of the Norwegian sniper. "We're not here to talk about dolphins. My op is classified."

"I'm not? Then what am I here for?" he asked, grinning a stupid smirk.

Merk stepped over to a table next to Peder and poured a glass of water, saying, "No. You're here for—" and splashed the water in Peder's face. He recoiled. Merk grabbed his arm and pulled the

Norwegian down, smashing the glass over his head. He kicked a leg off the chair and threw the sniper hard to the floor. Merk pulled Peder's arm flat, twisting the hand at the wrist, grinding his elbow in Peder's jaw, pinning his head to the ground. Merk put a knee on Peder's flattened elbow, freeing his right hand that held a jagged shard of glass and waved it over the mercenary's eyeball.

Peder slapped the floor with his other hand, crying, "Uncle, uncle. Stop. Stop it."

Merk rolled over the sniper's back, sprung to his feet, and ripped his long-sleeve shirt open, tearing it off, revealing his burn-scarred flesh and the orange and silver "Broken Daggers" tattoo on his right breast. It was the tattoo of the Navy SEAL trident on Merk's biceps that told Peder everything he needed to know about Merk Toten, a former SEAL Team Six member.

Merk pulled a chair over and sat down waiting for the Norwegian to get up.

Peder shook his numbed hand and wrist, rubbing his elbow as he rose to his knees. He eyed Merk's warped flesh, which looked like melted candlewax. He wringed his wet hair with his fingers, and sat down in a new chair across from the dolphin whisperer, muttering, "Sorry, didn't know."

"Norseman, you do know something," Merk said. Peder looked in Merk's eyes and said nothing. "Let me help you. Norway has been soft on terror for a long time, but not you. In summer 2011, the socialists, forever on a terrorist holiday, allowed a super lone wolf to bomb government buildings with a slow-acting, large-volume fertilizer bomb, blasting out the facades in a shock wave. But the madman wasn't done. What did the Norwegian police and authorities do? Nothing. Your goddamn government did squat to prevent the lone wolf from taking a Sunday drive up the highway, past toll booths, cruise deep into the countryside, take a ferry ride, and assassinate seventy kids and adults at a summer camp island. Great shit. Impressive."

Peder stared at the navy dolphin trainer, who clearly showed his US Navy SEAL counterterrorism background. *"Ja,"* he finally spoke up. "Add the Norwegian telecom giant Telenor to the list of defense failures. In 2013, they were breached by Chinese or Iranian hackers, who injected fifty Trojan horses through a zip file in one email sent to all thirty thousand employees. The phishing attack allowed the hackers to sit and wait, like a sniper, like me, a finger on the trigger, and then on one late Friday night in Oslo wipe all the data from Telenor's executives' laptops, desktop, and mobile devices. That was really embarrassing."

"Yeah, it was," Merk agreed. "Now, I need your help. A terrorist strike on the West is in motion. And I'm going to stop it." Peder opened his mouth about to say something, but then stopped. He looked at the floor and then watched Merk step to a wall screen. With a remote, the dolphin trainer clicked on the drone image of the *Blå Himmel* supertanker anchored in Berbera. The image had two red circles embedded on it, one marking the roof of the bridge, where Peder fired the shots, and the other all the way across the deck to the bow, the blood pool where he felled Samatar. "What did you fire? . . . Two, maybe three shots?" Merk asked; Peder nodded. "Your job as a vessel protection detachment guard was to protect the ship from a pirate attack. But you left the tanker vulnerable to just that. Why? Did you make that decision?"

"Nay, the shipowner."

"Oh, the owner," Merk scoffed, asking, "Why single out a pirate a klick away? Why not shoot the other pirates scurrying across the deck, hundreds of meters closer to you?"

"Who knows why?"

"Goatshit. You know why!" Merk screamed and clicked the next image showing a split-screen of the dorsalcam images of the bombs that were planted underwater on the supertankers' hull. "Squarehead, don't play dumb with me." Merk clicked the next image showing a similar type of bomb used in underwater demolition to decommission an old oil rig. "This is your work from Norway's offshore oil industry, isn't it?"

"I didn't plant the bombs, I swear," he said.

"No, you made them, stored them on the tanker, for the pirates to plant on the hull when they brought the ship to port," Merk said. "They don't make bombs like that in Somalia."

A single tear broke down Peder's face. His hands began to tremble.

Merk noticed both and put the remote down, then said with force, "You and the pirates are goddamn pawns to something much bigger than hijacking ships. It's for a spectacular attack, isn't it? The two ships were taken by design. The piracy was a dry run, wasn't it?"

"*Ja*, shit."

"Shit? People are going to die. Radicalism is spreading. Who paid you to kill Samatar?"

"Don't know," his somber voice cracked.

"Who gave the order?"

"Korfa."

"Who does he work for?"

"Something, er, like . . . Svarte Occult."

"Black Occult? Who the hell are they? A splinter group?"

Peder shook his head *no*.

Merk ran Korfa through his mind. It all began to make sense. A hard rap banged the steel door. Merk ignored the noise and the shouts to open it.

He looked hard at Peder, saying, "If you're holding anything back, I will hunt you down in prison or your homeland. You got it?"

Chapter Fifty-Eight

D EEP IN THE bowels of Fordow nuclear fuel plant in Qom, Iran, Kim Dong-Sun emerged from the R&D laboratory. After vetting the missile engineer with questions that only she would know about her kidnapping in the Syrian desert with General Adad, Ferdows gave Quds security an all-clear that Kim Dong-Sun was one and the same person he worked with in Syria.

Ferdows took Dong-Sun on a brief tour of the plutonium enrichment plant.

In recent years, Qom had taken over 20 percent of the centrifuges processing yellowcake from the US-targeted Natanz facility. So the Israeli Stuxnet worm, planted in the computer system in June 2010, had no impact on Iran's overall capability to enrich uranium; neither did the nuclear treaty with the US in 2015. Stuxnet was a mere speed bump in the process. Jenny saw with her own eyes that Iran wasn't going to comply with any nuclear arms agreement.

Having written a brief in the round Korean script on what elements should be included in retrofitting a missile guidance system for a torpedo, she handed it to Ferdows and requested to be transferred to a project for her missile engineering expertise.

Ferdows studied the document, but couldn't read Korean. "This is?"

"The new design," Kim said without emotion. "If you need a translation, email it to my colleague at the Syrian missile site or to your contact in North Korea."

"I will. What does it say? Are you recommending a fix?" the scientist asked.

"Smaller capacitor inserted sideways will give you the eight centimeters you need," she pointed out on the sketch. "A tight fit. But don't use Silicon Valley's commercial GPS system. That's not reliable." He looked at her perplexed. "When you control the steering of a torpedo near the surface, you can't risk the satellites' triangulation being off," she replied. "Have the Syrian Electronic Army hack into the Pentagon and use the US military's GPS system. It's far more accurate."

"But that's hidden behind a strong firewall."

"Yes, for you, but not me," she said. "I can show the cyber Syrians how to get inside."

Ferdows nodded, thinking her recommendations over, especially the one about hacking the US military GPS network. That was a good piece of insight. "Anything else?"

"Yes. I am ready to fly to the new missile site at Lake Urmia you mentioned," she said. "By the way, what happened to the old missile facility?"

"Badr near Teheran? A few years ago, Badr missile site suffered an explosion that destroyed two buildings."

"How did that happen? Saboteurs?"

"The revolutionary guards, who run the facility as they do here, said it was sabotaged. It could have been an accident. . . . Who knows? The Guard Corps are rebuilding the site now, hardening the fifty missile silos there," Ferdows said.

She nodded and followed Ferdows into the communication room.

If I get out of Iran alive, one bomb will misfire, she thought to herself, calculating that when the Syrian Electronic Army hacked into the military GPS satellite network, she would have the Pentagon redirect the torpedo from harm's way and alert Merk about the Russian navy dolphins.

But for that to happen, she had to get out of Iran.

Chapter Fifty-Nine

THE HELICOPTER RIDE over the mountain ranges of Kurdistan in northwest Iran was about to deliver Jenny a great deal closer to Iraq, the Kurds, and pockets of ISIS, all less than one day's drive to the border. Her immediate goal of exiting the hardline country with the Ayatollah's vow to destroy Israel and attack America became her only task, her singular goal, her only mission.

Sitting in the cargo bay with armed revolutionary guards, she avoided eye contact. She shut her eyes to feign taking a nap. Jenny, dressed as Kim Dong-Sun, began to run a slew of what-if scenarios with their potential outcomes, good and bad, in her mind when the helicopter touched down before sunset at the Lake Urmia missile site.

The worst-case scenario: Jenny would be exposed by her North Korean colleagues for being an imposter, in which case she would have to fight her way out of the base and then find a way to leave the country to Iraq, which was close enough by vehicle, but not on foot. The latter would take days. She also understood the longer she met with the real Dong-Sun's North Korean fellow engineers and scientists at the new missile site, the greater the risk of her being exposed as a CIA spy.

Upon landing, Agent King needed to move quickly. She had to find the quickest, most discrete way to vanish, to make her way over the Kurdistan Mountains to the border of Iraq. She had to escape. She had to make it. She had to give all the intelligence she collected to the directorates in Langley so they could act, with terrorist city and targets still unknown.

* * *

THE HELICOPTER SLOWED down as it approached the base under construction. Behind it, the big bowl of depleted salt water Lake Urmia spoke about the severity of the region's drought, which like ISIS extended from Syria through northern Iraq to the northwest corner of Iran. Lake Urmia looked like Las Vegas's dying Lake Mead—with Iran's overbuilding of dams accelerating its death. Urmia once was a favorite resort for thousands of Iranians. She saw several abandoned houses with ghost docks on the far side of the lake, a stark reminder of the summer days when Iranians used to flock to the resort to bathe and water ski.

Out the window in the foreground, Kim Dong-Sun saw three helipads, a long warehouse structure, and a parking lot half filled with Iranian, Russian, and Chinese-made cars. One of those cars, she posited, was going to come into play as her exit strategy.

When the helicopter landed, the Revolutionary Guards Corps walked Dong-Sun across the helipads to the rear entrance of the building. The door opened and an Iranian military officer greeted her. He led her to a debriefing room, where she was introduced to an Iranian scientist, a European engineer—*a defector?* she wondered—and what she feared was one of her North Korean colleagues. She didn't recognize the Korean engineer; and he didn't give her a hint that he knew Kim Dong-Sun either. So far, she was lucky.

The North Koreans greeted one another with a slight nod. In their native tongue, he congratulated her on the books and white papers she wrote over the years, shaping the missile program from duds falling short of their mark to a new, more robust, more accurate generation of North Korean missiles and guidance systems, stolen from American defense contractors.

She saw a set of plans spread out across the table. Aware of her homeland custom, she could neither point to her colleague nor wave him to pass the plans across the table—since in Korea it was considered rude and bad Western manners. Instead, she lowered her hand, turned it with her palm open facing up, and moved her hand forward. The North Korean engineer bowed to her request and slid the plans across the table to her.

"What do you want to see, Lady Kim?" the Iranian scientist asked.

Also lucky for Jenny, she had studied the satellite, drone, and spy plane images a month before on the Lake Urmia base being built. She noted a third helipad had been built since she saw the recon photos, but recalled there were no silos excavated as of that date, while the parking lot had doubled in size from what she recalled in the helicopter arriving to the base.

Jenny had also spent days studying the shrinking salt lake, some 85 percent in less than two decades. A bad mix of changing climate and man-made pressures caused Lake Urmia's death spiral. With drought the real threat to the region, the lake would soon dry up. Iran had hired a Belgium environmental science and engineering firm to restore the lake. The European company, which was hacked by the NSA, had previously resurrected the Dead Sea from a similar fate. But she doubted they would have success in Iran. Too many dams, built too fast. But then she realized Lake Urmia's restoration project was going to be Jenny's ticket out of Iran.

Dong-Sun spread the plans open. She studied the topography, where the missile pads would be installed in Phase II, and where the half dozen silos would be excavated, cored, and sleeved in Phase III of the project. She pointed to the south bend of the lake, asking "Is this where the shoreline resides today?"

"Good question," her North Korean colleague said.

"I believe that's the shoreline today," the Iranian scientist said, not quite sure.

She put the drawings together, rolled them up, and said, "I need to go outside and conduct a survey of the missile silo locations."

"I will come with you," her colleague said.

"No. I need to work alone. I think clearer when there's silence, the absence of chatter. Then I need to sleep on what I observe," she said. "By morning I will have an answer."

"I will send a guard to accompany you," the Iranian scientist said, insisting, "He will be quiet. He doesn't speak Korean or English."

Knowing she couldn't say no to the Iranian watchdog, Kim Dong-Sun nodded. She believed there would be no way to walk the shoreline alone. If she had to take out someone to make her escape, it might as well be a revolutionary guard sentry. She looked at her colleague, saying, "Wait for me for dinner. I will be back in two hours."

He nodded to her. They saluted each other.

Dong-Sun headed out of the office with the guard in tow. She stepped out into the setting sun as she exited the building. She would need to wait for dusk before she would attempt her escape, first by neutralizing the watchman, then searching for a car to steal in the parking lot. Outside, she noted that there was only one surveillance camera on the far end of the lot. She wondered if the lone closed-circuit TV cam was operational or even had its lens installed and software tested and operational.

Jenny walked the shoreline, past salt shapes, salt figures, and salt mounds, shadowed by the Iranian guard. She thought about the Book of Genesis and Lot's wife, when the woman of lore stopped to look back at the destruction of Sodom—the fallout from a comet, Jenny now knew—and was turned into a pillar of salt.

The engineer looked behind Dong-Sun and identified the old shoreline with water markings on boulders. She saw a line of survey stakes driven into the ground, showing where a couple of the missile silos would be installed. She marked up the layout drawing, adding notes for more stakes to those locations.

When dusk finally arrived, Jenny began to make her move. She placed the plans on the ground and used large rocks to keep the wind from rolling the plans back up. Then she waved the guard over and asked him to take a look at the layout on the plans and the shoreline across the lake. As she pointed to the buildings around the rim of the lake, she showed the structures on the plans with the piers extending out into the dried lakebed. The guard looked over at the buildings, and then down at the plans, and then back again. As he studied the rim of the lake, Jenny lifted a heavy rock, raised it over her head, snuck behind him, and smashed the guard in the back of the skull, knocking him out cold, if not killing him, Cain and Abel style.

His slackened body collapsed on the plans; rills of blood dripped over the blueprints.

Jenny tossed Kim Dong-Sun's hat toward the edge of the lake, suggesting she went missing in the water. Adjusting her eyes to the darkness, she backtracked her footprints to mislead those who found the guard that something bad happened to her, too.

At the edge of the parking lot, Jenny scanned the other side of the new base building for people—clear—while moving furtively toward the cars. With only two light poles installed, she needed to stay out of the lights to find a vehicle to snatch.

Jenny picked up her pace. She read about the history of bank robbers, how many who were successful planned little, taking only the risk to show up and improvise—which often caught the police in a different location, unable to respond. She took the same now-or-never approach on timing, too; that no one would come looking for her or the guard for another hour; that no one would arrive at the base that night to witness her escape; and that no emergency or fire drill would empty the building with the Revolutionary Guards Corps and missile scientists spilling out into the parking lot while she made off with one of their vehicles.

Timing and luck would play a pivotal role in aiding her escape.

Along the back of the parking lot, she combed the vehicles, hoping that the base didn't have some strict policy on turning in the keys to the security personnel until it was time to leave. Jenny stayed low, sliding from car to car, pulling at locked door handles, peeking inside to see what tools or equipment she could steal. By the fifteenth or so car, she had found all the doors were locked and, other than a few Iranian newspapers and food wrappers in the front seat, the cars were empty, not worth breaking into.

Half dozen cars later, Jenny found an unlocked door. She slinked inside and searched for keys under the visor, no; under the seat and floor mat, no; and in the glove box, no. It too was empty. So she pried open the plastic housing of the ignition, ripped the colored wires from the steering column, leaving the neutral wire dangling, and hot-wired the car, starting the engine. She put the car in reverse, lifted the break, feathered the clutch, and rolled backward, eyeing the gas tank. She was in luck: There was half a tank of gas to travel over the mountainous roads, some washed out to a single lane in the lowlands and some bedded with gravel. She had enough fuel to take a one-way ride to the Iraqi border and on to the ISIS-repelled town of Erbil, where she would rendezvous with the Kurdish leader Behar.

Without fanfare, CIA clandestine operator Jenny Myung King left the world of Kim Dong-Sun behind. She drove by the under-construction and unmanned guardhouse. Unarmed, except for maybe a tire-iron in the trunk, she felt naked, exposed, but full of relief.

Driving west on Iran Route 26 took Jenny down through the mountains to Iran's Kurdish-inhabited border city of Piranshahr. There she had a CIA asset that could drive her across the border to meet Behar. And when Jenny made it across the border without firing a single shot, she had a story to tell her "no gun" hero boyfriend Merk Toten how she accomplished the feat.

Jenny cracked the window and peered outside to the stars in the night sky.

She looked at her fingers gripping the steering wheel and eyed the black splatter dots and black streaks coating them. It was the blood of the Iranian Guard. The night was calm.

Chapter Sixty

U NDER THE GIANT canopy at Camp Lemonnier, the marines and the CIA and FBI agents joined the on-base SEALs, Merk, some of the NMMP team, along with the Azure Shell negotiators, Dante Dawson and Christian Fuller. They attended the twin memorial service for slain SEAL Commanding Officer Nico Gregorius and drowned Special Forces veterinarian Lt. Morgan Azar.

Their bodies were placed in flag-draped caskets, ready for the next day flight back to the United States via Dover Air Force Base in Delaware for final burial at Arlington Cemetery.

The Navy Marine Mammal Program team began planning the return of navy dolphins, Tasi and Inapo, Lt. Merk Toten, and half of the bioteam of biologists, technicians, assistants, and veterinarians to the United States, with the balance of NMMP staff being returned to Qatar for ongoing surveillance duties in the Strait of Hormuz and the lower Persian Gulf.

With moving closing words from a marine brigadier general on "sacrifice" followed by a solemn prayer given by the naval chaplain, the CIA agents and SEAL Lt. Commander Kell Johnston escorted Merk to the intel fusion center. A tall, well-groomed ONI attaché, dressed in navy white uniform, told Merk that the sea-mines planted near the *Shining Sea* were stolen from the last Iraq War, when the NMMP dolphins cleared mines from the Tigris and Euphrates Rivers delta in the Persian Gulf in 2003.

Merk remembered the operation, since it was that mission that sparked his interest in navy dolphins as a member of SEAL Team Six. He had met the NMMP dolphin master who had trained the half dozen dolphins that were involved in the mine-clearing operation in the confines of the shallow waterway, where naval minesweeping craft couldn't enter.

On the sea-mines planted around the container ship, Merk told the ONI attaché that the bombs planted on the starboard hull of the *Blå Himmel* were made by the Norwegian sniper, who was a diver familiar with oil rigs, undersea welding, tech dives, and marine engineering projects and inspections. In taking in the former SEAL's observations, the ONI attaché asked Merk the relevance. He replied, "Not one device can be traced to al Qaeda, ISIS, Iran, Syria, Yemeni affiliates and offshoots, or the Somali pirates."

Those words stopped the attaché cold. Merk and the others continued to the door, showed their ID badges, which were scanned by marine guards, who let them into the fusion center one at a time.

Merk sat down in front of the wall screen. The ONI attaché entered last and closed the door behind him. He fixed his eyes on the dolphin whisperer; Merk eyed him back, and said, "The new war is here, isn't? This isn't the Paris terrorist attacks or the bombing of a Russian plane over the Sinai." The room fell silent. All eyes fell on Merk. "So I will break protocol."

"Lt. Toten, what do you mean by that?" the Asian American CIA agent asked.

"We're chasing a fenemy . . . a 'faceless enemy,'" he began to explain. "Sure, we know who they are. They're the usual suspects. Let's tag them with blame. Al Qaeda, some splinter group in Africa or Yemen, AQAP, bin Laden's offspring, the Taliban, al Nursa, ISIS butchers, Somali pirates, Syrian rebels, the Iranian Quds force. Call it that and their names will pop up."

"Your point being?" the ONI attaché sitting next to Merk asked.

"What if the hydra-head was connected? A lead brain overseeing fringe elements?"

"That would be worse than Western converts or the ISIS-embedded flood of Syrian refugees to Europe and North America," the attaché agreed.

"A super alliance. An alliance with a common goal to attack our interests, distract us, decoy us, divert us, bait us, to get us to chase our own tail, to blame others, to hunt ghosts in shadows, to put America in its place, with a long-term goal to destroy our freedoms. What would the next evolution of the al Qaeda and ISIS doctrine look like? Yet be cloaked in stealth."

The intel officers at the table looked at one another, wondering where Merk was going with the insight. Merk sat forward, took three glasses of water, and aligned them in a triangle. "Syria-Somalia," he said, touching one glass, then the second glass, "Iran-Yemen," and then the third, "North Korea . . . this is not George Bush's 'Axis of Evil.' It's a new paradigm, run not at the top by each rogue entity, but by unseen middle layers. That's far more dangerous."

"Come again?" Kell Johnston uttered. "The planning doesn't come from fanatics and dictators, but from military generals and warlords fed up with taking orders from their leaders?"

"Now throw in borderless al Qaeda, American and Euro jihadists, the Somali pirates, their ilk, and all the copycats and wannabes," the ONI attaché added with a look of concern, coming to grips with a cold new reality. The CIA agents gazed at one another.

Merk pointed at the attaché, saying, "Every piece of intel we gather is either a false lead, a trapdoor, a diversion, or some item that can't be verified, that can't be traced back to its rogue source, yet falsely accuses another party. And then we have another problem." He dropped a teabag into the middle glass of water and they watched the water change color, with the tea leaching out of the bag, spreading around the glass. "We need to read their tea leaves to know what they are planning to do next. Set off a dirty bomb, an incendiary device?"

"Okay, Toten, you're onto something," the Asian American CIA agent said. "We have another slice of evidence for you." He aimed the remote at the wall screen and clicked images of a US drone and a Longbow Apache attack helicopter that shot the inferior Iranian drone out of the sky. More infrared images showed that the wreckage of the drone had fallen into the outer bay off Zeila, near the shoals of Ceebaad Island, where Merk and the dolphins operated the night before, collecting intel on the hijacked ship. "We downed the Iranian drone three hours ago," he said. "Now do you think it's untraceable?"

Chapter Sixty-One

DAWN. WITHOUT INFORMING the CIA agents, Merk and the ONI attaché took Peder Olsen out of the brig and escorted him with a pair of MPs to a nondescript warehouse. Inside, Tasi and Inapo were housed until they were going to be transported back to the Naval Amphibious Base in Little Creek, Virginia.

"Hey, Toten?" Dante called out, running over.

Merk wheeled around to the hostage negotiator. He spotted the mobile phone in Dante's hand and put his hand up to halt him. He motioned the ONI attaché to take Peder into the warehouse, where he would join them in a moment.

"Merk, listen—"

"Dante, don't break my rules about PDAs and the biologic systems," Merk said, pointing at the mobile phone. "My op is classified. Turn the device off."

"What? You mean, your fins being stationed here?" he said, pointing to the warehouse.

"Turn it off, damn it," Merk said, growing incensed. "You breached my op's secrecy."

"I was just going to tell you—"

"Piss off, Dawson. You were inside enemy territory. You engaged the pirates in Hargeisa and at the border. You operated from a runway shared with a Syrian diplo jet," Merk said. "Ten-to-fucking-one Syrian Electronic Army hackers were on board. They scanned and hacked you." He snatched the phone out of Dante's hand and examined it. "Maybe they're listening now."

Merk held his finger to his lips to keep quiet, turned the device off, and handed it back to him. He moved away from his ex-SEAL commanding officer as if the man had contracted Ebola.

Inside the warehouse, Merk joined the ONI attaché, Peder Olsen, and a team of US Special Forces biologists and veterinarians, who were conducting last-minute prep work to get the dolphins ready for dry transport to the new Camp Lemonnier airfield, and then load them onto a C-5 Galaxy cargo plane that would fly them back to the US with half the NMMP team.

Merk led Peder between the two inflatable pools filled waist-deep with salt water. The pools were ringed with tall orange net fences.

"Are these your trained dolphins?" Peder asked.

"They are the ones who spotted your bombs under the super-tanker, and then the next day the sea-mines around the container ship in Zeila bay," Merk said, nudging Peder to stand between the pools. As Peder peered through the net at Tasi, Merk stepped back and nodded to Inapo in the other pool.

The dolphin fluked around in a circle and on the rotation whipped his tail, lashing a rope of water over Peder. The netting vibrated; the pool water sloshed back and forth like an overflowing bathtub. The Norwegian sniper shook off being doused, with water streaming down his face, dripping on the floor. He glared at Inapo, saying, "*Ja*, hell, I'm all wet, thank you."

Inapo bobbed up and down in the pool, laughing, mocking the drenched Norwegian. Peder wringed his clothes and shook his hands dry. Inapo sculled backward on his tail and belly-flopped, splashing Peder again. Thoroughly soaked, he swore in all the Scandinavian languages at the dolphin, threatening to roast Inapo for dinner, when, from behind, Tasi splashed the Norseman with a flume of water. Peder turned and sneered at Tasi to stop—when both dolphins splashed him with furious whipping of their tails, chasing him behind Merk.

Peder raised his hands in surrender, backing away from the pools.

The dolphins spun around, clicking, squealing victory whistles, laughing, nodding.

Everybody broke out in laughter at the Norwegian mercenary's expense.

"*Ja*, go get changed. We're leaving to Ramstein AFB in an hour," Merk said.

Chapter Sixty-Two

MERK SAT IN the flight deck of the C-5 Galaxy with the pilot, copilot, navigator, cargo master, and ONI attaché, waiting for the long runway to clear out a trio of incoming C-17 Globemaster III transport planes. The ONI attaché pointed to the first two planes, noting they were from the 18th Air Support Operations Group at Pope Field, North Carolina. It was the third aircraft that drew his attention: The 53rd Electronic Warfare Group from Elgin AFB, Florida.

Camp Lemonnier, which housed 1,800 servicemen and special operations forces, and the latest CIA drone base, was getting bigger, faster. As asymmetrical warfare became the future of the twenty-first century, it all added up to more than drone surgical pinpricks and air strikes to prevent the reemergence of ISIS and its savage attacks.

"Cyberwar is entering a new phase of nastiness," the ONI attaché said. "The cyber assault team is being flown here to bore into the Syrian Electronic Army and Iran's cyberterrorists deployed by the Revolutionary Guards Corps."

"That's one threat to the US, but not the main one," Merk said. "Why go after the hackers with computer code? Why not take out their bunkers? That will send a message."

Not expecting to hear that from Merk, the former SEAL turned pacifist dolphin trainer, the ONI attaché exchanged glances with the cargo master. They watched the last Big Bertha C-17 Globemaster III land heavy, fully laden, rolling across the runway, which had been expanded a few years back to receive the larger transport planes.

The jumbo jet reversed engines, slowing down as it rode toward the end of the runway. The copilot signaled everyone to take their seats.

Once airborne, Merk would go back to the cargo bay to debrief Peder Olsen.

Chapter Sixty-Three

TWO-DOZEN SOLDIERS FROM the 4th Platoon, Brave Battery, 2nd Battalion, sat with their gear, backpacks, and duffel bags on one side of the fuselage. Some were chatting up a storm, others were half asleep, a nod away from deep slumber. Across from them, four MPs stood watch over Peder Olsen, whom they seated in a folding chair as the mercenary tried to grab some shut-eye.

With a tablet under his arm, Merk climbed down from the flight deck and headed over to him. He put the tablet on Peder's lap. "Take a look at these. Tell me what you think."

Peder shook himself awake and looked up at Merk and then at an underwater photo of a rusty boiler-type vessel sitting on the sea-floor. "*Ja*, okay. From where did you get this?"

Merk pulled up a chair and sat next to him, saying, "From your years as an offshore oil diver and a special forces expert in your homeland, show me." He handed the Norwegian a stylus to mark photos on the tablet that intrigued him or sparked questions.

For the next half hour, Peder swiped back and forth through the photos that Tasi and Inapo had captured underwater of the illegally dumped drums, barrels, and oversized boilers off the coast of northern Somalia. Instead of the discarded oil drums being repurposed for Syrian barrel bombs they were used to store waste—toxic, radioactive waste.

Merk glanced at the photos now and then, and thought of the young boy he had met at the cove, his corroded skin, his arms covered in rashes and boils. Then Peder studied one close-up photo. It showed the backside of the half-buried boiler. He enlarged the image, turned the tablet sideways to read a faint inscription or serial number next to the welded seam of the lid on the container. It appeared as if the lettering had been grinded off, not faded from decay, barnacles, or rust. But erased. "Have you showed these to anyone?" Peder asked.

"You're the first," Merk said. "Can I trace the nuclear waste inside those containers?"

"How do you know it's hot?"

Merk flipped through the gallery of photos, scrolled down, showing graphs of the nuclear probe readings Tasi took. For the first time, it dawned on Merk: Tasi was pregnant when he sent her down to search for, locate, and probe the toxic waste—but he didn't know that she was six months pregnant. The readings from the yellowcake refuse, the nuclear waste, or the spent fuel rods punched him in the gut. He felt his shoulders go slack as a stone pressed against his heart with dead, cold weight.

He then thought back to the shock wave created by the blast from the sea-mine blowing up the Iranian fishing trawler. Did that have any impact on Tasi? Did it affect the mother-to-be or her unborn calf? *Damn it,* he thought, knowing he was a fool. He should've listened to Morgan Azar and kept the dolphins out of harm's way. He now regretted more than ever the terrible risk he took, for Azar, for Inapo, for Tasi and her offspring. Now Merk had to see to it that Tasi wouldn't be sent back to the Navy Marine Mammal Program in Point Loma; that he, and only he had to look out for her welfare and that of her calf; and that whatever mission grew out of the terrorist threat he had to make sure he worked with the dolphins, protocol and risks be damned.

"Is that it?" Peder asked, picking at his flaking sunburnt skin.

"You help me, I will help you," Merk said, staring aimlessly at the back of the cavernous fuselage. "I need to know where the hot load came from."

"I have an idea. But I'll need this corner of the image blown up. Err, re-colored and rendered with contrast lightened so I can see it better."

"Roger that," Merk said. "When we land in Ramstein, you're going to be debriefed by an FBI counterterrorism expert. Don't worry, I'll be sitting with you in the meeting."

Chapter Sixty-Four

THE C-5 GALAXY landed on time at US Ramstein AFB. After taxing from the main runway, the transport plane pulled into the hangar, where the base's military police met with the cargo master holding the flight manifest, observation log, and cargo inventory sheet. The ONI naval attaché deboarded the plane and greeted the base MPs.

A cordon of MPs led Merk, the ONI attaché, and Peder Olsen to waiting SUVs that drove them to Building No. 413. Ramstein Air Force Base Headquarters had been built inside a forest perimeter, which contained the base golf course, massive runway, and the nerve center of the US Drone Program, all housed in the confines of thick, tall pine trees.

The MPs took Merk and Peder down into the HQ's intel room, where Merk Toten and Peder Olsen were introduced to FBI Special Agent Diane Wheelhouse. The auburn-haired agent was well dressed in a business suit and heels, her fingernails manicured with Ferrari-red nail polish. Special Agent Wheelhouse wore prescription sunglasses. She firmly shook Merk and Peder's hands, and then made the ONI attaché go to the next room. There, he joined CIA analysts, a pair of FBI counterterrorism agents, and other DIA intel officers in an adjacent soundproof room, where they would watch and listen as the debriefing unfolded.

Merk sat down with the Norwegian mercenary.

"As I said, I am FBI Special Agent Wheelhouse. I will be conducting this interview, which is being recorded," she said in a direct manner. "I'm jetlagged, landing only an hour before you did from LA.

216

That's nine time zones away. So what did this navy . . ." she looked at her notes, ". . . dolphin trainer tell you?"

"Er, what do you mean?" Peder asked.

"Your expectations? Did he promise you the world? Like, you're going home today?"

"Nay, not at all," he said, his facial muscles tightened, glancing over at Merk.

"Good. Today this is your home," she said, clicking a remote.

A wall screen behind Merk showed a split-screen of joint US-Norwegian intelligence agents rummaging through Peder Olsen's house in Stavanger, Norway, and Norwegian police officers rifling through his summer cabin up in the mountains. She clicked the next image that showed a live shot of still more Interpol agents going through the offices and home of the *Blå Himmel* shipowner in Bergen. She clicked another image, pulling up emails and cloud services that Peder had used, then zoomed on a half dozen emails addressed to a charity organization in the Puntland autonomous state. "You recognize these emails? What does P.O. stand for?"

"Pratique Occulte," he said, sinking in the chair.

"*Black Mass?* Nice. Is that the new terrorist group with no affiliation to any other org?"

"Uh, *ja*, I suppose. Um, how did you know the name?"

"It's my job to know. I get around. Who was on the receiving end of your emails?"

"Warlord Korfa." His voice cracked.

"It wasn't him. You were communicating with a CIA asset from Kenyan intelligence code-named Nairobi. She has just been confirmed tortured and murdered. Her raped, bloodied body dumped this morning by her pirate captors. The same terrorists who hijacked the supertanker you were supposed to be guarding, but instead you helped steal," the FBI special agent said, holding up a flash drive. "You used one of these to inject malware into the tanker's nav system, didn't you?"

"My god . . ."

"God's not here. Nairobi is just one person in a growing list of people who will die," she said, slamming the notepad on the table.

She tapped a pen on the table. "Both she and Korfa are being used to mask a much greater enemy alliance," Wheelhouse said, pointing the pen in his face. She clicked the next image, showing the bombs planted on the hull of the tanker.

Peder felt sick to his stomach. He nodded, admitting those were the bombs he had made for the pirates and stored on board the ship before he killed Samatar and escaped.

"Tell me about the bombs," Special Agent Wheelhouse said, pushing the edge of the table into Peder's chest to get his full attention. "Spit it out," she shouted. "You two are not the only bomb experts in this room. What do you think I studied for my master's degree after 9/11? What did the FBI teach me at Quantico after that?"

Diane Wheelhouse adjusted the focus of her high-tech sunglasses, capturing all sorts of biometric data from Peder's reactions: facial contortions, body movements, thermal reactions, the tics, tells, and much more, relaying the data stream to the observation room next door.

* * *

IN THE OBSERVATION room, the intel agents and officers were impressed with how FBI Special Agent Wheelhouse steered the interrogation, drawing out all kinds of biometric data and emotional response so the analysts in the room and back in Langley and Quantico could use it to dive deep into the psyche of the Norwegian sniper. They needed her to turn Olsen over to become an informant.

"I thought the director told her to go easy," an FBI counterterrorist expert said.

* * *

IN THE INTERROGATION room, Diane Wheelhouse hammered away at the facade, at the manhood of Peder Olsen. "What's the makeup of the plastic explosives you used?"

"Let's see . . ." He sighed. "The accelerator blasting cap tubes were—"

"Not the trigger, the material. Tell me," she said, glancing down at the tablet.

"C'mon, Peder, what did you use?" Merk asked, leaning across the table.

"*Ja, ja.* They probably found it," he said, exasperated. "Uh, it was Semtex-H . . ."

"From where?" Wheelhouse pressed, raising her voice again.

"Libya. Err, the same kind of plastique used in the 1988 Lockerbie bombing."

"What else went into the brick?" Merk prodded.

"A few chemicals that introduce more internal oxygen to speed up the expansion of the blast, you know . . . titanium microfibers to guarantee flashpoint," he said, looking lost.

"Well, we know it's not slow-acting fertilizer or one of Assad's chlorine barrel bombs, don't we. How many more of these bombs did you make?" she asked, texting a message to the agents next door in the observation room.

"What do you mean, more bombs?"

"Where are you storing the rest of the material? Who was your goddamn supplier? People are going to die," Wheelhouse yelled. The special agent stood up and stabbed her finger into Peder's flaking, sunburnt forehead. "Wake up, troll, or you might find yourself dead."

"Umm . . . Agent Wheelhouse, you want to lighten up a little," Merk said.

"Hell no. Get in line, sailor," she said. She shook her head at Peder and clicked the final image of a digital map of Olsen's black market network. "Hey, Viking Virus, you recognize any of the names in your network tree on the screen?"

Peder looked at the Venn diagram connecting him to clouds of terrorist organizations in Libya Dawn with the bomb-makers, warlord brothers in the Somali Pirates, Yemeni al Qaeda, and the Syrian Electronic Army. Diane pressed the remote adding a top-level cloud, showing new links down to the middleware of pirates, ISIS, and al Qaeda affiliates backed by an image of Syrian General Adad, Iranian nuclear scientists, and North Korean missile engineers.

"Svarte Occulte," Peder mouthed, shocked by what he saw.

"Olsen, you are a pawn in all this, just a minnow. You know that?" she said. "A lot of people are going to die in the next couple of weeks, unless we intercept them, disrupt their plans, roll up their terrorist network. Do you understand? If it happens, you will die. I'll see to it."

Peder nodded *ja*.

"Korfa has gone missing. He or someone in his inner circle will carry out the attack in the US. The FBI needs to drill down into his network. Are you going to help? Or should the Bureau send you back to Norway in a body bag?" she asked.

His eyes watered; he took a breath. "There's an American I've been chatting with . . ."

"Really? Who was it?"

"I don't know his name. No emails . . . never any emails or texts. Phone calls only made from the shipowner's office. Er, he had a Russian accent," he said.

"Do you have his number?"

He shook his head. "It changed every week. He always called from a new burner phone."

Diane turned around and looked up at a hidden camera in a light fixture, saying, "Do you hear that? Check all of Peder's phone records—after work hours—the loading dock, and go back to the *Blå Himmel* crew who were just released. Confirm Olsen's story."

She waved for Merk to leave the room. When he stepped out and closed the door, she took a picture of Peder with the tablet, informing him, "You cooperate, and you might end up in a cozy prison in Norway. You screw me, I'll make sure you spend the rest of your life in a shit hole prison in Yemen."

Chapter Sixty-Five

I N T H E O B S E R V A T I O N room, Diane Wheelhouse handed over the high-tech glasses to the CIA station chief of Kaiserslautern—"K-Town"—where Ramstein AFB was situated in southwest Germany. The agent told him that she needed to go over some notes with the navy dolphin trainer, to grab some R&R, and then pick up the intel discussion in the morning.

"Great job, Special Agent Wheelhouse." The FBI counterterrorist expert congratulated her for extracting a ton of information from the Norwegian sniper in a short amount of time.

"It's Agent Roundhouse to you," she said amid laughter of the other agents.

Overhearing her words with the station chief, the ONI attaché informed Merk, "Go debrief with her. But don't leave the base. You and I will have dinner late."

"Roger that," Merk said, eyeing the medals on the attaché's white uniform; there was no Purple Heart or medal for bravery.

* * *

O U T S I D E, S P E C I A L A G E N T Wheelhouse flashed her FBI credentials to an FBI driver of one of the SUVs, slipped him 100 euros, and told him she needed the vehicle for a few hours, after arriving jet-lagged from Los Angeles. She opened the backseat door for Merk, who stepped in and closed it. Wheelhouse climbed into the driver's seat, clicked the seat belt lock, and drove down the winding base road to the main gate.

Special Agent Diane Wheelhouse looked at Merk in the rearview mirror, and slowly pulled off a red-auburn wig. She unfurled her long jet-black hair, hand-combing the silk strands down her shoulders. She took off the sunglasses and eyed Merk in the mirror again, this time radiating warmth with her black eyes. Jenny King smiled broadly for the first time in months.

"Jesus, Jenny, you were good in there," Merk said.

"Is that all you have to say, in what . . . almost a year?" Jenny asked.

"My god, great to see you. What's up with your pasty white skin?" he said.

"I played Ms. North Korea," she replied, and cooed in a sexy voice—"So Merk, what should we do in Ramstein? Go bowling? Stay at the base inn? Drink beer with the ensigns?"

"Well, I-I-I—"

"Well, I reserved a suite at a luxury hotel in Kaiser-whatever."

"Kaiserslautern," Merk said, completing the Germanic name. "You do know it's called K-Town by the troops here. My father loved the place. It was a party town back in his day."

"The only K-Towns I know are Koreatowns. And they're located in New York, DC, LA, and Seoul." She pulled up to the gate guardhouse, powered down the window, and asked the MP who approached the vehicle, "I just landed from Camp Lemonnier in North Africa. Do you know any good restaurants nearby?"

The guard first mentioned there was a good German beer hall in the center of K-Town, and then, perhaps trying to flirt with her, said, "Oh, no, wait . . . there's Charles BBQ and the African Grille," he said excitedly, opening the gate for the attractive Asian woman.

Jenny thanked the guard and drove through, with Merk sitting behind her, out of view of the MP. "Okay, Blue, you can come up for air now. We're off base."

"Are we following orders tonight?" he asked with a smirk.

"When have we ever followed orders?" Jenny asked, turning the SUV onto the main road. She headed toward the city of Kaiserslautern, with a population of 100,000 people.

It would be her night to finally let loose, to get lost with her lover and polar opposite in emotion and personality—she the gun aficionado, he the "no gun" hero.

Chapter Sixty-Six

IN THE GRAND hotel suite, Jenny ordered room service, while Merk prepared to take a whirlpool bath in the oversized bathtub. He shouted, "Hey, King, why are you living large tonight?"

She popped open a bottle of champagne. "I've been earning two paychecks for the past nine months. Haven't been able to spend any money from either one. Funny thing is I'll never see what I earned in my North Korean bank account."

"What else?"

"The Revolutionary Guards Corps . . . I was lucky if the pigs bathed every third day. Many reeked of body odor, the spices they ate bled through their stinking pores. Talk about gross," she said. "Reminds me of that dry seaweed smell from the crack of your dorsal fin. Do you still carry that fine odor, honey?"

"You know, another two months inside the Iranian nuclear facility, and your white skin would turn porcelain white."

"And then what, honey? I thought you are attracted to me any way I come," she cooed.

"Yeah, that's great and everything, but . . ." he began to say, but when he turned around his naked, tall, lean body to her—she grinned, holding two glasses of champagne. Wearing only a towel wrapped around her breasts and torso, she handed both flutes to Merk. He put them down by the whirlpool and turned back to admire her standing naked when the towel hit the floor, as she flipped a bar of soap in her hand. "So that's why they call you Special Agent Glass-figure-house—"

"Madhouse to you, sailor," she said and drilled the bar of soap into his chest. She lunged at him, pushing him down into the

224

whirlpool. She tugged at his hair and kissed him on the face, on his lips, and over his mouth, their hot, wet tongues thudding, nurturing one another. She grabbed his cock and stroked it, rubbing her supple breasts and hard nipples against his body. Jenny massaged his balls, running his groin against hers, kissing him passionately. Merk bit her lips, kissing down her chin and swan neck, sliding his tongue over her breasts, as he sucked on her nipples, biting them, then kissing them softly, clutching her buttocks.

"Hmmm, roger that," she swooned, running the tip of his penis against her vaginal lips, arousing her clitoris to stir an orgasm. Being naked with Merk fired up her hollows hot and wet.

Merk slid inside Jenny. He began to make love to her in the bathtub, in the water, where he was born in the sea. Like teenage lovers who hadn't seen each other since summer, Merk and Jenny groped and humped in unison. She kissed him, pulling on and twisting his wet locks, biting and sniffing the strands. He thumped her, nibbling on her earlobe, caressing her neck.

Room service entered and, upon hearing the lovemaking emanate from the bathroom, left the cart of food and stepped out of the presidential suite.

"Do you love your fins more than me?" she whispered, riding him faster, faster.

"Huh, uh . . . you . . . of course," he said, felt a shudder, breathlessly licking her shoulder. "One fin is . . . pregnant."

"By you?" she teased, squeezing her thighs, pumping up and down.

"No," he chortled, delirious, and rolled her over in the tub, pumping her harder.

She wrapped her legs around his waist allowing him to thrust all the way inside her—deeper, stronger, faster. She moaned; he snorted until . . . he felt the pressure build and her body tremble as they climaxed together in a wild, jolting hot spasm.

They spent the rest of the evening in bed touching one another, kissing, caressing, and talking about life late into the night. They didn't need sleep; they needed each other without the wind-blown sand of the Mid-East or the toxic water from the Gulf of Aden.

Chapter Sixty-Seven

"**B**LOWING UP MOSUL," Jenny shouted, "destroying Muslim shrines, tombs, and icons, the Paris attacks has turned the world against ISIS. But this new group—Pratique Occulte—operates in the shadows with big ambitions to take down their enemy. That scares me. They work like me."

Agent King stared out the CIA-chartered jet window to the cotton-ball clouds below. Disguised as a private business jet flying across the Atlantic Ocean to Washington, DC, Jenny sat with Merk and a young female CIA analyst in the plane's digital room. Wearing glasses and dressed in a business suit, Jenny let the analyst lead the meeting. She thought the presence of an outsider peering into their unique worlds, into their separate missions, would benefit discovery and connect the terrorist links they might have overlooked.

The trio went over details and observations that Jenny and Merk had made during their missions. With Peder Olsen being detained by the FBI Counterterrorism Unit at Ramstein AFB, Merk questioned whether he would be of use anymore. But the Norwegian sniper did tip Merk off that the radioactive waste sitting that Tasi found came from Germany. Like the country's march toward clean, renewable energy by decommissioning its nuclear reactors in the south, it came with a cost, with a dirty, seedy underbelly. Merk posited the idea that if Peder did hire a planner, bomb-maker, or some type of scout in the United States, the fact that the mercenary was in US protective custody made it unlikely he would be sought after anymore.

Listening to that reasoning, the CIA analyst coaxed Merk and Jenny to see what dots beyond Olsen could be connected, what common traits or trends might be pulled from their missions, and what extraneous data could be discarded. The process of elimination began on that flight. What US cities would Pratique Occulte target? What landmarks in those cities? And what type of weapons or bombs could they use from the water?

That got Jenny thinking. She turned to Merk and inquired about the pirate hostage negotiations: Who was in charge? How did it go down? And was there any digital image or recording to analyze? Knowing that Dante Dawson was involved, Merk accessed the Navy's Blue Cloud, used a biometric scan, and entered a secure vault containing the Somali mission, where the records were kept, including the trade of cash for hostages at the Somalia-Djibouti border. He opened video clips and still images, rummaging through them, trying to pick an outlier, when his eyes seized on the small-frame pirate wearing a gas mask.

Merk played the audio. They listened to the chat between Dante and the gas mask man, who spoke through a mobile app. "Who's the tango?" Merk asked, referring to the terrorist.

"Can't make out his face. But look there." Jenny pointed to a shock of straight black hair. "That's not a Somali's wild locks. It's groomed."

Merk then noticed lighter brown skin between a glove and the long sleeve on the man's wrist, asking, "Is that Mid-Eastern blood? . . . Egyptian? . . . Yemeni? . . . Syrian?"

"Could be Iranian," the CIA analyst said, typing the file name in an email and sent it to digital analysts in Langley to see what they would come up with in their search for an identity to the mystery pirate. Jenny sent the same information to CIA Agent Alan Cuthbert, who had kidnapped her in the desert.

As they waited for replies, Jenny scrawled a list of items on a Smart Board:

- *Missing fissile material from Iran's Fordow nuke facility*
- *ISIS-stolen uranium from Iraq university*
- *ISIS-stolen chemical weapons from Syria and Iraq? What type of gas agents?*

- *What kind of dirty or suitcase bomb?*
- *Syrian missile site and Syrian Electronic Army collaboration?*
- *Iranian guidance system for torpedoes*
- *Russian navy dolphins in Canada or US? How many?*
- *North Korean missile guidance technology—stolen from America*
- *Korfa's US connections and network?*
- *Middle East man in gas mask—a dark omen?*

* * *

MERK SHOWED THEY had to work on the list from the top down. He told them to think in terms of cloaking data, erasing digital bread-crumbs, leaving few electronic prints that could be traced back to the *fenemy* of Iran, Syria, Yemen, North Korea, and Somali pirates.

They knew sleeper cells were probably inside the United States already. On the gaps and bottlenecks of information, Merk, Jenny, and the CIA analyst ran through obvious targets for a sea-level bomb delivery. The usual terrorist targets of Boston, New York, Philadelphia, Miami, Baltimore, and Washington, DC, all fit the bill on the Eastern Seaboard, while the West Coast's big three of Seattle, Los Angeles, and San Francisco made the list. Then Merk added, "What about San Diego? Home to the Pac Rim Command, the Navy SEALs in Coronado, and NMMP on Point Loma?"

Jenny sat back and opened her eyes wide. "I got it. When's Memorial Day?"

"In two weeks," the CIA analyst said, lifting her glasses, eyeing Jenny and Merk.

"New York City's Fleet Week, that's it," Jenny said with clarity. "A few years ago, Fleet Week didn't happen because of the stupid sequester. But now . . ." As Jenny searched for a list of politicians and dignitaries attending Memorial Day celebration, her tablet pinged.

She opened Cuthbert's reply, looked at the picture of the gas mask man side by side with a small Arab man wearing glasses, lurk-ing in the back of the crowd at the drone strike protest in Jaar, Yemen. There the man stood outside the terrorist safe house the CIA bombed. She digitally blew up his face, clicked open a metadata tag, and read the caption: "'His name is Bahdoon. A psychiatrist educated in France' . . . so the French name, *Pratique Occulte*, makes sense."

"He's the brains behind Korfa's Somali muscle," Merk added.

"There's another problem," Jenny said. "If Bahdoon met Dante at the border and the SEA hackers breached his mobile phone . . . well, Merk, they know who you are."

Chapter Sixty-Eight

A FTER SPENDING MORE than eight hours in meetings with Jenny, her superiors, teams of analysts, and clandestine operators, the CIA put Merk up for the night at Langley. In the morning, he ate breakfast with Jenny and the CIA director in his seventh floor corner office.

The plan was moving forward. While they finished egg whites and bowls of fruit, two stories beneath them, a team of CIA analysts began to connect the dots with NSA intercepts, the National Reconnaissance Office, and other intel agencies that matched Bahdoon to Qas, the Syrian Electronic Army hacker, and General Adad, and the Somali warlord brothers. From there they knew the contacts supplied to them via Agent Jenny King on the Iranian scientists and the North Korean missile engineers.

The last gap they had to close was Korfa. Why did he order Peder Olsen to kill his brother Samatar? What would the Somali pirates gain from their pact with Pratique Occulte?

Narrowing the gap with Olsen's Russian contact in America would prove difficult; Merk wrote it off. Instead, he told the CIA director that Olsen was now contaminated goods; he was radioactive and no longer needed as a fall guy to pull off a terrorist operation.

For Merk, the next phase was all about getting the supplies and pods of navy dolphins to New York without detection. That meant coordinating with SEAL teams, who would dress both in civilian clothes and military uniform to begin the search for the dirty bomb from either Iran or a stolen chemical weapons cache from Syria.

The claim of several Russian-trained dolphins and a couple of torpedoes deepened the nature and threat of the attack. But King's eyewitness account did bear out that dolphins and torpedoes were going to be used in some form, and that would limit the terrorist attack to one US city, and not two like during the 9/11 attacks that struck New York and Washington.

Chapter Sixty-Nine

M ERK DROVE THROUGH Gate One at Naval Amphibious Base Little Creek, escorted by a guard to Gate Three and the base Pass Office. There he was given restricted clearance to the base. They drove him to a storage facility by the shore at Crescent Cove.

The boats and craft usually moored in the slips of the cove had been moved out to other marinas around the base. That was to facilitate the temporary installation of Marine Mammal Systems holding pens, where Tasi and Inapo took residence. Portable veterinary clinics were set up around the slips on land in tents and mobile trailers, while trainers and EOD divers began to ferry rubber boats into the slips.

Before Merk could reconnect with the dolphins he trained overseas, a SEAL Team Two commanding officer and an ONI official had to debrief him. They led Merk into the storage warehouse. Inside, Merk noted the building had little insulation and no soundproofing. He requested acoustic soundboards with cones be installed to dampen background noise that would impact the dolphins, while preventing passersby from eavesdropping.

The ONI liaison entered the request on a tablet, captured pictures of the bare corrugated metal walls, and sent the photos in with the request.

Merk told them the building had to be converted on the fly to receive more sea mammals from NMMP San Diego. It had to be ultra-clean for the veterinary clinics to operate, treat the dolphins, give medical checkups, feed them, and store, prep, and process food. He then requested two emergency generators be delivered in case of a storm or blackout.

Sitting down in chairs around a dolphin's transport hardbox, the ONI official asked Merk about his thoughts on how he would sweep the waterways around New York City with the marine mammals. Merk shook his head at the man in uniform, and then looked at the Team Two CO. "Sir, I can't answer that question with any confidence until one, I review a map with contours tonight; two, know how many biologic systems will be under my command; and three, confirm the first two with an aerial flyover and swim-by of Manhattan."

"Fair list. Anything else, Lt. Toten?" the Team Two CO asked.

"Yes. What other minesweep ops, equipment, choppers, drones, and seaborne gadgets can Big Blue send to New York for Fleet Week?"

"Good call, Toten. Let me look into that," the ONI official said.

"If the navy sends in the cavalry, it will scare off the tangos. Then we'd lose them until they blow up another target in a different city," Merk said. He turned to Team Two CO: "Sir, Big Blue better coordinate our efforts with the CIA or we might screw this up. I need to be part of those discussions and learn what the biosystems will be exposed to."

"Roger that, Merk," he said. "Your sea daddy Admiral Quail Sumner has already set that pre-recon meeting up for tomorrow at 1100 hours. It will be held at the Pentagon."

"That works, sir."

They stepped outside. Merk strolled around Crescent Cove docks and slips, inspecting the dozen floating ten-by-ten enclosures that had been installed. They were moored between the slips as temporary holding pens. Coolers and fish cleaning tables were erected on each one of the floating pontoons that supported a marine mammal pen.

Tasi and Inapo swam around their enclosures. Below the surface, each enclosure was draped with netting that allowed the marine systems to swim out of the cove to be taken to sea for training exercises. Both dolphins looked in good shape. They were relaxed, rested, well-fed, out of the stressful environment of the Strait of Hormuz and the Somalia coast. They enjoyed the sun and warm weather along the Virginia coast, a setting familiar to both of them.

In adjacent pens, a pair of Atlantic bottlenose dolphins had been flown up from the Florida Keys, their littoral training exercise cut short by the national security emergency. Having never worked with those navy dolphins before, Merk observed their behavior, tuned into their traits. One appeared to be rambunctious, the other docile and relaxed. Neither one measured up to the gregarious Tasi or the obsessive-compulsive Inapo.

Within seventy-two hours, six to eight more dolphins flown in from the navy Marine Mammal Program on Point Loma peninsula, across San Diego Bay, would join the quad of biologic systems. More MMS personnel would be flown in from Coronado SPAWAR to support the mobile veterinary clinics and mobilize the staging area in New York City.

Merk met with the veterinary clinic supervisor. Together they double-checked supplies, reviewed inventory including food, gear, and dolphin accessories, such as GPS tags, dorsalcams, nuclear probes, and the types and amounts of food they would need in Little Creek and then in New York. Merk voiced his concern about the low number of transport hardboxes—about half of what would be required—but said he would make due with whatever SSC San Diego would provide for the operation.

The supervisor told Merk that he would call NMMP and follow up to finalize the details.

Minutes later, a CIA agent and the Team Two CO drove Merk to the Naval Network Command Center at the Oceana Naval Air Station in Virginia Beach for a meeting that would get the ball rolling.

Chapter Seventy

I NSIDE, THE NAVAL Network Command Center, Merk, the CIA
agent, and the Team Two CO met with the SEAL Team Two Navy
Commander (O-5). He was a tall, trim, graying man with an angular
face and creased forehead. They saluted the commander; he saluted
back, motioning them to take a seat. Via a videoconference on a wall
screen, he put Merk in touch with NMMP Director Susan Hogue in
San Diego—they hadn't spoken since the death of Morgan Azar.

After a quick round of introductions, the navy commander spoke
to Director Hogue, saying, "We need to move fast and coordinate
our efforts on the fly with SPAWAR. We need to do so under a total
press blackout. No FBI, no local police privy to NMMP counter ops."

"No tripping the alarm bells that will chase the terrorists away.
I'm fine with that plan," Director Hogue said, understanding the
absolute need for secrecy of the operation. She focused on Merk:
"Lt. Toten, we need a full list ASAP of what you're planning to do for
the marine surveillance in New York, including Mobile Vetlab items,
quantity, gear, etc."

"Yes, Director Hogue. We can start by sending MK-4 mine-detecting systems and MK-6 combat diver systems to Little Creek, until I
find a temporary home for them in New York. The NMMP team can
load the transport plane with accessories, transport slings, devices,
and teams of personnel, just like we were sending the systems overseas," he said.

When she received and confirmed the order, she would email
the list back to Merk and the SEAL navy commander, and other
officials on a need-to-know basis in the Pentagon.

Merk turned to the ONI official and the navy commander. He asked for a list of all navy ships, aircraft, and drones that would be in New York for the Fleet Week and Memorial Day celebrations. He needed to see what the SEALs, CIA, and other spy agencies were planning in terms of deploying drones, divers, land-based cams, underwater cams, and helicopter sweeps searching for nuclear materials. He felt the latter would pose problems, as the sensitive scans would tag the wrong kind of radioactive material, generating a slew of false positives, such as medical X-ray machines and nuclear density gauges used by inspectors testing soil compaction. Giving off hot reads would add layers of complexity, coordination issues, and confusion, while overt stress by the authorities might scare off the terrorists.

The CIA agent showed Merk a digital map of radioactive sensor buoys that ringed the waters thirty miles out in the ocean, in Long Island Sound, and off the 137-mile coastline of the Jersey Shore. Set up in the shipping lanes and routes of local pleasure craft and fishing boat traffic, the buoys could detect nuclear material being smuggled into the US from box carriers and cruise ships, to yachts and sailboats.

Merk was impressed with what he saw. But he pointed out that the stolen nuclear material was likely already in the New York area, having been smuggled across the porous border of Canada and New England. He told Director Hogue and the others that he was going to conduct the waterborne searches himself, in order to do it right, and that going the path of a hundred cooks would only jeopardize the operation. The data would flow from him and the dolphins to them and the other intel agencies in real-time analytics.

The navy commander concurred, warning, "We have no room for error in New York. Tens of thousands of lives are at stake, including your own."

Merk understood that. Failing to prevent an attack of that magnitude would kill lots of people and ruin numerous military and political careers. The collective guilt from such a debacle would be overwhelming. So he grabbed a pad and sketched the island of Manhattan, locating small islands in the East River he drew from memory, then the Hudson River, from the tip of Manhattan north past West Point, sketching the bridges and tunnels that crossed the rivers.

Chapter Seventy-One

MERK SPENT THE morning in the water with Tasi to make sure she was healthy enough for recon duties in New York. Had it been any other operation, at any other time, in which the lives of thousands of people weren't exposed to an overhang of a massive terrorist attack, he would have sent her back to NMMP to give birth.

In the cove, Merk cupped his hand on Tasi's beak. She rode him around underwater. First in a figure eight, then in an ever-widening loop, more than once grazing his side against the netting of the enclosures. Surfacing at near minute intervals to allow Merk to catch a breath of air, while she burst a breath through her blowhole, Tasi dove under and propelled him out to Little Creek inlet and the sea beyond.

There, Tasi surfaced with Merk for a breath, and then returned to the cove where she glided over the sandy bottom. She allowed Merk to feel the strength of her flukes. With a powerful thrust, she showed she was fit for duty—*no excuses*. He got the message. He tapped her to speed ahead, slow down, then motioned her to circle around a mooring line. In each turn and transition, the dolphin proved agile, nimble, and responsive. Still, Merk needed to give the pregnant dolphin rest before her next assignment and more down-time in between surveillance runs once they arrived in New York.

The decision to take Tasi along was Merk's alone. NMMP Director Hogue ordered that she receive health status and swim updates of the system on a daily basis, as a second check.

The NMMP had lost only one dolphin in its combat history of more than sixty years. And Merk remembered that dark day all too well. Neither Navy SPAWAR nor NMMP wanted to scuff its sterling record in New York Harbor. With the recent death of Lt. Morgan Azar, Merk didn't want to put anyone or any MM system in harm's way.

Merk toweled off. He watched the assistant handlers feed Tasi, Inapo, and the other dolphins. He met with the supervisor of the Mobile Vetlab clinic to make sure the hardboxes and the fleeced-lined stretchers were ready to move the dolphins when the time came to fly north to New York City.

* * *

ON THE HELICOPTER flight from Little Creek to the Pentagon, the SEAL Team Two navy commander joined Merk in going over the logistics of sneaking a dozen navy dolphins and tons of supplies into the City that Never Sleeps without raising an eyebrow.

When they landed, they were taken to a fifth floor conference room to meet with Naval Special Warfare Command, which oversaw all Navy SEALs and covert operations, including the implementation of the navy Dolphins with the Explosive Ordnance Disposal Mobile Units—EODMO.

Having received word that Lt. Toten didn't want the systems exposed in New York by telegraphing to the terrorists that the DoD was going to use every detection system in its arsenal to intercept a dirty bomb, the Special Warfare admiral signaled an engineer to run a presentation.

The first slide in the deck showed a naval helicopter with a laser detection system that pinpointed objects that dolphins tagged as suspicious. In a Midwest accent, the admiral noted: "Lt. Toten, because it's Fleet Week and there'll be military exercises plus an air show, we'll use a helicopter to fly around the harbor and laser-tag any discovery made by the MM systems. The show the navy puts on will be of a training exercise variety that shouldn't draw suspicion."

"Yes sir, Admiral, I agree. The dolphins won't use floating markers or buoys to broadcast their locations in the water. Since a visitor might see a dolphin or two, I request that the systems won't be saddled with anti-foraging muzzles or other hardware that's easy to spot. We need to take a Spartan approach to keep the op in stealth mode," Merk said, and then asked, "What other tools or equipment is the navy planning to use in the harbor?"

The engineer clicked the next slide. The admiral nodded to the engineer to answer Toten's question: "The US-3 is an Unmanned Surface Sweep System or sea drone." The image showed a thirty-six-foot-long, torpedo-shaped speedboat with magnetic and acoustic sweep capabilities.

A drone . . . dolphin drone, Merk thought, recalling what Jenny told him what she saw at the Fordow nuclear enrichment facility in Iran.

"Lt. Toten, if the US-3 wasn't cool in a kind of *Star Trek* way, I wouldn't deploy it. But under the same principle of Broadway theater for the Fleet Week crowds, we'll deploy the US-3 to cruise up and down the Hudson River under the auspices of showing off the navy's new unmanned drone. Remember, Fleet Week is a big recruiting tool for the armed services."

"Yes, I am aware of that, sir. The helo and US-3 will dovetail nicely with the armed forces showcase. Admiral, are there any other details about the op I should know?"

"Affirmative. Just one addition to your request for MK-4 and MK-5 EOD Mobile Units," the admiral said. "Because some waters in New York have low visibility, Special Warfare Command ordered a pair of MK-8 mine-detecting, mine-neutralizing dolphins to be flown direct to New York. When you set up there, be ready to receive them."

"Sir, what are the names of those systems?" Merk asked.

"Ekela and Yon," the engineer said. "It appears you have worked with those systems before."

"Affirmative, sir. As a pod on a covert op, no less," Merk said, wondering how those dolphins were doing. He would soon find out.

Chapter Seventy-Two

"**R**UTHLESS, MERK. YOU have to be ruthless," Jenny said, wearing a blonde wig and holding a black baseball cap in her hand. Dressed in gray slacks and a white blouse, donning glasses, she gave yet a different look, style, and persona with the disguise. "We're going to fly in the back door of New York through Westchester County Airport. A diplomat will escort us from there. You will be undercover until agents drive you to a CIA safe house in lower Manhattan," she explained. "Like my plan?"

"Incognito, like you." Merk checked out her blonde tresses, handing her a flash drive.

* * *

THEY LIFTED OFF without incident. Jenny and her team of CIA operators went over details that were streaming in from the New York State Intelligence Fusion Center. The two-hour flight was all the time Merk needed to decompress, grab a power nap, and think about the best way he should go out in the city and draw attention to his visit. Only he knew he would use himself as bait, as chum, to draw the terrorist tiger sharks out in the open. He would keep Jenny in the dark about that tactic, knowing that without taking such risk they would know next to nothing about Pratique Occulte's planned attack, except that it was going to originate in water around New York City.

* * *

GOING AGAINST FBI and ONI advice, Merk spent all of five minutes in the safe house in Manhattan's Tribeca neighborhood. He didn't care about protocol, potential threats to his life, or being a marked man. In the latter, he wanted to roam around in public to be seen and followed, as long as that meant flushing the terrorists out so they could pursue their quarry. If there were Syrians, Somali pirates, Iranian agents, or Yemen Shia warriors embedded in New York, he wanted to find out who they were and draw them out in the open.

So he began the chum operation by moving around the city, checking water extraction points for the dolphins, landmarks for Black Mass targets, and obstacles in the rivers for the systems to avoid; above all, to find a staging area for the Navy Marine Mammal systems to be housed and secure 24/7. NMMP needed space as much as secrecy, a place with easy access to the water that could hold a battalion of fifty marine biologists, armed security guards, assistant trainers, handlers, and veterinarians who were assigned to Merk to oversee Operation Free Dive.

Merk scouted the piers, warehouses, and the Intrepid Aircraft Carrier Museum along the Hudson River from the rooftop of a west side midtown hotel, drinking a light beer, enjoying the view. He saw old navy vessels in port, but not a Littoral Combat Ship that could be used to search the Hudson River for subsurface anomalies.

He took a subway down to the new World Trade Center, and strolled along the miles-long walkway of Battery Park City to the southern tip of Manhattan. He rode the Staten Island Ferry back and forth, eyeing the Statue of Liberty and Ellis Island on the New Jersey side of the harbor, and Governors Island and Brooklyn's industrial waterfront on the east port. Merk watched a cruise ship enter escorted by a tugboat, and scanned the Brooklyn Armory out toward the Belt Parkway, with the Verrazano-Narrows Bridge looming in the background under the noonday sun.

After a quick bite, Merk strode through the streets that Hurricane Sandy submerged in the fall of 2012, from Wall and Broad Streets, to Pearl Street and many other narrow avenues. On one of the New York Stock Exchange's blocked roads—to prevent a car bomb from going off—he watched a security guard circle an SUV holding a stick with a tiny mirror to search for bombs that might be planted under the vehicle.

Merk picked up a rent-a-car, using his real name and PenFed credit card. He drove across the Brooklyn Bridge. Not only was he out and about, leaving a long physical trail, but he left an electronic one as well. He took it one step further and kept his mobile phone on, inviting access to his location. He drove along the Brooklyn waterfront and didn't notice federal vehicles, police cars, or terrorists shadowing him. He was alone; his plan seemed to be failing.

Having seen enough, he took the Brooklyn-Queens Expressway on-ramp and drove on the elevated section of the highway by the Brooklyn-Battery Tunnel. He glanced out to the harbor and saw a dark, abandoned, concrete structure with the name NEW YORK PORT AUTHORITY GRAIN TERMINAL faded on the giant box's side.

After giving the old, tall structure a long look, he raced out to Coney Island. There he drove by the New York Aquarium, where dolphins used to put on a show. He doubled back heading west on the Belt Parkway around Bay Ridge and back toward Manhattan. He passed under the Verrazano-Narrows Bridge, rolled down the window, surveying the half dozen chemical and container ships moored across the harbor, waiting their turn to unload cargo heading into port, or riding out a storm before sailing to the Atlantic Ocean.

As Merk drove, eyeing the long-hull ships anchored across the narrows on the Staten Island side of the harbor, he realized the scope of finding bombs in and around the eleven-mile long island of Manhattan was going to be a vast, long, and monumental task. It would prove especially true when factoring in that he was going to deploy no more than a dozen dolphins to cover such large bodies of water.

As he drove the last stretch on the Belt Parkway toward Leif Ericson Park at 66th Street and Fourth Avenue, Merk looked out at the ships on the long throat that led into New York Harbor between northern Staten Island and Bay Ridge, Brooklyn. Consumed in deep thought, Merk failed to notice a dark green car shadowing him in his right blind spot. He lifted a mobile phone to take a picture of a Chinese flagged freighter across the channel, when the car slammed into the front right panel of Merk's vehicle, ramming it against the concrete median barrier. Brakes screeched. In a jolt airbags deployed from the steering column and door panel. The seat belt pulled taut as Merk's face slammed into the airbag, scraping his cheek and forehead.

Merk heard a car door open and knew the assassin was coming for the kill. Locked in place, he frantically searched his pants pocket, pulled a knife out, and cut the seat belt away. With his left hand, he reached down for the seat recliner to lower the seat back when the first rounds swept across the windshield, ripping the interior of the car, bursting the airbag, blowing the rearview mirror apart. With all his force, Merk slammed his back against the seat, snapping the recline lock all the way back, in effect breaking the seat. That allowed him to roll into the backseat and pop open the rear door.

More bullets strafed the vehicle, chewing up the windows, roof, and hood of the car. The seats were being torn to pieces as Merk slithered low out of the vehicle. He looked under the car and saw a pair of black boots with jeans, as the assassin stopped to reload the next magazine.

In the cacophony of shells tearing into the vehicle a third time, other vehicles screeched to a halt; horns honked; people abandoned their cars and SUVs, screaming as they fled and retreated from the ambush. Merk rose up the concrete median barrier, glimpsed the head of the lanky assailant—a Middle Eastern man with olive skin, cropped brown hair—and rolled over the wall into the southbound lane of traffic. And then—

A car reacted to the firing and jammed on the brakes. Sliding into the concrete barrier, it just missed hitting Merk. Two more cars avoided the new crash, while other southbound vehicles skidded and screeched to halt, with a couple of them colliding in fender-benders.

The terrorist stepped cautiously around the front of the vehicle. He peered inside the cab, seeing the shredded airbags, cut seat belt, and surveyed the broken seat pushed to the back—nothing. He looked down at the asphalt, but didn't see a trail of blood. He peered down the Belt Parkway, noticing the cars on his side of the northbound lanes had stopped, with other desperate motorists backing away, while others still abandoned their cars and fled on foot.

The assassin turned away from the panic and toward the median divider. . . .

On the other side of the barrier, Merk pinned his back against the concrete, making his body area small. He looked up at the crash victim in the car, and watched the injured man raise his head, his one eye opening with blood streaming down his face. The airbag in his vehicle didn't deploy. When his open eye widened with fear, the injured man tried to close the door in a futile attempt to escape. Merk kicked it shut and reached up as the gunman stuck the assault rifle over the side. Merk grabbed hold of the hot barrel, pulling the assassin down.

Bursts of gunfire pelted the asphalt around Merk, like the nose of a jackhammer, hitting him with spats of flak from the shrapnel and asphalt. The assassin's trembling hands refused to let go, as the weapon's recoil tried to shake Merk's strong grip. Merk refused. He reached up and pulled the terrorist over the barrier, slamming his face into the blacktop. Merk rolled on top of him and headbutted the assassin in a jarring blow. Blood poured from the assassin's nose.

With speed, Merk chopped the side of the assassin's head and then struck his throat, cracking cartilage with a fierce blow, knocking the terrorist out cold. Merk's killer instinct had returned. With rifle in hand, Merk pivoted on one knee, raised the barrel as if to fire the weapon, and watched the other terrorist scramble back to the green car, jump in it, and drive off.

Injured, bruised with scrapes to his face, a welt on his head and blood running from his nose and lips, Merk pulled the magazine out and watched the green car speed away. The car dashed off the parkway on the Belt's last exit.

A piercing whistle droned through Merk's ears and burrowed into his skull. Dazed, Merk tried to shake the whistling sound, to no avail.

He searched the roadway on the northbound side, looking for his mobile phone. Some fifty feet back up the road he saw it lying in three pieces. Holding the rifle in one hand and the magazine in the other, Merk stepped to the crashed car, opened the door, and asked the injured driver if he could use his cell phone to make a call on behalf of the US Navy. The injured man nodded in pain.

Merk gave the rifle and magazine to the bloodied man to hold; he looked up in wonder. "I hate guns," Merk said, tapping Jenny's number. As it started to ring, he put two fingers on the man's bloody neck and felt his pulse. Merk made a gesture to the injured man letting him know that he was going to live, when Jenny King answered the call.

"Hey, Memo, are you listening? . . . A tango tried to take me out on the Belt Parkway. His partner escaped in a banged-up green Buick," Merk said.

"Got it, Blue," Jenny replied, not wanting to use Merk's name either for OpSec reasons. "You and I will need a secure way to communicate going forward. I was right. SEA hacked Dante's smartphone in Somaliland. The tangos know what you look like."

Sirens wailed and chirped in the background; the police were on their way.

Merk felt relieved. He realized that for the first time in months he was standing on US soil. It was good to be home, even if he was under the duress of a terrorist attack.

Chapter Seventy-Three

POLICE CRUISERS AND motorcycles escorted the ambulance after it picked up the unconscious terrorist on the Belt Parkway, placed him on a gurney, and put the gurney into an ambulance with a pair of FBI agents making sure the handcuffed terrorist wouldn't come to and try to escape.

A CIA agent filed Merk into a black SUV with dark tinted windows. He slid over to the middle seat next to an upset Jenny King, who gave her lover a hard look as a CIA medic stepped in, closed the door, and attended to the cuts and abrasions Merk suffered in the car crash and firefight. The medic said in a demure voice, "You don't follow rules, do you?" Merk smiled.

"Don't ever pull that crap again. Next time ask me to cover your dorsal fin. You grab an assault rifle from a terrorist and do what? You give it away?" Jenny shouted in disbelief.

"Will I be on the news tonight?"

"The news? Hell yes," she said, flicking his ear with her finger. "Merk, you're not a SEAL anymore. This is the twenty-first century and social media dominates." She held up her mobile phone. "Look at the Twitter feeds coming out of the local TV stations. . . . Pictures taken by drivers of the accident." Jenny showed him the pictures and videoclips of Merk dazed, of him hiding behind the median barrier, of him wrestling the assassin, of him handing the rifle while tending to the injured driver as he made a call, of him inspecting the bullet-ridden crashed rent-a-car. "Very photogenic. I'm sure the admirals and Director Hogue will be pleased to see this."

"Okay, okay, got it. So I went viral . . . Kim, er King, whatever your name is."

"Kiss off, Merk."

"Jenny," he whispered, nodding his head across the narrows to a chemical tanker ship moored off Staten Island, "Look at that ship. The cargo is already here."

She leaned over and blew in his ear, "What cargo?"

"The items you saw in Iran's nuclear facility. The torpedo . . . the animals in the picture of Russian navy dolphins . . . they're all here," he said. "I know it. It's churning my gut."

Stunned, she sat back, knowing he was right. Guarding the container ports, airports, and borders now was a useless exercise, a waste of money. But there was no turning around the Titanic of big government and getting it off red alert status. Jenny surmised that the only items left for the terrorists to transport across the ocean would be a handful of operators: Korfa, Bahdoon, and a few others. But even they, she now believed, were already in the New York City area, which gave her the chills. If she could use an alias and a disguise many times, if she could impersonate a North Korean missile engineer, she knew Korfa and Bahdoon could step into someone else's shoes, too, do the same as her, and enter the United States without trouble. Add betrayed Somali refugees, Yemeni sympathizers, and American jihadists, and the Pratique Occulte sleeper cell was already operating in the United States.

"Did you read my report on what happened to the dolphin recon in the Strait of Hormuz? Iran must be behind Pratique Occulte," he said.

"Yes, I did. So you traded your friend's life for more intel. It's a horrible tradeoff, but with Iran and national security, I would make that trade every time," Jenny said with relish. Her mobile phone vibrated. "Merk, the intel was critical. It matches up with everything I saw in the Iranian nuclear plant. And how Bahdoon screwed Cuthbert with the false intel on the terrorist safe house in Yemen. It was all a ruse to deliver bad publicity to the United States and draw away CIA drones so Iran could lay mines. They nearly pulled off a great one-two punch, if it weren't for you and your fins."

Jenny read the text alert: "They found the green car . . . abandoned in downtown Brooklyn. Manhunt is on the way for the other tango, believed to be in the subway."

Chapter Seventy-Four

Inside the New York Intelligence Fusion Center, which unified the city and state police forces after 9/11 with federal agencies, from the FBI and the Department of Homeland Security to the CIA and NSA, an FBI special agent showed Merk dozens of screens on the live media wall. Surrounded by New York City's new Command and Control Unit, deploying most of its 500 counterterrorism-trained Hercules Teams, Merk felt more like a SEAL than a dolphin trainer.

Merk took in the angles, monitors, sensors, traffic cams, social mining sites, closed circuit TVs, NSA-hacked mobile phone data—emails, texts, photos, and video—and other audiovisual feeds from around the five boroughs and waterways of New York City, and saw what was missing. He whispered the discovery in Jenny's ear.

"Lieutenant Toten, would you care to share your thoughts with the rest of us?" the FBI special agent said, watching Merk whisper in Agent King's ear again.

"Sure." Merk turned to the special agent. He stepped over to the screens, waved his hands about, saying, "For all of this visual virtuosity and digital analytics, you're missing a key piece to the puzzle."

"Which is what, precisely?" the skeptical FBI special agent asked.

"You won't find squat with your technology," he said.

Jenny averted her eyes at Merk's cringe-worthy statement.

"Come again? We've spent more than 100 million dollars on sensors, cameras, data analytics, and drones of all sizes," the special agent said defensively.

"Wrong sensors," Merk noted. "You need to locate a hot load with a low radioactive signature. It's not going to advertise itself. It will be masked."

"We have a chopper flying over Staten Island right now," the annoyed special agent said, pointing to a top screen that showed a live shot over the ocean side of the borough.

"Right? You're trying to locate heat from backpack nukes, the kinds that our Special Forces carried into war zones. You ever seen or worn one of those?" Merk asked, silencing the special agent and the entire room. "One FBI helo for multiple devices won't cut it."

"Uh, Lt. Toten . . ." the New York City DHS Director spoke up. "We have two more radiation detecting helicopters en route to JFK. They are due to arrive at 2200 hours."

"Zulu," Merk added with navy flair. "That'll be good for tomorrow, good for the ground and good for parts of the sky. But it won't do any good if the mini nukes are transported or planted in the waters around Manhattan." Merk looked around at agents and police officers that surrounded him. "You want to stop the worst terrorist attack in US history and keep your names out of the media about this impending attack, then you're going to need more than helos."

"What Lt. Toten is saying," Agent King spoke up, "is we need to get on the same page and coordinate our efforts. New York has done a lot since 9/11. But you haven't faced this threat vector before, even with your overseas officers." With that, Jenny led Merk to a soundproof conference room, whispering in his ear, "You know, Merk, for a dolphin-loving introvert you're one talkative man." She goaded him into the glass room, locked the door, and sat at the table across from him.

His NMMP laptop had been delivered and placed on the table. Merk turned it on, took out a pair of mobile phones from a utility belt, each downloaded with a mobile app of the Dolphin Code software, and said, "This is how we're going to communicate when we're apart, like dolphins. No one can hack our conversation, not even the NSA." He spun the laptop around showing the color-coded keyboard, the commands organized by colors, groups, and tasks.

"Like fins? How's that going to work, Blue?" she asked, tapping the menus on the Dolphin Code app. "Pretty cool. Not bad for a geek who likes to swim more than have sex."

Merk shook his head at her last comment, "Low blow."

"Hmmm, I believe you would like that right about now." She fiddled with the app.

He spoke into his mobile phone, saying, "King likes to hold wood."

She looked up at him, grinned, and chortled, "Never on the first date." As she heard the words spoken by Merk, she heard dolphin trills come out of the speaker of her mobile phone. It startled her. Jenny looked at the screen and now saw his words—*King likes to hold wood*—written out in text format. "What the hell . . . ? How did you do that?"

"I didn't. DARPA did with my input. That and a few trained fins," he said with a wry smile. "If our phones are hacked, the cyber thief will only see sound waves."

"Data obfuscation."

"Dolphin obfuscation."

"Pure genius, Merk," she said, standing up. She picked up a remote, aimed it at a plasma screen. "The terrorist who attacked you today was part of the P.O. sleeper cell. He has a refugee visa from Homs, you know, that Syrian destroyed city. What the hell is he doing with Korfa? Unless he went to the other side?" She clicked the next slide, showing the other terrorist, the one who drove away, being arrested, handcuffed, pulled out of a New York subway, and thrown into an armored police vehicle. "The NYPD Hercules Team made the collar. He's of Syrian descent, too, from Dabiq, with an older and forged visa that predates Syria's 2011 civil war."

"Okay. Enlighten me."

"They are assassins only. There may be more; the world now knows what you look like. But if we're going to stop the attack vector, we have to intercept Bahdoon, take out Korfa and his Somali henchmen, and capture the core of the Syrian Electronic Army that's here in New York. We don't do that, they'll green-light the operation and detonate whatever devices they have."

"Let's start with Korfa," Merk said. "He's determined, but a sacrificial lamb for Pratique Occulte. If you were a well-known Somali pirate, where would you hide in New York?"

"In plain sight."

"What? Does Somalia have an office here in the city?"

"You mean, a consulate or embassy? Sure, it's on East 61st Street and York Ave," she said, confirming the address on her mobile phone.

"What about the United Nations?"

"Christ," she looked at him in surprise. "My god, brilliant. The UN is international territory. It's a safe haven. He'd be protected there."

"Practically untouchable," he pointed out.

"We need to make a short list of the most likely locations of where the warlord would hide and have those buildings watched 24/7."

"And you'll need to break into one of those places to hunt him down," he stated. "We're not dealing with the cherry founder of WikiLeaks. Korfa is one dangerous MF."

Chapter Seventy-Five

L ATE THAT NIGHT, disguised as a livery cab driver with Indian features, Merk visited the first of three sites. He drove by an empty warehouse in the Brooklyn Navy Yard off Flushing Avenue, between the Williamsburg and Manhattan Bridges. But he felt the location was set too far back from the water to be effective; he also didn't like operating below the higher vantage points of both bridges, where he and the dolphins could be watched. And there was too much traffic and activity, so he scratched the Navy Yard off the list of possible sites for the MMS staging area.

He drove out to the Brooklyn Armory Terminal, but came away with the same reservation about the site. Although it was ideally suited, located on the waterfront with sweeping views of the harbor and lower Manhattan, it was too busy for an industrial area.

Merk then drove to the abandoned, black concrete structure he saw the day before in Red Hook, near the Brooklyn-Battery Tunnel in the New York Port Authority Grain Terminal. He learned city officials had long referred to the terminal as the "Magnificent Mistake."

For Merk, the dirty, soot-covered, concrete box structure was isolated, well fortified for protecting the NMMP Mobile Vetlab Unit and to keep the navy dolphins from prying eyes. More critical, the structure appeared bombproof. It was a bunker. The tall structure offered a commanding view to scout New York Harbor from its upper floors and roof.

So he parked the car and climbed up the rusting metal stairs in a decayed stairwell covered with graffiti. The cracking and chipping of paint reminded him of the Somali boy's scarred arms. On the roof, he peered around. On the backside, he saw cars, buses, and trucks stuck in traffic on the BQE overpass, which could see him and other navy scouts or snipers, so he would have come up with some sort of blind to obstruct their views. Other than that, the Magnificent Mistake was a prize location to run a stealth dolphin operation.

Merk used the Dolphin Code mobile app to communicate his findings to NMMP, which in turn shared the information with the CIA, the navy brass in the Pentagon, and the New York Intelligence Fusion Center through a direct high-speed, fiber-optic pipe.

Merk spent another twenty minutes on the roof. He peered down at a chemical tanker unloading its cargo at a nearby terminal. He looked below to a rusty trolley stuck, frozen in time, on the abandoned tracks in Red Hook. He photographed the Gowanus Canal on the terminal's backside and knew it was polluted, just not as badly as it was back in the 1970s and 1980s.

He figured he could ferry the dolphins through the canal and out to the East River to be inserted in cleaner water, and upon return hoses would spray the bad chemicals and pollutants off their epidermis. He also made a mental note to tell the trainers, helpers, and marine biologists to make sure they instructed the dolphins to swim above the surface in the canal and not dive under, to prevent contaminated water from filling their blowholes. The Vetlab team would have to take water tests, in case any of the marine mammals became sick with infection or virus.

Merk made his way down the building, floor by dirty floor. He looked out broken windows to the lights of New York Harbor, at the dilapidated grain feed equipment and broken conveyor belts lying about. The air had an acrid, musty odor to it. He made a mental note to set up fans and humidifiers. The Navy Dolphin Mobile Team would have to draw power to the building or get it turned back on by Con Edison without any questions being asked.

Outside of a fast retrofit, Merk felt lucky he had stumbled on something of immediate value. He and the marine mammal systems could hide in New York City in plain sight, just like Korfa.

Chapter Seventy-Six

B Y THE TIME Merk and Jenny arrived at 0600 hours at the grain terminal, navy personnel were already removing trash and debris from the ground floor, taking the refuse out to a Dumpster in bags and large chunks. A couple of chemists were testing the water around the abandoned facility to determine whether the presence of toxins and heavy metals could harm the dolphins' lungs, immune systems, and epidermis. Merk didn't want a repeat of a vulnerable system, like Tasi, being exposed to toxic waste.

Those who worked outside on the grain terminal grounds wore hazmat suits, since that was the cover story the Pentagon and NYPD used to chase curious people away.

Inside the ground floor, a crew of carpenters began laying down sleeper planks and then subfloor plywood over the dirty and degraded concrete floor. Other laborers installed acoustic-absorbing foam panels on the walls, as if the two-foot-thick walls needed more soundproofing.

Jenny looked around at the unfolding operation, nudged Merk in the side, reminding him, "We need to finish this off, Merk. Don't forget, be ruthless."

"How about you?"

"I got a break on Korfa," she said, picking up the backpack and handing it to Merk. She leaned over and whispered, "We tapped the Somali embassy on 61st Street. It appears he has a few friends in high places. The phone calls have been traced back to the UN."

"So he's here."

"You told me Korfa was in the UN. But you never told me how to get him out."

Merk gave her a look, grinned, and opened the backpack, pulling out an oversized plastic pistol. He loaded a plastic dart with a metal tip into the handgun.

"What's this?"

"Korfa's sleeping pill," Merk said, then fired a shot at a sheet of plywood. The dart struck in a burst of purple ink, sticking in the wood. "A tranquilizer dart for dolphins."

"Cool. Really, cool. What's with the dye?"

"Need to know when the dart hits a dolphin. The dye washes off in salt water after a few days." He pulled the dart out and handed it to Jenny.

She studied it, asking, "Okay. But how can I get the dart gun past UN security?"

"You don't have to. Just carry a couple of darts into the UN and stab him—"

"If I get that close."

"Let Korfa convulse for show. When that happens, call an ambulance and take him to a hospital off UN grounds." He gave her a new dart. "C'mon, King, you like to throw things."

Jenny held the dart with a finger on the tail and tossed it hard, exploding it in the purple dye across the plywood. "Yes. That'll work fine the next time I seduce you."

Merk's Satcom vibrated. It was NMMP Director Susan Hogue calling for an update. "Toten here," he answered, listening to his boss, and then replied, "Yes, director, I've seen the pictures. There's more? . . . Of course there is, it's on the Internet. Affirmative." He ended the conversation with his boss and stared at Jenny, telling her: "They believe NMMP's on-premise servers and Pentagon Cloud have been hacked. They're trying to confirm it."

"More pictures of you on the Belt after the scuffle?" Jenny said. She pulled a Heckler & Koch MK23 pistol with a silencer out of her jacket pocket, and showed the firearm to Merk, saying, "Time to retaliate."

"You can't bring that into the UN."

"Maybe not."

He held up the spent dart, and reminded her, "We need Korfa alive."

Chapter Seventy-Seven

INSIDE THE WHITE House Situation Room, the CIA director and Pentagon military leaders looked at a wall screen with the president, the secretary of state, and the secretary of defense. The president gave the green light to bomb what the NRO's intelligence unit estimated was General Adad's 40 million dollar private jet parked on an airstrip in a northeast Syrian desert—a former ISIS stronghold. They looked at a live UAV image of the jet sitting on the tarmac at night, through an infrared lens. A blur. Little detail. It was a long shot. All they had to go by was some Red Cell analysis, along with known locations of Agent King's movements in the same area months before when she scouted the desert for the new missile launch site guised as North Korean missile engineer Kim Dong-Sun.

A four-star army general requested to see the spy photos of the Syrian jet parked on the runway in Hargeisa Airport a week earlier. A CIA engineer showed a split-screen of the two jets side by side. The jets looked like twins to all who were present.

"That's Adad's bird, all right," a navy admiral confirmed on a gut feeling. "Blow it to hell."

"Mr. President, permission to fire?" the army general asked.

The president signaled yes, by moving two fingers in a chopping motion.

The army general gave the order by telephone to CIA drone reachback operators in Fort Meade. Ten seconds later, the drone fired the first of three Hellfire rockets at the jet.

Within seconds, the trio of Hellfire missiles blew apart the fuselage and wings of the jet, sheering the nose off, blasting the tail section back from the wreckage in a skidding fireball. The bursts of flames lit up the infrared lens.

As the blast radiated outward, in ascending fiery clouds of smoke and debris, the CIA director remarked, "That should send Syria and its Black Mass affiliates a loud message."

"Well done, gentlemen," the president said, congratulating the DoD executives.

Chapter Seventy-Eight

A S SHE WAITED for the arrival of the North Korean Army uniform, Jenny secured access to an empty upper floor apartment
across First Avenue from the United Nations Headquarters.

Tudor City was an elevated, tree-lined, eleven-building enclave
built in the late 1920s on the east end of 42nd Street. Rising above
the city streets, the tall brick buildings encompassed a pair of parks
with stairs that swept down to 42nd Street and First Avenue, built at a
time when factories and slaughterhouses stood where the UN headquarters would eventually be built. The pair of Tudor City buildings
that faced the East River had small windows to prevent residents
from looking at the industrial eyesores of the day.

In that rented one-bedroom apartment, Jenny and a geeky CIA
digital engineer set up a surveillance nest. They took turns: One of
them watched the UN's front entrance, driveway with international
flags, and North Lawn, and peered into the iconic, all-glass, newly
renovated headquarters with binoculars. The other agent reviewed
a marked-up set of plans, trying to identify where inside the UN
Korfa might be hiding. Once Jenny got inside, she would need as
few places as possible to search for the warlord.

"How are you planning to break into the UN? You going in disguised as a journalist?" the CIA digital engineer asked.

"No. I'm going to be the North Korean missile engineer Kim
Dong-Sun one last time."

The digital engineer nodded, knowing cyber teams from the NSA
and CIA had started to hack into UN communications networks, sifting through thousands of emails, cloud notes, and millions more

texts and instant messages generated in the last month to see when Korfa, whether by name or code name, popped up in the UN data dump. The longer the spy agencies hacked the UN nerve center, the more Jenny believed Korfa operated off the grid, leaving little to no electronic footprint to be discovered. Terrorists had learned how to go dark thanks to Edward Snowden, a traitor in Jenny's eyes, who should one day be tried for treason.

She chose the General Assembly Building, which had been closed down for a complete construction overall until the GA's 69th Session in September 2014. The GA was the main area to search, with the Security Council, the Secretariat's Cafeteria, and the Dag Hammarskjöld Library as other areas to probe. For her, they would all become hot nodes in her intense manhunt.

On a hacked blueprint of the newly renovated UN building, Jenny circled the second floor and the Secretariat's Cafeteria as two places to begin the search. If she went in as a kidnapped North Korean asylum seeker, maybe UN security would lead her to Korfa.

The intercom buzzer rang.

"That's Dong-Sun's gear," Jenny said.

"Really?"

"Yes. When I enter the UN, where are you going to be?"

"In the van parked across the street."

Jenny patted the data engineer on the shoulder. He answered the intercom buzzer, telling the front desk to let the delivery be made to the apartment.

Kim Dong-Sun's clothes had arrived from Langley.

Chapter Seventy-Nine

THE FIRST HALF dozen dolphins arrived at McGuire Air Force Base in New Jersey. They were shipped up the New Jersey Turnpike in ordinary rent-a-trucks, then were transferred onto a US Coast Guard ship and ferried across the Hudson River to the Brooklyn grain terminal.

Because of the ongoing security investigation into the network breach, the NMMP's usual communication line to inform Merk the dolphins were on their way was not used. Instead, he received one secure phone call telling him in code the marine mammal systems' estimated time of arrival. That was it.

The whole military hacking spy game was one of the reasons why Merk, in concert with DARPA computer architects, engineers, and scientists, created the Dolphin Code software. If communications were ever hacked, the stolen data would amount to little more than strings of acoustic noise that couldn't be deciphered. So the translation of more than 200 directives from the color-coded keys would be impossible. Only a handful of directors and admirals with the highest levels of navy security clearance had access to the Dolphin Code Rosetta key, which was kept offline in vaults at three different secure locations around the country.

Set up in twenty-four hours at the grain terminal, the MMS Mobile Vetlab Unit received the Pacific bottlenose dolphins, Ekela and Yon. Merk had trained the pair in Hawaii more than a year before for an operation in Southeast Asia. Now the biosystems were back under his command in waters with the industrial noise signal of a big port city that would be foreign to them.

Merk reminded himself of being a carpenter, of his father telling him to "use the tools you got," when he removed the dolphins from the slings and hardboxes. He placed them on stretchers, fed both during dual medical checkups, then set them in a rubber boat, covered in poly sheets to protect their sensitive skin from the sun's ultraviolet rays and snooping eyes by local boaters. With a young assistant, Merk rode Ekela and Yon out to the harbor, steering clear of the thousands of tourists and commuters aboard the Staten Island ferries.

The Coast Guard ship, carrying Tasi and Inapo and two other dolphins from NMMP San Diego, crossed paths on the way to the grain terminal. The Coast Guard captain flashed a light, signaling Merk that four more biologic systems were being delivered.

If Pratique Occulte's plan of attack were pushed up to the next day, Merk would have a lot of water in and around New York to cover with only a half dozen systems. Six dolphins to search a dozen or so moored international ships, to stand guard and scan landmarks such as the Statue of Liberty, the Intrepid Museum, cruise ship terminals, the Chelsea Piers, the ferry slip at Whitehall Station, the South Street Seaport, and up the East River on Roosevelt Island. It would be a tall order for drones to carry out. And that's not to mention all the points on the Brooklyn and New Jersey sides that flank the city.

The navy got bogged down in delivering the mine-detecting helicopter, too. That meant the sonar sweeping capability and the unmanned drone ship—both of which would cover a great deal of real estate up and down the harbor and rivers—would have to wait. In true government bureaucratic fashion, the logistics had become a headache, bordering on nightmare.

That afternoon, things got worse. Jenny sent Merk a coded text about the Pentagon's retaliatory strike of General Adad's jet. The parked jet was empty with no one wounded and zero casualties. In her anger at the shortsightedness of their superiors, she noted the casualties would mount on the US side of the Atlantic Ocean, because "the US sent the wrong message to the renegade general in Syria. Pratique Occulte will definitely strike now."

Merk texted Jenny back: "Be a carpenter. Use the tools you have." In a way, he was reminding himself of the predicament, that the Pentagon had put a crimp into his search plan.

Off Staten Island, around the bend from the ferry terminal, Merk steered the rubber boat to a Chinese-flagged, black-hulled cargo ship *Hang Sun*. He pulled the poly sheets off the dolphins, checked their dorsalcams and GPS tags, and signaled them to roll into the water.

Once in the harbor, he gave a second hand-sign directing Ekela and Yon to swim around the medium-size vessel, and return giving him one of three signs: first sign, raising a left or right flipper to signal some object had been found; second sign, a tap of their beak in his palm telling him they found a mine, bomb, or torpedo; and third, an echolocating click to signal "all clear."

If they gave the tapping sign, Merk would place an emergency call to the Pentagon to summon navy SEAL divers, who were stationed nearby, to race out and inspect the object. Dorsalcam images, if not too blurry, might confirm what a discovered object might be: a false positive or a potential real threat. Like everything else with Operation Free Dive, the SEAL divers wouldn't arrive until later that day.

The navy dolphins were taught to ignore empty cans, drum barrels, and containers they could differentiate with their sonar from solid explosive packs and sea-mines. A dolphin's sonar is so sensitive and accurate that it could tell whether the hull of a ship came from Swedish steel or Japanese recycled scrap metal, by measuring the steel's density at a distance.

With their GPS tags, Merk watched the dolphins' progress above surface and below the vessel. The digital pings showed their movements on a digital map of New York Harbor superimposed on the laptop screen.

Ekela followed the mooring line down to the anchor that was buried in sediment. The dolphin found nothing, returned to the surface, breathed a pinch of air through her blowhole, and then swam around the bow before she dove below surface to search again.

Yon swam under the keel, filming the length of the seaweed-clad hull.

Nearly half hour later, the dolphins returned with both of them clicking in staccato bursts. Merk knew they didn't find anything that was threatening; the dorsalcam images he downloaded confirmed as much.

Merk drove the dolphins to a pier at the end of Belt Parkway on the Brooklyn side of the harbor. Seeing people were fishing on the pier, Merk cut the motor halfway across from the *Hang Sun,* and allowed the dolphins to dive in the water and swim under the pier. With Yon towing a DPod to the pier, Merk watched their movement underwater via the dorsalcams.

Ekela darted down one row of pylons, weaving in and around them, grazing fishing lines, stirring a few people to believe they had fish nibbling on their hooks. Yon worked the other side of the pier, surveying for bombs or the odd object with side-sweeping echolocating clicks. Like the *Hang Sun* cargo ship, the pier was clean.

When the dolphins returned from the foray, Merk received a text from the navy SEAL team. They were at the NMMP staging area and were going to take Tasi and Inapo and the other pair of mine-searching dolphins out to the harbor to join the search.

Merk welcomed the news. But he needed a lot more help if they were going to find and interdict a mini nuclear device from detonating in the city waters.

Chapter Eighty

FOR JENNY IT was all or nothing. At knifepoint, she made the digital engineer punch her in her ribs. The blow knocked her to the floor. She squirmed, sucking for air.

Curled in a ball, she lifted a bare foot and ordered the engineer to club the sole of her foot with a towel-bar she'd ripped off the bathroom wall. The blow drove shooting pain through her foot with an electrical jolt that shot up her spine. After the spasms subsided, Jenny straightened her body on the floor and stretched for several minutes, stilling the numbness. She gathered her senses, breathed short breaths, part bikram yoga, part Merk teaching her dolphin breathing techniques, until she was able to climb to her feet and limp to the bathroom. If she was going to lie her way into a secure facility like the UN, the pain and bruises had to be real.

In the bathroom, Jenny scrubbed her face clean, removing all signs of makeup. She looked behind the bathroom door, saw dust on the floor, squatted down, and rubbed the grime on her face, giving the impression she had been held captive in some cellar in the city.

Dressed one more time as North Korean engineer Kim Dong-Sun, making sure the collar was crooked, Jenny exited the apartment by the back stairs. At the ground floor, she disabled the alarm and stepped through a fire door, out onto the street in full view of UN headquarters.

With her clubbed foot still sore and throbbing, Jenny limped to the intersection across First Avenue from the UN's main gate at the Visitor Centre overlooking the North Lawn.

A few passersby noticed her strange military getup and pronounced limp. But it was New York; on the opposite side of town sat Times Square, where adults dressed up as superheroes and nude women to drain tourists of money. Was the disguise a ruse, a Communist fashion statement, or was she from a rogue nation? Jenny ignored the gawkers and hobbled across the street.

A couple of security guards questioned her in English.

Jenny spoke fast in a breathless, fast-paced Korean, like a fire hose turned on high. The obscure words confused the guards, who didn't understand the foreign language. She gave a guard a handwritten note in English and a forged North Korean passport to the other guard. She waited for a moment, and then shouted at the guards to hurry and let her into the UN.

The note read, "Seeking asylum from CIA abuse."

By charter and treaty, the United Nations was international territory and no part of it resided in the United States or New York City, where it physically existed. In short, the UN was out of the jurisdiction of US officials at the federal, state, and local levels.

The first guard handed the note to the other, saying, "This woman is from North Korea. Can you believe it? How did she come all the way to New York from overseas?"

Reading a second note, the other guard said, "She's an army colonel kidnapped by the CIA. Wow . . . that's why she's here. She must have escaped."

"Kidnapped?" the first guard said, flipping through the pages of her passport to see if it had been stamped by customs agents entering the United States. But the guards didn't find any US stamp. In fact, the last stamps were months old, with one belonging to Syria and then a few weeks later from when she entered Iran. But neither country showed an exit stamp. The first guard asked Dong-Sun for a US visa. She looked blankly at the guard, shrugged, and shook her head pretending not to understand, then said in thick Korean accent, "Ghost plane."

Jenny pointed to the first note that requested asylum from the US for fear she would be attacked again, kidnapped, and tortured in the CIA's rendition program. She then handed Merk's flash drive to the other guard with a note wrapped around it, with a label reading: "Toxic Illegal Dumping by the West in the Gulf of Aden."

The guard gripped the flash drive and motioned the other guard to take her inside.

Stunned, the guard led Jenny through the gate. He spoke on a radio requesting the chief of security and a Korean translator to meet the North Korean visitor.

At the metal detector, Jenny as Dong-Sun emptied her pockets and took off her military hat. She removed the hat and handed it to the guard. He put it in a container and ran it through the X-ray machine. She placed a wallet, a pen, some Syrian and Iranian coins, and North Korean money in another basket. As the female X-ray examiner studied the contents in the baskets, Jenny watched the guard out of the corner of her eyes.

Stone-faced, emotionless, with her eyes not making contact with any one guard, Kim Dong-Sun stepped through the metal detector, wearing a short wooden chopstick that pinned her hair in a ball on the back of her head. The chopstick didn't trigger the alarm.

Another UN security guard swept a metal-detecting wand over her limbs, then up and down her torso. She neither blinked nor moved, standing like a statue, giving a sniper's stare straight ahead. The guard waved her to step through.

After a short wait, a security detachment led Kim Dong-Sun upstairs to the second floor library and asked her to take a seat until a translator arrived.

The guards spoke to one another, mentioning she was like the other asylum seeker that came to the UN the day before from Somalia. Pretending not to listen, the UN security detail confirmed for Jenny that Korfa was on the premises. She sat still and waited, staring at a glass of water that was offered to her, with her face devoid of emotion.

When the Korean translator arrived, she took Dong-Sun into an empty office with a view of First Avenue. There, she was offered to sit down and tell her story.

In Korean, Jenny said, "The CIA agents kidnapped me twice. First in Syria, then inside the Iranian border. They flew me to America and did this to me." She pulled up her army jacket and undershirt, showing the fresh bruise on her ribs. "They beat my foot. Why? What did I do? I don't know. Doesn't America respect women? Doesn't America respect North Korean Army officers? Doesn't America respect civil engineers? I am an engineer."

"Tell me, what questions did the CIA ask you?" the translator inquired.

"Look—" Dong-Sun pointed out the window to a government van parked across the street with the digital engineer and two other CIA agents waiting inside, who were all part of Jenny's team. "Arrest them," she shouted. When the translator only nodded, writing down notes, Jenny stood up and shouted a screed about torture, about waterboarding and punishment, about food and sleep deprivation, and other forms of abuse and torture to break her will. "But it didn't break my will. I was strong. That's how I escaped. That's why I'm here. Now I want to go home. But they want to kill me. They want to hunt me down." She pointed to the van again.

In glancing at the van, the translator replied in Korean, "You're going to have to stay here tonight until we can get representatives from Pyongyang on the phone tomorrow to speak to the US State Department, which is closed right now." The translator tapped her watch.

Kim Dong-Sun gave a stiff nod and was led to the lounge area behind the library until arrangements could be made on-site for her to sleep somewhere in the newly renovated UN headquarters. The translator led Jenny into the lounge, where the Somali warlord Korfa was playing chess with another man, the diminutive Bahdoon. She asked to go to the bathroom.

Inside, Jenny locked the door. She opened the cuffed sleeves on the army jacket, removed the false buttons, ripped open a sewn seam, and pulled out tubes of one dart from each sleeve. In each button was a mini-packet of liquid tranquilizer she poured into the two tubes.

She removed the chopstick, twisted it open breaking a glue seal, removed two needles, and attached each one to the darts. She checked the inky fluids inside the plastic darts, then stored one dart in each jacket pocket along with the broken chopstick. She bit her lip, saying to the mirror, "I can't believe they are both here. Wow, two birds in the hand, Jenny." She flushed the toilet and washed her hands. Shaking her hands dry, the now-armed Kim Dong-Sun stepped out of the bathroom. The translator handed her a laptop and offered her a seat near Korfa's chair. The Korean missile engineer whispered to the translator, "Who is he?"

"He's an exile from Somalia. He couldn't go to the Somali consulate in New York, since the US government calls him a terrorist," the translator explained.

Jenny dropped the laptop on a sofa next to Korfa. He looked up at her in a cold stare. She eyed him back and shouted in Korean, "Swine. You are rude. I can't stay in the same room with a pirate. I'm an army colonel. I'm a missile engineer. Not a killer beast like this animal."

Confused by the language, but not by the tone of her voice, Korfa stood up and towered over her, drilling a colder stare. But the 105-pound engineer stood firm. He started jabbering in his Somali tongue, shouting in her face. When she had enough, she kicked the chessboard over, chasing Bahdoon away as a fight was about to break out.

The translator stepped between them. Jenny tossed her aside and struck Korfa in the temple with a lightning blow. Stunned, he threw a punch. But in his telegraphing it, she ducked under his fist and, pulling out a dart, stabbed it in Korfa's side. Feeling the pinch of the needle, the hot fluid injected into him, Korfa wrestled her down, knocking over the coffee table and chairs. On the floor, Jenny plunged the second dart into his thigh—enough tranquilizers to immobilize 1,000 pounds of dolphins—driving the needle deep, before quickly pulling it out.

As the translator and Bahdoon jumped in to separate them, Korfa lost strength and then consciousness. The translator pulled Jenny off, while she slid the darts into her jacket pockets.

UN security rushed in and examined Korfa. They kept Kim Dong-Sun away from the motionless warlord. One security officer put his finger on Korfa's pulse, shouting, "Call 9-1-1. Get an ambulance, fast. He's fading."

What the security officer and the UN staff didn't know was the sedative artificially lowered Korfa's heart rate to what appeared to be a life-threatening level. Jenny showed her hands, covered with purple dye, complaining, "Is the dog dying? What color blood do Somalis bleed?" Jenny knew she could only snatch Korfa; grabbing both terrorists would be too risky.

Not wise to the purple dye as part of the animal tranquilizer, the translator rushed Jenny to the bathroom to wash up. The security officer put a pillow under Korfa's head; he checked his pulse, which stabilized at a low rate, and then waited for the ambulance to show up.

Three minutes later an ambulance pulled up to the UN.

A minute after that, security guards rushed EMT workers into the lounge, rolling a gurney. They checked Korfa's vital signs, put an oxygen mask over his face, placed the oxygen cylinder on a rack, and then put him on the gurney, strapping him down. The EMT technicians raised the gurney and rolled Korfa out, following the security officers, who led the way.

Dong-Sun emerged from the bathroom with the translator, checking her uniform for holes and tears, then her hands and skin for cuts and scrapes. With the room clear, except for a pair of security guards taking a statement from Bahdoon, Jenny asked to be taken to another room and to have dinner before she would give her statement about the fight.

The translator sat Dong-Sun down in the library next door and told her to wait there until she returned. Given the second gift in less than an hour, Jenny looked up at a security camera and broke the seal to a locked fire door, triggering the alarm. She headed down the stairs and broke out of the building, limped across First Avenue, and disappeared in Tudor City.

Chapter Eighty-One

TWO HOURS LATER at the CIA's downtown safe house, Korfa came to, aroused by smelling salts.

Dressed in black, Jenny splashed water in the warlord's face. He shook his head, trying to rise out of the chair, but found his wrists bound to the armrests. She kicked Korfa in the balls—he doubled over in pain, coughing, spitting on the floor. He soon realized he had been stripped out of his clothes, wearing only boxer shorts. He saw two Band-Aids stuck on his skin where Jenny had stabbed him with the darts. She stared at the buffalo hump on his shoulder.

"Good hangover?" Jenny asked, slapping Korfa in the ear.

"Who the fuck are you?" Korfa shouted. "Why am I here? I demand to know."

"That's my question for you," she said, putting the barrel of a pistol to his head. "Why aren't you in your homeland, Somalia? Why did you come here?"

"Uh-uh-uh . . ."

She smacked him with an open palm, shouting, "I didn't hear you. Try again. How did you get into the United States? Who are your enablers?"

Korfa lifted his head, blinked, wriggled his eyelids, and just stared at her.

"Time is running out. My government just blew up General Adad's lair," Jenny said, playing a short clip of the Syrian jet being blown up on a tablet.

Korfa looked up at her in shock. "What do you want from me?"

"The details on the bombs," she said. "They're going off soon, aren't they?"

"I don't know the details."

"Lies!" she shouted, slapping the warlord in the face. "I need names, places, the bombs."

"I'm a knight, not a king or queen," he said, referring to chess pieces. "But you're a dead pawn when I am freed."

Chapter Eighty-Two

"LATER? WE'RE SIX fins short, minus one drone boat—" Merk shouted, getting in the face of the SEAL lieutenant commander from Little Creek, who stood at the boat launch of the grain terminal.

"The drone will be here tomorrow," the Team Two lieutenant commander said.

Merk's smartphone vibrated. He looked at a text message from Jenny telling him she had captured Korfa and to come over to the CIA safe house in Manhattan to question the warlord. Merk showed the text to the lieutenant commander, saying, "Do you want to meet this bastard?"

The officer read the message, saying, "Hell, yeah. Let's bolt."

Merk went inside the main floor of the Vetlab Clinic inside the grain terminal. He stood by Tasi. She was placed in a fleeced-line sling suspended over a table, allowing a biologist to draw blood from the dolphin's median notch on the tail. The biologist showed Merk the vial of blood, saying, "Need to compare this draw to the baseline we took when the system arrived."

"What? Every twelve hours?" Merk asked, annoyed, petting Tasi, talking softly to her. He eyed the biologist: "We need her in the water to have any hope of finding the device."

"Yes. But this is what Director Hogue wants. Tasi's pregnant," the biologist said.

Merk ignored the biologist. He put his arm around the dolphin and flashed the sign of two fingers forming a dorsal fin over his heart, reminding her to be strong.

Tasi whistled, knowing she would return to searching New York Harbor.

Outside, Merk climbed into a black SUV with the lieutenant commander driving. As he drove the battered road toward the gate guarded by a Special Forces detachment, who were guised as EPA engineers in hazmat suits, he said, "You know, Toten, you left your SEAL balls back in Somalia."

"Really? My brains, too?"

"Yeah, the fins have clouded your head. You gotta think like the pirates."

With that last line, Merk stuck his foot over on the driver's side floor and slammed on the brakes. The SUV skidded to a stop at the gate; the guards jumped out of the way.

"Are you crazy?"

"Gotta go back." Merk popped open the door.

"Toten, what am I going to do with the Somali pirate?"

"Grill him. See if *he* has balls."

The SEAL gave Merk a dirty look. Merk hopped out of vehicle and sprinted back to the grain terminal.

Inside, Merk pushed through the congestion, grabbed his laptop, and ran upstairs to be alone. On the third floor, he sat down at a café table with a couple of chefs sitting in a nearby lounge, taking a coffee break. He began to pull up dorsalcam images of the bombs planted on the starboard hull of the supertanker *Blå Himmel*. The only details he was missing from the videos were in his mind: *Who planted the bombs in the harbor? And when were they planted after the ship was brought to port?*

He banged the table, yelling, "Damn it!" He stood up and paced, shouting to the ceiling, "Korfa, you allowed me to get close . . . you allowed me to film the rigged ships . . . you watched the fins and me to see how we operated. Shit. Why have I been so blind?"

Merk knew a scuba diver had attached the bombs on the supertanker after it was ported, using something like a magnet or adhesive. But when did the diver plant the bombs? Was there more than one diver? Did it happen after Merk fended off the Somali pirates in the skiff he stole? Or earlier, when he met the children with the toxic lesions on their skin? And were they watching him now? If he and the dolphins cleared a ship or pier, would that give Pratique Occulte an opportunity to double back and plant a device with no worry of being caught?

What Merk needed to look for were divers who could move at a moment's notice to plant a bomb or launch the Iranian torpedo. He pulled up a digital map showing New York Harbor. With his finger he marked six areas where the divers could enter the water and plant the bombs without much trouble. They could either die with the explosion, like an ISIS suicide bomber, or slip out of the water and disappear on foot, by car, or public transportation, like the Boston Marathon bombers. If the terrorists delivered Russian dolphins to New York, the new wrinkle represented a different problem for Merk and his dolphins to sniff out and defend against.

"Lt. Toten?" a voice shouted downstairs.

"Up here," he yelled. Merk digitally marked the first location: a seawall between South Street Seaport and the Brooklyn Bridge. He circled the second location on the Brooklyn side of the East River with a loading dock, container cranes and warehouses not far from the grain terminal. On the third location, he selected a ship sailing into New York port—that would be passing through in the morning. He needed the next day's manifest of all the cargo ship deliveries. The fourth target had to be the Statue of Liberty Ferry in Battery Park, as the exit strategy from an island would trap the terrorist—if he chose to live.

The fifth site he envisioned was the Chelsea Piers, while the sixth he figured to be the piers flanking the Intrepid Museum at 42nd Street by the Circle Line cruise terminal.

Thinking like a pirate, Merk numbered the six targets in priority. The top three were the cargo vessel sailing into the harbor, the Intrepid Museum, and the Brooklyn pier in that order. He knew the other three locations, and still more minor ones, needed watching. But since the last six dolphins weren't going to arrive until dawn, he had to plan ahead to get the most out of them.

A pair of FBI special agents entered the room—one a short female dressed in a business suit was the special-agent-in-charge (SAC), the other a young, bearded man wearing coveralls to blend in with the local citizens in Williamsburg and downtown Brooklyn. They sat on either side of Merk, checking out his laptop and the color-coded keyboard. He closed it.

The female SAC opened her laptop and showed Merk a map of the five boroughs and North Jersey, from Hoboken and Jersey City to Fort Lee and the George Washington Bridge. Dozens of blue and red stars populated the map in a shotgun spray, touching all zip codes.

"The red stars are where FBI and state police helicopters managed to get positive, false positive hits on radiation sources from medical devices, X-rays, MRI scanners in dental and doctor offices, and the like," she said. "The blue stars are where the probes picked up nuclear density gauges."

"Nuke what?"

"Soil compaction equipment that uses trace amounts of radiation to power the ground-penetrating probes," the male special agent explained.

"So these blue tags are . . . construction sites, engineering and inspection offices, where the gauges are stored. Correct?"

"Yes, Lt. Toten. They're also from pickup trucks, personal vehicles, and the homes of where the inspectors live, before they drive to a site the next day," the SAC said.

"What about on the water? In the harbor, bays, or rivers?" Merk asked, noticing that, with the exception of one marina in New Jersey behind the Statue of Liberty, there were no stars in the harbor or anywhere around the island of Manhattan.

"Just the one in Jersey. The source of the hit hasn't been determined yet," the SAC said.

Merk stood up and headed downstairs to the ground floor.

"Okay, we'll put more agents on board the commuter ferries in the morning," the SAC called out, heading down the rusted stairs behind him.

"Now you're talking. As long as your agents dress like New Yorkers and not FBI agents, they'll be fine," Merk said, stepping into the ground floor Vetlab.

He handed his laptop to a lab technician, answered the phone, and listened to Jenny berate him for not coming to the safe house to grill Korfa. He let her carry on and vent her frustration for succeeding and failing at the same time in capturing the warlord, but getting zero intel out of him in the way of operational plans.

After another minute of Jenny spewing guilt and profanities, Merk cut in, saying in a stern voice, "King? Listen. The bombs are not in the water yet. They'll be there tomorrow when tango divers deliver them to the drop points. Bring Korfa to me."

Chapter Eighty-Three

M ERK ASSISTED THE MMS mobile veterinary crew in receiving
the last of the biologic systems.

They cleared out the ground floor clinic of the first batch of dolphins, Tasi and Inapo, Ekela and Yon, and a pair of MK-8 dolphins.
They sent those pods on night patrols, with each pod overseen by
two-man EOD divers in RHIB boats. Two pods swam up each side
of the East River to check around piers and bridge abutments; Tasi
and Inapo cruised along the seawall of Battery Park City, where the
Hurricane Sandy storm surge had breached lower Manhattan, flooding the Wall Street area for a week and closing the Brooklyn-Battery
Tunnel for a month.

At night, the navy RHIBs resembled police patrol boats. The main
danger for EOD divers and the dolphins was the hazard of being
struck by a boat or ferry, since poor visibility engulfed the harbor.
Merk reminded the divers of that, to keep their heads on a swivel,
and keep their eyes and ears open. They needed to record the times
and routes of the ferries, and match them to a GPS waterway database maintained by the NY State Intelligence Fusion Center.

With the new arrivals—two pairs of MK-6 Atlantic bottlenose dolphins and one pair of MK-8 spinner dolphins, the first of their kind
in NMMP's long history—Merk got the staff of trainers, feeders,
nutritionists, biologists, veterinarians, assistants, and the navy SEALs
who provided security at the grain terminal on the same page. He
told them his gut: "The schedule for the bombing will be pushed up
from Memorial Day Weekend to likely Thursday morning, which is
tomorrow. I feel our operation is being watched in the harbor."

Merk glanced to the door and saw Jenny standing at the threshold, watching him take charge of the onsite NMMP team. He ambled over and greeted her.

"Korfa is outside," Jenny said, looking on as the professionals treated, fed, and prepped the six new-arrival systems to be turned loose within the hour.

Merk nodded and stepped out of the grain terminal.

The Little Creek lieutenant commander and CIA digital engineer flanked an SUV; a pair of armed CIA agents stood behind the vehicle. They opened the hatch and pulled out the blindfolded pirate. Merk strode over to Korfa. To the shock of everyone, he removed the blindfold.

"Hey, Toten, what're you doing?" the lieutenant commander asked, drawing a pistol.

"Grilling the Somali," Merk said, wiping dirt, sleep, and grime out of Korfa's eyes. "He needs to see who he's going to talk to." He checked the welt on the warlord's face and glared at Jenny. She said nothing. Merk led Korfa, his hands cuffed in front of him, to the grain terminal and ribbed Jenny: "Bully." She averted her eyes from his gaze.

"Toten, you got OpSec Level Five inside," the lieutenant commander declared.

Jenny and the lieutenant commander trailed Merk, who escorted the warlord inside the mobile dolphin laboratory. He led Korfa out of the dark city night and into the "Magnificent Mistake" abandoned more than half a century ago. Merk took the pirate out of the slums of Hargeisa, out of the poverty and deserts of Somaliland, out of the tense meetings with Yemeni al Qaeda, AQAP, al-Shabaab, and Syrian generals, out of negotiations for hostages, out of ferrying migrants in a dhow, out of the temptation to pirate and hijack foreign ships, out of forming Pratique Occulte with Bahdoon and General Adad, and ushered him into the modern world, into Merk's domain of big data, cloud analytics, technology, and US Navy dolphins.

When Korfa stepped across the threshold into the NMMP Mobile Vetlab, where teams of scientists, assistants, and personnel worked tirelessly to get the dolphins checked, fed, and out to the harbor to conduct subsea surveys, his eyes opened wide. The pirate was amazed at how the US military had transformed the run-down concrete building into a high-tech marine mammal lab.

Merk led Korfa around the lab with a pair of armed navy SEALs shadowing them. He took the warlord over to see the MK-8 minesweeping dolphins, saying, "This is the US Navy's latest technology, its latest weapon in its arsenal, spinner dolphins. . . . A trained dolphin like this one is what I used in Berbera and Zeila to recon the hijack ships."

Merk gave Korfa a fish to feed the dolphin. A trainer flashed a sign; the spinner opened its mouth and Korfa dropped the fish on its tongue. After the animal swallowed the fish, it received a syringe of kelp juice with vitamins. A lab technician turned on an oversized battery-powered toothbrush and began brushing the dolphin's yellow, conical-shaped teeth.

"Tomorrow, these mammals are going to stop the double bombing," Merk declared.

"Triple bombing," Korfa corrected, checking Merk's eyes. There was no reaction.

Despite Jenny trying to beat the answer out of the pirate, Merk had just pried the first piece of intel out of the warlord by building a bond, an affinity with him. He led Korfa to the back of the building and up the metal stairs to the third floor café. He waved three assistants on coffee break to leave, and for the chefs to prepare a hot meal for his guest. He sat him down, held up his cuffed hands, and pointed to the lieutenant commander to unlock the handcuffs. With a pissed-off look, Merk glared at the SEAL. The hard look forced Jenny to step forward. The lieutenant commander shook his head, ordering the SEALs to take seats at corner tables, while radioing more SEALs to come up to cover the exits.

Jenny unlocked the handcuffs and tossed them to the CIA digital engineer. She stepped into the kitchen and pushed a cart with snacks, juice, and water over to Korfa. The warlord pointed at cranberry juice; Merk handed it to him and opened a bottle of water for himself.

Merk opened his laptop, clicked through folders, and opened images of the bombs Peder made for the pirates to plant on the hull of the supertanker. "Here's the first ship you hijacked."

"Not going to ask me about the New York plan?"

"What, the triple bombing? . . . No; why would I do that when I know how it's going down?" Merk said, using psychology to earn the pirate's trust, while goading him to talk without the threat of beating him. "Korfa, we'll come back to the tanker in a minute." Merk clicked open the video files of the dorsalcams capturing rusty containers dumped offshore. He pulled up an audio recording of the radioactive decay screeching higher as Tasi nosed the nuclear probe closer to the container. Inapo's dorsalcam filmed the action from afar.

"What's that?" the warlord asked, not understanding the discovery or why the navy dolphins were searching the Gulf of Aden's seafloor for toxic waste.

"Your freedom point," he said. "I met a Somali child in a cove. The boy had scars and lesions on his skin worse than mine." Merk rolled up his sleeve and showed his burn scars. "This was from a fire. The boy I met . . . his came from radioactive waste leaking to the surface."

"Yeow, cup . . ." Korfa uttered, his voice sad. "Many Somali children like the boy you met, they used to go fishing, used to swim, now scared, scarred. They don't play in the sea."

Merk's mobile phone vibrated. He opened a message and saw an alert that the next pod of dolphins was being sent out to the harbor. He slid the phone across the table to Korfa, saying, "I promised the boy that I'm going to find out who did the illegal dumping. These files are now with a government body that will take action for the illegal dumping."

Merk opened the photos of the supertanker. "Korfa, you came to New York to fulfill a vow you made against the United States. That's why you're here. You had your brother killed during the hijacking, because he had gone over to the dark side of ISIS. But Bahdoon and his Iranian sponsors are no better. They will use you and then stomp your carcass when they're finished with you."

The warlord nodded; he knew that was true.

Chapter Eighty-Four

I NSIDE A DARK, second floor abandoned office at the half empty South Street Seaport, Bahdoon and the Syrian Electronic Army engineer Qas viewed multiple New York City street cameras that he had hacked into. The engineer watched downtown Manhattan street views and intersections, switching from block to block, down the East River to the southern tip of Manhattan and around the waterfront up Battery Park City. Bahdoon scanned the empty streets in and around the old, decaying Domino Sugar refinery plant. The only traffic he saw was the ebb and flow across the Williamsburg Bridge, just south of the factory's yard on the water.

"How does it look?" Qas asked in Arabic.

"All clear. Any signs of the American dolphins?" Bahdoon asked. He turned on a burner mobile phone, dialed a number, and waited for a man to answer the call. When he heard a Russian tongue on the other end, he said, "Let's meet tomorrow for lunch."

The shorthand code to an Occulte sleeper point man was an "all go" directive, instructing the Russian to release a pair of Iranian Navy dolphins into the East River now.

Bahdoon leaned over to Qas and watched the hacker take control of the South Ferry Terminal's rooftop camera. Qas remotely redirected its aim from the Staten Island Ferry slip and pointed the lens a hundred yards out to the dark waters of the harbor. He controlled the camera, first picking up small bow waves from a police whaler putting around the Battery Park seawall. It then tracked a party yacht farther out, heading in the opposite direction. As he swiveled the camera around, zooming the lens in and out, it picked up ripples in the surface. Qas enhanced the contrast of the infrared lens and zoomed on the wavelets. He and Bahdoon saw a dorsal fin slice through the water, a dolphin rolling through the surface taking a breath with its blowhole.

"Where there's one navy dolphin, there are two," Qas said.

With those words, the second navy dolphin breached a little farther out.

"Should we go after them?" Bahdoon asked.

"No, not yet. Let's learn where they are operating first, so we can kill the trainer," Qas said with a hyena laugh, scratching his battle scar.

Bahdoon switched city camera locations to the Brooklyn waterfront, looking for activity across the river. "Do you have access to cameras on Governors Island?" he asked in English.

"Not yet. Will soon," Qas said, opening a different city operating system and database. He typed lines of code to override the preprogrammed and time-synced commands.

*   *   *

ON THE VACANT, decaying concrete pier of the Domino Sugar plant a couple of Russians took the cab off the bed of a six-wheel, heavy-duty pickup truck. A third Russian, the point man, stood lookout. He scouted the streets at the front of the building, the deck on the Williamsburg Bridge above, and panned the bend of the East River—clear of police patrols.

The burly men pulled tarps off a pair of Iranian Navy dolphins. The men checked the dolphins' conditions, fiddled with GPS tags strapped to their pectoral fins, and poured jugs of water over their epidermises to keep them moist.

The point man strapped anti-foraging cones with spikes over the beaks of each dolphin so they wouldn't be distracted searching for food in the rivers of New York. He lowered the tailgate, jumped in the truck, and backed it up to the edge of the pier. He and his men climbed into the bed, stood on each side of one dolphin, grabbed hold of the 500-pound mammal's flippers and tail fluke and heaved the creature out of the tailgate.

The first dolphin flew off the truck bed, landing in the river in a thunderous splash.

The men looked around to see if anyone had heard the splash. The point man barked orders to push the second dolphin into the water. They launched the other dolphin out of the pickup truck. It dove into the river in a spray, disappearing in a wash of foam.

The men jumped off the truck, closed the tailgate, and scanned the river. They didn't see the dolphins again. The mammals swam away, leaving no trace of their arrival.

* * *

BAHDOON RECEIVED A text from the point man that the Iranian dolphins had been delivered to the East River. "They're in," he said, referring to the dolphins swimming south to the harbor.

"Will they perform?" Qas asked.

"Yes. The Revolutionary Guards Corps had help from Russian trainers," Bahdoon said.

He removed his glasses and inserted contact lenses, so he wouldn't stand out in public. He patted Qas on the back, saying, "Allah be with you," and stepped outside the office.

In the corridor, Bahdoon selected two of four Somali guards to go with him, leaving the other duo behind to protect Qas, who remotely monitored the police, navy, and United States Coast Guards' activities.

Chapter Eighty-Five

ACROSS THE RIVER at the grain terminal, Merk watched the last pod of the spinner dolphins being carried outside on stretchers and loaded into a rubber boat. He approached CIA Agent Alan Cuthbert, who just arrived, saying, "I need your help to go upstairs and hang out with Korfa."

"What for, Toten?" the agent asked.

"Company. Don't want him bored. Chat with him. Strike up a conversation. Ply him with beer and wine. I don't care, as long as he talks and keeps talking. Tell him I screwed you."

"Am I going to wear a wire?" Cuthbert asked.

"Damn, you're good," he said. "Yeah, we need a transcript so your team at the CIA, mine at NMMP, and ours at the Pentagon and Fusion Center can have bathroom reading material."

Merk slid the laptop into a waterproof bag, stuffed that into a backpack, then took his gear out to a rubber boat that he would operate alone. Going solo gave him the flexibility to move quickly to any pod. With the navy dolphins trained to spot enemy divers, other dolphins, mines, and torpedoes in the water within a kilometer, no matter how dark or murky, Merk would have the ability to react fast when something broke. The only restraint he had: just half of the dozen dolphins were fitted with nuclear probes.

The SEAL lieutenant commander followed Merk outside and handed him the port manifest of the ships coming and going in New York Harbor that Thursday. Merk took the one page, double-sided manifest laminated in plastic, and listened to the lieutenant commander reassure him: "Toten, if you need backup, ping me. I'll be stationed on Governors Island with four platoons of SEALs, EOD divers, and Team Six snipers."

"Ready for war in an urban setting, huh? I'm sure New Yorkers will love that."

Chapter Eighty-Six

JENNY AND THE digital engineer drove around lower Manhattan on the East River looking for a sedan with diplomatic plates registered to Kenya. To her, it was a sick inside joke with Pratique Occulte. She understood the historical reference given by the propagandist Bahdoon. Osama bin Laden's attack on the West began with the US embassy bombings in Kenya on August 7, 1998, eight years to the day after the American military forces arrived in Saudi Arabia for Operation Desert Shield in preparation for the First Gulf War in 1990.

Al Qaeda always chose significant dates to attack Western targets. It was one of the tools terrorists used to instill fear in exploiting psychological warfare. That's why she scoffed at the Obama Administration denying and then running interference on the September 11, 2012, attack of the US diplomatic mission—a.k.a. CIA Station—in Benghazi, Libya, when the building was under fierce gunfire and then overrun by 150 al Qaeda terrorists: a terrorist attack; not a video.

From that day forward, she would do whatever it would take, use whatever means and force necessary, to eliminate the world's bad actors, dictators, and terrorists, laws be damned. That was the ruthless side she wanted to unleash in Merk, which he had once possessed as a SEAL cold warrior.

In less than a month, Agent King had used a rock to bludgeon an Iranian guard at Lake Urmia missile facility to make her escape from Iran; a catch basin to kidnap and stow a North Korean missile engineer in the desert of Syria to get inside General Adad's inner circle; a dolphin tranquilizer to snatch a Somali pirate warlord from inside the United Nations; and a red-haired wig to pump the Norwegian Special Forces sniper of intel at Ramstein Air Force Base.

Jenny didn't care. Results, not laws or tactics, were what drove her to win at every phase in the shadow war. She wasn't going to let an ideologue politician, a deluded CIA deputy director, a green manager, or a lawyer get in the way of defending New York City from an attack that would dwarf 9/11 in magnitude and horror, the number of fatalities and wounded, not to mention the collateral damage and psychological scars it would leave for decades.

Jenny was keenly aware of anniversary dates—Fleet Week and Memorial Day—and their iconic meanings. Both the Kenyan mall attack and Benghazi station would pale in comparison if Pratique Occulte succeeded in setting off a dirty nuke somewhere in New York Harbor, and then blaming another organization in doing the evil deed, like the terror twins of ISIS and al Qaeda.

So she replayed videoclips sent to her in a five-hour delay from the Intel Fusion Center. It showed the Kenyan sedan picking up Bahdoon when he bolted the United Nations and ran across the North Lawn. UN security cameras, along with a traffic cam at 46th Street and First Avenue, filmed the Yemeni psychiatrist scurrying across UN Plaza. Additional cameras at 48th Street captured Bahdoon climbing over and scaling down a wall before leaping to the waiting car.

That was five hours ago, she thought, pissed at the delay. She knew Twitter's tweets were instantaneous. So why did it take the fusion of the CIA-DHS-NSA-FBI-NYPD five hours to send her the video? Did a team of analysts have to review and get agency clearance before releasing it? Whatever happened to real-time data in the Digital Age? She was disgusted.

As she replayed Bahdoon dashing across the UN lawn over and again, she wondered: *Did the US's seventeen intelligence agencies and military armed forces take the 140-pound geek with glasses in Bahdoon as a serious threat? No. Did they not fear a few Somali pirates drifting around the city with a dirty nuke? No again. Or did they not care to notice them because of their skin color and the poor clothing they wore?*

In the fenemy, there was no Osama bin Laden bogeyman or ISIS caliph to put on the FBI's most wanted list.

Chapter Eighty-Seven

A T THE GRAIN terminal, two teams of navy SEAL snipers ran up the exterior stairwell wearing night-vision goggles, carrying weapons and gear. One team fanned out across the south end of the roof. They kicked open a door to the dirty, dilapidated, three-story control bridge office that overlooked New York Harbor to the south toward the Verrazano bridge. On the north end of the terminal roof, the second team of SEALs took position, with four snipers hiding inside a narrow lookout tower with a commanding view of the southern tip of Manhattan.

In position, SEAL snipers began to search the water and edge along the harbor as they tried to spot any unusual activity or person out of place.

*   *   *

FED UP WITH the inertia, Jenny sent a text message to the Intelligence Fusion Center to dispatch CIA and FBI agents on patrols to canvas Battery Park City, the West Village, Tribeca south of the Holland Tunnel, the Chelsea Piers and West Side Drive, neighborhoods along the East River, and down the Brooklyn waterfront looking for the Kenyan-plate car and Bahdoon.

The police sent her a text message that the E-ZPass electronic toll system of the sedan crossing the bridges and tunnels had not been used in the past forty-one hours. Jenny concluded the vehicle was either still in Manhattan or had driven over to Brooklyn on one of the free East River spans in the Queensboro, Manhattan, Williamsburg, and Brooklyn bridges.

Based on that likelihood, Jenny concentrated her forces in lower Manhattan. She secured additional help from NYPD patrols to canvass the Brooklyn piers and waterfront.

Chapter Eighty-Eight

AN HOUR LATER, a police cruiser found the Kenyan-licensed sedan parked at a Brooklyn waterfront restaurant parking lot. Police and FBI vehicles raced to the restaurant. Jenny and the CIA digital engineer showed up several minutes later.

Agent King got out of the car and took control of the scene. The police entered the closed restaurant and searched for suspects hiding inside. They found the chef and a couple of assistants cleaning the kitchen, but no one else.

Not wasting time, Jenny called for a helicopter with FLIR to search the area. She wanted to see if any human heat-signatures would pop up in a night search along the river and waterfront streets, the way the image of the final wounded Boston Marathon bomber was found hiding in the boat in a backyard in 2013.

Jenny strode to the river. She looked past the Brooklyn Bridge. A football field out from where she stood, right in front of her, a police whaler cruised down the middle of the river heading to the harbor. What she didn't see was the two Iranian dolphins swimming on either side of the boat's wake. The rogue dolphins were trained to swim in stealth, take as few breaths as possible, temporarily shutting off their echolocating sonar—like SEALs going radio silent—until they reached the open water of the harbor. The anti-foraging devices helped remind the marine mammals of that. They used the boat's wake to mask their movements from other navy dolphins, which were canvassing both sides of the river, but not the shipping lane in the middle.

Jenny took out a pair of night-vision binoculars and aimed it toward Red Hook, where the Brooklyn-Battery Tunnel plunged under the East River, connecting Kings County to Manhattan. She panned the rooftops of the terminal buildings, scanned the warehouses and piers, snapping photos with a high-tech cam. She sent those pictures directly to Merk and the CIA, bypassing the Intel Fusion Center.

It wasn't spite that drove her, but incompetence and the interagency turf war that, since the failures of 9/11, still hadn't fully rid itself of ego and deadwood. Agent King didn't have time to explain, educate, or coddle managers and department heads. She had to move fast, be flexible; there was no time for chain-of-command decision-making or problem solving by committee.

Jenny returned to the abandoned sedan and met with the FBI Special-Agent-in-Charge and two NYC police detectives. She showed them images on her smartphone she took of the Atlantic Yards, the waterfront terminals and warehouses, saying, "We have a lot of ground to cover beyond this car." She knew the bomb squad was a waste of time; she felt the vehicle parked out in the open on the Brooklyn side of the river was a ruse by Bahdoon to throw police and FBI off his trail—and it worked.

For a water detonation to achieve maximum damage, Brooklyn was the place to go: Lots of areas to hide, in full view of Wall Street and government buildings on lower Manhattan, with swaths of water frontage to slip into unnoticed and plant a device or two.

Merk was right, she thought.

The police popped open the trunk of the abandoned vehicle. Swept it for radioactive material. It was clean. They then summoned their bomb-sniffing dog. The German shepherd pranced around the vehicle, sniffing the ground, then the bumper. The dog climbed into the trunk. It sniffed and barked, raising its paw to signal alert. Dog, alert. The dog made a hit.

The FBI agents called in bomb technicians to check the sedan for explosive materials, det cord, triggers, and any residue of accelerant. Jenny knew it would be the latter, a honeytrap set by Bahdoon that would gum up more valuable resources.

The terrorists were experts in planning, in tying up resources with diversions to lead first responders astray while the real plot unfolded. That was the hallmark of an al Qaeda strike, from which Bahdoon took the model, borrowed heavily, and shaped as his own.

Unlike the FBI, Jenny didn't care about trace evidence. That was all the FBI ever cared about, drips and drabs of facts for some future court case. She was never fond of US courts. As an arena of action to settle disputes, the court system lacked her killer instinct.

*   *   *

JENNY WENT ON foot, flanked by the pair of CIA agents. They ambled toward the Brooklyn Container Terminal along the water-front. She reasoned the piers, loading cranes, and buildings were as a good place as any to search for clues on where the terrorists might launch an attack from, use to leverage, and decipher what their plan might be to strike the city.

When they reached the pier outside the gate, Jenny saw railroad tracks cut under the perimeter fence. She took out her smartphone, viewed the railroad tracks on a digital map, then texted Merk a warning.

Chapter Eighty-Nine

"**I**'M NEAR YOUR site," read Jenny's decrypted Dolphin Code message on Merk's mobile phone. He thought about it for a moment and realized she was roaming around the Brooklyn waterfront by Red Hook near the Magnificent Mistake grain terminal.

He texted her back: "Not there . . . I'm out in the harbor."

It would be another minute before she replied. Merk drifted off Battery Park City in the rubber boat, waiting on a response from Tasi and Inapo's underwater survey, when Jenny texted: "Tangos smoked out in the open. What's our blind spot?"

Searching for an answer, he thought about it and mouthed the words *blind spot*, looking around the harbor. *That's it,* he thought. He saw swaths of dark open space, few lights in the nightfall, gaps between a ferry to Jersey City and a booze cruise circling around the tip of Manhattan. He noticed that night there weren't as many military, law enforcement, or spy agencies out on the water. *Why? What were they waiting for?* he wondered.

Merk felt like he sat in the rubber boat with Morgan Azar in the Strait of Hormuz: alone, without the cover of drones, with backup teams miles away. Except now he wasn't spying on an Iranian fishing trawler laying sea-mines in the Persian Gulf, but searching for a bomb, a device, a torpedo, a terrorist, anything that would stand out in New York Harbor. Merk sensed Pratique Occulte was going to launch the attack that night. He felt it when he saw the video of Bahdoon being flushed out of UN headquarters, making an escape. Time was no longer on the United States' side. Whatever his schedule was, Bahdoon was going to accelerate it to ensure success.

Merk sent Jenny a message: "What are our weak points?"

"Our weak spots. Lack of intel on where and when the attack will take place," Jenny replied. *You're right, King,* he thought. *We are blind. How do we change that?*

"Keep hunting," Merk texted Jenny, and put the mobile phone down. With a swipe he awoke the laptop to see where the six pods of dolphins were located at that moment.

Behind him, deep sonorous rotor blades thudded the air, fast approaching. Merk felt the power and vibrations in his chest. He knew it was a military helicopter. He turned and looked up at the blinking lights of a wide-body Navy minesweeping helicopter— finally—the one that the admiral ordered when Merk first arrived at Little Creek. But the helicopter showed up in New York City at night, not during the day for Fleet Week show. That meant if terrorists were watching the Hudson River, they would see the helicopter wasn't part of the Memorial Day air show, but a high tech snooper that could detect all sorts of bombs and devices in the water.

Angered by the untimely arrival of the helicopter and the lack of the robotic drones in the water he was promised, Merk flipped the night-vision goggles down and read the laminated marine log of ships coming to and from New York Harbor. He saw the ships that were docked, the tankers that were in port, and those that were going to embark the next two days out to the Atlantic Ocean.

Then he looked up and saw in the darkness a silhouette of an EOD RHIB following two dolphins in front of the Statue of Liberty. They were heading north up the Hudson River. "What the hell?" Merk said, radioing the EOD divers. They failed to answer the call. A moment later, they sent a text to him, reading: "Navy sea daddy ordered us to retask to the Intrepid."

They were going to the Intrepid Sea, Air, and Space Museum at 46th Street on the West Side Highway. The Pentagon, in its cover-its-ass mode, shorted Merk a pair of navy dolphins. Instead of a dozen, he had now only ten at his disposal, and they were scattered. They had been summoned to guard the ships and submarines ported around the museum. What irritated Merk more than losing a pair of MMS was the third-party way in which he learned about the change in plans. He didn't hear about it from the Pentagon, Centcom, an admiral, or Director Susan Hogue at the Navy Marine Mammal Program, but from EOD divers under his command in the field. Flush with anger, he smacked the outboard motor and punched a box of flares.

* * *

JENNY FLASHED SIGNS dispatching three two-agent teams to search the Brooklyn Container Terminal buildings one by one. Over the roof of a warehouse, she saw the bridge and, to the right, the container boxes stacked on top of the cargo ship's foredeck. Above them the tall container lift sat idle against the night sky. She looked at the marine log on the smartphone, read the name of the Chinese flagship, then glanced over at a chemical tanker ship moored behind it.

Seeing the second ship triggered a reaction. It was the same empty feeling she had when General Adad's soldiers escorted the CIA agents, disguised as journalists, back to the missile site in the Syrian Desert. A knot in her stomach tightened; she texted Merk.

* * *

ONE POD OF Navy dolphins weaved back and forth under the length of a supertanker moored off Staten Island. The lead dolphin scanned the hull with the nuclear probe, while the trailing dolphin clicked the ship's bottom with its sonar, searching for cavities or anomalies.

In the rubber boat, Merk watched the underwater survey of the infrared dorsalcams on the laptop. He switched to the next pod conducting a swim-by of a cargo ship anchored outside the Verrazano bridge near the Belt Parkway. But he had lost the third nuclear tracking pod to the systems guarding the Intrepid Aircraft Carrier Museum. He knew the pair of marine mammals would spend the rest of the night protecting the navy ships moored upriver; that left Merk's current deployment of MM systems spread too thin to be effective. He had to take the risk of pulling back the outer pods. He did so, putting his career and the dolphins' lives on the line.

Chapter Ninety

E YEING THE CHEMICAL ship, Jenny moved toward the loading pier. She put a call into Langley, requesting a drone, deployed over New York City, to be retasked to scan the Red Hook area in search of suspicious actors or activity.

She received a text message from Merk that he was splitting the East River twin pods. One would continue north to conduct surveillance of the river around the United Nations and Roosevelt Island by the Queensboro Bridge. The other pod was called back to survey the ships at the Brooklyn Container Terminal.

Informed that the terminal was run by a private company and not the City of New York, Jenny called the NY State Intelligence Fusion Center and told them to review the terminal's security cameras' videos in an electronic search for Korfa's men or Bahdoon.

The more she studied the marine terminal in front of her, the more she saw something amiss. Like Merk, she began to think like a terrorist. By sunrise, she knew there would be a swarm of laborers, dockworkers, and managers coming to work that would make a morning detonation tempting for any terrorist—but on the Brooklyn side of the river. Blue-collar workers as the target for Pratique Occulte made little sense, however.

She scanned down the piers, spotting a freight train parked by the stern. The second ship was confirmed to be a special chemical vessel, not a cargo or container ship. She read the marine log. The offloading of chemicals would continue at seven in the morning.

Jenny directed her team to head to the ship, as she pulled up the name of the vessel with its bill of lading of what was being transported. A quick search of the list spooked her: 20,000 dead-weight tons of liquid chlorine stowed on board in protective drums. The chlorine would be transferred via special hoses to a chemical-transport railcar. That explained the railroad tracks.

Chapter Ninety-One

A TEXT FROM Jenny showing a photo of the chemical ship carrying chlorine gas alarmed Merk. There was no time for him to scream at agency heads in New York or top brass in the Pentagon. He had to act fast. He sent a text to the EOD diver boat monitoring the MK-4 dolphins in the lower East River, directing them to conduct a swim-by of the loading dock by the chemical ship.

Unable to see from where a threat might arise, Merk picked up and tracked the navy helicopter flying down the Hudson River, fifty feet above the water, sweeping its sonar side to side trying to detect objects, from torpedoes to mines. Eyeing the silhouette of the minesweeper swerving as it cruised downriver, he saw a glint of light, a glow like a torch on the water out of the corner of his eye. Merk shut off the motor, kneeled down, and picked up a secure Satcom. He looked across to Jersey City and saw the Hudson River Ferry coast toward the Battery Park City landing, a quarter klick to his right. He pressed a number on the Satcom, and then hit a key on the laptop directing Tasi and Inapo to swim over and intercept the incoming boat.

"EOD Two here," the SEAL diver said.

"Check the Staten Island Ferry starboard and port hulls," Merk ordered into the Satcom, changing the plans for the EOD dive team from the chemical tanker to the Staten Island Ferry filled with hundreds of people. Were two ships going to be blown up simultaneously?

Merk put the Satcom down. On the laptop's triple-split screen, he watched the dolphins. The center pane showed a digital map of the Hudson River with the dolphins' locations tracked by GPS tags. On the right pane, he watched Tasi's POV of the dorsalcam skimming the surface. On the left screen, he glimpsed Inapo rising, breaching, stealing a breath with the blowhole as rolls of white water washed over his melon, before diving down again heading toward the ferry.

Seeing the dolphins would reach the ferry in less than thirty seconds, he picked up the laptop to watch the survey of the boat's hull when the minesweeping helicopter flew overhead and straight out to the harbor, where another Staten Island Ferry headed toward Manhattan. Merk opened the metal flare box. He took out a loaded flare gun, unclicked the safety latch, and then waited for the dolphins to reach the boat. He took aim at the ferry—"This is for you, Azar."

Tasi dove under the bow wave of the ferry, while Inapo tracked her movement outside, passing the boat. The dolphin sliced through the wake and circled back to follow the boat.

Underwater, Tasi zigzagged along the port side of the ferry with the nuclear probe, but didn't pick up a reading. She fluked down to the bottom and shot back up to the starboard side, while Inapo cut across the hull, spying on a cylindrical, cigar-shaped object. Trained to identify and tag torpedoes buried in sand, to see one out in the open attached to the hull had to be like pinging the round sphere of a sea-mine in the Strait of Hormuz. It didn't belong.

Tasi swam alongside the torpedo. She moved the nuclear probe side to side, sweeping it across the back, middle, and front of the small brass torpedo. But the probe didn't pick up a single hit of any kind. No static feedback. No detection of radiation. Not even a minor leak.

* * *

ON THE RUBBER boat, Merk sat back in disbelief. *Why isn't the torpedo hot with waste?* he wondered. *Did Jenny swallow disinformation during her visit of Iran's nuclear plant?*

He sent a message to Tasi to double-check the torpedo. Nothing. A third time. Again, no reading. Was it a decoy? Did Tasi find a decoy? Or did the nuclear probe malfunction? What about the tor-pedo? Was it packed with a different kind of explosive?

Not liking the latter possibility, Merk continued to aim the flare gun at a point ahead of where the ferry would be in a few seconds and then fired.

The hot projectile shot out in a comet streak of bright white light. It sizzled toward the cabin of the ferry and burst across the windshield, deflecting into the water in a spat of smoke. Seeing the warning shot, the captain slowed the ferry down to a crawl before he hit the engines hard and shut them off. The boat plowed into a swell, arresting its momentum; it rocked back and forth and lurched in undulating waves slowing the craft down to drift and bob.

Merk read a number on a chart and called the ferry captain, tell-ing him to stay put as he called for backup to arrive. He picked up the Satcom and called the Intelligence Fusion Center to confirm they were viewing the same torpedo object fastened to the starboard hull of the ferry. He requested emergency boats to remove the pas-sengers and a SEAL ordnance disposal team to disarm and remove the torpedo.

He then called the EOD Two diver, saying, "You see the torpedo my fins probed with the dorsalcam? That's what you're looking for on the bottom of the ferries. Like remoras on sharks."

* * *

IN THE SOUTH Street Seaport dark office, Qas and a team of Iranian Revolutionary Guard hackers had broken into the NMMP on-prem-ise cloud and breached its firewall.

The penetration occurred through a router, an email loaded with a Trojan horse link that was opened by one of the dolphin han-dlers at the Point Loma headquarters from Merk's email address. The hack enabled Qas to spy on the same dorsalcam images and GPS tracking movements of the navy dolphins in and around the rivers and harbor of New York City.

Qas glanced at a second laptop and watched the Iranian Navy dolphins seek out the EOD divers and MK-4 team heading toward the Staten Island Ferry. The Syrian engineer retasked the Whitehall Ferry Station roofcam and swiveled it back toward the incoming ferry, which was a few hundred yards out and closing. He wanted to watch the intercept by the navy dolphins, as Bahdoon had suggested, and then get the video uploaded to social media sites and channels to continue the viral, negative propaganda surge against US imperialism.

The Syrian Electronic Army engineer sent a coded message to Bahdoon and watched the GPS dots close on one another. Qas stood up, stepped over to the door, and banged on it twice.

One of the Somali guards tapped the door back. He and the other guard picked up their barrel-bags and headed up the fire stairs to the roof. They were about to become a new layer in the plan to trap and kill the US Navy dolphin trainer Merk Toten.

Inside the office, Qas logged off, closed the laptop, stuffed it into a backpack. He killed the lights and headed out the door, bolting down the long dim corridor in the opposite direction of the Somali guards, heading up the stairwell to the roof of the three-story structure.

Like operating from the tent in the Empty Quarter Desert, when Qas hacked into the navigation system of the supertanker and guided it to the Somali pirates' ambush, he wanted to stay ahead of US intelligence agencies and the military that were hunting for him.

Outside, the Somalis knelt on the roof. They assembled sniper rifles, attached scopes, and aimed, zoomed, and adjusted the sighting as they panned the lower part of the East River, from the Brooklyn Container Terminal across to Governors Island.

Through the scopes, they scanned the black water, waiting for the action to come to them.

Chapter Ninety-Two

MK-4 DOLPHINS SWAM on both sides of the RHIB, while the EOD divers angled toward the Staten Island Ferry that was slowing down to make a broad turn to dock in the slip.

The EOD diver flashed a hand-sign for the dolphins to swim ahead and quick-search the ferry, when out of nowhere one of the Iranian dolphins rammed its anti-foraging cone, armed with a steel spike, into the hindquarter of the US Navy dolphin. The jarring blow wounded the creature. The EOD divers watched in horror as the Iranian dolphin rammed the mammal again, snapping the spike off and rolling the injured dolphin underwater.

One diver lifted a spear gun; the other pulled out a pistol as they searched the inky dark water for a sign of the rogue animal.

The other MK-4 Navy dolphin darted under the RHIB, hunting for the attacker, when the Iranian dolphin struck the injured dolphin again as it floated to the surface to breathe. The EOD diver called Merk, shouting, "Mayday, mayday, we got a dolphin war."

The EOD diver fired the spear gun at the rogue dolphin, grazing its dorsal fin with the spear. Wounded, it tried to swim away when the second Navy dolphin headbutted the Iranian dolphin in the belly, flipping it over. Stunned and injured, the rogue dolphin dove below. The divers pulled the wounded navy dolphin on board and attended to the metal shaft impaled in its side. The dolphin squirmed in shock, in need of immediate medical care.

* * *

RESPONDING TO THE mayday call of the EOD divers, Merk led Tasi and Inapo racing down the seawall of Battery Park City, rounding Whitehall Station.

They headed toward the RHIB bobbing in the wake of the Staten Island Ferry, which slowed its engine as it bounded off timber pilings of the ferry slip.

At that moment, Merk realized the ferry hadn't been checked for a planted remora-type device. He pounded the gunwale in Morse code taps and dashes, signaling Tasi to swim over to the ferry as he and Inapo continued on to the EOD divers.

Merk swept the rubber boat behind the RHIB so as not to rock it with the wake of his rubber boat. He pulled up alongside. Inapo joined the other navy dolphin and dove down to the harbor floor to finish off the injured rogue dolphin.

"What do you have?" Merk shouted over the idling motor.

"Our system was attacked by a rogue fin," the EOD diver shouted back, showing Merk the steel spike sticking out of the dolphin's side.

"Just one?" Merk asked, puzzled. "Makes no sense. They operate in pairs."

The EOD diver shrugged, holding up one finger.

"No way," Merk said, scanning around the harbor. First to the Staten Island Ferry that just docked, but was not letting passengers off, then over to the chemical ship, Jenny started to search at the Brooklyn Container Terminal, and back across to Governors Island, where a mini fleet of SEALs in four RHIBs raced out, heading around Manhattan to the Hudson River ferry that was drifting with the torpedo still attached to its starboard hull.

Merk took out the mobile phone and texted Jenny to keep her head on a swivel for a second Iranian dolphin. He waved the EOD divers to take the injured dolphin back to the grain terminal to be treated by the NMMP veterinarian staff for the injury it sustained.

Inapo breached behind Merk, squealing.

Merk turned to Inapo tilting his side, nodding, whistling that the first rogue dolphin was at the bottom of the harbor. Merk replayed Inapo's dorsalcam video and saw that he and the other MM system took turns beating and ramming the wounded mammal into submission, driving its lifeless body into the muddy trough, where it succumbed to its injuries and drowned.

The video showed a raw aggression, a nastiness that few people are aware of in dolphins, not realizing that even the trained ones are often as wild as their wild brethren. Merk saved the digital file to the NMMP cloud.

Merk opened a new window to Tasi's dorsalcam and watched her sweep back and forth under the broad hull of the ferry. She didn't find any remora-type device attached, so that ferry, at least on the bottom, appeared clean.

He raised his hand to give Inapo an order when two shots were fired. One clipped the water near the outboard motor to find the range; the second shot struck the starboard gunwale, puncturing a hole in the air chamber, blowing rubber pieces in a blast of shrapnel that strafed his body and the back of his head as he turned away.

The plastic and metal grains blew across Merk with a hissing sound of air that spurted out of the ruptured chamber. He ducked, feeling the sting of the pieces spray his wetsuit; the smell of burnt rubber and cordite from the high-powered shells froze him momentarily. The next two shots missed, spraying water off the other gunwale. The sniper had the range, but not the sight.

Not wanting to be shot, Merk hit the deck. He reached back for the motor, cranked the throttle, and took off. Lying on his belly, he blindly steered the lopsided rubber boat using the tops of the lower Manhattan skyline as reference points, trying to race out of the range of the rifles.

Out in the open, vulnerable to a sniper's line of fire, Merk figured the shots came from nearby Governors Island or farther back from one of the Red Hook buildings. Either way, it gave him one of two options other than being shot. He could jump into the river, which would buy him time to survive and enable him to hitch a ride with a dolphin, or race up the East River far away.

More shots struck the water. Sporadic at first, then the gunfire blew in a staccato stream.

* * *

ON THE ROOF of the grain terminal, the two teams of SEAL snipers heard the shots. The engineers scouted the rooftops of buildings below and along the point of Red Hook. Then one SEAL saw muzzle-fire light up behind a mechanical bulkhead on the roof of a low-rise building.

"Open fire," the lieutenant commander ordered, standing between the engineers.

The eight SEAL snipers shot at the mechanical roof, dumping the load, with the bullets chewing up and breaking off brick and metal in a hail of bullets. Several shots pierced the water tower on top of the building, with water beginning to leak out and flood the roof.

The lieutenant commander called his counterpart on Governors Island, sitting directly across from the apartment building on the opposite side.

* * *

ON THE DECK of the chemical ship, Jenny heard the gunfire. She saw the rubber boat race a zigzag path across the river toward the FDR, but she didn't see anyone steering the boat. She took out a pair of night-vision goggles and tracked the rubber boat when a new round of gunfire erupted north from what she figured was the South Street Seaport building. She called the Intel Fusion Center, requesting SWAT and paramilitary teams to descend on the East River pier.

Her smartphone vibrated a message: "Drone en route." She looked up at the night sky to spot the UAV. She opened a mobile app that uploaded a 3-D map of New York City with an icon of the drone flying down the East River. She opened a second app and now saw what the UAV operators out of Fort Meade watched with infrared, as they maneuvered the drone, armed with Hellfire missiles, toward the new nest of snipers.

* * *

ON THE ROOF of the low-rise apartment building, bullets sprayed the brick bulkhead from both directions. The three Russians, who had offloaded the Iranian dolphins in the East River, were now cowering behind the parapet as shrapnel of brick, mortar, steel, and glass rained down on their wounded bodies; water poured across the deck from the shot-up water tower.

A Black Hawk helicopter took off from Governors Island. It circled around the harbor. Hovering, it swung into position and opened fire, suppressing the snipers further, blowing apart the precast parapet. Bullets struck and hit two of the snipers, wounding one in the arm and shoulder, blowing apart the head of the other. The third Russian crawled toward the corner of the roof, but, in doing so, was now exposed to the snipers on the roof of the grain terminal.

A pair of SEALs shot and wounded the third Russian in the legs, immobilizing him.

* * *

IN THE RUBBER boat, the gunfire from the rear was replaced by sniper shots from the front. Bullets tore apart the rubber boat; they were heavy caliber. Merk picked up the metal flarebox and laptop trying to shield himself, as he attempted to kneel up and roll into the water. But as he rose a shell blew apart the laptop. He felt the next bullet would find its mark and kill him—when Tasi leapt out of the water . . . arched over the rubber boat . . . and speared Merk in the chest, knocking him into the river as the next shot ricocheted off the falling flarebox.

Underwater, Tasi drove Merk down.

More shots struck the rubber boat above in muted punches; other bullets broke apart upon hitting the water surface, which acted like concrete and shredded the shells to pieces.

* * *

ON THE DECK of the chemical tanker, Jenny knelt behind the wall. She took out a folding-stock assault rifle, and patiently waited to acquire where the gunfire came from. About a half mile away, up and across the East River, she saw muzzle-flashes of the snipers' rifles. She took aim and fired an automatic stream of bullets, raking the rooftop in the vicinity of the snipers.

She switched on an open mic on her vest and called in the location of the snipers on the South Street Seaport roof as she continued to suppress the snipers with return fire.

* * *

ON THE ROOF of the Seaport, the Somali gunmen came under fire. Bullets struck and danced around them, smashing glass windows on the floor beneath them, and an office to the rear. When the gunfire stopped for reloading, they sprang and ran to the stairwell, when up above them the CIA drone angled down, circling like a hawk, with the Hellfire missiles armed, chasing them in the opposite direction. They raced across the roof with a fresh round of bullets spraying around them. One bullet clipped the lead Somali in the ankle, dropping him to the deck. The other guard ran toward the edge of the building at the elevated FDR Drive.

A few more strides . . . a swarm of NYPD and CIA agency vehicles pulled up to the building. SWAT snipers yelled "Freeze!" from down below as they trained assault rifles on the lone Somali sniper stopping at the edge of the roof. He held up his hands and looked back at his wounded mate squirming in pain.

FBI agents stormed out of the rooftop stairwell, aiming machine guns at the Somali. He trembled. A tear of defeat upwelled in his eye as he dropped the rifle and kneeled down.

The rampage was over, but not the threat. There was still a bomb ready to go off somewhere in New York City.

Across the river . . . Tasi swam Merk toward the chemical ship that Jenny had boarded.

Chapter Ninety-Three

G RIPPING THE DORSAL fin, Merk rode Tasi to the chemical tanker.

On deck, Jenny pointed to the rear of the ship and ran to the stern, shouting, "Merk, get out of the water. This tanker is loaded with chlorine."

Merk waved her off and slipped on the dive goggles. He tapped Tasi and she dove them under the hull in a powerful thrust.

Out in the river, EOD divers raced over to the chemical tanker. They dropped anchor next to a micro-buoy—a navy dolphin had flagged it as an area searched earlier in the day.

Underwater, Merk panned the bottom of the algae-clad hull, but saw nothing as they swam under and rose on the other side by the pier. As they breached, taking a full breath, Merk watched Inapo glide over to them. He lifted the dive goggles and signaled the EOD divers that he would come over. He grabbed on to Inapo's dorsal fin and rode over to the RHIB.

When they reached the boat, the EOD divers pulled Merk on board. He tossed the goggles off, put on a weight-belt, slapped swim fins on his feet, and pulled a dive mask with a maskcam over his head; the divers fitted a tank of trimix gas onto his buoyancy control vest and rolled him overboard.

"Stay alert. There's another rogue dolphin out here. They always swim in pairs," Merk warned, and inserted the regulator in his mouth. He cupped his hand over Tasi's snout and let the pregnant dolphin propel him back to the chemical tanker.

In navy SEAL fashion, the high-tech rebreather left no trail of air bubbles to track Merk's movement underwater. The EOD divers had access to Merk's maskcam video only, but could message him on the dive-watch he was wearing.

* * *

ON THE SHIP, Jenny got word of a "hot pursuit" in Brooklyn off Hamilton Avenue under the BQE Expressway near the Sanitation Department facility. She looked over the side for Merk, but didn't see any sign of him. He was gone. She motioned the EOD divers that she had to leave. They waved back signaling they would get word to him.

As Jenny deboarded the ship, the EOD divers uploaded the tanker's spec sheet and confirmed it was unloading liquid chlorine. They saw the two ships docked at the Brooklyn Container Terminal had been searched hours earlier separately by FDNY and NYPD, and then four hours before by tandem MK-8 spinner dolphins. Each search cleared the vessel as clean. But after hearing Merk's story about the dolphins surveying the hijacked supertanker run aground in Somalia and hearing about the terrorist safe house turned into a drone-struck school in Yemen from Alan Cuthbert, she began to think like Bahdoon and that he would plant and arm the bombs at the last possible hour. Merk was right. The terrorists were already in the city with the bombs, just that they were mobile and not planted yet, like the Brussels airport bombing in 2016.

* * *

TOPSIDE, CIA AGENTS searched the ship for crewmen and dock-workers, who might be still on board the vessel, to evacuate them. Jenny ran over to the railcars that were being filled with liquid chlorine in the complex chlorine transfer operation. She couldn't believe what she saw. They weren't going to continue to unload the contents of the ship the next morning; they were doing it right then and there that night. And no one from the Intel Fusion Center, federal or local, had put a stop to the operation.

She clicked photos of the bulk chlorine liquid tanks, noting they had one liquid transfer line that connected the ship's tanks to a transfer hose with a remote shutdown valve. With her smartphone, she videotaped the canister of dry air that was being pumped into the tank at high pressure to suppress any vapor flash; the hoses had emergency isolation valves on both ends. She recorded the chlorine vapor flowing into a giant scrubber, filled with a caustic solution, tagged with the symbol for danger on the outside of the scrubber vat, all of which circulated through an educator. A heat exchanger that pumped cold water removed the heat from the air, while the liquid turned into a vapor filled into the railcar.

The two workers involved with the transfer operation wore fire-retardant suits with neck-dams, masks, and aerators. It was at that moment that Jenny grasped the magnitude of the danger of what a bomb could do to the ship.

Jenny grabbed the foreman and ordered him to shut down the operation, showing her CIA badge and assault rifle. The foreman called the terminal manager. After a conference call with the NYPD, the foreman shutdown the chlorine transfer operation. Not trusting anyone, Jenny stood by to make sure they shut the process down in a hurry, but safely, and then cleared the area. She asked the foreman how many railcars had been filled with the transfer of liquid to chlorine gas, to which he held up four fingers. She ordered him to move the railcars out of the terminal.

Jenny King turned back to the ship, signaled an agent on the deck. She called him on the smartphone and asked how many chlorine tanks were still to be emptied in the bowels of the ship. After an on-deck conference, he flashed eight fingers.

Upset, Jenny accessed the Fort Meade CIA agents operating the drone and opened a window on her smartphone, where she viewed a live aerial shot of what looked like the Pratique Occulte propaganda merchant Bahdoon on the run. He was on foot, dressed in black, wearing Body Glove shoes, dripping a trail of water.

She figured he had to have been in the river in the past thirty minutes.

Jenny called the digital engineer to come over and pick her up. They had to head to the Third Avenue roadway under the BQE to intercept the terrorist mastermind.

Chapter Ninety-Four

UNDERWATER, MERK RODE Tasi as she swept the nuclear probe along the tanker's starboard hull by the pier. In the darkness, he listened for the probe to sound an alert, but like the decoy torpedo, the device didn't detect any sign of a dirty nuke or hot load.

At the bow, Inapo located a pair of devices attached to the fore of the chemical tanker and swam back, tapping his beak on Merk's shoulder twice, alerting him there was a bomb attached to the ship. Merk pushed Tasi to swim ahead, then latched on to Inapo when, suddenly, the dolphin reacted to an unseen threat. Unnerved, Inapo twisted and dumped Merk, and darted down the hull of the ship.

At the bow, the second rogue dolphin struck Tasi, hammering her against the steel hull. The wild creature headbutted a dazed Tasi again, knocking the nuclear probe off her beak. The animal tail-whipped Tasi and speared her into a pier piling.

Just as the rogue dolphin was about to finish Tasi off, Inapo torpedoed the creature broadside, smashing it back, driving it off the pregnant dolphin. But instead of fighting or holding its ground, the kamikaze dolphin corkscrewed around Inapo and slipped away, swimming toward the bombs attached to the hull to try to detonate them by ramming.

Peering through the dive mask, Merk stared down the rogue dolphin and slammed his forearm on the dolphin's melon as its beak smashed into his dive mask, cracking the lens open like an eggshell. Water rushed into his face. It overwhelmed his senses, blurred his vision, constricted his ability to breathe.

315

As water filled the cavity, Merk ripped the dive mask off and gulped one last breath from the regulator before he discarded it. He crossed his lower legs, unclipped the weight-belt, letting it sink, and braced for the next blow. The rogue dolphin speared him, snapping his head against the hull. Battered, he expelled his last breath, crossed his arms, and blocked the dolphin trying to hit him in the face again. The force of the blow against his arms slammed the back of his head into the hull, rocking him to near blackout.

Programmed to finish him off, the rogue dolphin fought with Merk instead of trying to detonate the bomb. That delay, that hesitation allowed Inapo to soar back and slam the dolphin into the hull, knocking it out cold. Tasi flew over, ramming the concussed dolphin down into the murky depth, where it spun around upside-down, mouth ajar, tongue sticking out, sinking in a lifeless drift below.

Inapo nosed Merk up to the surface. Fighting the easing pressure that drove him to pass out from the rapid ascent, Merk's face broke the surface. He cleared his mouth, blew a couple of breaths, gasping for air, hyperventilating until his lungs emptied and filled with air again.

Tasi rose up and joined Merk. She cleared her blowhole in a spray, inhaling a breath. She rubbed her beak against his face. Feeling her wet, coarse skin, he grinned and latched on to her as she swam him around the tanker and over to the EOD divers.

Merk let go of Tasi and grabbed on to the RHIB. He was bleeding from his face and forehead; a welt crowned the back of his head, which he rubbed.

"Where's your dive mask?" the lead diver asked, handing him a towel.

"Smacked off by a dead dolphin," Merk said, pressing the towel to his forehead. "Call in backup teams; we got two devices at the starboard fore."

Merk reached for the radio on his scuba vest and called Jenny, informing her that the ship was rigged to blow. Then he told the EOD divers to go over and disarm the twin bombs, neither device being radioactive. But a chlorine-laden ship was all the blast material the terrorists needed to unleash holy hell and maximum destruction.

Chapter Ninety-Five

M ERK HELD ON to Tasi and Inapo as the EOD divers raced over to the chemical tanker. He bled from a cut to the cheek and a gash to the forehead. He floated by the EOD RHIB until the backup SEAL teams arrived and hauled him out of the water.

Merk picked up a Satcom, pressed a global emergency number that connected him with SEAL Team Two command in Little Creek, the admirals at the Pentagon, Jenny, and the NYPD, FBI, DHS, NMMP, and CIA at the Intelligence Fusion Center, and shouted: "The chem tanker is hot. Syria hot. And ready to blow." He took a breath. "It's fully loaded with chlorine. Clear the area. Clear Brooklyn waterfront. Clear lower Manhattan . . . Now, now, now."

Merk knew if there was acetylene in the vicinity the torch gas wouldn't need any flame to ignite. What he didn't know was Jenny had started the evacuation process at the terminal.

* * *

ON THE OTHER side of the vessel, Jenny heard the frantic call. She cleared the foreman and workers away from the chlorine transfer operation, waved her agents off the ship, and then ran toward the digital engineer driving over to pick her up.

The car fishtailed around and skidded to a stop. The front door flung open. Jenny hopped in, closed it, and spoke to Merk, saying, "I'm out of there. On Bahdoon's tail now."

"Jenny, is there any acetylene gas on the dock?" Merk asked on a different channel.

"Not that I saw. Maybe. Why?"

He didn't answer. The digital engineer sped toward the gate. Jenny rolled down the window, aiming the assault rifle at the guard to open it. He complied, opening the gate as the car drove out of the terminal, nearly clipping the guard. "What's hot?" the digital engineer asked.

"A bomb to detonate a bigger bomb," she said, feeling a rush of adrenaline kick in. "Merk's dolphins found two devices planted on the chem tanker. If the chlorine goes off a lot of people are going to die gruesome deaths."

"What the f—you mean? . . ." he began to say in disbelief.

"A mega bomb," she said, pointing down the street. "Not radioactive, but a chain reaction of chlorine liquid to gas. . . . Head to Third Avenue under the BQE. Bahdoon is on foot."

The digital engineer weaved in and out of cars, swerved through a stop sign, drove down an empty sidewalk, chasing a stray dog into traffic, and dodged hitting a slew of vehicles.

He drove around the ramps and walls of the double-stacked BQE intersection that tied to the Brooklyn-Battery Tunnel, located a half-mile from Third Avenue.

* * *

BACK AT THE terminal, near the chemical tanker, stood a toolshed.

Inside, a dozen acetylene gas tanks were turned on, open full, with gas filling the shed, leaking out the seams and cracks, enveloping the area.

Chapter Ninety-Six

THE EOD DIVERS listened to Merk as they viewed the dorsal-cam images the dolphins had captured of both devices. They shook their heads as Merk crawled into another dive team RHIB that would ferry him and the dolphins out of harm's way over to Governors Island.

As the RHIB drove Merk away from the disposal operation, the backup team of EOD divers steered their craft around the bow of the chemical tanker. From the photos and videos they analyzed, there didn't appear to be any timing device that would trigger the bomb. So they tied off the boat to the pier, away from the first planted bomb, in order not to disturb it.

One EOD diver put on an air tank, swim fins, and dive mask. He slipped into the river and reached back into the boat, lifting a waterproof sack filled with tools, and slung it over his shoulder.

He dove underwater, swimming first under the keel to make sure that bottom hull and port side were clear of remora bombs. Once confirmed they were safe, he made his way under the bow to the starboard side, and flippered along the hull to the bomb.

The diver opened the sack, twisted a chemlight on, inserted it in a slot on his wet suit vest, and pulled out a magnifying lens to study granular detail of the device, from how it was attached to the hull—metal clamps with some type of waterproof adhesive—to what the bomb was packed with, Semtex-H with titanium microfiber accelerator, he figured. He noted the device didn't have a det cord, timer, or an obvious way to trigger the bomb remotely.

Why? the diver wondered. He took out a wand and ran it over the bomb, confirming it was non-radioactive, but still appeared lethal.

There were two of them positioned near the bow, adjacent to the cargo hold where the last eight chlorine gas tanks remained, fully laden.

Chapter Ninety-Seven

B ROOKLYN POLICE OFFICERS shutdown Third Avenue, Brooklyn, under the BQE Expressway.

At 62nd Street, the NYPD's Hercules team and SWAT unit cordoned off the far end of the broad roadway, which ran three lanes wide in each direction with a broad parking area that divided the center median. A cell of four armed Navy SEALs snipers stood at 50th Street. A group of FBI agents took tactical positions behind the steel columns on the center island, while on both sidewalks more agents and police officers aimed guns and rifles from behind vehicles, light poles, parking lots, and storefronts.

At the first light of dawn, CIA agent and gun enthusiast Jenny King couldn't believe all of the firepower and show of force for one cornered terrorist, Bahdoon, who weighed a little more than she did. The Yemeni psychiatrist stood in the middle of the roadway, donning a gas mask, just as he did when he traded hostages for cash at the Somali-Djibouti border with Dante Dawson and Christian Fuller of the Azure Shell hostage negotiation team backed by US Marines.

Jenny saw the photos. This time, Bahdoon stood alone with no hostages. But still he felt he was in charge, in a position of strength and power. He had leverage. In his right hand he held a remote stem, a transmitter to detonate a bomb. And the bomb appeared to be in the black metal box resting on the pavement. He put his foot on the box, mimicking a pirate, then took it off and gently kicked the device. What kind of explosive was stuffed in the box was another question that no one seemed to know.

Restrained by a burly sergeant, a bomb-sniffing canine barked and yelped, pointing at the box. Jenny watched the German shepherd and figured the bomb was real by the dog's reaction. Was it packed with explosives, such as dynamite? Or did it contain a chemical or nerve agent? Or was it a hybrid of both gas and a C-4 type explosive spiked with shrapnel?

Bahdoon looked around, surrounded by agents, police, and a wall of firepower. The reason no one had fired at him yet was the remote he gripped in his hand. If it was a pressure detonator, then if someone shot or killed him, he would release the grip on the pressed-down button, drop the remote, setting off the black box bomb.

For the first time she could remember, Jenny witnessed a terrorist negotiate over an unexploded ordnance. That gave Bahdoon leverage in keeping the police and agents at bay, and from shooting him. And that didn't sit well with Jenny at all.

Understanding the implications, Jenny stepped out of the car, carrying an assault rifle. She showed her CIA credentials to police officers, told them and an FBI special agent-in-charge that she would talk to the terrorist Bahdoon. "You see that bastard. He's the propaganda czar of the new terrorist group Black Mass," she said to the FBI SAC. "He's the evil man who lied about the school in Yemen being destroyed by a CIA drone last month. He staged the scene with bodies of children flown in from Syria. And I took down his terrorist operation in Syria."

"He's the one on the Yemen school drone strike?" the SAC asked, lifting a shotgun.

"No school. Terrorist safe house. His name is Bahdoon. He's a psycho psychiatrist. A murderer. A terrorist. An enemy of the world. Like ISIS, he's the ultimate propaganda machine," she said, staring at Bahdoon wearing the gas mask.

"A bad MF," he said.

"Not for long. The drone strike lie ends today, here and now."

Jenny stepped past a pack of armed officers, moving furtively out into the open, closing on the Pratique Occulte leader, less than a block away. She felt her heart race. Step by step, marching forward.

She aimed the assault rifle at Bahdoon's gas mask, shouting, "We found your bombs on the hull of the chemical tanker. They are being disarmed."

With a smartphone in his hand, the terrorist spoke through a mobile app to Jenny, and said in a machined voice, "Are you sure you have found them all?" He glanced behind him, eyeing the armed agents training weapons on him.

"We stopped the torpedo, too," she said, stepping closer.

"That's close enough," he said via the smartphone, motioning her to stop.

"Sorry, I love close-quarter combat. Up close and personal," she said, ignoring his gesture to stop. "I should have taken your ass down inside the UN when I grabbed Korfa."

"That was you?" he said, a bit surprised by the revelation.

She sighted the scope at his scalp above the gas mask. "You see, when I was in Syria and Iran, I stood a lot closer to the enemy than where you are right now. I killed one Iranian Quds soldier by smashing a rock against his head. You should have seen all the brain tissue ooze out."

"That's enough," he shouted into the mobile app. "Put down your weapon or I will blow us up." He put his foot on the box again.

"I trained rebels in Syria to overthrow that government that failed to fight the ISIS pussies," she said. "I trained the Free Syria Army on how to shoot, how to sabotage, how to avoid sarin gas attacks and Assad's chlorine barrel bombs. Now I'm going to take down Pratique Occulte."

"Try and I will kill all of us," he said, unzipping his wet suit top, revealing that he also wore an explosive vest underneath.

"Two bombs. What's with the vest, al Qaeda amateur hour?"

"I swear, I'll blow us up," he warned, waving the remote detonator in his hand.

Jenny sighted Bahdoon's neck, as if she saw through the gas mask breathing hose and canisters. She scoped the crosshairs on his neck right above the plastic explosives vest. And in a blink of an eye, she fired a shot that tore through his collarbone, shattering it in half. The blast toppled Bahdoon to the ground, wounding him.

The law enforcement officials behind Bahdoon jumped back, others retreated many steps, yet still others dove and hit the ground. Bahdoon was still alive. He was still holding the remote detonator, but writhing on the pavement. Neither bomb had gone off.

With a trembling hand, Bahdoon held up the remote. Jenny fired the next salvo, blowing the device and several digits off his hand, chasing the agents to the rear, scrambling farther away as the remote bound and bounced across the asphalt, coming apart at cowering SWAT team members, who flinched and ducked for cover in anticipation of an explosion that didn't go off.

Disarmed, badly wounded, and now impotent by failing to detonate the black box, Bahdoon rolled over, pulling the gas mask off his face, screaming in agony. With his good hand, he reached down to the bottom of the vest, feeling for a ripcord, which Jenny couldn't allow him to pull. So she took aim and fired a third volley into the back of the terrorist, severing his spine. His hand fell limp to the pavement; his legs slackened.

Jenny held up a fist, holding the government agents and police officers back as she strode to the psychiatrist. She stepped on Bahdoon's ankle, digging her heel into his foot, but there was no reaction. She knew he was paralyzed, fading fast. Bahdoon's breaths were labored . . . soon hissing like a trapped snake . . . a gasp of expiring air, to which she remarked, "Karma."

A pool of blood spread around him.

While he was still alive, Jenny placed the hot barrel of the assault rifle against his face. "I'm going to go to your hometown in Yemen and hunt the rest of your dogs and pigs down. Bleed them. Kill them one by one." She added with salt, "You're not forgiven, you're destroyed."

Chapter Ninety-Eight

I N THE WATER off Governors Island, Merk sat in the RHIB as the
lead EOD diver peeled off the top of Merk's shredded wet suit.
He cut away and pulled off strips of rubber, exposing the grains and
shrapnel of plastic, metal, and rubber that had been sandblasted
against his skin, on his side, head, forearm, and back when the snipers opened fire on him.

In disrobing, Merk revealed the burn scar he suffered from the
mission that went south off the coast of mainland China. Without that
hellish nightmare, without Merk healing for a year from the burn
wounds, bedridden, sitting idle as a log, recovering from numerous
skin grafts, he wouldn't have become a pacifist; he wouldn't have
learned how to communicate with dolphins.

"Are you sure you don't want to go back to Dolphin One?" the
lead diver asked, pointing to the blackened grain terminal. "You'll
get better treatment there."

"I'm good," Merk said, peering at the chemical tanker and
the ongoing EOD operation to disarm and dispose of the bombs
attached to the hull.

The other EOD diver offered Merk a gas mask. He shook his
head, saying, "The wind."

"What about it?"

"It blows in the opposite direction than it did on 9/11. Today it
blows toward Manhattan." Merk looked over at the morning light
shining on the army trucks that lined the FDR Drive. Troops, donning gas masks, turned away cars, ordered citizens to go inside buildings or seek shelter in the tunnel that connected the FDR Drive with

West Street around the tip of Manhattan. He held up a rag, dipped it in water, and said, "This is all I need if the chlorine leaks."

The lead EOD diver nodded, using tweezers to pull out fragments from Merk's flesh.

*　*　*

AT THE CHEMICAL tanker, the EOD scuba diver surfaced with an inflatable bladder and the first bomb. Another pair of EOD divers carefully received and handled the device. They put it inside a lead-lined bag, lowered that into a steel gangbox, and slowly steered the RHIB toward Governors Island, where they would take the bomb into an underground bunker—turned into a disposal lab—and disarm it with robots and bomb technicians, wearing full Demon W Class-2 Suits with face shields and aerators, manufactured by Radiation Shield Technologies, in case the nuclear-detecting probe that Tasi used to scan the device malfunctioned.

In the other boat, Merk put on a navy-blue tee shirt as he watched the first bomb, stowed in the gangbox, be lifted on land, put on a cart, and driven to the center of the island to the freight elevator that would take the device underground for disposal. When Merk saw the cart disappear behind a bend of trees, he radioed the second cell of EOD scuba divers to remove the last remora bomb from the hull of the chemical tanker.

Underwater. The divers examined the surface area, seams, and canister—light metal wrapped in a plastic sheath—to see how the device was attached to the hull.

The second bomb was attached differently than the first. A single screw had been inserted through a metal lip on the canister and drilled into the ship's steel hull. No waterproof adhesive was used. It looked like a rush job to attach. One diver aimed a flashlight, while the other one took out a screwdriver. He tried to turn the screw, but the head just spun around. He felt the screw threads were stripped. The EOD diver checked the lip and signaled to cut the screw-head so the bomb could be removed off the hull.

The diver took out a mini rotary-saw and began to carefully grind the metal screw below the head. He then used a small crowbar and pulled on the screw, trying to free the bomb, when—a massive explosion caved in the hull in a concussion blast. The energy wave crushed the divers against the pier in a massive shock wave, blowing the steel hull open, slicing a huge gouge in the storage well that held the eight liquid chlorine tanks, ripping them apart in secondary explosions.

The blast was so powerful that it lifted the entire laden ship up a meter, before rocking it up and down in huge hull waves. Mooring lines snapped, tearing the vessel free. A klick away, Merk felt the shock wave vibrate in his chest and sternum.

The waves rippled out of the blast zone, pushing the ship out, before it listed on its side, taking on water as tons of liquid chlorine no longer under compression spilled out and reacted to the water, turning into a gas. Plumes of yellowish-green chlorine gas began to drift around the ship and envelope the pier. The broken tanks of compressed liquid chlorine poured out, mixing with the water and, in the evaporating process, expanding, becoming a huge gaseous vapor.

On the pier, the blast blew shrapnel and big chunks of steel through the chlorine transfer station, setting off a fiery explosion that blew open the pressurized mixture of chlorine in the tanks, railcars, and scrubber in an immense gas cloud spreading across the concrete deck. The shed where the acetylene tanks were stored blew apart in a massive ascending fireball.

* * *

IN THE GRAIN terminal, the veterinary clinic team, the SEALs, along with Jenny and the digital engineer, who had just arrived, heard the loud explosion around the bend of the Red Hook Marine Terminal.

Shaken by the force of the blast, Jenny ran upstairs to get a better view.

On the third floor, Korfa drank a cup of tea when the explosion rocked the building. He stumbled out of the chair, knowing the bombs had just detonated. The Somali warlord clutched his chest to feign a heart attack. One of the shaken SEAL guards came over to Korfa to see if he needed medical attention, when the pirate tossed hot tea in the guard's face, swatting the firearm out of his hand. He pushed the guard aside and dashed toward the grain elevator entrance in the front of the building, with the elevator shaft running down to the river.

Knowing Bahdoon's bombs had detonated, Korfa had nothing left to live for. He didn't want to be tied to the blast and be branded a terrorist. And he didn't want to be blamed for one of the worst acts of terror in modern history, when he considered himself a liberator.

Korfa threw a chair behind him to block the other SEAL from giving chase. The SEAL took out a pistol and fired a shot at the fleeing warlord but missed, with the bullet ricocheting off the concrete wall. Korfa ran into the hallway leading to the boarded grain elevator shaft. The other SEAL fired a second shot that missed Korfa, who now sprinted and crashed through the plywood protection, which snapped in half. His body hurled over the cracked plywood board. Korfa plunged three stories below, smashing his head and shoulders on a pile of rubble in the elevator pit that broke his neck, instantly killing him, his body impaled by rebar.

At the rear stairwell, Jenny heard the gunshots and ran through the third floor to the SEALs standing by the elevator shaft. She stepped between them and saw Korfa sprawled at the bottom of the pit. The Somali pirate had committed suicide. He was now dead like his brother, Samatar.

Jenny nodded to the SEALs and dashed back through the third floor and raced up nine more flights of stairs to the roof.

On the roof, Jenny joined the SEAL snipers and engineers, who were watching the toxic cloud waft across the East River.

"Oh my god," she mouthed, staring at the unusual sight. She called Merk's Satcom and smartphone, but there was no reply. She feared the worst. But then the lieutenant commander pointed to the RHIB boat drifting in front of Governors Island. Jenny took his binoculars and zoomed on the boat. Jenny saw Merk and the EOD divers watching the chlorine cloud form around the crippled, listing ship.

* * *

SHOCKED, MERK AND the EOD divers waved police and Coast Guard boats to evacuate the East River by the South Street Seaport and those agents on the helipad by Whitehall Station. The wind blew the lethal cloud to float across the East River.

Angered by the bomb going off, Merk Toten had had enough. He was no longer conflicted. His navy dolphins were in the water and he had no clue whether they had cleared the chemical tanker before the bomb exploded and the chlorine spilled out. He knew they would die if they surfaced and breathed the chlorine gas instead of air.

With EOD divers fixated on the gas clouds, Merk dipped the sonar-whistle in the water, calling Tasi and Inapo to swim over to his location. Within half a minute, both dolphins surfaced behind the RHIB, out of view of the EOD divers. Merk flashed a sign for Tasi and Inapo to dive below. He pulled off the tee shirt, slipped on swim fins, grabbed a dive mask, snorkel, and a pair of needle-nose pliers and rolled overboard without the EOD divers knowing he left them.

Merk dove down to the bottom of the harbor, expelling breaths now and then through the snorkel. He greeted both dolphins, pulling Tasi toward him, and with the needle-nose pliers he removed the dorsalcam and GPS chip from her dorsal fin. He hugged the dolphin, then removed the same items off Inapo's dorsal fin. When he finished, he dropped the pliers to the riverbed, flashed a hand-sign of a dorsal fin over his heart, signaling they were free.

With the hand-sign, Tasi and Inapo nodded and floated over to Merk, rubbing their heads and beaks on his face, and then swam away . . . their tailfins fluking . . . their silhouettes fading in the grey water. . . .

Merk rose to the sunlit surface.

* * *

ON THE ROOF of the grain terminal, Jenny and the SEALs watched Merk surface and climb back into the rubber boat. The EOD divers appeared to ask him what he had done underwater, but he shook his head and waved them off, not interested to discuss it.

Jenny wondered, too. Knowing that she had taken out Bahdoon, that Korfa had killed himself, and that the last of the bombs went off, all she could do now was watch the gas cloud enshroud lower Manhattan and pray people had run for their lives to seek cover.

Chapter Ninety-Nine

A MONTH LATER on the summer solstice, a salvage barge anchored off the coast of Somalia in the Gulf of Aden lifted the last of a half dozen rusting tanks that held the radioactive waste a German nuclear contractor had illegally dumped in the sea that Tasi and Inapo had found on the seamount.

With the operation overseen by the USS *New York*, live images streamed back to the Pentagon and the UN, showing the retrieval of the toxic waste.

*   *   *

ON THE SAME day in the White House Situation Room, the CIA director, army general, and navy admiral, along with several cabinet members and intelligence officials watched live as a night-time double strike unfolded on plasma screens. A true Navy SEAL double tap.

Launched by the black diamond-shape of a F-117 Nighthawk, which flew above the clouds, the bunker buster bomb drilled into the ground, igniting a percussion blast, blowing open the steel-reinforced cap to General Adad's bunker. The blast wave crushed everybody in the top level instantly. But the bunker buster projectile carried on, drilling down into the next concrete level, when its more lethal second payload—a tactical nuke—blew open the floor slab, burying the bunker levels below ground, killing everyone inside with a lethal fiery, radioactive blast.

"Was that bunker buster the nuclear-tip option?" the president asked.

331

"Affirmative, Mr. President. A B-61. That was payback for the fifty-six New Yorkers who died from the chlorine gas bomb," the CIA director said.

"Excuse me, Mr. President," the navy admiral chimed in. "The next earth-penetrating weapon is about to hit its target at oh-one-hundred hours Tehran time. It will strike the hard target in three minutes and counting. The Fordow Nuclear Plant will be hit by the next B-61 bunker buster. That should get the mullahs' attention."

Chapter One Hundred

D AWN THE NEXT day. Merk's cell phone vibrated with a message. Under covers with Jenny in a Washington, DC, five-star hotel suite, he read it out loud: "Two trained dolphins spotted off Long Beach Island, NJ . . . Jesus," he sat up. "Today's the day we go find them."

Merk and Jenny showered, packed up, and took an Acela train to Philadelphia's 30th Street Station. There they rented a car and drove across the Ben Franklin Bridge on Route 70 East heading toward Long Beach Island. At a circle in the Pine Barrens, Merk took Route 72 East, driving through a long green corridor flanked by scrub pine forests and sand—the New Jersey Pine Barrens being one of the great watersheds in the Garden State.

Merk handed Jenny his smartphone and told her to search his contact list for the Holgate Marina and reserve a powerboat to charter. "Guess I no longer have to swim off my anger about the health of the dolphins," he said.

"What did NMMP Director Hogue say about Tasi and Inapo disappearing?" Jenny asked, texting the marina on the availability of a powerboat.

"What could she say? She probably figured I had a hand in it. But after the bomb going off and the chlorine spill, she knew the navy was lucky not to lose a couple of more systems. Can you imagine video of dolphins on the news dying in the line of duty? It's one thing for people to die in a drone strike, for extremists to kill and slaughter people, but it's whole different orbit to see beautiful animals die," he said.

"Merk, you once told me that navy dolphins are trained to return to the nearest base when out at sea."

"Yes. Like a million times around the world for the past half-century, with few exceptions."

"So what will prevent Tasi and Inapo from returning to the naval base at Virginia Beach in, say, a few weeks, as they swim south?"

Merk looked at Jenny and, with a slight grin, said, "Because I untrained them."

At the Holgate Marina on the bay side of Long Beach Island, Merk and Jenny carried a couple of barrel bags and a cooler on board a twenty-five-foot bowrider powerboat. Merk drove the boat out of the marina, cruising south around the marshlands of a national wildlife refuge at the southern tip of Long Beach Island.

Once out where the ocean surf met the bay, Merk pushed the throttle down and rode the bowrider over a series of waves, cresting and slamming through the last swell, and then opened the power, cruising the boat up the ocean side of the long barrier island.

Knowing that fishermen had spotted two Navy-like dolphins on the northern part of the island off Barnegat Lighthouse, Merk decided to take a chance trying to reunite with Tasi and Inapo. He had released both dolphins to the wild a month ago in New York Harbor, after the bomb blew open the chemical tanker and the chlorine spread across the waterfront and over the East River to lower Manhattan. Merk would soon learn the effective range of the sonar-whistle and whether he would be lucky enough for the dolphins to respond to their whistle-names if they were still in the area.

Dropping anchor, Merk stripped down to a bathing suit. He put on oversized swim fins, grabbed a dive mask and the sonar-whistle, and then plunged in the water. Jenny took off her tee shirt, wearing a white bikini underneath, applied suntan lotion to her now-tanned skin—no longer the pasty white of the North Korean engineer Kim Dong-Sun she had impersonated for a year.

Underwater, Merk turned on the sonar-whistle and wrapped its string around his wrist, swimming about. He leisurely circled the boat, floating, swimming backward, and doing the sidestroke and then the breaststroke; other times he gently flippered around. He checked the anchor line as he swam by, and made a figure eight in front of the bow. He roamed around, sometimes on the surface, sometimes beneath it, all the while keeping the sonar-whistle in the water to ping the high-pitched whistles of Tasi and Inapo's birth names.

After a couple of hours, Merk tied the sonar-whistle to the ladder. He climbed on board to have lunch with Jenny. She had turned over on her stomach, catching sun as she read an e-book on the Pacific War in World War II.

"Any luck?" she asked, sitting up, adjusting her sunglasses.

"Not a peep," he said, taking a kale smoothie from the cooler.

She grabbed a mango smoothie and sipped. "Did we miss them?"

"Maybe. Let's stick around longer. I don't think they made it as far south as Brigantine in less than a day."

"Okay. Why not?"

"It took them a month to mosey their lazy tails halfway down the Jersey Shore. They don't appear to be in a rush. Maybe it's the Atlantic bottlenose dolphins migrating north from Florida up here and to Long Island. It's summer. So who knows what they bumped into?" Merk said, downing the kale smoothie. "Maybe they're part of a pod or a herd now."

"How did you do it?" Jenny asked.

"Do what?"

"Deprogram them. Doesn't that take several months?"

Shielding his eyes from the sun, Merk looked in Jenny's eyes and said, "It started at the beginning of my training with them, about a year ago. I taught them that if I got hurt, like what happened to Morgan Azar, they would have to go survive on their own. I broke several NMMP cardinal rules with Tasi and Inapo. The biggest was bonding with them, which the program frowns upon. But out of view of handlers and navy personnel, I broke down the barriers, turned their shyness into strength, made them resilient, and turned that all into self-reliance. I made Tasi and Inapo support each other without me. They would survive in the wild only as a pair." Merk chugged water and then wiped his mouth with the back of his hand. "Like you and me."

Out of nowhere, Tasi breached off the side, arcing high through the air and splashing down. Then Inapo surfaced, sculling backward and splashed water across the bow, playfully laughing at Merk and Jenny, who both got soaked. Not wasting time putting on the swim gear, Merk dove into the water. Jenny stood up, removed her wet sunglasses, and toweled off. She lifted the other cooler on the seat, opened the lid, and began to toss fish into the sea.

Tasi rode Merk around in a circle; Inapo darted over and snatched the fish floating on the surface. Tasi fluked over, as Merk let go of her dorsal fin. Jenny fed Tasi three mackerels in a row. Each time, the dolphin opened her mouth and gulped the fish whole down her throat.

Jenny climbed down the ladder eased into the water. She enjoyed the mirth of swimming with the Navy-trained dolphins. For the next half hour, the foursome played around, toyed with each other, mimicking emotions and mirroring one another.

The bond for Jenny was surreal after all she had been through in the coarseness of war and the male-dominated cultures of Syria, Iran, and North Korea. She realized how much her job had taken a toll on her psyche, her spirit, her body and well-being, and how much she missed being with Merk, being a part of his unique, special bond the dolphin whisperer had with his dolphins. They would always be his dolphins. It was truly a gift.

Freeing Tasi and Inapo, not once but twice, took a strong person. She sat on the ladder and watched Merk end the swim. He gave the dorsal fin sign over his heart with two fingers, and said, "Be as strong as your last breath."

With that, Tasi and Inapo whistled, swam around Merk one last time, and darted off. They dove under the boat, heading south.

Merk and Jenny climbed on board and watched the dolphins swim away in the high shining summer sun.